FEB 1 5 2013

Zygmunt Miłoszewski, born in Warsaw in 1976, is a star of Polish fiction. His first novel, *The Intercom*, was published in 2005 to high acclaim. In 2006 he published a novel for young readers, *The Adder Mountains*, and in 2007 the crime novel *Entanglement*. The latter received the High Calibre Award for best Polish crime novel of the year and was made into a feature film. *A Grain of Truth*, the sequel to *Entanglement*, also featuring State Prosecutor Teodor Szacki, was published in 2011 in Poland.

P9-EMR-065

NAPA COUNTY LIBRARY
580 COOMBS STREET
NAPA, CA 94559

Also available from Bitter Lemon Press
by Zygmunt Miłoszewski:

Entanglement

A GRAIN OF TRUTH

Zygmunt Miłoszewski

Translated from the Polish
by Antonia Lloyd-Jones

BITTER LEMON PRESS
LONDON

BITTER LEMON PRESS

First published in the United Kingdom in 2012 by
Bitter Lemon Press, 37 Arundel Gardens, London W11 2LW

www.bitterlemonpress.com

First published in Polish as *Ziarno prawdy*
by Wydawnictwo W.A.B., 2011

This edition has been published with the financial support of
The Book Institute – the © POLAND Translation Programme

Bitter Lemon Press gratefully acknowledges the financial
assistance of the Arts Council of England

Copyright © Wydawnictwo W.A.B., 2011
English translation © Antonia Lloyd-Jones, 2012

All rights reserved. No part of this publication may be
reproduced in any form or by any means without written
permission of the publisher.

The moral rights of the author and the translator have
been asserted in accordance with the Copyright, Designs, and
Patents Act 1988

A CIP record for this book is available from the British Library

ISBN 978–1–908524–02–7

Typeset by Tetragon

Printed and bound in UK by CPI Group (UK) Ltd, Croydon, CR0 4YY

For Marta

"In every legend there lies a grain of truth."

– FOLK SAYING

"Half the truth is a whole lie."

– JEWISH PROVERB

"It is the prosecutor's duty to strive to establish the truth."

– ETHICAL PRINCIPLES
FOR THE PROSECUTOR

1

Jews are celebrating the seventh day of Passover and
are commemorating the crossing of the Red Sea. For
Christians it is the fourth day of Easter week. For
Poles it is the second day of a three-day period of
national mourning declared after a hotel fire in Kamień
Pomorski in which twenty-three people were killed. In
the world of European Champions League football Chelsea and Manchester United go forward to the semi-finals, and in the world of Polish football some fans of
ŁKS, the Łódź team whose main rivals are a team called
Widzew, are charged with inciting racial hatred by
wearing T-shirts inscribed "Death to Fucking Widzew-
Yidzew". Police Headquarters issues a report on crime
figures for March — compared with March 2008, crime
has risen by eleven per cent. The police comment: "The
economic crisis is forcing people to commit crimes."
In Sandomierz it has already forced a saleswoman at
a butcher's shop to sell cigarettes free of excise
duty under the counter, and she has been detained.
In the city it is fairly cold, as throughout Poland,
and the temperature does not exceed fourteen degrees
Celsius, but even so it is the first sunny day after
an ice-cold Easter.

I

Ghosts certainly don't appear at midnight. At midnight there are still late films running on TV, teenage boys are having intense thoughts about their lady teachers, lovers are gathering strength before the next go, long-married couples are having serious conversations about "what's happening to our money", good wives are taking cakes out of the oven and bad husbands are waking up the children in their drunken attempts to open the front door. There's too much life going on at midnight for the spirits of the dead to be able to make a proper impression. It's quite another matter shortly before dawn, when even the staff at petrol stations are nodding off, and the dull light is start-ing to pick beings and objects out of the gloom whose existence we had never suspected.

It was approaching four in the morning – the sun would be up in an hour – and Roman Myszyński was fighting off sleep in the reading room at the State Archive in Sandomierz, surrounded by the dead. Around him towered stacks of nineteenth-century parish registers, and even though most of the entries concerned life's happy moments, even though there were more baptisms and weddings than death certificates, even so, he could smell the odour of death, and couldn't shake off the thought that all these newborns and all these newly-weds had been pushing up the daisies for several decades at least, and that the rarely dusted or consulted tomes surrounding him were the only testimony to their existence. Though actually, even so they were lucky, considering what the war had done to most of the Polish archives.

It was bloody cold, there was no coffee left in his thermos, and the only thought he could formulate was to berate himself for the idiotic idea of founding a firm that specialized in genealogical research, instead of taking on a junior lectureship. The salary at the college was low but regular, and came with free health insurance – nothing but pluses. Especially compared with the jobs at schools which his friends from the same year at university had ended up in – just as badly paid, but enhanced with non-stop frustration and criminal threats from the pupils.

He glanced at the huge book lying open in front of him, and at the sentence finely inscribed by the parish priest at Dwikozy in April 1834: "The applicant and witnesses are unable to read." That really would have said it all, as far as Włodzimierz Niewolin's noble ancestry was concerned. But if anyone still had doubts that perhaps the father of Niewolin's great-great-grandfather who presented his child for baptism was just having a rough day after wetting the baby's head, his profession was enough to dispel them – peasant. Myszyński was sure that as soon as he rooted out the marriage certificate, the Marjanna Niewolin mentioned in the birth certificate – fifteen years younger than her husband – would turn out to be a serving wench. Or maybe she was still living with her parents.

He stood up and stretched vigorously, accidentally jogging an old, pre-war photo of the Sandomierz market square that was hanging on the wall. He set it straight, thinking that somehow the square in the postcard looked different from today. More modest. He peered out of the window, but the market-square frontage visible at the end of the street was shrouded in the dark mist of daybreak. What nonsense – why should the old market square look any different? Why on earth was he thinking about it? He should get down to work if he wanted to reconstruct Niewolin's past and get back to Warsaw by one o'clock.

What else might he find? He shouldn't have any trouble with the marriage certificate, and Jakub and Marjanna's birth certificates must be somewhere too – luckily the Congress Kingdom of Poland was fairly kind to the archive researcher. From the start of the nineteenth century, thanks to the Napoleonic Code, in the Duchy of Warsaw all the registry documents had to be drawn up by the parishes in two copies and delivered to the state archive; later on the rules had been changed, but even so it wasn't bad. It was worse in Galicia, and the eastern Borderlands were a real genealogical black hole – there was nothing in the Warsaw archive relating to territory east of the River Bug but the remains of some documents. In other words, Marjanna, born *circa* 1814, shouldn't present a problem. As for Jakub, the tail end of the eighteenth century was still not too bad; the priests were becoming better educated, and apart from in the exceptionally lazy parishes, the books were generally complete. In Sandomierz it was a help that during the last war neither the Germans nor the Soviets had sent them up in smoke. The oldest documents dated from the 1580s. Earlier than that, the trail broke off – it wasn't until the Council of Trent in the sixteenth century that the Church had come up with the idea of registering its flock.

He rubbed his eyes and leant over the outspread records. What he needed were the marriage certificates from Dwikozy dating from the previous two years, and maybe he'd look for the mother at once. Née Kwietniewska. Hmm. A small alarm bell rang in the researcher's head.

Two years had passed since the time when, against everybody's advice, he had founded his company, Golden Genes. He had had the idea for it while gathering material for his thesis at the Central Archive of Historical Records in Warsaw, where he kept coming across people with a mad look in their eyes, ineptly seeking information about their ancestors and trying to draw up their family tree. He helped one lad out of pity, one girl because of her stunningly beautiful bust, and finally Magda, because she was so sweet, with her great big genealogical chart, something like the Tree of Jesse. It ended in Magda and her chart coming to live with him for half a year. Five months too long – she moved out with tears in her eyes and the knowledge that her great-great-grandmother Cecylia was a bastard, because in 1813 it was the midwife who had had her baptized.

Then he had decided he could take advantage of the genealogical craze and sell his ability to make use of the archives. As he registered the business, he was very excited by the prospect of becoming a historical detective, and it never entered his head that the name Golden Genes would mean that every, literally every single client would first ask if it had anything to do with Gene Wilder or Gene Kelly, and then try their best to make a silly joke about "taking down your jeans".

Just like in the opening pages of a crime novel, at first he spent most of his time waiting for the phone to ring and staring at the ceiling, but finally the clients had shown up. From one case to the next, from commission to commission there were more and more of them, unfortunately not for the most part leggy brunettes in stockings. There were two types who came along most often: the first type were complex-ridden, bespectacled men in tank tops with a look on their faces that said "But what have I ever done to you?", whose lives had turned out so badly that they were hoping to find their meaning and value in their long-since-decomposed forebears. With humility and relief, as if they had been expecting this blow, they accepted the information that they were the descendants of no one from nowhere.

The second type – the Niewolin type – made it understood from the start that they were not paying to be told that they came from a clan of drunken carters and worn-out whores, but rather for their crest-bearing noble ancestors to be found and the place where they could take their children to show them that here stood the manor house in which Great-Grandfather Polikarp recovered from the wounds he sustained in the Uprising. Any uprising would do. At first Roman was painfully honest, but later on he realized that his was in fact a private firm, not a research institute. As evidence of the nobility meant bonuses, tips and further customers, let there be nobility. If anyone were to form a view of Poland's past based on nothing but the results of his research, they would soon come to the conclusion that despite appearances it was not a land of primitive peasants, but of distinguished gentlefolk, or at least prosperous burghers. Although he twisted things a bit, Roman never lied – so far he had usually just dug around in an offshoot of the family until he found some lord of the manor.

The worst thing of all was to come upon a Jew. The historical arguments that in inter-war Poland ten per cent of the citizens were Jews, as a result of which one might well find an ancestor of the Jewish faith, especially within the Congress Kingdom, which covered the heart of the country, and Galicia, did not convince anyone. It had happened to him twice – the first time he was sworn at, and the second time he almost got hit in the face. At first he couldn't get over his amazement, then he spent a few days brooding on it, and finally came to the conclusion that the customer is the boss. He usually brought this issue up during the initial conversation, and if it turned out to arouse excessive emotion, he was ready to sweep any chance Izaak under the carpet. However, it had happened extremely rarely – the Holocaust had chopped off the crown of the Jewish genealogical tree.

And now if you please, Marjanna Niewolin, née Kwietniewska, had appeared in the nineteenth-century records. It wasn't always the case, but surnames derived from names of months – in this case "*kwiecień*", meaning "April" – were often the names of converts, after the month in which the baptism took place. The same went for names containing days of the week, or starting with "Nowa-", meaning "new". The name "Dobrowolski" – meaning "good will" – could also indicate the fact that an ancestor had voluntarily converted from the Jewish to the Christian faith. Roman liked to believe that the motive behind these stories was love, and that people faced with a choice between religion or emotion, had chosen the latter. And as Catholicism was the dominant religion in the Most Serene Commonwealth of Poland and Lithuania, the conversions were usually in that direction.

In fact, Roman could drop that lead; as it was, he was surprised Niewolin's documented roots went back so far. But firstly he was curious, and secondly he was annoyed by that arrogant bastard toting a signet ring with a space on it for a crest.

On his laptop, Roman fired up one of his basic tools – a scanned copy of the *Geographical Dictionary of the Polish Kingdom and Other Slavonic Countries*, a monumental work dating from the late nineteenth century, where every village located within the borders of the pre-partition Polish Republic was described. He looked up the entry for Dwikozy, to find out that it was a village and a grange that was formerly Church property, consisting of seventy-seven houses and 548 inhabitants. Not a word about a Jewish community, which was natural, considering there was usually a ban in force on Jews settling on Church estates. In other words, if Marjanna came from a local family of converts, he would have to look in the nearest towns, Sandomierz or Zawichost. He browsed the scanned pages, and discovered that in Sandomierz there were five Jewish hostelries, a synagogue, 3,250 Catholics, fifty Orthodox Christians, one Protestant and 2,715 Jews. Whereas in Zawichost, of a population of 3,948, there were 2,401 people who professed the Jewish faith. A lot. He looked at the map. Intuition told him that Zawichost was a better shot.

He drove off the thought that he was wasting time, got up, did a few squats, winced at the sound of his knees cracking, and left the reading room. He flicked the switch in the dark corridor but nothing happened. He flicked it a couple more times. Still nothing. He looked around hesitantly. Although he was an old hand at spending the night in the archives, he felt uneasy. It's the *genius loci*, he thought, and sighed with pity at his own tendency to fantasize.

Losing patience, he pressed the switch once again, and after a few flashes the stairwell was flooded with pallid fluorescent light. Roman looked down the stairs at the Gothic archway leading from the administrative part of the building into the archive. It looked somehow – how should he put it? – menacing.

He cleared his throat to break the silence and headed downstairs, thinking how the story of Niewolin and his great-great-grandmother née/converted Kwietniewska gained a curious touch of spice from the fact that the Sandomierz archive was housed in an eighteenth-century synagogue. The reading room and the staff offices were in the *kahal* building tacked onto the house of worship, which would have been the administrative headquarters for the Jewish community. The actual records occupied the synagogue's main prayer hall. It was one of the most interesting places he had seen in his career as a detective of the remote past.

Downstairs, he pushed open the heavy iron door studded with nails. The nutty smell of old paper struck his nostrils.

The old prayer hall was in the shape of a large hexagon, and had been adapted in a peculiar way to meet the needs of the archive. An open-plan cube had been constructed in the middle of the room, composed of steel walkways, stairs and, above all, shelving. The cube was not much smaller than the entire room; you could walk around it along the walls, or you could go inside it, into a labyrinth of narrow little corridors, or climb to the upper levels and immerse yourself in the old records there. Its structure made this metal scaffolding into a sort of overgrown *bimah*, in which instead of the Torah you could study registers recording births, marriages, taxes and sentences. Bureaucracy as the holy scripture of the modern era, thought Roman. Without putting on the light, he walked around the scaffolding, running his hand over the cool plaster. He reached the eastern wall, where only a few decades ago the Torah scrolls had been kept in the alcove known as the *aron ha-kodesh*. Roman switched on his torch and the light forced its way through the particles of dust densely rising in the air, picking out of the darkness a golden gryphon holding a tablet with Hebrew writing on it. He suspected it was one of the Tablets of Stone. He aimed the light higher, but the wall paintings situated nearer to the vaulted ceiling were flooded with darkness.

To the tune of a metallic echo, he ascended the steep open-plan stairs to the highest level. There he found himself close to the ceiling. As he walked between the shelves full of records, he started inspecting by torchlight the pictures of signs of the zodiac that adorned the upper part of the room. He frowned at the crocodile. A crocodile? He glanced at its neighbour – Sagittarius, the archer – and realized the crocodile was meant to be a scorpion. Perhaps there was a reason for it being a scorpion. All he could remember was that in Judaism you weren't allowed to represent people. He went up to Gemini, the twins. In spite of that fact, they were represented as human figures, but without heads. He shuddered.

He reckoned he'd had enough of this expedition now, on top of which he had noticed a sea monster wrapped about a small round skylight. Here was Leviathan, the spirit of death and destruction, surrounding a patch of grey light as if it were the entrance to its underwater kingdom, and Roman became ill at ease. He felt a sudden need to get out of the archive, but just then, from the corner of his eye, he noticed something moving on the other side of the aperture. He shoved his head inside the monster, but he couldn't see much through the dirty glass.

On the far side of the room a floorboard creaked. Roman jumped, painfully banging his head against the wall. He cursed and crawled away from the skylight. There was another creak.

"Hello, is there anyone there?"

He shone the torch in all directions, but all he could see were registers, dust and signs of the zodiac.

This time something creaked right next to him. Roman gasped aloud. It took him a while to calm his breathing. Fantastic, he thought, I should treat myself to even less sleep and even more coffee.

At an energetic pace he followed the metal walkway towards the steep stairs; there was a thin railing separating him from the dark hole yawning between the staircase and the wall. As the top level of the scaffolding was also the level of the windows that admitted light into the hall, he passed some very strange contraptions used for opening and cleaning them. They looked like small drawbridges, now raised to the vertical position. To get to the windows, you had to release a thick rope and lower the bridge so that it reached across to the window alcove. Roman thought it rather a curious mechanism – after all, neither the scaffolding housing the records, nor indeed the thick walls of the synagogue were likely to be going anywhere, so they could have been kept permanently lowered. Now it made him think of a battleship with raised gangways, ready to set sail. He swept the entire structure with the beam of his torch and walked towards the stairs. He had only taken a single step when a mighty bang filled the room, a shock ran through the staircase, and he lost his balance, only failing to tumble down the stairs because he seized the railing with both hands. The torch fell from his grip, bounced off the floor twice and went out.

As he straightened up, his heart was beating with dizzying speed. Quickly, feeling slightly hysterical, he inspected his surroundings. The drawbridge he had walked past had fallen. He gazed at it, breathing heavily. Finally he burst out laughing. He must have accidentally disturbed something. Physics – yes; metaphysics – no. All quite simple, really. Whatever, it was the last time he was going to work after dark among all these great-great-grand-corpses.

He blindly groped his way up to the drawbridge and grabbed the rope to pull it vertical again. Of course it was jammed. Swearing like a trooper, he crawled up to the window alcove on his knees. The window looked out onto the same bushes as the aperture guarded by the sea monster.

The world outside was now the only source of light, and it was extremely feeble light. Inside it was almost impossible to see a thing, and outside the break of day was changing into a springtime, still timid dawn; out of the darkness loomed trees, the bottom of the ravine surrounding the old town, the villas built on the opposite side of the escarpment and the wall of the old Franciscan monastery. The black mist was changing into grey mist, but the world was foggy and out of focus, as if reflected in soapy water.

Roman stared at the spot where he had seen something moving earlier – in the bushes just below the remains of the fortifications. As he stared hard, a sterile white shape stood out of the sea of grey. He wiped the window pane with his sleeve, but despite the sophisticated drawbridge mechanism, evidently no one was too keen on cleaning it very often, so he just smeared dust across the glass.

He opened the window and blinked as cold air swept across his face.

Like a little china doll floating in the mist, thought Myszyński, as he gazed at the dead body lying below the synagogue. It was unnaturally, unsettlingly white, shining with lack of colour.

Behind him, the heavy door into the old synagogue crashed shut, as if all the spirits had flown out to see what had happened.

II

Prosecutor Teodor Szacki couldn't sleep. Dawn was breaking, and he hadn't slept a wink all night. Worse yet, that little nymphomaniac hadn't slept at all either. He'd have been happy to pick up a book and read, instead of which he was lying there without moving, pretending to be asleep. He felt scratching behind his ear.

"Are you asleep?"

He smacked his lips a few times and muttered something to fob her off.

"Coz I'm not asleep."

He had to use all his will-power not to let out a loud sigh. Tense all over, he waited to see what would happen. Because something was going to happen, he was sure of it. The warm body behind him moved under the duvet, chuckling like a character in a cartoon who had just thought up a plan for world conquest. And then he felt a painful nip biting his shoulder blade. He leapt out of bed, only just holding back a very strong expletive.

"Have you gone crazy?"

The girl leant on her elbow and gave him a truculent look.

"Sure, I must be crazy, because somehow I got it into my head that maybe you'd want to make me feel good again. Jeezus, I'm just impossible."

Szacki defensively raised his hands skywards and fled into the kitchen for a smoke. He was already at the sink when he heard her call flirtatiously: "I'm waiting." You can wait all you like, he thought, as he put on a fleece. He lit a cigarette and switched on the kettle. Outside the dark-grey roofs stood out against the pale-grey common, separated from the pale nothingness of Sub-Carpathia by the darker ribbon of the Vistula. A car crossed the bridge, two funnels of light moving through the fog. Everything in this image was monochrome, including the white window frame coated in peeling paint, and the reflection of Szacki's pale face, milk-white hair and black top.

What a bloody dump, thought Szacki, and took a drag on his cigarette. Its red glow added some colour to the monochrome world. What a bloody hole he'd been sitting in for several months now, and if anyone had asked him how it had come about, he'd have shrugged helplessly.

First of all, there was the case. There's always some case or other. That particular one was a thankless pain in the arse. It had all started with the murder of a Ukrainian prostitute at a brothel on Krucza Street in central Warsaw – less than a hundred yards from Szacki's office. Usually in that sort of situation finding the corpse was the end of the matter. All the pimps and tarts would be off in minutes, for obvious reasons no witnesses would be found, and anyone who did come forwards couldn't remember a thing; you counted yourself lucky if you actually managed to identify the body.

This time things had turned out differently. A good friend of the dead girl had appeared, the corpse had gained the name Irina, even the pimp had gained a handsome face on a facial-composite portrait from memory, and the connection with the Świętokrzyskie province, which centred on the city of Kielce, had appeared once the case had started to get going. Szacki had spent two weeks travelling around the Sandomierz and Tarnobrzeg areas together with Olga (who was the friend), an interpreter and a guide, to find the place where the girls were being kept after arriving in Poland from further east. Olga told them what she had seen from various windows, and sometimes from behind car windscreens, the interpreter interpreted, and the guide wondered where that could be, while at the same time spinning rustic yarns that drove Szacki up the wall. A local policeman did the driving, making it plain with every twitch of his facial muscles that his time was being wasted because, as he had stated at the very start, they had closed down the only brothel in Sandomierz that summer, and along with it they had got rid of Kasia and Beata, who made a bit of extra cash on the game after work at a shop and a nursery school. The rest were small-time slappers from the catering college. But in Tarnobrzeg or Kielce – there it was quite another matter.

Nevertheless, finally they had found a house in an out-of-the-way spot in the industrial part of Sandomierz – it was the house they were looking for. In a greenhouse converted into a bedroom, they found a petite blonde from Belarus breathing her last, wasted away by gastric flu; apart from that there was no one there. The girl kept repeating on and on that they had gone to the market, and that they'd kill her. Her fear made a great impression on the rest of the expedition – but none whatsoever on Szacki. Whereas the word "market" set him thinking. The bedroom in the greenhouse was pretty big, besides which the property included a large house, a workshop and a warehouse. Szacki imagined Sandomierz on the map of Poland. A backwater with two amateur good-time girls. Churches by the dozen, quiet and sleepy, nothing going on. Not far from Ukraine. Pretty close to Belarus. Two hundred kilometres to the capital, even less to Łódź and Krakow. Altogether not a bad spot for a trafficking hub and a wholesale outlet for live goods. The market.

It turned out there was a market, and quite a big one too – a large bazaar known to the locals as the mart, a place that sold everything and anything, situated between the Old Town and the Vistula, right on the bypass. He asked the policeman what went on there. All sorts of things, he replied, but the Russkies take care of business among themselves – if you start interfering in that, you'll only mess up the statistics. Occasionally the police pick up a kid with knock-off CDs or grass, so it won't look as if they're not interested.

On the one hand it seemed pretty unlikely that any gangsters could be so stupid as to traffic in people at a bazaar. On the other, there was a reason why these people weren't busy colliding hadrons or floating companies on the stock exchange. And, in fact, the bazaar was outside the jurisdiction of the city.

They took away the sick girl, who could hardly stand, went off and found it – two large vans among the sweet stalls, supposedly full of clothes, but in fact containing twenty girls chained up, all of whom had come here in search of a better world. It was the Sandomierz police force's biggest success since the time they had recovered a stolen bicycle, for a month the local papers wrote about nothing else, and Szacki briefly became a small-town celebrity. The autumn had been beautiful.

And he liked it here.

And then he thought: what if?

They were having a drink at the Modena pizzeria not far from the prosecutor's office, he was already quite well oiled, and he asked in a naive way if they happened to have any vacancies. Yes, they did. It only happened once every twenty years, but just at that moment they did.

And so he was to start a wonderful new life. Pick up girls in clubs, go running along the Vistula each morning, revel in the fresh air, have some adventures, feel uplifted, and finally find the greatest love of his life and grow old with her in a house covered with vines somewhere near Piszczele Street. So it'd be a short walk to the market square, to be able to sit down at the Mała Café or the Kordegarda restaurant and have a cup of coffee. When he first moved here, this image was so vivid that he even found it hard to call it a plan or a dream. It was a reality which had entered his life and started to take effect – simple as that. He could remember the exact moment when he had sat on a bench outside the castle, basking in the autumn sunshine, and seen his own future so clearly that the tears almost came to his eyes. Finally! Finally he knew exactly what he wanted.

Well, to put it subtly, he had been wrong. To put it unsubtly, he had thrown the life he had spent years building down the toilet in exchange for a sodding pipe dream, and now he was left with nothing, which felt so terrible that it even gave him a sense of exoneration for his own bad behaviour. Absolutely and exactly nothing.

Instead of being the star of the capital city's prosecution service, he was an outsider who prompted mistrust in a provincial city, which was in fact dead after six p.m. – but unfortunately not because the citizens had been murdering one another. They didn't murder each other at all. They didn't even try to commit murder. They didn't commit rape. They didn't organize themselves into criminal gangs. They rarely attacked one another. Whenever Szacki mentally browsed the catalogue of cases he was working on, he got a bad taste in his mouth. It couldn't be true.

Instead of a family, he had loneliness. Instead of love, loneliness. Instead of intimacy, loneliness. The crisis triggered by his pitiful – as well as brief and mutually unsatisfying – affair with a journalist, Monika Grzelka, had pushed his marriage into a hole from which it had no chance of digging itself out. They had carried on a bit longer, as if for the good of the child, but by then it was in its feeble, dying phase. He had always thought he was the one who deserved more, and that Weronika was dragging him down. Meanwhile, less than six months after their final parting she had started dating an up-and-coming lawyer a year younger than herself. Recently she had casually informed Szacki that they had decided to live together at the man's house in Warsaw's Wawer district, and that maybe he should meet and talk to Tomasz, who was now going to be bringing up his daughter.

He really had lost everything there was to lose. He had nothing and nobody, on top of which, of his own free will, he had become an exile in a place he didn't like and that didn't like him. Calling Klara, whom he had picked up in a club a month ago and then sent packing three days later, when in the light of day she didn't seem either pretty, or intelligent, or interesting, had been an act of desperation, the ultimate proof of his downfall.

He stubbed out his cigarette and went back to the monochrome world. Only briefly – some long red fingernails appeared on his fleece. He closed his eyes to hide his irritation, but he couldn't muster the courage to be cruel to the girl, whom first of all he had seduced, and to whom now he was still giving false hopes that there might be something between them.

He went to bed like a good boy to perform some boring sex. Klara wriggled away underneath him, as if trying to make up for the lack of tenderness and fantasy. As she gazed at him, she must have noticed something in his face that made her try even harder. She squirmed and began to moan.

"Oh yes, fuck me, I'm yours, I want to feel you deep inside."

Prosecutor Teodor Szacki tried to control himself, but he couldn't, and burst out laughing.

III

No corpse looks good, but some look worse than others. The cadaver lying in the ravine below the medieval walls of Sandomierz belonged to the latter category. One of the policemen was mercifully covering the woman's nakedness, when the prosecutor appeared at the scene of the murder.

"Don't cover her up yet."

The policeman looked up.

"For goodness' sake, I've known her since nursery school – she can't lie there like that."

"I knew her too, Piotr. It doesn't really mean anything now."

Prosecutor Barbara Sobieraj gently raked aside some leafless twigs and kneeled beside the corpse. Tears blurred her view of it. She had often seen dead bodies, usially dragged out of car wrecks on the bypass, sometimes even the corpses of people whom she knew by sight. But never anyone she knew personally. And certainly not an old friend. She knew, surely better than others, that people commit crimes and that you can fall victim to them. But this – this couldn't be true.

She coughed to clear her throat.

"Does Grzegorz know yet?"

"I thought you'd tell him. After all, you know…"

Barbara glanced at him, and was just about to erupt, but she realized the Marshal – as this policeman was known in Sandomierz – was right. For many years she had been a close friend of the happy couple, Elżbieta and Grzegorz Budnik. At one time there had even been a rumour that if Elżbieta hadn't come back from Krakow when she did, then who knows – some people had already heard hints that Barbara and he were an item. Gossip and ancient history, but actually, if anyone was going to tell Grzegorz, it should be her. Unfortunately.

She sighed. This wasn't an accident, it wasn't a mugging or an assault or a rape committed by drunken thugs. Someone must have put himself to a lot of trouble to kill her, then carefully to undress her and lay her in these bushes. And that too… Barbara was trying not to look, but every now and then her gaze went back to the victim's mutilated neck. Slashed repeatedly from side to side, her throat looked like a gill, thin flakes of skin, with bits of the veins, larynx and oesophagus visible between them. Meanwhile the face above this macabre wound was strangely calm, even smiling a little, which, combined with the unusual plaster whiteness of the skin, gave it an unreal, statue-like quality. It occurred to Barbara that maybe someone had murdered Elżbieta in her sleep, or while she was unconscious. She seized onto this thought and tried hard to believe it.

The Marshal came up to her and placed a hand on her shoulder.

"I'm awfully sorry, Basia."

She gave him the nod to cover up the corpse.

24

IV

Holes like this one do have their good side: nothing's ever far away. As soon as he got the call from the boss, with a sigh of relief Szacki abandoned Klara and left his rented bachelor pad in the apartment block on Długosz Street. Small, ugly and neglected, it had one advantage – its location, in the Old Town, overlooking the Vistula and the historic secondary school founded by the Jesuits in the seventeenth century. He emerged from the building, and walked to the market square at a rapid pace, slipping on the wet cobblestones. The air was still bracing, as in winter, but one could sense this was already the tail end of it. As the fog grew thinner with every step, Szacki hoped today would be the first of the beautiful spring days. He really did need some positive emotion in his life. Some sunshine and warmth.

He walked across the entirely deserted market square, passed the post-office building located in a fine tenement house with arcades, and reached Żydowska Street, with the glow of the flashing blue lights already visible from afar. It struck a sensitive chord in him – the sight of police light-bars in the mist was part of a ritual. The early morning call, extracting himself from Weronika's warm embrace, getting dressed in the hallway in the dark, and planting a kiss on the sleeping child's forehead before leaving. Then a drive across the capital as it came to life, the street lamps going off, the night buses driving down to the depot. On site, Kuzniecow's sceptical smirk, then the corpse, and coffee at Three Crosses Square. And a clash with his grouchy lady boss at the prosecution service. "Our offices appear to be in different dimensions of time and space, Prosecutor Szacki."

He was feeling nostalgic as he passed the synagogue building and, holding on to some branches, made his way down the escarpment. He immediately recognized the "principled pussy" by her shock of ginger hair. She was standing with her head drooping, as if she had come to say a prayer for the dead rather than conduct an inquiry. An obese cop had his hand on her shoulder, joining her in her pain. Just as Szacki had supposed – a city where there were more churches than bars was bound to leave a painful mark on its citizens. Barbara

Sobieraj turned towards Szacki, and was too surprised by the sight of him to hide the scowl of dislike that crept over her face.

He nodded to everyone in greeting, went up to the corpse and un-ceremoniously lifted the plastic sheet that was covering it. A woman. Between forty and fifty. Hideously slashed throat, no sign of other injuries. It didn't look like an assault, more like a bizarre crime of passion. Well, finally a decent corpse. He was just about to cover the body again, but something was bothering him. He examined it again from head to foot, and visually scanned the crime scene. Something wasn't right, something definitely wasn't right, but he had no idea what, and it was a very unsettling feeling. He tossed aside the plastic sheet, and some of the policemen turned their gaze in shame. Amateurs.

Now he knew what was wrong. The whiteness. The unreal, unnatu-ral whiteness of the victim's body. But there was something else too.

"Excuse me," said Sobieraj behind him, "that's my friend."

"That was your friend," snapped Szacki in reply. "Where are the technicians?"

Silence. He turned around and looked at the fat policeman, who was bald with a bushy moustache. What was his nickname? The Marshal? How original.

"Where are the technicians?" he repeated.

"Marysia's just coming."

Everyone here was on first-name terms. Nothing but old friends, blast them, a small-town clique.

"Send for a team from Kielce, too. Tell them to bring all their toys. Before they get here, cover the body, cordon off the area within a radius of fifty metres and don't let anybody in. Keep the gawpers as far away as possible. Is the detective here already?"

The Marshal raised his hand, staring at Szacki as if he were from outer space and looking enquiringly at Sobieraj, who was standing dumbstruck.

"Great. I know there's mist, it's dark and there's bugger all to see, but everyone in these buildings" – he pointed at the houses on Żydowska Street – "and those ones" – he turned round and pointed at the villas on the other side of the ravine – "must be interviewed. Maybe there's

26

someone who suffers from insomnia, maybe someone's got prostate trouble, maybe there's a crazy hausfrau who makes soup before going to work. Someone might have seen something. Got it?"

The Marshal nodded. Meanwhile Sobieraj had regained her composure and was standing so close that he could smell her breath. She was tall for a woman – their eyes were almost on the same level. Country girls are always handsome creatures, thought Szacki, waiting calmly to see what would happen.

"Excuse me, but are you conducting this case now?"

"Yes."

"And might I know why?"

"Let me see. Because for once it has nothing to do with a drunken cyclist or the theft of a mobile phone at a primary school?"

Sobieraj's dark eyes went black.

"I'm going straight to Misia," she hissed.

Szacki reached into the deepest, unexplored depths of his will-power to stop himself from snorting with laughter. Good God in Heaven – they really did call their boss Misia.

"The quicker, the better. It was she who dragged me out of the sack, where I was passing the time in a madly interesting way, and told me to deal with this."

For a moment Sobieraj looked as if she was about to explode, but she turned on her heel and walked off, swinging her hips. Narrow, unappealing hips, reckoned Szacki, as he watched her go. He turned to address the Marshal.

"Will someone from the criminal investigation department be coming? Do they start work at ten?"

"I'm here, sonny, I'm here," he heard a voice behind his back.

Behind him on a folding fishing chair sat an old boy with a moustache – almost all of them here had moustaches – smoking a fag with no filter. Not his first. On one side of the seat lay several torn-off filters, and on the other several dog-ends. Szacki masked his own surprise and went up to the old cop. His snow-white hair was cut short, his face was furrowed, like a Leonardo self-portrait, and he had pale, watery eyes. On the other hand his well-trimmed, modest moustache was jet black, which gave the old boy an alarmingly demonic look. He must have been about seventy. If he was younger, evidently there had been plenty of astonishing ups and downs in his life. He gazed with a bored expression as Szacki stood in front of him and offered his hand.

"Teodor Szacki."

The old policeman sniffed, discarded his fag-end on the correct side of the chair and shook hands without getting up.

"Leon."

He held onto Szacki's hand and took advantage of his help to get up. He was tall, very skinny, and under his thick jacket and scarf he probably looked like a vanilla pod – thin, bendy and wrinkled. Szacki let go of the old boy's hand and waited for the next part of the introduction. Which did not come. The old man glanced over at the Marshal, who bounced up to them, as if he was on elastic.

"Inspector?"

Surely that was a mistake – too high a rank for a cop from the provincial investigative branch.

"Do as the prosecutor said. Kielce will be here in twenty minutes."

"Take it easy – it's almost a hundred kilometres," protested Szacki.

"I called them an hour ago," muttered the old boy. "And then I waited for you prosecutors to roll up. Good thing I brought my folding chair. Coffee?"

"Sorry?"

"Do you drink coffee, Prosecutor? The Ciżemka opens at seven."

"As long as we don't eat anything there."

The old boy nodded with respect.

"He may be young and from outside, but he learns quickly. Let's go. I want to be here when the kids with the toys turn up."

V

The dining hall at the Ciżemka, as the hotel with the best tourist location in town was called – on the market square, by the street that led to the cathedral and the castle – was everything that restaurants in civilized cities had ceased to be a decade ago. It was a large, un-welcoming space with tables covered in an underlay as well as a top cloth, and high-backed chairs upholstered in plush. There were lamps on the walls, and candelabra hanging from the ceiling. Tapping her heels, the waitress had to cross such a large expanse that Szacki was sure the coffee would go cold on the way.

It hadn't gone cold, but he could taste a distant hint of dirty dishcloth in it – a sign that the espresso machine was not top of the list of items to be cleaned on a daily basis at this smart Sandomierz facility. Does that surprise me? thought Teodor Szacki. Not in the least.

Inspector Leon drank his coffee in silence, gazing out of the window at the pinnacles of the town hall. Szacki might as well not have been there. He decided to adapt to the old boy's pace and wait patiently until he found out what he had been dragged here for. Finally the policeman put down his cup, coughed and tore the filter off a ciga-rette. He sighed.

"I will help you." He had an unpleasant voice, as if it were badly oiled.

Szacki gave him an enquiring look.

"Have you ever lived outside Warsaw?"

"Only now."

"In other words you know bugger all about life."

Szacki did not pass comment.

"But that's no sin. Every youngster knows bugger all about life. But I will help you."

Szacki's irritation was rising.

"Does that help only cover carrying out your duties, or something else on top? We don't know each other, so it's hard for me to judge how kind-hearted you are."

Only now did Leon look at the prosecutor for longer.

"Not very," he replied without smiling. "But I'm extremely curious to know who butchered that clown Budnik's wife and threw her in the bushes. Intuition tells me you're going to find out. But you're not from round here. Everyone will talk to you, but no one will tell you anything. Maybe that's a good thing – less information means a purer mind."

"More information means the truth," put in Szacki.

"The truth is the truth – floating in a cesspool of superfluous knowledge doesn't make it any truer," wheezed the inspector. "And don't interrupt me, young man. Sometimes you'll be struggling to understand who really did what with whom and why. And then I will help you."

"Are you friends with all of them?"

"I'm not good at making friends. And don't ask me questions that aren't relevant or I'll lose my good opinion of you."

Szacki had a few relevant questions to ask, but he kept them for later.

"And I'd prefer us to remain on formal terms," concluded the policeman; Szacki didn't let it show how very much he liked that proposal. He nodded his consent.

VI

There were more and more gawpers, but luckily they were standing there politely. Szacki caught the name Budnik coming from the conversations being held in hushed tones. For a moment he wondered if he needed to know who the victim was right now. He realized that he didn't. What he needed now was a very careful inspection of the crime scene and the body. The rest could wait.

He and Inspector Leon, who in the meantime had acquired the surname Wilczur, stood next to the body, which was now surrounded by a screen, while the technician from Kielce took photographs of it. Szacki carefully examined the precisely slashed throat, which looked as if it had been carefully sliced to make anatomical specimens to go under slides, and was furious that he still couldn't identify the unbearable buzzing in his head. Something wasn't right. Of course he would find out what, but he would prefer to understand it before he got down to the interviewing and the search for experts. The head of the inspection team came up to them, a friendly thirty-year-old with bulging eyes and the look of a judo fighter. After introducing himself, he fixed his fish-like gaze on Szacki.

"Just out of curiosity, where have you landed from, Prosecutor?" he asked.

"From the capital."

"From the Big Smoke itself?" He didn't try to hide his surprise, as if the next question were going to be whether Szacki had been kicked out for drink, drugs or sexual harassment.

"As I said, from the capital." Szacki loathed the expression "the Big Smoke".

"But did you get into trouble, or something like that?"

"Something like that."

"Aha." For a moment the policeman waited for this heart-to-heart to continue, but he gave up on it. "Apart from the body there's nothing, we haven't found any clothes, handbags, or jewellery. There are no signs of dragging, and no evidence of a struggle either. It looks as if she was carried here. We've made casts of the tyre tracks lower down and the footprints that were fresh. It'll all be in the report, but I wouldn't count on much, except from the autopsy."

Szacki nodded. Not that he was particularly excited. He had solved all his cases by relying on personal, not material evidence. Of course it would be nice to find the murder weapon in the bushes and the murderer's identity card, but he had long since realized that nice wasn't an everyday occurrence in Teodor Szacki's life.

"Commissioner!" yelled one of the technicians rootling about in the bushes on the escarpment.

The goggle-eyed man indicated for them to wait, and ran off towards the remains of the medieval wall, which had once tightly girded the city and now served mainly as a shady place for knocking back cheap, traditional Polish apple wine. Szacki headed after the technician, who was squatting by the wall, raking aside some still leafless twigs and last year's grass. Goggle-Eyes reached out a gloved hand and cautiously picked something up. Just then the sun broke through the clouds and shone keenly on the object, dazzling Szacki for a moment. Only after blinking several times to dispel the black spots dancing before his eyes could he see that the technician was holding a bizarre knife. He carefully put it into a sealed evidence bag and held it out in their direction. But the tool must have been devilishly sharp, because thanks to the mere weight of it, the blade pierced the bag and it fell to the ground.

31

That is, it would have fallen, if the squatting technician hadn't caught it at the last moment by the handle. He caught it and gazed at them.

"You could have lost your fingers," said Goggle-Eyes calmly.

"You could have contaminated the murder weapon with your blood, you cretin," said Wilczur calmly.

Szacki looked at the old policeman.

"How do you know it's the murder weapon?"

"I assume it is. As we've found a precisely slashed throat under one bush and a razor as sharp as a samurai sword under another, there might be a connection between them."

"Razor" was a good word to describe the knife, which Goggle-Eyes was putting into another bag, this time more cautiously. It had a rectangular blade as shiny as a mirror, but with no sharp tip and no curvature. The dark wooden handle was very fine compared with the metal part, completely inappropriate. Whereas the blade itself was huge – about thirty centimetres long and ten wide. A razor, a razor for shaving a giant with a face the size of a delivery van. Both the metal part and the handle – at least at first glance – were undecorated. It wasn't a collector's toy, but a tool. Maybe it was the murder weapon, but above all it was a tool with some application other than shaving the legs of the Fifty-Foot Woman.

"Finger prints, trace evidence, blood, secretions, DNA material, chemical analysis," listed Szacki. "As fast as possible. And I want detailed photographs of this charming object today."

He handed Goggle-Eyes his business card. The man put it in his pocket as he gazed suspiciously at the large razor.

Wilczur tore the filter off another cigarette.

"I don't like it," he remarked. "Much too fanciful."

VII

Prosecutor Teodor Szacki had no luck with his bosses. The last one had been a technocratic bitch, as cold and attractive as a corpse dug out from under snow. Many a time, as he had sat in her office absorbing smoke and putting up with a person totally devoid of femininity trying to make a feminine impression on him, he had wondered if he could possibly do worse. Not long after, malevolent fate had answered that question.

"No really, please try it." Maria Miszczyk, who to Szacki's horror was called Misia, her nickname, in a most unbusinesslike way by everyone at work including herself, pushed a cake platter under his nose. The cake consisted of layers of something like chocolate brownie, plain sponge and possibly meringue.

His boss smiled at him radiantly.

"I put an ever-so thin layer of plum jam under the meringue. I've still got some left over from the autumn. Go on, please have some."

Szacki didn't want it, but Miszczyk's friendly smile was like the stare of a cobra. Stripped of his mind's control, his hand reached out for the cake, and in obedience to the woman's will it took a piece and stuffed it into Szacki's mouth. He smiled wryly, showering his suit in crumbs.

"All right then, Basia, tell us what this is about," said Miszczyk, putting down the platter.

Barbara Sobieraj – known informally as Basia – sat stiffly on a leather sofa, separated from Szacki, who was comfortably ensconced in a matching armchair, next to a small glass table. If Miszczyk had wanted to create a homely atmosphere in her office by taking the average furnishings of the typical Polish small family house as her model, she had achieved her aim.

"I'd like to know," said Sobieraj, either unable, or simply not trying to hide the grievance in her voice, "why, after running my own investigations for seven years at our prosecution office, I'm being kept off Ela's murder. And I'd like to know why Mr Szacki is to run it, whose achievements I don't deny, but who doesn't yet know the town and its particulars all that well. And I'd like to add that I was sorry to find out about it in this way. You could at least have warned me, Misia."

Miszczyk's face looked genuinely worried in a motherly way. There was so much warmth and understanding radiating from her that Szacki could sense the smell of the nursery-school canteen. He was nice and safe – the teacher lady would be sure to solve the problem so that no one felt sad any more. And then she'd give them a hug.

"Oh, I know, Basia, I'm sorry. But when I found out about Ela I had to act quickly. Normally this sort of case would have waited for you. But it's not a normal situation. Ela was a close friend of yours. Grzegorz was involved with you. You were friends with them, you often met up. A lawyer could use that against us."

Sobieraj chewed her lip.

"Apart from which, emotions are no help in an inquiry," Szacki delivered the final blow, took another piece of cake and answered her murderous look with a smile.

"You know bugger all about my emotions."

"It's blissful ignorance."

Miszczyk clapped her hands and looked at them as if to say: "Children, children, you really must stop it now!" Szacki forced himself not to drop his gaze, but to resist the reproach in her gentle, doe-like, motherly eyes.

"You can snipe at each other afterwards, my loves. Now I'm going to tell you about your professional position."

Sobieraj twitched and quickly started talking. How many of these neurotic birds had Szacki seen in his life? Legions.

"I hope that—"

"Basia," Miszczyk stopped her mid-sentence, "I'm happy to hear your views and suggestions. I'm always happy to listen, you know that, don't you? But right now I'm going to tell you about your professional position."

Sobieraj shut up on the instant, and Szacki looked closely at Miszczyk. She was still the mummy with gentle eyes, the smile of a children's therapist and a voice that recalled the scent of vanilla and baking powder. But if the last remark she had made were stripped of its form, it would sound like a firm put-down.

Miszczyk poured them all more tea.

"I knew Ela Budnik, and I know Grzegorz too, just as everyone here does. We don't have to like him or agree with him, but it's hard to overlook him. This will be – already is a major, well-known inquiry. A situation where it's run by a friend of the victim—"

"And of the main suspect," put in Szacki.

Sobieraj snorted.

"Please watch what you say. You don't know the man."

"I don't have to. He's the victim's husband. At this stage that makes him the main suspect."

"And that's just what I'm talking about." Sobieraj raised her hands in triumph. "That's why you should keep right away from this case."

Miszczyk waited a moment until there was silence again.

"That is exactly why Prosecutor Szacki will not only not keep away from this case, but will run the inquiry. Because I want to avoid a situation where the corpse, the suspects and the investigator are a gang of old friends, who only the other day were making a date for a barbecue. But you're right, Basia, that Mr Szacki is new here. That's why you're going to give him advice, help and information about everything to do with the city and its residents."

Szacki sighed with relief as a large piece of cake squeezed past his gullet. We're in for lots of fun, he thought. Sobieraj sat motionless on the sofa, changing into one great big sulk. Miszczyk cast a maternal eye at their cups and the cake platter, and then turned it one hundred and eighty degrees.

"There's more jam on this side," she said in a theatrical whisper, taking a piece.

Szacki waited a moment, realized that the audience was over, and got up. Miszczyk waved her hand to say that as soon as she finished her mouthful she'd have something else to say.

"Let's meet here at seven p.m. I want to see the first witness statements and a detailed investigation plan. Send all the media to me. If I see any personal animosity obstructing you in this case…"

Sobieraj and Szacki fixed their gaze on the boss's plump, crumb-coated lips in unison. She smiled at them warmly.

"…I'll give you such hell you'll never forget it. And the only job open to you in any public institution will be scrubbing the floors at the nick. Is that clear?"

Szacki nodded, bowed to both ladies and took hold of the door handle.

"Presumably I'm to hand the rest of my cases over to someone else."

Miszczyk smiled softly. He realized it was a completely unnecessary question. He was actually insulting her by imagining she might not have thought of that. It must all have been arranged by now, and the secretary would be removing the documents from his office.

"You must be out of your mind. Get back to work."

VIII

Prosecutor Teodor Szacki was standing in his office, looking out of the window and thinking that the provinces had their plus points too. He had a large office all to himself, which in Warsaw would have been divided into three two-person rooms. He had a nice view of green fields, residential buildings and the towers of the Old Town in the distance. He had a twenty-minute walk to work. He had a safe with the files for his eight current cases in it – exactly ninety-seven fewer than in Warsaw six months earlier. He had the same salary as in the capital, and the excellent coffee in his favourite café on Sokolnicki Street cost him less than five zlotys. And finally – he was ashamed of the fact, but he couldn't hide his satisfaction – he had a decent corpse. Suddenly this hellish, sleepy hole seemed an altogether bearable place.

The door slammed. Szacki turned round, adding the thought that he also had a partner who had made PMT into a way of life. He automatically adopted his cold, professional prosecutor's mask as he watched the principled pussy, Basia Sobieraj, approach him with a folder in her hand.

"This has just arrived. We should look at it."

He pointed to the sofa (that's right, he had a sofa in his office) and they sat down next to each other. He glanced at her bust, but couldn't see anything interesting there because it was shrouded in a completely asexual black polo neck. He opened the folder. The first picture showed a close-up of the victim's slashed-open throat. Sobieraj audibly took a gulp of air and looked away, and Szacki was about to pass comment, but he felt sorry and kept his spiteful remarks to himself. It wasn't their fault or their shortcoming that all the people here added together had seen as many corpses in their entire lives as he had in a single year.

He put aside the pictures of the corpse.

"Anyway, we have to wait for the examination. Will you be coming to Oczko Street?"

She stared without understanding; he had automatically referred to the forensic unit in Warsaw.

"Sorry – to the hospital. For the autopsy."

There was a flash of fear in her eyes, but she quickly took control of herself.

"I think we should both be there."

Szacki agreed, and laid out on the table about a dozen pictures of the razor, carefully photographed from all angles. According to the ruler underneath it, the razor was more than forty centimetres long, with the rectangular blade alone accounting for about thirty of them. The handle was covered in dark wood, and there was something engraved on the brass fittings. Szacki looked for a close-up. The faded inscription said: C.RUNEWALD. On one of the close-ups he noticed the photographer's hand reflected in the polished, mirror-smooth blade. A lady photographer, married, judging by the wedding ring. The silvery blade was entirely free of stains, scratches or chips. Undoubtedly a masterpiece of the art of metallurgy. An antique masterpiece.

"Do you think it's the murder weapon, Mrs Sobieraj?"

Szacki was already finding all these politenesses tiresome, and in the course of the investigation they were bound to become intolerable.

"I think it's all very odd and theatrical. A naked corpse with a slashed throat, an antique razor-machete dropped nearby, no sign of a fight or a struggle," he said.

"And no blood on the blade."

"Let's see what the guys at the lab can find. I think there'll be blood, some trace evidence, DNA. The knife will tell us more than the person who planted it there would like."

"Planted?"

"So neat, clean, and untouched? Someone did that on purpose. Even with squalid crimes of passion every drunken thug remembers to take the murder weapon with him. I don't believe it was left in those bushes by accident."

Sobieraj took a pair of reading glasses out of her handbag and started closely examining the pictures. The thick brown frames suited her. It occurred to Szacki that if the razor-machete was a message, they'd have to find someone who could interpret it. Bloody hell, what sort of specialist could deal with that? An expert on cold steel? Or on militaria? Metallurgy? Or works of art?

Sobieraj handed him the photo with the close-up of the wood-encased handle and took off her glasses.

"We'll have to look for an expert on cold steel, best of all a museum curator. They might have heard of this firm."

"C. Runewald?" asked Szacki.

Sobieraj snorted with laughter.

"Grünewald. Maybe it's high time for a pair of specs, Mr Szacki."

Szacki opted for peace. No smirk, no nervous reaction, no retort.

"It's high time you told me all about the victim and her family."

Sobieraj was put out.

IX

Prosecutor Teodor Szacki was dissatisfied. Sobieraj's account of the Budniks had provided a lot of information, but also a lot of feelings. In his mind the victim had ceased to be just the result of an illegal act for which someone must be held responsible and bear the penalty. The victim's husband had ceased to be prime suspect. Thanks to Sobieraj's colourful, emotional account they had become too much like real people of flesh and blood; the border between information and interpretation had been crossed. In spite of himself, as he thought about the victim, Szacki could see a smiling teacher, giving ecology lessons on bike rides. Her husband was not just a candidate for a stretch in the nick, but also a social campaigner capable of fighting to the bitter end over every, even the most minor affair, as long as it was for the good of the town. Szacki doubted whether there was any independent councillor anywhere else in Poland who was quite so good at persuading the entire council to vote unanimously – for Sandomierz. Enough, enough, enough – he didn't want to think about the Budniks until he had talked to the old policeman, who had already made it clear that he wasn't entirely sold on these secular saints.

He tried to occupy his thoughts by looking for information about the mysterious razor-machete, and that was the second reason for his dissatisfaction. Teodor Szacki mistrusted people in general, and people with hobbies in particular. He regarded passion and devotion to a passion, especially one for collecting things, as a disorder, and people inclined towards that sort of fixation on a single subject as potentially dangerous. He had seen suicides caused by the loss of a coin collection, and he had also seen two wives whose misdeeds were to rip up a priceless stamp and to burn a first edition of Jarosław Iwaszkiewicz's pre-war short stories. Neither was still alive. The husbands who had murdered them had sat over their corpses in tears, saying over and over again that they simply didn't understand.

Meanwhile, the world of knives turned out to be full of enthusiasts and collectors, and there was even a periodical called *Thrust*, the mission of which – as the authors claimed – was "to provide you, dear Reader, with reliable information on top-quality knives and related topics. There are also plenty of curiosities, for example in our next issue 'The Whip', which may seem an exotic topic in the context of knife-collecting, but is about an item that has been made here in Poland since ancient times. A series of articles on cold steel will speak for itself."

Whips, sabres and butcher's knives – what a charming hobby, thought Szacki, cringing, as he immersed himself in chat-rooms full of debate about blades, handles, sharpening methods, chiselling, carving and stabbing. He read the outpourings of a writer who made samurai swords by hand, he read about the "Father of the Modern Damast Knife" who had mastered the technique of reproducing Damascus steel, he looked at pictures of army daggers, hunting knives for dressing game animals, foils, bayonets, rapiers and broadswords. He had never imagined humanity produced so many different kinds of sharp object.

But he couldn't find the razor-machete.

Finally, in an act of desperation he took a few photos of the probable murder weapon with his mobile phone and sent them to the editors of *Thrust* by e-mail, asking whether they meant anything to them.

X

The spring had come and gone, and that evening Teodor Szacki was feeling the cold as he walked along Mickiewicz Street towards the Modena pizzeria, where he had arranged to meet Wilczur. The old policeman had refused to be persuaded to meet in the market square, claiming that he couldn't stand "that bloody museum", and Szacki had lived in Sandomierz long enough by now to know what he meant.

Sandomierz really consisted of two, or even three towns. The third was the so-called works on the other side of the river, a memento of the days when the Reds had tried to change the bourgeois, churchy, historical town into an industrial city and had erected an enormous glassworks there. This dismal, ugly district looked intimidating, with a closed-down railway station, a hideous church and a vast factory chimney, which every minute of the day and night destroyed the panorama of Sub-Carpathia visible from the high left bank of the Vistula.

Town Number Two was the Sandomierz where life actually happened. Here there was a smallish housing estate of fortunately not too invasive blocks, here there were residential districts with one-family houses, schools, parks, a cemetery, an army unit, the police, a bus station, smaller and larger shops, and a library. It was the typical Polish provincial town, maybe a bit less neglected, and its hillside location made it more attractive than others. Yet it wouldn't have stood out from countless Polish holes, were it not for Town Number One.

Town Number One was the picture-postcard Sandomierz of TV cop show *Father Mateusz* and classic writer Jarosław Iwaszkiewicz, a little gem set on a high escarpment, whose panorama delighted everyone without exception, and which in his time Szacki had fallen in love with. He was still capable of taking a walk onto the bridge merely in order to see the historic houses banked up on the hillside, the dignified Collegium Gostomianum, the towers of the town hall and the cathedral, the Renaissance gable of the Opatowska Gate, and the solid mass of the castle. Depending on the season and the time of day, this view looked different every time, and every time it was just as breathtaking.

Unfortunately, as Szacki knew all too well now, it was a view which only made a very Italian, Tuscan impression from a distance. Once you were on the inside of the Old Town, everything was very Polish. Sandomierz was too far away from Krakow, and above all too far from Warsaw to become a holiday resort like Kazimierz Dolny. Which it deserved infinitely more, being a beautiful town, and not just a big village with three Renaissance houses and a few dozen hotels, so that every Polish company chairman had somewhere to roger his mistress. Its location off the beaten track meant that Sandomierz's lovely old-town streets exuded boredom, emptiness, Polish hopelessness – it really was nothing but "a bloody museum". In the afternoon the school tour groups disappeared, the old residents of the tenement houses shut themselves at home, not long after the few shops closed, and a little later so did the bars and cafés. As early as six p.m., Szacki had sometimes walked right across the Old Town, from the castle to the Opatowska Gate, without meeting a living soul. One of the most beautiful towns in Poland was deserted, dead and depressing.

Szacki really did feel better once he had got to the end of Sokolnicki Street, left the Old Town and started walking along Mickiewicz Street to the Modena. Cars appeared, and people; the shops were still full at this hour, there were kids glued to their mobile phones, someone eating a doughnut, someone running for the bus, someone shouting to a woman on the other side of the road to say, "Coming, coming, in a moment." Szacki breathed deeply, and was afraid to admit it to himself, but he was badly missing the city. So badly that even the modest substitute for it offered by this part of Sandomierz made the blood run quicker in his veins.

The Modena was a provincial dive that stank of beer, but he had to grant it to them, they served the best pizza in Sandomierz here, and thanks to their delicious "Romantica", armed with a double helping of mozzarella, Szacki's cholesterol level had jumped more than once. Just like a typical cop, Inspector Leon Wilczur was sitting in the blackest corner with his back against the wall. Without a jacket he looked even thinner, and Szacki was reminded of the hall of mirrors at a holiday fun fair. It was impossible for a person to be quite so skinny, like a fake head set on top of some old clothes for a joke.

Without a word he sat down opposite the old policeman, and a whole set of questions flew through his mind.

"Do you know who did it?"

Wilczur's look acknowledged the question.

"No. Nor do I have any idea who could have done it. I don't know anyone who would have wanted to. I don't know anyone who could gain from this death. I'd have said no one from round here, if not for the fact that it must be someone from round here. I don't believe in the idea of a wandering stranger putting himself to so much trouble."

That really did answer Szacki's key questions, even if he had been intending to answer each of them in person. Time to move on to the supporting ones.

"Beer or vodka?"

"Water."

Szacki ordered water, as well as Cola and a Romantica. After that he sat and listened to Wilczur's scratchy voice, while mentally drawing up a record of the divergences between the old policeman's account and Sobieraj's mawkish delivery. The dry facts were the same. Grzegorz Budnik had been a Sandomierz councillor "for ever", i.e. since 1990, with unfulfilled mayoral aspirations, and his late wife Elżbieta (Ela for short), fifteen years his junior, was an English teacher at the famous "Number One" – in other words the grammar school that occupied the building of the old Jesuit college – ran an arts club for children and was active in every possible kind of local cultural event. They lived in a small house on Katedralna Street, apparently once occupied by Iwaszkiewicz, the famous writer. Not particularly wealthy, childless, ageing philanthropists. With no political colouring. If one were forced to look for labels, he would have been a Red because of his past on the National Council, and she a Black – a conservative, traditionalist – because of her involvement in church initiatives and mildly professed Catholic faith.

"In a way that is a symbol of this town," Sobieraj had said. "People of very different views, with different past histories, in theory from opposite sides of the barricade, but always able to see eye to eye when it came to the good of Sandomierz."

"In a way, that is a symbol of this dump," said Wilczur. "First the Reds and the Blacks each had something to prove by turns, and finally they realized they could see eye to eye for the good of business. Not for nothing is the city council in an old Dominican monastery with a view of the synagogue and the Jewish district. So they'd never forget what's good for *gesheft*," he said, dropping in a Yiddish word. "I'm not going to give you a history lecture, but to put it briefly, under the Reds the town was yuk. Tarnobrzeg was fine and dandy with its sulphur deposits, and eventually there was the glassworks across the river, but here it was educated types up to their tricks, dubious intellectuals, and priests, to make matters worse. In Warsaw, Sandomierz wasn't even mentioned on the road signs, only Tarnobrzeg. This place was nothing but misery, indigence and a bloody open-air museum. The new era came along, people rejoiced, but not for long, because suddenly it turned out this wasn't a town, just a secular growth on the healthy tissue of the Church. They changed the cinema into a Catholic Centre. They started holding masses in the market square. They set up a statue of John Paul the size of a lighthouse on the common to have an excuse from then on why no event should ever be held there, and now it's just a place where the dogs shit. And so it became a bloody open-air museum again, more churches than pubs. And then the Reds came back to power, and after a moment's consternation it turned out that if there's good *gesheft*, then oy vey, oy vey, everyone can benefit.

If a shop or a petrol station can be put up on recovered church land, everyone gets a cut, everyone will be happy."

"Did Budnik take part in that?"

Wilczur hesitated, and ordered another bottle of mineral water with a gesture worthy of single-malt whisky.

"In those days I was working in Tarnobrzeg, but people used to talk."

"This is Poland, they always talk. I have heard that he was never mixed up in anything."

"Not officially. But the Church doesn't have to be public about these things – it can sell whatever it wants for as much as it wants and to whomever it wants. It was quite strange that first of all the town was happy to hand over plots of land to the Church, as part of the recompense for Communist injustices, and then the Church immediately sold them as sites for a petrol station or a supermarket. No one knows who bought them or for what price. And Budnik was a great advocate of the idea of rendering unto God the things that are God's, and rendering unto the Jew the things that are the Jew's."

Szacki shrugged. He was bored, he was tired of the fact that all Wilczur's statements had a negative tone, permeated with Polish poison, as sticky as the tables at the Modena.

"There are deals like that the length and breadth of the country – what's the significance of that? Did it earn Budnik enemies? Was there someone he didn't take care of? Or didn't take care of the right way? Did he do deals with the Mafia? So far it sounds to me like village scams, a scoop for the local school magazine. But nothing you slash someone's wife's throat for."

Wilczur raised a skinny, wrinkled finger.

"Maybe land isn't worth as much here as in central Warsaw, but no one gives it away for nothing."

He stopped talking and became pensive. Szacki waited, watching the policeman. He was trying to think of him as an experienced local cop, but there was something about the inspector that he found repulsive. He looked like a tramp, and this quality was so integral to him that however he dressed and whatever he drank he'd always resemble a vodka-soaked tramp. There were no rational reasons for it, but Szacki's trust was melting away by the minute. He missed Kuzniecow. He missed him very much.

"You can see what this town is like," Wilczur continued. "It may still be sleepy, but it's a gem of a kind that's very rare in Poland, with the makings of a new Kazimierz Dolny or even better. They'll build a marina, set up a couple of spas, the motorway will run past from Warsaw to Rzeszów and on to Ukraine. A stretch of motorway from Warsaw to Krakow in the other direction, and in five years there'll be a queue of BMWs here every Friday from both directions. What'll the profit on a plot of land be like then? Tenfold? Twentyfold? A hundredfold? It doesn't take a genius to see it coming. And now please think. You know Sandomierz, it has lots of money and big plans. Hotels, restaurants, residential areas, tourist attractions. There are absolutely billions in this land. And you know that, but at most you can put up a dog kennel in the garden of your villa, because all the city's land for investment goes back to the Church in a hail of glory, after which it quietly ends up in the hands of the most trusted types who know the right people. Where do you live?"

"I'm renting a place on Długosz Street."

"And have you checked how much a flat costs here? Or a house? Or a plot of land?"

"Sure. A sixty-square-metre flat costs about two hundred thousand, and a house is three times as much."

"In Kazimierz Dolny a flat that size costs from half a million to a million, and for a house there's actually no upper limit, but the conversation starts at a million in the case of a hovel on the edge of town."

Szacki imagined taking out the biggest possible loan and buying three flats here in order to become a happy rentier in a few years' time. Nice, very nice.

"OK," he said slowly. "Next question: who's the most pissed-off builder of a dog kennel in the garden of his villa?"

In response Wilczur tore the filter off a cigarette and lit it.

"You have to understand one thing," he said. "No one here likes Budnik."

Szacki started to fidget; he had been expecting the shrewd local policeman, but he was dealing with a paranoiac.

"I've only just been painted a picture of Mr and Mrs Budnik in nothing but pastel tones, beloved by all, secular saints. Is it true he brought the *Father Mateusz* TV series here?"

"It's true. They were going to film it in Nidzica, but Budnik knew someone at the TVP channel and persuaded them to choose Sandomierz."

"Is it true that thanks to him the scrubland on Piłsudski Boulevard is becoming a park and a marina?"

"True as true can be."

"Is it true he had Piszczele Street refurbished?"

"Absolutely true. That even impressed me – I was sure there was no hope for that murderer's and rapist's alley."

It occurred to Szacki that he had never heard of any rapes or murders occurring in Sandomierz, not counting in the local eateries, where flavours were murdered and palates were brutally assaulted. He kept that comment to himself.

"So what's it about?" he asked.

Inspector Wilczur made a vague gesture, designed to imply that he was trying to convey something that couldn't be conveyed in words.

"Are you familiar with the noisy social campaigner type of person who can't bear opposition because he's always in the middle of some crusade?"

Szacki said he was.

"He was that type. Never mind if he was right or not, he was always bloody infuriating. I know people who voted for his ideas just so he'd shut up. So he wouldn't keep hanging around, pestering them on the phone at night and rushing off to the newspapers."

"Small beer," remarked Szacki. "It's all small beer. An irritating social campaigner, doing his small-time provincial deals; it's all small beer. They didn't slash his tyres, or smash his windows, or kill his dog. They cruelly and deliberately butchered his wife."

Sobieraj's judgment of the victim had been unambiguous. She was wonderful, good, with no faults at all, open-hearted, even if her husband was sometimes over-aggressive in his crusades and annoyed people, in her presence everybody melted. She helped, she advised, she took care of things. She was goodness incarnate, full of all that was best from head to toe. Prosecutor Sobieraj had delivered a totally non-objective paean in her honour, and then burst into tears. It was embarrassing. But nevertheless credible. Meanwhile, Szacki had a problem with Wilczur's account. Something didn't match up. He didn't yet know what, but something wasn't right.

"Mother Elżbieta of the Angels, that's what they called her," said Wilczur.

"After the character in Iwaszkiewicz's story, 'Mother Joanna of the Angels'? She was a madwoman."

"Mrs Budnik wasn't," said Wilczur, shaking his head. "Not in the least. Goodness personified."

"The woman in the story was insane."

"You know that, and so do I, and she knew it too, and she hated that nickname. But that's what they called her – they thought it was a compliment. And I'll be frank with you – she wasn't my cup of tea, but she deserved every compliment. She really was a good person. I won't keep repeating myself, but I'm sure everything you've heard about her and have yet to hear about her is true."

"Perhaps she was irritating too? Too much social conscience? Too Catholic? I don't know, maybe she bought too little at the local bazaar? This is Poland – they must have hated her for something, bad-mouthed her behind her back, envied her something."

Wilczur shrugged.

"No."

"No, and that's all? End of brilliant analysis?"

The policeman nodded and tore the filter off a cigarette; Szacki felt an overwhelming sense of resignation. He wanted to leave for Warsaw. Now. This minute. At once.

"What about the relationship between them?"

"People usually pair up with partners in the same league, I'm sure you're aware of that principle. The beautiful with the beautiful, the stupid with the stupid, the prodigal with the prodigal. Whereas Mrs Budnik was from two or three rungs higher than her husband. How should I explain it to you?..." Wilczur fell into thought, which made his face take on a ghostly, corpse-like expression. In the dim light of the pizzeria, behind a veil of cigarette smoke, he looked like an incompetently animated mummy. "People only put up with him because she chose him. They think, too bad, he may have a screw loose but essentially he's right, and if there's a woman like that at his side, he can't possibly be bad. And he knows that. He knows it's contrary to nature."

Sobieraj had said: "I'd like a man to be that much in love with me for all those years. I'd like to see that sort of adoration in someone's eyes every day of the week. From the outside they may have looked ill-matched, but they were a wonderful couple. I would wish anyone that sort of love, that sort of adoration."

"He adored her, but there was something sordid about that adoration," said Wilczur, exuding his poison, "something possessive, clinging, I'd say. My ex was working at the hospital over ten years ago, when it became clear that Mrs Budnik wouldn't ever have children. She was in despair, he wasn't at all. He said at least he wouldn't have to share her. It was a passion, for sure. But you know what people with passions are like."

Szacki did know, but he didn't want to agree with Wilczur, because he was finding him less and less likeable, and any fraternizing with this individual seemed abhorrent. Nor did he wish to prolong the discussion. Two people had told him about the Budniks today, but he felt as if he still knew bugger all – this emotionally stamped quasi-knowledge was of no use to him at all.

"Have you questioned Budnik?" he asked at the end.

"He's in a terrible state. I asked him a few technical questions, I'm leaving the rest to you. He's under discreet surveillance."

"Where was he yesterday?"

"At home."

"And where was she?"

"At home too."

"Sorry?"

"So he claims. They watched television, snuggled up and went to sleep. He got up at dawn for a glass of water, and she wasn't there. Before he'd had time to get really worried, he got the call from Basia Sobieraj."

Szacki couldn't believe his own ears.

"That's a load of crap. The silliest bunch of lies I've ever heard in my entire career."

Wilczur nodded in agreement.

XI

Prosecutor Teodor Szacki tossed into the bin the leftover cold meat and cheese that was festering in the fridge, a half-eaten tin of pâté and a piece of tomato; for a moment he hesitated over the contents of the frying pan, but finally the day-before-yesterday's bolognese sauce ended up in the rubbish too. The greater part of the food he had cooked. He had made far too much, enough for a three-person family and some chance guests. In Sandomierz he had no family, no friends or acquaintances and guests; as it was, he had to force himself to cook at all, because the ritual of standing on his own at the cooker and eating alone was dreadful. He tried to eat with the radio or the television on, but this fake version of someone else's presence just made matters worse. He couldn't swallow a bite, the food stuck in his throat, and he was starting to think of eating as such a tough, depressing activity that after every meal it took him a long time to recover. And he was finding it more and more arduous.

He went shopping as if it were a punishment. He was learning to buy less and less. At first, as with the cooking, he automatically got as much food as ever, accustomed to the fact that however much he bought, it would all disappear from the fridge. Someone would make themselves a sandwich, someone would come home hungry, or have a snack in front of the evening telly. Here there was just him. First he gave up buying anything that was in a packet. The packs of cold meat and cheese were too big for one person, and he was throwing things away on a daily basis. He started buying by the weight, but still bought too much. Two hundred grams of smoked sausage, a hundred and fifty, a hundred. One day he was standing by the till in a shabby co-op on the market square. One bread roll, a pot of cottage cheese, a small carton of orange juice, fifty grams of ham and a tomato. The checkout girl joked that he didn't have much of an appetite. He left without a word, somehow kept a grip on himself on the way home, but once he got there he cried as he made himself breakfast, and when he sat down at his plate with two sandwiches on it, he sobbed hysterically, and couldn't stop; there were tears and snot smeared across his face. And he went on howling, rocking backwards and forwards, unable to tear his misted gaze from the ham sandwiches. Because he realized he had lost everything he loved, and would never get it back again.

Since moving from Warsaw he had lost fifteen kilos. People didn't know him here – they thought he'd always been a skinny guy. But his suits were hanging off him, his collars had become too loose, and he had had to burn extra holes in his belts with a nail heated on the gas.

He thought of throwing himself into a whirl of work, but there wasn't that much work to do here. He thought of going back to Warsaw, but he had nothing to go back to. He thought of finding someone for company who wouldn't just be there to share the bed, but he hadn't the strength. He did a lot of lying down, and a lot of brooding. Sometimes he felt that things were better now, that now he was standing on solid ground, but then the ground would give way and he'd have to take a step back again. He couldn't see what was there behind him, but he took that step. On the other side of the crevasse was his old life, there was Weronika bustling about, Helka, Kuzniecow and his friends. Light, noise, laughter. Where he was, on one side there was darkness, and on the other the crevasse. Another day, another landslip, another step backwards. Finally he was surrounded by darkness on all sides, but even so, each day he took another step backwards. He had come to terms with the idea that that's how things were going to be from now on.

He poured a little water into the dirty frying pan and put it down on the cooker. He'd clean it up eventually.

It can't be like this, it occurred to him, as he pushed away the conscious thought that this conviction had come to haunt him every day. It can't be like this. People go on living in harmony after a divorce, they sometimes make friends and bring up children jointly, Demi Moore was at Bruce Willis's wedding and vice versa, you don't have to sleep in the same bed or live in the same flat to be a family. After all, he, Weronika and Helka would always be a family, regardless of what had happened and what would happen.

He reached for the phone – he still had Weronika on speed-dial. Except that now it said "Weronika", not as it once had, "Kitten".

"Yes?"

"Hello, it's me."

"Hello, I can see that. What do you want?"

She didn't have to be friendly. He realized that.

"I'm just calling to see if everything's OK. How you are, how's Helka?"

There was a short silence.

"Again?"

"What do you mean, again? I'm sorry, but is there a time when I can call and find out how my daughter is?"

He heard a sigh.

"Your daughter's fine, I've been nagging her to do her homework, she's got a test tomorrow." She sounded tired and unenthusiastic, as if she were completing an unpleasant task, and Szacki could feel a lump of aggression rising in his throat.

"What's the test on?"

"Nature. Teo, is there something in particular? Sorry, but I'm quite busy."

"In particular I wanted to find out when my daughter is coming here. I get the impression you're obstructing her contact with me."

"Don't be paranoid. You know she doesn't like going there."

"Why so? Because as soon as she starts to visit me, then her step-father will have competition and your wonderful new relationship won't be quite so wonderful?"

"Teo…"

"Well all right, but she has to understand that I live here now."

He hated himself for letting a plaintive tone creep into his voice.

"Explain it to her yourself."

He didn't know how to answer that. Helka was reluctant to talk to him and reluctant to listen. She liked her new home, and not her father's bachelor den, which was two hundred kilometres away. At one time she had tried to hide her disgust, but lately she had stopped bothering.

"All right, in that case maybe I'll come there."

"Maybe. As you wish. Teo… please, if you haven't got anything in particular…"

"No, thanks, kiss my little bunnikin for me. OK?"

"OK."

She was waiting to see if he'd say any more; he could feel her reluctance and impatience. He caught some sounds coming from the other end. The television was on, a pot was clattering, and someone laughed, a child. Weronika hung up, and in the little flat on Długosz Street in Sandomierz unalloyed silence reigned.

Szacki had to do something to avoid thinking. Work – he did after all have a proper case at last. He must prepare a case hypothesis, do some thinking, prepare the operational stages and draw up a time-table. Why wasn't he doing it? Normally he'd have had three exercise books full of notes by now. He impetuously flipped his laptop open to look for information and get ready for tomorrow's interrogation of Budnik. The man must have featured a great deal in the media, both he and his wife. He should look through some editorials, gossip, and reports from sessions of the City Council. Everything. The unique sound of being teleported from Myst Island informed him that a new message had come in.

From: editor@thrust.com
Subject: Re: Prosecutor asking about razor-machete
To: teodor.szacki@gmail.com
Date: 15 April 2009 19:44 CET

Hello,

You gave me a proper fright with the word "Prosecutor" – I thought we'd infringed some paragraph of the law by showing pictures of too big knives :-) But to get to the point, I had to ask a few serious collectors in order to confirm my own identification, and they all agree that your "razor-machete" is a *chalef*, a knife for the ritual slaughter of animals as used by a *shochet*, a Jewish butcher.

From the dimensions one may conclude that it is designed for the slaughter of cattle (the smaller ones are for poultry and lambs), and from the condition that it could still easily be used in many a kosher abattoir. You ought to know that knives for ritual slaughter must be in a perfect state, and the slightest scratch, chip or bump renders them unusable. The blade is tested with a fingernail before and after each use, the point being that only a perfectly sharp knife can cut the oesophagus, larynx, main jugular vein and artery at a single stroke, and such are the conditions for ritual, kosher slaughter. The Jews believe that this is the most humane and painless way of killing (how much truth there is in that is another matter).

I hope this is helpful, and that the knife – by the way, I love the definition "razor-machete" – has not been used for any ignoble purpose ;-)

Yours sincerely,

Janek Wiewiórski
Editor

Szacki read the e-mail several times, no longer thinking about his personal problems at all. So in a churchy city with an anti-Semitic past he was supposed to conduct an inquiry into a case involving the murder of a well-known social benefactress, who had been ritually slaughtered like a cow in a Jewish abattoir.

Someone knocked at the door.

This is going to be a bloody mess all right, thought Szacki, at the same time reproaching himself for the unfortunate choice of words, and opened the door. Klara was standing on the other side of it as naked as the Lord God had made her. He looked at her lovely, supple body, her pert young breasts and the chestnut locks tumbling down her neck. And he smiled happily and encouragingly, without feeling anything for her at all.

But the smile was sincere. Prosecutor Teodor Szacki had a case, and he was very happy about it.

2

For Jews in the diaspora it is the solemnly observed final day of Passover, for Christians it is the fifth day of the Easter Week and for Poles it is the final day of national mourning following the tragic hotel fire. The Polish Army is celebrating Sapper's Day, actress Alina Janowska her eighty-sixth birthday and the Warsaw stock exchange its eighteenth. In Włocławek the municipal guard picked up a priest and his altar boy, in their vestments, both roaring drunk and aggressive. They turned out to be laymen who had pinched the outfits from one of their mothers, a seamstress. A British firm has found enormous deposits of gas under Poznań, and according to the British press, the piece of music most often played at funerals is Frank Sinatra singing *My Way*; also high on the list is *Highway to Hell* by AC/DC. In the second leg of the quarter-finals of the UEFA Cup the winners are Dynamo Kiev, Shakhtar Donetsk, Werder Bremen and Hamburg, who face fratricidal encounters in the semi-finals. Sandomierz is outraged by the relocation of its vegetable market, which must vacate its site to make way for a car park serving the new stadium. Whatever their views on this matter, all the citizens have another cold day. The temperature does not rise above fourteen degrees, but at least it is sunny, with no rain.

I

Prosecutor Teodor Szacki did not like cold weather, stupid cases, incompetent lawyers or provincial courts. That morning he got a triple dose of all of them. He glanced at the calendar: spring. He looked out of the window: spring. He put on his suit and coat, threw his gown over his shoulder and decided to take an invigorating walk to the courthouse. By the time he reached Sokolnicki Street, where he slipped on the frosted cobblestones, he knew it was a bad idea. Somewhere near the Opatowska Gate his ears went numb, at the water tower he had no feeling in his fingers, and when at last he turned into Kościuszko Street and entered the dirty-green courthouse, he had to spend a few minutes recovering, blowing on his frozen hands. It was like the North Pole in this bloody, windswept dump – damn the place, he thought.

The courthouse was ugly. Its solid bulk may have looked modern when it was built in the 1990s, but now it looked like a gypsy palace converted into a public service building. Its steps, chrome railings, green stone and irregular surfaces didn't suit the surrounding architecture, or even the building itself; there was something apologetic about its green colour, as if it were trying to hide its own ugliness against the cemetery trees. The courtroom consistently followed the style of the rest of the block, and the most eye-catching item in this space, which looked like the conference room at a second-rate corporation, were the green, hospital-style vertical blinds.

Scowling and disgusted, Szacki was still mentally bemoaning his surroundings once he had put on his gown and sat down in the seat reserved for the prosecution. On the other side he had the defendant and his counsel. Hubert Huby was a nice old fellow of seventy. He had thick, still-greying hair, horn-rimmed spectacles and a charming, modest smile. The defence counsel, probably a public service lawyer, was the picture of misery and despair. His gown was not done up, his hair was unwashed, his shoes weren't polished and his moustache hadn't been trimmed – he prompted the suspicion that he probably smelt bad. Just like the whole case, thought Szacki with rising irritation, but finishing off all his predecessor's cases had been a condition for getting the job in Sandomierz.

Finally the judge appeared. She was a young lass who looked as if she'd only just graduated from high school, but at least the trial was under way.

"Prosecutor?" said the judge, giving him a nice smile after completing the formalities; no judge in Warsaw ever smiled, or if he did it was out of malice, when he caught someone in ignorance of the regulations.

Teodor Szacki stood up and automatically adjusted his gown.

"Your Honour, the prosecution upholds the arguments proposed in the indictment, the defendant has confessed to all the charges, and there is no doubt about his guilt in the light of his own statements and those of the injured parties. I do not wish to prolong the case, I am filing for acknowledgement that the defendant is guilty, that by means of deceit he repeatedly led other individuals to submit to various sexual acts, which covers all the characteristics of the crime described in Article 197, paragraph two of the Penal Code, and I am filing for the court to impose a punishment of six months' imprisonment which, I stress, is the bottom limit of the punishment stipulated by the legislator."

Szacki sat down. It was an open-and-shut case, and he just wanted to get it over and done with. He had deliberately demanded the lowest possible sentence and had no wish to discuss it. In his thoughts he was endlessly composing a plan for his interrogation of Budnik, juggling topics and questions, changing their order and trying to envisage scenarios for the conversation, to be ready for every possible version. He already knew Budnik was lying about the final evening he had spent with his wife. But then everyone tells lies – it doesn't make them into murderers. Perhaps he had a lover, maybe they'd had an argument, maybe they'd had a quiet few days, or maybe he'd been drinking with his mates. Back a bit – he should cross out the lover, because if Sobieraj and Wilczur were telling the truth, he was the most infatuated husband on earth. Back again – he couldn't cross anything out, in case it was a small-town, thick-as-thieves conspiracy, God knows who, why and for what reason he should be told anything. Wilczur did not inspire trust, and Sobieraj was a friend of the family.

"Prosecutor," the judge's strident voice shook him out of his lethargy, and he realized he had only heard every third word of the defence counsel's speech.

He stood up.

"Yes, Your Honour?"

"Could you take a stance on the position of the defence?"

Bloody hell, he hadn't the slightest idea what the position of the defence was. In Warsaw, apart from exceptional circumstances, the judge never asked for an opinion, he just got bored listening to both sides, withdrew, passed sentence, job done, next please.

Here in Sandomierz the judge was merciful.

"To change the classification of the crime to Article 217, paragraph one?"

The content of the article flashed before Szacki's eyes. He looked at the defence counsel as if he were a madman.

"I take the position that this has to be a joke. The counsel for the defence should familiarize himself with the basic interpretations and jurisdiction. Article 217 concerns assault and battery, and is properly only applied to minor fights, or when one politician slaps another one in the face. Of course I understand the defence's intentions – assault and battery is a privately prosecuted indictment, subject to a punishment of one year at most. There is no comparison with sexual abuse, for which the penalty is from six to eight months. But that is the crime your client has committed, sir."

The defence counsel stood up. He gave the judge an enquiring look, and she nodded.

"I would also like to remind the court that as a result of mediation almost all the injured parties have forgiven my client, which should result in a remission of the sentence."

Szacki did not wait for permission.

"Once again I say: please read the Code, sir," he growled. "Firstly, 'almost' makes a big difference, and secondly, remission as a result of mediation only applies to crimes subject to up to three years' imprisonment. The most you can petition for is extraordinary commutation of the sentence, which in any case is ridiculously low, considering your client's exploits."

The lawyer smiled and spread his hands in a gesture of surprise. Too many films, too little professional reading, Szacki thought to himself.

"But has anyone been harmed? Did anyone suffer any unpleasantness? Human affairs, involving adults…"

A red curtain fell before Szacki's eyes. He silently counted to three to calm himself down. He took a deep breath, stood up straight and looked at the judge. She nodded, her curiosity aroused.

"Counsel for the defence, the prosecution is amazed both at your ignorance of the law and of civilized behaviour. I would remind you that for many months the defendant Huby went about houses in Sandomierz county kitted out with a white gown and a medical bag, passing himself off as a doctor. That in itself is a felony. He passed himself off as a specialist in, I quote: 'palpation mammography', and suggested prophylactic examination, with the aim of making the women bare their chests and give him access to their charms. Which comes under the definition of rape. And I would also like to remind you that he assured most of his 'patients' that their bosoms were in good health, which might not have been true and could have led them to abandon their plans for prophylactic tests, and thus to serious health problems. In any case, that is the main reason why one of the injured parties refused to agree to mediation."

"But in two of the ladies he felt a lump and prompted them to get treatment, which as a consequence saved their lives," retorted the defence counsel emphatically.

"Then let those ladies fund a reward for him and send parcels. What concerns us here is that the defendant committed an illegal act and must bear the consequences, because it is against the law to go about the houses telling lies and fondling women. Just as it is against the law to go about the streets knocking out people's teeth in the hope that later on at the dentist's some more serious problems will be discovered and treated."

He could see that the judge was having to stop herself from snorting with laughter.

"And the case has led to a serious discussion within the province about preventive action and the need for mammograms," said the relentless defence lawyer.

"But is this a formal motion?" Szacki felt weary.

"These are circumstances that should be taken into consideration."

"Your Honour?" Szacki looked enquiringly at the amused judge.

"The session is closed. The sentence will be announced on Monday at ten. Mr Prosecutor, would you please come to my office for a moment?"

The judge, whose name, as he discovered from the case list, was Maria Tatarska, had an office as ugly as the rest of the building, equally nastily decorated in dirty-green colours, but at least it was spacious. Szacki knocked and was invited to enter just as Judge Tatarska was taking off her gown. An electric kettle was already burbling away on a cabinet.

"Coffee?" she asked, hanging up her court uniform.

As Szacki was on the point of replying yes, please, one spoonful, no sugar, lots of milk, Judge Tatarska turned to face him, and he had to concentrate on making sure no signs of his emotions appeared on his face. And on trying not to swallow his saliva in a theatrical way. Under her gown, Judge Tatarska was a regular sex bomb, with the body of a girl from a centrefold, and the amount of cleavage revealed by her purple blouse would have been thought daring in a night club.

"Yes, please, one spoonful, no sugar, lots of milk."

They chatted for a time about the case, while she made them both coffee. Small talk, nothing interesting. He imagined she had brought him in here for some purpose. Other than the pleasure of communing with his professional coolness, gaunt figure and ashen face of a guy due to turn forty in a few months' time, who had spent the winter feeling depressed and neglecting his physical fitness. He knew he looked like a state official. Usually he couldn't care less, but right now he would have liked to look better. He also would have liked her to get to the point, as he had to leave in the next five minutes.

"I've heard a few things about you, about your cases – my colleagues in the capital have told me." She was looking at him closely. Szacki didn't answer, but waited for her to continue. What was he supposed to say? That he knew of her by hearsay too? "I won't say we made any special enquiries when the rumour went round that you were staying on here. You must have realized by now that personnel changes are not an everyday event in the provinces. From your perspective it can't have been obvious, but in our little world it was a minor sensation."

He still didn't know what he was meant to say.

"I also looked in the press, I read about your cases – some of them are first-class crime stories, well-known ones. I was intrigued by the murder that happened during Hellinger's Constellation Therapy."

Szacki shrugged. Hellinger, Devil take it, if not for that case, if not for the affair, if not for the old secret police stories, right now he'd probably be eating boiled eggs in tartare sauce on Solidarność Avenue, and arranging with Weronika for one of them to pick up the child from school. If it weren't for Hellinger, he'd still have a life now.

"In my time I've been very interested in Hellinger. I even went to Kielce for a constellation, but they cancelled it and I didn't feel like going a second time. You know how it is, a single woman, long evenings, too much thinking. Thinking there might be something wrong with her, maybe she needs therapy. Stupid thoughts."

Szacki couldn't believe his own ears. She was trying to pick him up. This sex bomb with legal training was trying to pick him up. He braced himself, the old habit of a married man. He braced himself at the thought of the flirting, the rendezvous, the lying, the text messages sent on the sly, the phone set to silent, and the office hours wasted on meeting up in town.

And he realized the married man's habit was just that – a habit, second nature, but only that. He was free, he was single, he had a flat with a view of the Vistula. He could make a date with a girl from the provinces and roger her standing up in the kitchen. Simple as that. Without any pangs of conscience, without any scheming, subterfuge, or pussyfooting about innocent friendship.

He had to fly. But he made a date for the evening. Hellinger, of course, that was quite a case, he'd be happy to tell her about it.

Except that he'd have to stand Klara up.

II

WITNESS INTERVIEW TRANSCRIPT. Grzegorz Budnik, born 4th December 1950, resident at 27 Katedralna Street, Sandomierz, higher education in chemistry, chairman of the Sandomierz City Council. Relationship to parties: husband of Elżbieta Budnik (victim). No convictions for bearing false witness.

Cautioned re criminal responsibility under Article 233 of the Penal Code, his statement is as follows:

I met Elżbieta Szuszkiewicz in the winter of 1992, during the "Winter in the City" campaign, when she came here from Krakow to run drama workshops for children. I had never met her before, although she had spent her childhood in Sandomierz. In those days I used to coordinate all events held at the town hall. I couldn't help noticing her because for some people that sort of campaign is drudgery, but she produced such a good show with the children at the end of the festival that they got a standing ovation – it was Stories for Children *by Isaac Bashevis Singer. She was young, not yet thirty then, beautiful and full of energy. I fell head over heels in love, without any real hope – I was a provincial official, and she was a big-city girl who'd been to drama school. But two years later we got married in Sandomierz cathedral on the Sunday after Easter. Unfortunately we never had any children, though we very much wanted to. When it turned out we would have to go through all those medical procedures, we considered adoption, but finally we realized that we would continue to look after children through our social activities. I less so, in view of my duties on the council, but Ela devoted herself entirely to it. She taught at a school, but mainly she organized events, brought in artists and devised the most fantastic workshops. It was our common dream to set up a special place, an arts centre for children, where we could organize entire summer camps, like the American ones. But we kept putting it off, there was always some issue of the day to take care of. We were supposed to get it off the ground this year, to look for property and take out a loan.*

Our life together worked out well, there was only the occasional quarrel, we had a good social life, maybe a bit less these days – the winter is so long, and our place is at its best when you can sit in the garden.

Szacki felt worn out. The short transcript was the result of a three-hour conversation. Budnik went off into digressions, or long silences, sometimes wept, and occasionally felt obliged to affirm how very much he loved his wife, and to tell an anecdote from their life together. At times he was so genuine that Szacki's heart was bleeding. But only at times – besides that, the prosecutor's nose for lies could smell something nasty. Budnik was definitely telling the truth about one thing – his feelings for his wife were movingly real. But apart from that, he was lying through his teeth.

My wife and I spent most of the last few days together. Over the winter we had worked a lot, so we had decided to spend Easter on our own at home, just the two of us. In any case, we had nowhere to go and no one to invite. My sister had gone to visit our brother who lives in Germany, and Ela's parents had gone to Zakopane. They were all supposed to be coming now, on Sunday, for our fifteenth wedding anniversary, we wanted to have a party, a sort of second wedding. We hadn't met up with anybody since Saturday; that is, we saw people we know at the blessing of the Easter food. We didn't go to the cathedral for it, but to Saint Paul's, to have a bit of a walk. No one after that. On Sunday we slept in too late for the Resurrection Mass, had a modest, but festive Easter breakfast, read a bit, chatted a bit and watched a bit of telly. That evening we went for a walk; after the walk we looked in at the cathedral, but not for mass, and said a few prayers together at the Holy Sepulchre. I can't remember if anyone else was there, there must have been someone. We actually spent the whole of Monday in bed – Ela had a sore throat, it was terribly cold this Easter. On Tuesday she was still feeling unwell, there was nothing we needed to do, so we both stayed at home. Just in case she wouldn't be feeling up to it, we cancelled a visit to our friends, Olga and Tadeusz Bojarski. I can't remember, but I think my wife must have called them on Monday evening or Tuesday morning. I went to the office for a while on Tuesday, and a few people saw me there. I came home in the afternoon, I brought us some food from the Trzydziestka restaurant. Ela was feeling better, she looked quite well, and we were even sorry we'd called off our get-together. In the evening we watched a Robert Redford film on Channel One, about a prison, I can't remember the title. And then we went to bed. Very early, I had a headache. I didn't get up in the night. I haven't got any prostate problems. When I woke up, Ela wasn't there. Before I'd had time to start worrying, Basia Sobieraj called.

"I'm glad you're questioning me. It could be hard for Basia to do it."

"I'm questioning you because I am in charge of the inquiry. Emotional considerations have nothing to do with it."

Grzegorz Budnik nodded in silence. He looked awful. After hearing all the stories about the legendary councillor, Szacki was expecting a portly gent with a moustache or a salt-and-pepper beard, a receding hairline and a waistcoat buttoned over his belly – in short, a classic MP or mayor from the television. Meanwhile, Grzegorz Budnik was like a retired marathon runner: small, thin and wiry like a predatory animal, as if there wasn't a single cell of fat in his entire body. Probably capable in normal circumstances of beating many a heavy from the provincial gym at arm-wrestling, today he looked like someone who had just lost a long fight against a deadly illness. His short ginger beard could not conceal his sunken cheeks, and his sweaty, unwashed hair was sticking to his skull. He had dark rings around his eyes, which were red from crying and clouded, probably from tranquillizers. Slumping and closed in on himself, he reminded Szacki more of the Warsaw vagrants he used to question almost every day, rather than a staunch councillor, chairman of the City Council, who put fear into the other officials and his political opponents. The picture of destitution and despair was completed by a large plaster, crookedly glued to his forehead. Grzegorz Budnik looked more like a homeless drifter than a civic official.

"What happened to your forehead?"

"I tripped and hit it on a pan."

"A pan?"

"I lost my balance, waved my arms about and hit the handle of the frying pan, the frying pan leapt up and bashed me on the head. It's nothing serious."

"We'll have to do a forensic examination."

"It's nothing serious."

"Not because we're worried about you. We have to check in case it's the result of a fight or a wounding."

"Don't you believe me?"

Szacki just stared. He didn't believe anyone.

"You know, of course, that you can refuse to make a statement or answer specific questions?"

"Yes."

"But you prefer to tell lies. Why is that?"

Budnik sat up proudly, as if that might add truth to his testimony.

"When was the last time you saw your wife?" Szacki didn't let him get a word in.

"I told you…"

"I know what you said. Now please tell me when you really saw your wife for the last time and why you lied about it. If you don't, I'll put you on remand for forty-eight hours, charge you with murdering your wife and apply to the court for your arrest. You've got thirty seconds."

Budnik slumped again even more, and contrasting horribly with his pale complexion, his red eyes filled with tears, reminding Szacki of Gollum in *Lord of the Rings*.

"Twenty."

Gollum, hissing "My precious!", incapable of existence without his treasure, addicted to a thing that could never be his. Was that what the relationship between Grzegorz and Elżbieta Budnik had been like? A provincial Gollum, the ugly-mug do-gooder and the city girl, beautiful, clever and good, a Premier Division star making a guest appearance in the youth league. Why had she stayed here? Why had she married him?

"Ten."

"But I told you…"

Without twitching a muscle, Szacki tapped out a number on the phone while at the same time extracting a charge sheet from his desk.

"Szacki here, put me through to Inspector Wilczur please."

Budnik put his hand on the phone hooks.

"On Monday."

"Why did you lie?"

Budnik made a gesture as if he wanted to shrug but lacked the strength. Szacki pulled the transcript towards himself and clicked his ballpoint.

"Well then?"

I am changing my statement. I saw my wife Elżbieta for the last time on Easter Monday at about two p.m. We parted on bad terms, we had started to argue about our plans: she insisted time was running out, that we were only getting older and that if we were ever going to make our dreams about the centre come true we had to start doing something at last. I preferred to wait for next year's local council elections, and to run for mayor, because if I won, everything would be easier. Then, as typically happens when you argue, we started reproaching each other. She accused me of putting everything off until later, and for politicizing in just the same way at home as at the office. I told her she was being unrealistic, thinking you only have to want something very much and it will all become fact. We were shouting and hurting each other's feelings.

"O God, when I think the last words I ever said to her were that she should take her sorry arse back to Krakow…" Budnik began to sob quietly. Szacki waited for him to calm down. He felt like having a smoke.

Finally she took her jacket and left without a word. I didn't chase her, I didn't go looking for her, I was furious. I didn't want to apologize, I didn't want to say sorry, I wanted to be on my own. She had plenty of friends – I suspected she'd gone to see Barbara Sobieraj. I didn't get in touch with her on Monday or on Tuesday. I read, watched television and drank some beer. By Tuesday evening I was starting to miss her, the Redford film was good, but I was sorry to be watching it alone. My pride wouldn't let me call that evening; I thought in the morning I'd go over to Barbara Sobieraj's place or call her. I covered up these facts because I was afraid our quarrel, and the fact that I hadn't gone looking for her, would look bad and would incriminate me in the eyes of the law.

"Didn't it occur to you that these facts might have significance for the inquiry? Isn't finding the murderer important to you?"

Once again Budnik all but shrugged.

"No, it's not. Nothing's important to me now."

Szacki handed him the transcript to read through, while at the same time wondering whether to lock him up or not. He usually listened to his instinct on such matters. But his compass was confused. Budnik was a politician, a provincial one, but a politician, in other words a professional liar and hoodwinker. And Szacki was certain that for some reasons, which he would be sure to discover, he hadn't told him the whole truth. Nevertheless his grief seemed genuine. Totally resigned grief at an irrecoverable loss, not the quaking, fear-filled grief of a murderer. Szacki had had rather too many opportunities to observe both these emotions and had learnt to tell them apart.

He took a file full of photos out of the drawer and filled in the heading on an exhibit form.

"Have you ever seen this tool?"

At the sight of the photo of the razor-machete Budnik went pale, and Szacki was amazed it was actually possible for skin as chalk-white as his to do that.

"Is that…"

"Please answer the question."

"No, I've never seen a tool like that before."

"Do you know what it's for?"

"I have no idea."

At about four p.m. a touch of warmth finally appeared in the sunshine, a shy hint of spring. Prosecutor Teodor Szacki turned his face to the sun and drank Cola from the can.

After interrogating Budnik he had met up with Wilczur and told him to find anyone who might have seen them over Easter. At church, on a walk, in a restaurant. Every bit of the interview had to be checked, every acquaintance questioned. Kuzniecow would have got palpitations halfway down the list of demands, but Inspector Wilczur just nodded his gaunt head; in his black suit he looked like Death taking an order for the harvest. Szacki felt ill at ease in the old policeman's presence.

Now he was waiting outside the police station for Sobieraj, to go on a romantic walk with her to the city hospital. In fact he was surprised they had an anatomical pathology department here – he had been sure they would have to go to one of the bigger cities, Kielce or Tarnobrzeg.

He lazily opened one eye when he heard a car hooting. Sobieraj was waving to him from some characterless piece of junk. He sighed and dragged himself to his feet. An Opel Astra.

"I thought we were going to walk there."

Why is it always the case that the smaller the hole, the more usual it is for everyone to go everywhere by car?

"Three quarters of an hour each way? I don't much fancy it. Not even with you, Prosecutor."

In three quarters of an hour I could walk to Opatów and do a tour of every village on the way, Szacki had it on the tip of his tongue to say, but he got into the car. It smelt of air freshener and stuff for cleaning plastic, and must have been several years old, but it looked as if it had only left the showroom yesterday. The ashtray was empty, the speakers were putting out smooth jazz, and there were no crumbs or little bits of paper anywhere. In other words she was childless. But she was married, she had a ring, she must have been about thirty-five. Didn't they want them? Couldn't they have them?

"Why couldn't the Budniks have children?"

She cast him a suspicious glance as she joined the traffic on Mick-iewicz Street. They were driving towards the exit for Warsaw.

"He couldn't, right?" Szacki pressed on.

"Right. Why do you ask?"

"Intuition. I don't know exactly why, but it's highly relevant. The way Budnik mentioned it, as if in passing, as if lightly. That's how men talk who've heard so many times that it doesn't matter that they almost believe it."

She looked at him closely. They passed the courthouse.

"My husband can't have children either. I tell him it doesn't matter too, that other things are important."

"And are they?"

"Less so."

Szacki said nothing as they drove around the roundabout and past a hideous modern church, a pile of red bricks arranged in the shape of the gates of hell, ugly, oppressive, and totally unsuited to its sur-roundings and to this city in general.

"I have an eleven-year-old daughter. She lives in Warsaw with her mum. I feel as if she's getting more and more alien, fading from sight by the day."

"Even so, I envy you."

Szacki was quiet; he had been expecting anything but this sort of conversation. They came to what was rather grandly called the bypass and turned towards the Vistula.

"We've had a bad start," said Sobieraj, without taking her eyes off the road for a moment. Szacki wasn't looking at her either. "I was thinking about it yesterday, that we're both trapped by our own stereotypical thinking. To you I'm a stupid little provincial, and to me you're an arrogant jerk from Warsaw. And of course we can go on playing that game, except that I really do want to find Ela's murderer."

She drove off the bypass into a small side street and parked outside the surprisingly large hospital building. It was L-shaped with six floors, built in the 1980s. Better than he'd thought.

"You can laugh and call it small-town overdramatizing, but she was different. Better, brighter, purer, it's hard for me to describe. I

69

knew her, I knew everyone who knew her, I know this town better than I'd like to. And as for you, well, this is no time for bullshit, I know how many times you were offered a transfer to the regional court, to the appeal court, and what a career they predicted for you. I know your cases, I know the testimonials and the legends about Teodor Szacki with the snow-white hair, that brave defender of Justice."

Finally they looked at each other. Szacki held out his hand, and Sobieraj gently shook it.

"Call me Teodor."

"Basia."

"You've parked in a disabled parking space, Basia."

Sobieraj took a card out of the glove compartment with a blue logo on it symbolizing disability, and put it on the dashboard.

"Heart. Two attacks. I probably wouldn't be able to give birth anyway."

IV

"Artur Żmijewski should come and live here," said Szacki, as he looked around the tidy hospital admissions area, referring to the famous actor, popular for his TV roles as a priest-cum-detective in a show filmed here in Sandomierz, and as a doctor in a serial that had run since 1999. "He could ride his bike from his parish straight to his medical practice."

"He has been here anyway," replied Sobieraj, leading the way downstairs into the basement. "Rumour has it that when they were filming *Father Mateusz* he fell off his bike and had to be treated in hospital. It's a well-known story – have you really not heard about it?"

He waved his hand in an indeterminate way. What should he say? That no, he hadn't, because he hadn't been socializing, but had been going through a depression in solitude? He steered the conversation onto the hospital. He really was surprised – he had been expecting a dismal building stinking of mould, some sort of old army huts in the city centre, but although admittedly it had the feel of the 1980s, this one was almost attractively done up inside. It was modest and nice, the doctors were smiling and the nurses were young, as if they were making an advert for the National Health Fund. Even the autopsy room wasn't disgusting – compared with the Warsaw morgue inundated with corpses it was like a charming B&B alongside a barrack at a labour camp. On the one and only dissecting table lay the alabaster remains of Elżbieta Budnik.

Szacki tried to think of her as Budnik's wife, but he couldn't do it. He had never admitted it to anyone, but in the presence of corpses he was incapable of thinking about them as people who were recently alive; treating them like pieces of meat was the only thing that prevented him from going insane, even though he had had such a lot to do with death. He knew the same thing went on in the pathologists' heads.

As he stared at the unsettlingly white corpse, naturally he noticed some particular features. Dark blonde hair, a slightly turned-up nose, narrow hips with prominent pelvic bones, small breasts. She certainly would have looked different if she had had children. Was she pretty? He had no idea. Corpses are always just corpses.

His gaze kept constantly returning to the throat, slashed open repeatedly, almost right down to the spine – in the view of the Jews, and probably the Arabs too, it was the most humane way of inflicting death. Did that mean she hadn't suffered? He sincerely doubted it; nor was he convinced by the humanity of kosher abattoirs.

The door slammed. Szacki turned round, and by some miracle he managed firstly not to make a surprised face, and secondly not to step back at all. Dressed in an anatomist's gown, the newcomer appeared to represent some humanoid race of giants. Six foot six tall, as wide across the shoulders, with the physique of a bear, he could have piled coal into a boiler with his hands faster than with a shovel. Onto this enormous body was fixed a head with a kindly, beaming face, and the straw-coloured hair was tied in a small ponytail. A butcher from a long line of butchers, who had hacking carcasses in their genes. Could there have been a better place for him?

Overcoming his alarm, Szacki took a step forwards and held out a hand to say hello.

"Teodor Szacki, district prosecutor."

The giant smiled sympathetically and shyly, wrapping Szacki's palm in the warm mound of meat that was attached to his forearm.

"Paweł Ripper, pleased to meet you. Basia told me about you."

He didn't know if it was a joke, so just in case he took it at face value. The giant took a pair of rubber gloves from the pocket of his gown and pulled them on with a snap as he went up to the table. The prosecutors withdrew to some small plastic chairs placed against the wall. The doctor clapped his hands, and the shock wave set the door shuddering.

"Jeepers, she only just did a show with my kids."

"I'm sorry, Paweł. I'd have taken her somewhere else but I trust you. If it's too hard… I know you knew Ela…"

"It's not Ela any more," said Paweł, pressing a button on a Dictaphone. "It is the sixteenth of April 2009, external examination and dissection of the remains of Elżbieta Budnik, age forty-four, conducted by Paweł Ripper, forensic medicine expert, at the anatomical pathology department of the Health Maintenance Organizations Group in Sandomierz. Also present: prosecutors Barbara Sobieraj and Teodor Szacki. External examination…"

Luckily Ripper's large frame shielded most of the activities he was performing, so Szacki and Sobieraj could immerse themselves in conversation. There was no point in tormenting the giant with questions until he knew more than they did. Szacki told Sobieraj about his conversation with Budnik. Obviously, the victim had not reached Basia's place either on Monday, or ever, and the last time the two women had been in touch was on Sunday, when they had wished each other a Happy Easter over the phone.

"How did you know he was lying? Intuition?"

"Experience."

Then he told her about his correspondence with the knife collector's magazine called *Thrust*. As his tale continued, the blood drained from her face and her eyes grew larger and larger.

"Tell me you're joking!" she gasped at last.

He denied it, surprised by her reaction.

"You have no idea what that means, do you?" She had to raise her voice because of the background noise made by the saw with which Ripper was cutting through the breastbone.

"It means that whoever planted that knife is hoping the matter will leak out to the media and that the traditional Polish-Jewish hysteria will flare up – it'll be harder for us to work amid that hysteria, because we'll be spending more time at press conferences than doing our jobs," said Szacki. "But it's all right, I've survived that sort of storm before. The media will get bored with it all in three days."

Sobieraj was listening to him, while at the same time shaking her head. She winced as she heard an unpleasant cracking sound. It was Ripper, cutting through the cadaver's ribs.

"It won't be ordinary hysteria," she said. "The journalists will hang around here for weeks. Sandomierz is at the centre of the so-called legend of blood, and the history of Polish-Jewish relations alternates between either nice, friendly cohabitation or recriminations and bloody pogroms – the last anti-Semitic killings happened here just after the war. If someone, God forbid, uses the term 'ritual murder', it'll be the end."

"Ritual murder is a fairy tale," replied Szacki calmly. "And everyone knows it's a fairy tale that was told to children to make them behave, otherwise the big bad Jew would come and eat them. Let's not get hysterical."

"It's not quite a fairy tale. A Jew is not a wolf or a wicked queen, he's a real person, whom you can make complaints about. You know what it was like. The Christian mother would fail to keep an eye on her child, then up and scream that the Jews had kidnapped and murdered it. One thing led to another, and it would turn out that very few people actually liked those Jews – someone owed them some money, and as an excuse had come up, it wouldn't be such a bad thing to set fire to a few of those child-killers' cottages and workshops."

"All right, in that case it's not a fairy tale, but ancient history. There aren't any Jews, there aren't any workshops, there's no one to accuse, or to set on fire. Whoever planted that razor is certainly very keen for us to follow that trail."

Sobieraj let out a loud sigh. In the background Ripper was monotonously dictating for the record that each successive organ bore no signs of injury or pathological change.

"Wake up, Teodor. Sandomierz is the capital of the universe for the idea of ritual murder. The place where accusations of kidnapping children and the resulting pogroms were once as regular as the seasons of the year. The place where the Church endorsed that sort of bestial attitude, virtually institutionalized it. The place where to this day there's a painting hanging in the cathedral showing Jews murdering Catholic children. As part of a series about Christian martyrdom. The place where everything possible has been done to sweep that bit of history under the carpet. Now, as I think about it, my God, that is about as revolting as it gets…"

Szacki gazed at the dissecting table now revealed by Ripper, who was at a small table next to it, cutting up Elżbieta Budnik's internal organs. He would not have used the word "revolting"; the image before his eyes – an open corpse with the skin hanging to either side and the white tips of the ribs sticking out of the rib cage – was horrid, but not revolting. Death in its finality was characterized by physiological elegance. Peace.

"It's revolting that someone is trying to connect that with Ela and Grzegorz."

He gave her an enquiring look.

"All his life Grzegorz has fought against that superstition, fought to have it talked about the right way, as a black page in our history, and not some sort of eccentric tradition practised by our ancestors. For years on end he has tried to have the painting removed, or at least get it provided with an appropriate sign, saying it was still here as a memento of Polish anti-Semitism, a reminder of what hatred can lead to."

"And?"

"The Church has its own way of dealing with things like that. They haven't taken it down or put up a sign. When there was too much fuss about it, they hid it behind a screen, and hung a portrait of the pope on the screen, and they pretend it doesn't matter. If it was a mosaic on the floor rather than a painting, they'd probably have covered it with a rug."

"Very interesting, but none of that is of any significance. Whoever planted the ritual knife wants us to get involved in all that – paintings, history, legends, so we'll start traipsing around churches, sitting in libraries and talking to academics. It's a smokescreen, I have no doubt. I'm just worried it's a well-prepared smokescreen, and that if someone's putting himself to so much effort to send us up that track, he might be too clever for this case to be solved at all."

Ripper came up to them, holding in his gigantic paw a small plastic bag with a little metal object in it. His gown was surprisingly clean, almost without any trace of blood.

"My assistant will sew her up. Let's go and have a chat."

They drank coffee out of plastic cups. It was so disgusting that all the patients here must have ended up on the gastroenterology ward sooner or later, Szacki was sure of it. "Jack" – it turned out that really was his nickname, what a surprise – had changed, and in a grey polo neck he looked like a large boulder with a little pink ball on top.

"I'll tell you the whole story, but it's fairly self-evident. Someone cut her throat with a very sharp surgical instrument. But it wasn't a scalpel or a razor blade, because the cuts are too deep. The large cut-throat razor you showed me in the photos would fit perfectly. All that happened while she was still alive, but she must have been unconscious, otherwise she'd have defended herself, and it wouldn't look as if it were done with such…" – for a moment he sought the right word – "…precision. But she was undoubtedly still alive, because there is no blood in her. Forgive me for the details, but that means that at the moment when the jugular vein was cut there was still pressure in the circulatory system, capable of pumping blood from the body. She also has congealed blood in her ears, which probably means that at the moment of death she was hanging upside down – like, if you'll pardon the expression, a cow in an abattoir. What a screwed-up degenerate must have done that. He also took the trouble to wash her – she must have been covered in blood."

"We must look for the blood," Szacki thought aloud.

"You must also find out what this is," said Ripper, handing them the small plastic evidence bag. Szacki examined it carefully and gulped; the little bag gave off the faint meaty aroma of the anatomy lab. Inside there was a metal badge about a centimetre across the diagonal, the kind worn in a shirt or jacket lapel. Not with a safety pin, but a fat spike to which you have to attach a clasp from the other side. It looked old. As Sobieraj leant forwards to inspect the piece of evidence, her ginger hair tickled Szacki's cheek. It smelt of camomile. The prosecutor glanced at her brow, furrowed in concentration, and her dense freckles which were managing to break free from under a layer of foundation. There was something in this sight that he found touching. A little ginger-haired girl who had grown up and become a woman, but still wanted to hide the freckles on her nose.

"I've seen that somewhere before," she said. "I don't know where, but I'm sure I have."

The badge was red and rectangular, with no lettering, just a white, geometric symbol. It looked like an elongated letter S, except that it was more geometrical than that, with the two shorter legs at more of an angle to the longer one, and it looked very like half a swastika. From the lower shorter piece there was also a small tail sticking upwards.

"She had this in her clenched fist. I had to break her fingers to get it out," said Ripper as if to himself, as the mild gaze of his light-blue eyes hung on some point outside the window, perhaps on one of the old historical towers of Sandomierz.

Szacki meanwhile was looking at Basia the principled pussy's attractive profile, at the crow's feet next to her eyes and the laughter lines in the corners of her mouth, which told him she smiled a lot and had a good life. And he wondered why Budnik hadn't wanted Basia Sobieraj to question him. Because he didn't want it to be tough for her? Rubbish. He didn't want her to notice something. But what?

V

As Jack the Ripper's assistant was busy stuffing crumpled newspaper into the white corpse of the town's most beloved citizen by the light of the fluorescent strips at the Sandomierz morgue, prosecutors Teodor Szacki and Barbara Sobieraj were sitting on a sofa in their boss's office, each eating their third piece of chocolate cake, though they hadn't really felt like a second one.

They had told her about Budnik's interrogation, about the autopsy, about the badge with the strange symbol, and about the knife, which – perhaps – was a tool for ritual slaughter. Misia had listened to them with a maternal smile on her face, without interrupting, but occasionally putting in a fact to help them with their account, like the model graduate of an active listening course. Now they were done, and she lit a scented candle; the aroma of vanilla floated about the office, and together with the dusk falling outside and the amber light of the desk lamp it produced a nice, festive atmosphere.

Szacki felt like some raspberry tea, but he thought he might be going too far by asking for it.

"Time of death?" asked Miszczyk, extracting crumbs from her large, flaccid bosom, probably worn out by several children. Szacki gave her a hard stare.

"There's a problem with that, the range is quite large," he replied. "Definitely more than five or six hours, taking rigor mortis into account, in other words she was murdered at the latest on Tuesday at about midnight. And at the earliest? The pathologist claims she could even have been dead since Easter Monday. The blood was drained out of the body, which means it's impossible to draw any conclusions on the basis of livor mortis. It was as cold as hell, so the putrefaction hadn't started. We'll know more if it turns out someone saw her. For now, the period from when she left the house on Monday until midnight the next day comes into play. Of course that's supposing Budnik is telling the truth. She may just as well have been dead since Sunday."

"Is he?"

"No. I don't know exactly when he isn't telling the truth, but I'm sure he isn't. He's under round-the-clock surveillance. Let's see what comes of searching the house and grounds. For the time being he's the chief suspect. He lied to us and he hasn't got an alibi. Maybe she was a saint, but apparently things weren't going well between them."

"People always gossip like that when someone else is doing all right," protested Sobieraj.

"Every bit of gossip contains a grain of truth," retorted Szacki.

"What about other scenarios?" asked Miszczyk.

Sobieraj reached for her papers.

"We're provisionally ruling out homicide related to robbery or a sexual motive. There's no evidence of rape, and it's too elaborate for a mugging. I'm checking up on everyone she ran her campaigns with, her family, and friends from the theatrical world. Especially the latter. Ela had connections with the theatre, and you'll admit this has something of a performance about it."

"Fakery," commented Szacki. "But for the time being that's of secondary importance. Above all we're looking for the blood. We have to find evidence of the several litres of it that drained out of her. The police are going to search public places in the city and the suburbs, and all private premises that feature in the inquiry will be checked from this angle too."

"As we're on the subject of blood," said Miszczyk, then paused and sighed, finding it hard to broach the subject, "what about the ritual murder theme?"

"Naturally we're rounding up all the Jews in the area," said Szacki with a stony look on his face.

"Teodor's joking," Sobieraj quickly put in, before Szacki had uttered the final syllable of his remark.

"In all my life I never would have imagined you'd be on first-name terms so quickly! You're totally forbidden to talk to the press about the inquiry, especially Prosecutor Joker here – send them all to me. I'll do my best to make sure the rotten egg doesn't break."

Szacki had a ready-made opinion on that subject – not for this had someone gone to so much trouble – the killer clearly wanted it to leak out. He'd have placed a large bet on the fact that tomorrow morning it'd be hard to push one's way through the broadcasting vans here. But if Miszczyk was taking the press on herself, well then – not his circus, not his monkeys. He kept these considerations to himself, and also his view that the lady district prosecutor had just signed up for the centuries-old Polish tradition of sweeping things under the carpet. She could have had a brilliant career in the Church.

VI

Perhaps it was because Oleg Kuzniecow, the police detective he'd worked with in Warsaw, was completely different – burly, bawdy and jovial, always trying to get a stupid joke into every sentence. Perhaps it came down to the fact that he and Kuzniecow had known each other for years, worked together, drank together and used to meet up at each other's houses. Or maybe it was to do with the fact that Kuzniecow was a real friend of his, and that Prosecutor Teodor Szacki loved him like a brother. Maybe that was why he was incapable, he couldn't and didn't want to like Inspector Leon Wilczur.

It was quite another matter that Inspector Wilczur was rather far from being likeable. He had arranged to meet him in the "Town Hall" bar, a dreadful dive in the basement of a tenement house on the market square that stank of the cigarette smoke which had infused every bit of the decor for decades, and was full of weird customers and weird waiters. Szacki was sure that behind the scenes there were weird cooks weirdly preparing weird meat, so he limited himself to coffee and cheesecake. The cheesecake smelt of an old sofa which everyone sits on, but no one fancies cleaning. The coffee was real, but made in the cup.

Wilczur looked like a demon. In the gloom and the cigarette smoke, his deeply set yellow eyes shone feverishly, his pointed nose cast a shadow across half his face and his cheeks sank with every avid drag on his cigarette.

"A shot each, perhaps, gentlemen?" The waiter's tone was funereal, as if he meant a shot of fresh blood.

They refused. Wilczur waited for the waiter to go away, and then started to speak, occasionally glancing at the documents lying in front of him or at a small laptop. Which at first surprised Szacki. The inspector looked more like the sort of person whom one should spare the torture of explaining what text messages are.

"We know Budnik's version of events, and now we can supplement it with various statements. On Sunday they were definitely at the cathedral at about six p.m., and they definitely left before mass, which starts at seven. We have two independent witnesses to that. Then they went for a walk, and at a quarter past seven they were caught by a camera on Mariacka Street."

Wilczur turned the computer towards him. On a short recording he could see the vague outlines of a couple walking along arm-in-arm. Szacki magnified the image, and for the first time he was able to see Elżbieta Budnik alive. She was the same height as her husband, with dark blonde hair spilling down her sports jacket; she wasn't wearing a hat or a cap. She must have been telling him something – with one hand she was gesticulating vehemently; at one point she stopped to adjust her boot top, while Budnik went on a few paces. She caught him up in three small hops, like a little girl, not a mature woman. Next to the solemn Budnik, dressed in a brown raincoat and a felt hat, she looked like his daughter, not his wife. She drew level with her husband at the edge of the camera's range of view, and stuck her hand into his pocket. Then they disappeared.

"Everything's all right, isn't it?" Wilczur tore the filter off another cigarette.

Szacki knew what he meant. There was no visible tension between them, no argument or stubborn silence. There you had a couple out for walk on an Easter evening. It testified in favour of Budnik's story that they had spent the holiday period as usual, given each other a dressing-down, she had gone off and... and quite, and what?

"Didn't that camera catch her on Monday or Tuesday?" he asked.

"No, I had two people on the job of looking through everything from that moment until the time the body was found yesterday morning. Every single minute. She's not there. We checked this camera and another one by the castle – if you want to leave for the city from Katedralna Street you have to go past one of them. The only other way is through the bushes, or over the cathedral wall and across the garden towards the Vistula."

"What about the neighbours?"

"Nothing. But please look at this."

The second recording was from a camera on the market square, covering part of a row of restaurants including the Ciżemka, the Staromiejska, the Trzydziestka and that café whose name Szacki had forgotten, because he had never dropped in there. The camera clock showed it was Tuesday, shortly after four in the afternoon. There was nothing going on, just the occasional passer-by hovering about. The door of the Trzydziestka opened and out came Budnik, with two "laptops" – polystyrene food containers – in a transparent plastic bag. He headed energetically towards Mariacka Street, and quickly left the camera's field of vision.

Szacki knew perfectly well why Wilczur had shown him this piece of film.

"Interesting, isn't it?" The old policeman leant back in his chair, pressing himself so far into a dark corner of the room that part of him must have been in the next-door property by now.

"Very. Because if it's true that his wife left him on Monday..."

"Then why on earth take her dinner on Tuesday?"

"Which would tally of course, but with his first version of events, the totally improbable one that even he has dropped."

81

Wilczur nodded – in the gloom his prominent, pale nose stood out. Szacki was thinking. He had only smoked one cigarette today, so he had two more left. Intuition told him it would be worth saving them for his date with Tatarska, besides which, simply by being in this room he had smoked a packet and a half. Nevertheless, he took out a cigarette. Wilczur gave him a light. Even if he was surprised the prosecutor smoked at all, he didn't show it. He kept quiet while Szacki tried to sort out the possible scenarios in his head. The pieces went whirling around in his imagination, but each one was from a different set, and he felt as if he were forcing them to fit.

On Sunday the Budniks were still together. Then he appears on Tuesday at the restaurant and buys two dinners. But she only turns up on Wednesday, as an alabaster corpse in the bushes by the old synagogue. What happened?

Let's suppose they really did have a row on Monday. She left, and set off across the fields in a rage towards the Vistula, unobserved by the cameras. There a mysterious madman got hold of her and murdered her. But why in that case did Budnik buy two dinners the next day? Why was there no evidence of a struggle or any attempt to escape on the victim's body, why was there no sign of any blows?

Let's suppose they quarrelled on Monday so badly that Budnik battered his wife. Back a step – there were no marks on the body. Let's suppose they quarrelled so badly that he smothered her with a pillow that night. Or he murdered her in the cellar and drained out her blood. Back a step, there's no trace of blood anywhere in the house. In that case he drove her off to a secluded spot, murdered her there – back a step, the cameras hadn't recorded Budnik leaving by car. He carried her out wrapped in a tight bundle – because once again there aren't any traces – through the bushes to a secluded spot, murdered her and drained out the blood. To cover his tracks and make everything look normal, on Tuesday he went to the office, and got two dinners in order to have an alibi. That night, he went through the bushes again, dragged her to the other end of the Old Town and left her there. Does that sound credible? Totally and utterly, a thousand times no.

So maybe let's suppose he had the plan prepared for ages. That he had a motive which for the time being remains a mystery. He works at the city council, he knows the security system, the layout of the cameras. On Sunday he paraded past the camera, then dragged her out for a walk to a spot near where the body was found. So he wouldn't have to lug the corpse right across town. He stunned her, murdered her and bled her dry. Once it was all over, he left the body there.

"However you look at it, it's clear as shit, isn't it?" wheezed Wilczur out of his dark corner.

Szacki agreed. Unfortunately, he couldn't see any motives or proof, and the murder weapon had turned out to be as sterile as a surgical instrument made ready for an operation.

"Here's one more clip," said Wilczur, pushing the laptop towards him.

The image on the screen was completely white, the contours of the tenement houses so pale that they were virtually invisible. Szacki was reminded of *Silent Hill*.

"Where is that?"

"Żydowska Street. The camera is on the wall of the synagogue," – Szacki noticed that Wilczur didn't use the word "archive" – "set to face the castle. On the right there's the parking area, and behind that there are the bushes where Mrs Budnik was found. The recording is from Wednesday morning, a few minutes before we were notified. Please watch this."

As Szacki watched, several seconds went by, then minutes, then the thin mist cleared a bit as it started to get lighter; now he could see that the camera was above a street, not submerged in a bowl of milk. Suddenly at the bottom of the screen a black semicircle appeared, and Szacki shuddered. The semicircle was advancing down the street, and as it moved away from the camera, it became apparent that it was in fact the upper part of a hat shaped like a bowler, but with a very wide rim. Beneath the hat there was a black coat reaching to the floor, long enough to make it impossible to see any feet or shoes. The effect was ghostly, as the black phantom in the hat levitated for a moment in the grey milk, only to disappear entirely soon after. Szacki rewound the image and pressed pause. He very much wanted it to remind him of something else, but there was no helping it – there, floating in the mist shrouding Żydowska Street in Sandomierz, was the phantom of a Hasidic Jew.

He looked at Wilczur.

"Of course you know what used to be there in those bushes where they found Mrs Budnik," wheezed the policeman.

"The city walls?"

"First of all, they were higher up, and secondly, a long time ago, so you're wrong. It was the *kirkut* – her corpse was lying right at the very centre of the old Jewish cemetery."

The cold evening air was like medicine, an antidote for the "Town Hall" bar. Szacki took a deep breath, while Wilczur tied a scarf around his neck and lit a cigarette. Behind them a door crashed shut, one of the tramps came out and was now looking at them hesitantly.

"Mr Officer…"

"Give me a break, Gąsiorowski. How many times is it now? And it always ends the same way, right?"

"I know, Mr Officer, but—"

"But what?"

"But it's a week now since Anatol's been gone."

"Gąsiorowski, have pity on us. The police chase vagrants away, they don't go looking for them. And certainly not tramps from another county."

"But—"

"But there's nothing more to say. Goodbye."

The tramp disappeared behind a door. Szacki gave Wilczur an enquiring look, but he was in no hurry to explain, and Szacki realized he didn't have to know about every woe besetting the provincial police. They said a perfunctory goodnight.

"We must find out where Elżbieta's blood is," said Szacki, doing up the collar of his coat. It was icy cold again.

"In the matzos," muttered Wilczur and dissolved into the darkness.

VII

The windows are open, letting in a slight chill and the scent of the night. The antlers are asleep on the walls, and there are patches of blue light lurking under the tables, on the coat hooks and in the mirrors. My face looms out of the looking glass, as if from the bottom of a well. I know I can't stay here – with every shudder of the hands on the clock in the hall I'm taking more of a risk; in defiance of reason, my entire body is raring to run away. And yet I must hold out until Saturday. If I hold out until Saturday, if nothing happens by Sunday, if on Sunday evening I am free – then Divine Mercy Sunday will truly deserve its name.

VIII

Buying a decent bottle of wine in the most beautiful old town in all Poland turned out to be impossible. The shabby little shops had nothing but some weird-looking kvass, and finally he realized it would be quickest to nip down the steps that descended the escarpment and buy a bottle of Frontera at the Orlen petrol station on the bypass. He put this plan into action, also wanting to get a Wedel chocolate torte along the way, which seemed to him a nice souvenir of Warsaw where it was made, but unfortunately there wasn't any, so he bought a box of sweets that screamed of having been purchased at a petrol station, and a packet of condoms. He went back up the hill, trying not to sweat too much, because intuition told him he would be performing in the nude before the day was over. The rational side of his brain was telling him that although intuition always suggested the same thing to every guy, it was often proved wrong, but even so, he took care not to run.

Now he was standing in Judge Maria Tatarska's sitting room at her home on Żeromski Street, feeling surprised. Greatly surprised.

At the interior decor, firstly. By now he had realized that the absence he was usually aware of when he entered people's flats in Sandomierz was an absence of Ikea furniture. In Warsaw it was unthinkable for the average flat of a representative of the middle class not to have at least half its furnishings from the Swedish firm. Here, in the better homes, the Krakow-bourgeois style was de rigueur, in other words lots of fabrics carrying enough dust to kill an allergy sufferer, murky mirrors and heavy sideboards with plenty of drawers and shelves. The wealthier citizens without a pedigree lived in villas with wood panelling and holiday-home decor. The poor lived in blocks of flats, inside which there were brown room dividers and sticks of furniture dragged home from the market. He was expecting Tatarska to have the dusty bourgeois effect, or at most pastel modernity, imitation Ikea. But he saw... hmm, this room had something of the hospital ward about it. The colour white, chrome, mirrors and glass. The sitting room was white, quite literally white, so very white that on several of the shelves the books had been carefully covered in white paper, with the titles and authors' names written onto them by hand.

At the hostess's decor, secondly. Judge Maria Tatarska was wearing a plain red cocktail dress and red stilettos. Not that he had expected to see her in a fleece and flip-flops, but her outfit was too showy for a casual evening over a glass of wine. In the white interior she looked like a bloodstain, and perhaps the effect was intentional. Szacki shrugged internally, aware that she was watching him. He liked normal and ordinary, flashiness didn't impress him – at most it evoked pity that there are people capable of investing so much time and effort in things that don't matter.

At the decor of the courtyard, thirdly. Yes, above all the decor of the courtyard, because Judge Maria Tatarska's garden was a cemetery. Not metaphorically, but literally. Szacki had only ever seen it from the other side, from the main entrance, as he walked or drove past along Mickiewicz Street. The beautiful, tree-covered necropolis stretched almost all the way to Żeromski Street, which ran below it, and where there were various monumental masons' yards as well as Judge Tatarska's house. The upstairs sitting room was only a fraction above the level of the tombstones, right against the cemetery wall. The light pouring from the house was strong enough for Szacki to be able to amuse himself by reading the names carved in stone. He noticed to his alarm that there were three forty-year-olds there. Exactly forty years old. And he only had a few months left to his birthday.

He turned around, and saw the judge, sitting on the sofa with a glass of wine in her hand, the colours white and red with corpses in the background – how patriotic, thought Szacki, thinking of the Polish flag.

"A memento mori," she said, raising a foot in a red stiletto onto the sofa. She wasn't wearing any knickers.

3

Friday, 17th April 2009

For Catholics it is the sixth day of the Easter
Week, Orthodox Christians are celebrating Good Friday,
and for Jews the Sabbath begins at sunset, which in
Sandomierz is at 18.31. According to Michael R. Mol-
nar's hypothesis, exactly 2,015 years have passed since
the birth of Jesus Christ, and other people blowing out
the candles on a birthday cake today include Polish rock
star Jan Borysewicz, skiing champion Apoloniusz Tajner
and Victoria Beckham. The news in Poland is boring:
the prime minister is gaining support, the government
is losing support and the president is losing support.
Lech Wałęsa swears he was never a secret-police agent,
and may he drop dead if he's lying. In the world outside, the White House reveals that Bush allowed the
torture of prisoners, the EU announces that the number
of successful and unsuccessful terrorist attacks is
falling, the Scottish police publicizes the fact that
ten followers of the Jedi religion work for it, and the
Vatican expresses regret that the Belgian government
is criticizing Benedict XVI for criticizing the use of
condoms. In the cinemas there are film premieres for
Vicky Cristina Barcelona, directed by Woody Allen, and
the underappreciated *General Nil*, with a superb performance by Olgierd Łukaszewicz in the role of General

Fieldorf aka Nil. Warsaw football team Legia win 1—0
against Piast Gliwice, who play at home, and go to the
top of the Premier Division. There is spring in the air,
and in Sandomierz the maximum temperature is twenty
degrees, but not thanks to the sun — it's cloudy and
it's pouring with rain.

I

Prosecutor Teodor Szacki had had a classical education, and he knew
that Eros and Thanatos have always gone hand in hand, he knew the
legend of Tristan and Isolde, he had read Byron and also Iwaszkiewicz's short stories about doomed lovers; there had even been a time
when he couldn't get to sleep without absorbing a few drops of the
writer's erotic angst. But never before in his life had those two elements
combined so literally and in such an acute way. He woke up with a
hangover and the aftertaste of too much wine on his tongue, and
before he had realized where he was, he could tell it wasn't thirst that
had brought him back to consciousness, but an unbearable, throbbing
pain in his male member. As he gradually came to, the memories of
last night returned, when Tatarska had worn him out in ways that he
had never even seen in a porn film before now. It had seemed silly
just to disappear, because she evidently had great expectations, and
he didn't want to seem churlish, so he had taken part, without any
particular sense of commitment, in a series of erotic exercises, half
of which were tacky, half plain stupid, and all equally exhausting.
They might have been described as the sort of sexual adventure you
talk about for years, and remember for decades. But in fact Szacki
wanted to forget about the whole incident as quickly as possible. He
badly needed a shower.

He opened an eye, fearing he'd see the judge's body lying in wait for
him to wake up and – yet again during this visit – he was amazed. Half
a metre in front of his nose there was a window pane, and a metre
beyond that there was a wet gravestone, on which it said: "Watch

therefore, for ye know neither the day nor the hour." Szacki closed his eye; he didn't want to think about the fact that after all those bestial perversions he had woken up on a tombstone with an evangelical quotation from the parable of The Wise and Foolish Virgins as far as he remembered. How very much he wished he had been a foolish virgin last night, before whom the door was shut and who wasn't allowed in to the wedding feast, for Judge Tatarska to have said to him last night "Verily I say unto you, I know you not" and sent him packing. He turned his back on the earthly remains of fifty-two-year-old Mariusz Wypych and the quotation from the Gospel of St Matthew that was guarding him. The scene on the other side, within the house, wasn't much better – there lay Judge Tatarska, snoring on her back with her mouth open; her face was shiny and puffy, and her ample breasts were flopping to either side. In the light of the April day her sitting room was not snow-white any more, at best faded grey. Szacki looked at his watch, cursed and set off from the funeral home of iniquity as fast as he could.

An hour and a half later, washed and bathed, he was already at work, hoping the stinging he felt when he peed was just being caused by a bit of chafing, and not some mysterious infection. Strangely sure he had every one of last night's acts written on his face, he shut his office door and buried himself in the world of symbols. After an hour he knew it was even worse with symbols than with knives – the number of graphic signs and associations, the multitude of logos and web pages devoted to them – there were millions. He decided to make his search more systematic.

Naturally he started with the Jewish ones, and was soon feeling disappointed, because there weren't many of them. The Star of David, the Menorah, the Torah scrolls, the Tablets of Stone and, surprisingly, the hand of Fatima. He had always associated that symbol with the Arabs, but it turned out to be used in Jewish amulets too. Clearly with cultures it was the same as with spouses – the more alike they are, the more they jump down each other's throats. Szacki was reminded of the time when he had accidentally called some kosher lamb halal at a shop in Warsaw. The owner had almost exploded with rage. Szacki carefully looked through the letters of the Hebrew alphabet, but he couldn't find anything like it. Reading about the Kabbalah was interesting, but in none of the drawings or designs, in none of the mystical writings did he find anything that was even vaguely similar to the badge lying in front of him.

His fruitless research on Jewish sects led him to Christianity. Via Christianity he came to the cross in all its thousands of varieties, and for a moment he thought it might be a variation on the Orthodox cross, a symbol of half of it, some holy order perhaps – but no, it was none of those things

From the cross he came to the swastika. The ancient symbol appeared in many versions, and he examined each one, because the sign on the badge Mrs Budnik had been holding looked very like one half of the Nazi symbol, with a small tail added at the bottom. While he was about it, he wasted a few minutes looking at some pictures of the Bengali actress Swastika Mukherjee, who was an extremely appealing beauty. Admittedly, that morning he had vowed he would never have sex again, but he'd have made an exception for her. He was amazed how many Polish organizations had once made use of the swastika emblem before it became the symbol of Hitler and his plans for Aryan domination. Especially in the mountainous Podhale region it was a popular talisman, nowadays either shamefully hidden, or – as at the hiker's hostel in Gąsienicowa Valley – accompanied by the relevant explanation, so that no tourist should faint with horror. The traditionally Polish, Slavic swastika was called the *swarga*. This trail led him to Slavic symbols, and he laboriously inspected all the signs that appeared for example on earthenware from pre-Christian times, sculpted bas-reliefs, the labels on ritual cakes and the marks on traditional painted eggs and embroidery. And what did he find? Nothing.

His heart skipped a beat when he thought of the Freemasons (nothing), and when he immersed himself in the symbol-infested world of occultism, Satanism and other such nonsense, whose fans are always having things tattooed on their bottoms or sewn onto their jackets. Nothing there either.

He leant back in his chair; he had a headache from the hangover and from squinting at the computer. It was starting to look like a joke, as if someone had gone to the trouble of raking through all the symbols in the world to create a logo that wasn't like anything else. He must think. He stared at the monitor, where there were several different windows open, filled with reversed stars, ugly Satanic faces and charts testifying to the fact that there is a pentagram written into the Washington street map. There was also the runic alphabet, which riveted Szacki's attention. He had a stretch, and then got stuck into the new symbols. He discovered runes invented by Tolkien for *Lord of the Rings*, learnt the differences between individual forms of this old-Germanic alphabet, and finally achieved – albeit partial – success. If the little tail were erased from his symbol, it would look like the rune *eihwaz*. It was a magnetic rune, meaning a yew tree, the symbol of transformation, corresponding to the sign Aquarius, the perfect amulet for a spiritual leader, a state official or a fireman. Not even the Catholic saints covered such a broad spectrum of activities. But what was the result of all this? Absolutely zilch, sheer futility, a waste of time. And anyway, it didn't have the little tail.

Furious, he got up from his chair. He wanted to sleep, his head ached and so did his member, he had a bad taste in his mouth from the wine, and a bad moral taste in his mind from the sexual exploits, on top of which the weather was the sort that makes you feel like either going to bed or to the pub. The clouds hung low and it was drizzling non-stop with miserable, bloody annoying rain; the water was collecting on the window pane and dribbling down it in single trickles. He thought of Elżbieta Budnik, suspended upside down in a warehouse somewhere, and of the murderer watching as the blood leaked ever more slowly from her neck. Had he placed a bucket underneath her? Or a bowl? Or had he let it flow into the drain? The more detailed a scene he tried to imagine, the more a chord of desire quivered inside him for plain old human, not at all legalistic, justice. There was something charming about Elżbieta Budnik on the recording from the urban camera. A pretty woman, but with a hint of girlishness, a woman who hadn't forgotten what it meant to skip up to someone, to laugh out loud at the cinema and to eat waffles and whipped cream in the summer, letting a white spot get left on her nose. A woman who wanted to do things for children, workshops, shows, parties, most of them probably for free or for peanuts. Who must have already had the holidays planned, knew who was coming on what day, when there'd be an outing, when a concert, when a trip to the castle at Ujazd. Who was pleased when the mothers told her it was a pity for the children to go away for the summer when there was so much going on here.

She had been alive when he hung her upside down, and when he slashed her throat. First the bright arterial blood had gushed out in a mighty stream; it had frothed and then begun to flow down her face to the rhythm of the final beats of her heart.

For the first time Szacki felt how very much he wanted to see the culprit in court. Even if that meant examining, with a hangover, every bloody symbol humanity had ever created throughout its entire history.

He went back to the computer, wrote down what he had found about the rune *eihwaz*, and got on with the nationalist symbols. Perhaps rather than the Jewish trail it would make more sense to try the anti-Semitic one? Reading the nationalist websites was quite astonishing – he was expecting to find messages saying "Fuck the Jews with axes" or "Queers to the gas" spiced up with drawings in the style of pre-war anti-Semitic lampoons, but instead he found some smart, well-edited sites. Unfortunately the rune with the tail was nowhere to be seen. There was the notched-sword symbol of the Falanga Polish nationalist group, the skinheads' Celtic cross, and of course the homophobic "No Camping" sign. He was just about to give up, when out of a sense of duty he clicked on a site called *lesserpoland-patriots.pl* and gave a loud sigh of relief. There in the heading, as well as the emblem of the Polish Republic, was the rune with the tail, whatever it might be.

"Hallelujah!" he cried out loud, and just at that moment Sobieraj stuck her ginger head round the door.

"And praise be to the Lord!" she added. "This morning I described that mysterious symbol to my husband and he says it's called a '*rodło*', the symbol of the Union of Poles in Germany. And that we should probably go back to school if we didn't recognize it immediately. I dug around a bit and... have you got a moment?"

Szacki quickly minimized all the windows on his desktop.

"Sure, I was just sorting out the papers. And of course it's a '*rodło*', I must have been pretty dead-beat yesterday not to think of that."

Sobieraj gave him a meaningful look, but didn't pass comment. She sat down next to him, bringing a cloud of scent with her, rather a fruity cloud, a bit too fruity for early spring, and spread some sheets of paper on the desk. On one of them the symbol, the "*rodło*", was placed on top of a map of Poland.

"Look, Teodor." He couldn't think when someone had last addressed him as Teodor – probably a teacher at school. "The mysterious half-swastika with the thingumajig symbolizes the shape of the river Vistula on the map of Poland. It goes right, then straight at an angle to the mountains, then to the right. And the thingamajig is the spot where the Vistula flows through Krakow. The symbol came into being in 1933, after Hitler had taken power. The Nazis introduced the swastika, and banned the use of any other symbols except ones approved by them, and the Polish white eagle was totally out of the question – the ban on using it had been in force since Prussian times. And now look what our smart compatriots in Germany do. They create a symbol like this, and they tell the Germans it's a half-swastika. The Germans make clever faces, nod their heads and say: yes, quite, that makes sense. The real Germans have their complete, wonderful swastika, and the Poles in Germany only have half, *gut, gut, sicher, wery polite Polnischer schweine, verstehen?*"

"Why not *verstehen*? I everything *verstehen*!" said Szacki.

"Of course, for our lot this was the total opposite of the swastika, I mean the opposite of what it represented. The '*rodło*' was and is a symbol of the German Poles' connection with the Polish Republic."

Szacki nodded. "And what else? Does that union still exist?"

"Absolutely – from what I've managed to find out, it's pretty active, with a headquarters in Bochum. It's an organization that supports Poles living abroad, represents them officially, helps them when they're in trouble, like a sort of non-governmental consulate. They also have a strong national mythology, they were set up in the 1920s, they must have been operating in the era when the Nazis were on the rise, and you can guess what that means."

"Confiscation of property, delegalization, arrests, executions, death camps."

"Spot on. That's why nowadays the '*rodło*' is also a symbol of courage, the Polish spirit and indomitability in nationalist organizations, for example several scout packs use this sign."

"Nationalist meaning the sort who shout slogans like 'man and wife, family life'?"

"No, more like the reasonable nationalists, the patriotic types."

"Reasonable nationalists?" snorted Szacki. "Are we playing at oxymorons now?"

Sobieraj shrugged.

"Maybe it's unfashionable in Warsaw, but in the provinces some people like to feel proud of the fact that they're Polish."

"Yesterday you were telling me that being a genuine Pole could have very dark undertones in Sandomierz."

"Maybe I forgot to add that between rejecting the nation and burning down synagogues in its name, there's a pretty large area for reasonable people to claim."

Szacki didn't want to polemicize. He didn't like people who had hobbies; more than that, he was afraid of them. To him, the nation was a hobby – a passion which is totally unnecessary and doesn't help in any way, but which gets people so deeply involved that in unfavourable circumstances it can lead to terrible things. A prosecutor, to his mind, should not identify with the nation; he shouldn't believe in anything, and he shouldn't have a passion that envelops his mind in a fog. The legal code is very precise, it doesn't make divisions into better and worse, it doesn't look at faith and national pride. And the prosecutor is meant to be a servant of the code, a guardian of law and order.

Sobieraj stood up and leant against the window sill.

"Apropos burning down synagogues," she said, nodding at something outside.

Szacki looked out; on the other side of the street stood a Polsat TV van, and there were some technicians unfolding a satellite dish on its roof. Whatever – not his circus, not his monkeys. He considered further moves to take. Elżbieta Budnik had been holding the symbol of the Union of Poles in Germany, also used by some patriotic and nationalist organizations. They'd have to talk to the local nationalists, if there were any, check out the scouts and the right-wing activists.

"Jerzy Szyller is an honorary member of the Union of Poles in Germany," said Sobieraj quietly, as if to herself. "This case is getting odder and odder."

"And who is Jerzy Szyller?"

Prosecutor Barbara Sobieraj's ginger head turned slowly to face him. There were moments when Szacki found her pretty, in a nice, feminine way, not at all vulgar or blatant. There was amazement and disbelief painted on her pretty face, as if he had asked who was the last pope.

"You're joking, aren't you?"

No, he wasn't joking.

II

He listened to what Basia Sobieraj had to say about Jerzy Szyller, and as soon as she had left his office he called Wilczur and told him to come at once. He needed the antidote to yet another panegyric delivered by his freckled colleague. From her account emerged a handsome patriot, an honest businessman, a citizen who paid high taxes on time, a connoisseur of art, an erudite, sophisticated man. In short, yet another flawless person in Sandomierz, the city of flawless people, law-abiding, honest and noble, who only once in a while speared a Jew or two on pitchforks or slashed someone's throat and left them in the bushes.

Wilczur buried himself in an armchair without taking off his coat; he had brought the damp and the cold in with him, and his nose had gone red in the middle of his sallow face. The room at once became darker, so Szacki switched on the lamp and explained what it was about.

"Not a week goes by when we don't get some sort of complaint about Szyller," Wilczur began, tearing the filter off a cigarette. "He parked badly by the Opatowska Gate. The trees outside his office are blocking out the light. His dog shat right outside someone's door. He parked on the pavement without leaving the statutory one-and-a-half metres for pedestrians. He walked across Mickiewicz Street on a red light, causing a hazard for road traffic. He breaks the silence at night. He blew his nose by the monument to John Paul II, offending the religious sensibilities of the Catholic citizens of Sandomierz, and by the same token breaking Article 196 of the Penal Code."

"That last one is a joke, right?"

"No. Nor is it an exception. I wish I had a zloty a month from every citizen of Sandomierz who hates him like poison." Wreathed in a cloud of smoke, Wilczur became pensive, probably imagining what he would have spent such a fortune on.

"Do they hate him for any particular reason?"

Wilczur laughed hoarsely.

"You really have never lived in a small town before, Prosecutor. They hate him because he's rich and good-looking, and because he's got a big house and a shiny car. In the Catholic world that can only mean one thing – that he's a crook, an oppressor of the poor who has made a packet at the expense of others."

"And what's the truth?"

"The truth is that Jerzy Szyller is a businessman who's clever with property, deals in it here and in Germany, and specializes in sites that attract tourists. I've heard that in his time he used to buy plots of land from the peasants in Kazimierz Dolny. He also invests in infrastructure from time to time – for example that new hotel on Zawichojska Road is his. I know the tax people and various agencies have vetted him several times, he's clean. Quite an idiosyncratic type, but you'll discover that for yourself."

"What sort of relationship did he have with the Budniks?"

"There was certainly no love lost between him and Budnik – thanks to Budnik's scams and his efforts to hand land back to the Church several nice plots slipped past Szyller's nose. As for Mrs Budnik, I have no idea, but the guy's a bit of a philanthropist, and I'm sure he financed some of her enterprises for children. On the whole they were from different worlds. The Budniks belonged to the left-wing intelligentsia, and Szyller was more the type who has a red-and-white flag on a pole outside his house. To him they were a bit Communist, and to them he was a bit of a fascist – I'm sure they never had a barbecue together."

Wilczur suffered from the typical Polish tendency to make everything sound like invective, even if he was talking about someone positively or neutrally. That weary tone, that slight grimace, the single raised eyebrow, that way of dragging on his cigarette to mark each comma, then taking another drag and tapping off the ash to mark each full stop. His disdain for the world in general sullied everyone the old policeman spoke about.

"Szyller. Is he a Jew?"

A spiteful smirk flashed across the policeman's lips.

"Since the last political changes we no longer keep records of denomination or descent. But if you believe the informers, yes, one hundred per cent. As well as a pederast, zoophile and Devil-worshipper."

For effect Wilczur raised a hand with the little and index fingers held straight, and now he looked like Keith Richards's uglier, even more wrecked brother.

Szacki didn't laugh.

III

On the phone, Jerzy Szyller's low, refined voice announced in Polish and German that its owner cannot take your call at the moment, but would you please leave a message. Rather half-heartedly Szacki left one, but less than fifteen minutes later Szyller called back, apologizing for having been unable to answer earlier. As Szacki began to explain what he was calling about, he politely but firmly interrupted him.

"Of course I understand, in a way I was expecting this call, like myself, Mr and Mrs Budnik are public figures in Sandomierz, and we did," – here he paused, almost imperceptibly – "like it or not, maintain contact. I admit that I deliberately cancelled a trip to Germany because I foresaw that I might be necessary to the legal authorities."

"In that case please come to the prosecutor's office on Kosely Street."

"Well, unfortunately I'm not quite such an ideal citizen. I cancelled my trip to Germany, but I took the opportunity to see to some business in Warsaw. I'm still in the capital," – Szacki liked the fact that he used that word – "but the Friday rush hour will start before I leave… Would it be a major problem if we were to meet tomorrow? Do forgive my impertinence – of course I could hop in the car at once, but I'm afraid even if I do that I won't be with you before about eight."

Experience had taught Szacki that with every hour that passes from the moment when a corpse is found the case becomes more obscure, and the chances of finding the culprit diminish. He was just about to react sharply, but he told himself that a few hours didn't really matter.

"All right, let's meet tomorrow."

"At what time should I appear at the prosecutor's office?"

"I'll be at your house at three p.m." Szacki had no idea why he answered like that; it was sheer impulse, his investigator's sixth sense at work.

"Of course. In that case, see you tomorrow?"

"See you tomorrow," replied Szacki and hung up, wondering why Szyller had ended with a question. Was it that good manners wouldn't let him end a conversation which he hadn't started? Or was he letting himself have the thought that they might not see each other after all?

Just then, the boss's secretary put her head round the door.

IV

Prosecutor Teodor Szacki was an enlightened man who knew the basics of psychology, and was aware that negative identity formation is a blind alley. That a person should define himself in terms of positive emotions, in terms of what he likes, what makes him happy and brings him joy. That constructing his identity on what annoys and infuriates him is the start of the slippery slope towards embitterment, down which he descends ever faster until he finally becomes a malcontent seething with hatred.

He knew that, and always tried his best to fight against it, but there were moments when it was quite simply impossible. This was one of those moments. In his immaculate suit and matching tie, with his distinguished white hair and his stern expression, standing straight behind the improvised speakers' table, Prosecutor Teodor Szacki looked like the embodiment of the legal authorities. As he looked at the group of about a dozen journalists gathered on the other side of it, he concentrated on his breathing, and on restraining the disdainful scowls that were trying to appear on his face and that might get caught on camera.

Yes, the brave defender of Justice with the snow-white hair sincerely loathed the media. For lots of different reasons. Definitely because they were horribly, acutely, gut-churningly boring and predictable. Definitely because they made things up and told bare-faced lies depending on the needs of the moment, juggling the facts to make them fit their presupposed theories. Definitely because they produced a warped image of the world, giving every marginal extreme the features of the norm or a trend, because only then did that extreme gain a significance that justified harping on about something utterly irrelevant for twenty-four hours a day.

But all this would have been bearable if only the media were firmly placed in the same drawer as entertainment for the emotionally disturbed. One guy likes to watch football matches, another likes porn films involving animals, and another likes the TVN24 rolling news channel – different strokes for different folks. And if Teodor Szacki hadn't been a prosecutor, he'd probably have categorized journalists alongside people who enjoy satisfying Labradors, and then forgotten about them. Unfortunately, so many times had morons shouting about the citizen's right to information caused trouble in his investigations, so many times had they confused the witnesses by inflating the most sensational and gory aspects of the case, so many times, despite being asked and begged not to, had they published facts which set the inquiry back for weeks or months – that if the good Lord had turned to Szacki and asked which professional group should vanish into thin air on the instant, he wouldn't have hesitated for a moment.

And now, if you please, it turned out that even if the circus wasn't his, the monkeys most certainly were.

"Have you already singled out someone to accuse?"

"So far an inquiry is being conducted into the case, not against anyone. That means we are investigating various leads and interviewing various individuals, but we have not charged anybody," Misia replied smoothly, without removing the motherly smile from her face for a second. This was already the umpteenth stupid, incompetent question in a row, and Szacki noted to his horror that the hacks in the provinces were even stupider than the ones in Warsaw.

"How would you comment on the fact that the victim was brutally murdered with a knife used for ritual kosher butchery?"

Silence fell in the auditorium. On both sides of the table. Szacki was just about to open his mouth, when Sobieraj's resonant, pleasantly high-pitched voice rang out.

"Ladies and gentlemen, unfortunately it sounds as if someone is trying to encumber the investigation by spreading false rumours, and you are trotting after them like lambs to the slaughter, not necessarily the ritual kind. It is a fact that the victim's life was taken by cutting her jugular artery, in a very unpleasant way. It is a fact that a very sharp instrument was used for this purpose. But we are not aware of any ritual butchery. Neither kosher, nor halal, nor any other kind."

"So in the end are we talking about Jewish or Arab ritual?"

"Sir," put in Szacki, "we're not talking about any ritual at all. I repeat: none at all. Where on earth do you get these ideas from? Is there something I've failed to notice? Is there a fashion among you lot these days for calling homicide ritual murder? A tragedy has occurred, a woman's life has been taken, and we're pulling out all the stops to get the case solved and identify the perpetrator. The circumstances of this murder are in no way more unusual than dozens of the homicides

I have dealt with in the past, and I spent fifteen years with the city-centre prosecution service in Warsaw. And believe me, I've seen a lot."

Miszczyk glanced at him respectfully, for once without maternal approval. An ugly female journalist in a green top stood up, without introducing herself of course – probably everyone was meant to recognize her.

"Was the victim a Jew?"

"That's of no relevance to the inquiry," replied Szacki.

"So am I to understand that if the victim had been a homosexual, for example, that would be of no relevance to you either?" For some reason the ugly journalist seemed to be offended.

"It would have just as much relevance as the fact that she played chess or went fishing…"

"So you regard sexual orientation as a sort of hobby?"

There was a salvo of laughter. Szacki waited for it to pass.

"Everything that concerns both victim and suspects is of relevance to an inquiry, and everything is investigated. But experience shows that the motives for murder rarely lie in religious or other preferences."

"So where do they lie?" shouted someone from the back of the auditorium.

"Alcohol. Money. Family relations."

"But surely an anti-Semitic stunt of this kind deserves special treatment?" the ugly journalist nagged on. "Especially in a city of pogroms, in a country where anti-Semitism still thrives and where it reaches a point of xenophobic disturbances?"

"If you know of any anti-Semitic stunts, please report them to the police. I am not aware of anything of the kind, and the inquiry into the case of Elżbieta B. certainly has nothing to do with it."

"I simply want to write the truth. The Poles deserve the truth about themselves, not just whitewashed heroics."

A few people clapped, and Szacki was reminded of the way the journalists had applauded the extremely reactionary populist politician Andrzej Lepper when he had cackled and asked out loud: "How can you rape a prostitute?" Yes, that scene epitomized the truth about the Polish media. In fact he agreed with the ugly journalist's last comment, but nevertheless he had a growing feeling that all this was a pointless waste of time. He glanced at Miszczyk and Sobieraj, who were sitting motionless in front of the cameras, as if this lark were going to last all day.

"All right, please write the truth," he said; unfortunately he failed to conceal his disdain, he could see that on her face. "Maybe you'll blaze a trail for your colleagues. Last question, then we've got to get back to work."

"Are you an anti-Semite, Prosecutor?"

"If you're a Jew, then yes, I'm an anti-Semite."

V

He was furious. After the press conference he fled to his office to avoid talking to Miszczyk. He exchanged a few words with Sobieraj and called Wilczur to check on progress with the inquiry, but there wasn't any. No witnesses had appeared, no traces of blood had been found, reviewing the recordings from other security cameras hadn't produced any results and Budnik was sitting at home. Interviewing Elżbieta Budnik's other friends had merely confirmed that she was a wonderful person, a cheerful social benefactress, full of life. Not everyone had a high opinion of her marriage, but everyone said that "at least they were friends". The fatter the files grew, the more saintly Elżbieta Budnik became, the more no motive whatsoever was apparent, and the more frustrated Szacki felt. He had a hard time stopping himself from getting in the car and driving off to meet Szyller, to interview him at the Statoil petrol station in Kozienice, to do anything, discover anything at all just to push the case forwards.

In search of fresh ideas and fresh air he left the prosecutor's office, went past the stadium, where there was still a fuss going on in defence of the potato stalls, and started walking along Staromiejska Street towards Saint Paul's church, passing the villas of the Sandomierz elite and the modern Piszczele Park, established in the gorge of the same name. Szacki hadn't seen this place before it was done up, but apparently it had been a typical back alley dedicated to the patron saint of cheap plonk, where at any time of day you could lose your virginity against your own will. Szacki walked fast, briskly. It was warm enough for him to unbutton his coat, and the drizzle settled on the fabric of his clothes, cladding him in ethereal shining armour.

He reached the church and the graveyard picturesquely situated next to it; the clouds had dispersed enough to reveal a lovely view of Sandomierz Old Town up on the hill, from which Szacki was now separated by the gentle gorge. From here the city looked like a ship drifting across the common land, which was turning green by now. The soaring cathedral bell tower marked the prow, the tenement houses looked like containers standing on the deck, the town-hall tower rose like a mast right in the middle of the ship, and at the stern stood the solid figure of the Opatowska Gate. From here Szacki could clearly see the characteristic, stocky shape of the synagogue and the bushes extending below it, where the corpse had been found.

He started to walk downhill, towards the city, mentally multiplying the various possible scenarios. Each one began with the key assumption that either Budnik was the killer, or Budnik was not. Each one was just as senseless and improbable. His frustration rising, he walked faster and faster, went past the castle, and when at last he stopped outside the cathedral, he was terribly out of breath.

The cathedral was so-so, neither beautiful nor ugly, a pretty large Gothic red-brick block with baroque elements stuck onto the façade. Certainly every guidebook poured honey and icing onto this church, going on at length about its ancient history, but the building made no particular impression on Szacki, especially since he had found out that its finest feature, in other words the soaring bell tower, was the result of neo-Gothic reconstruction in the late nineteenth century. He walked up to the side entrance where there was a freshly written sign that must have been hung up there that day, saying: "Absolutely no filming or photography!!!" Clearly the media had already made their presence known to the clerics.

He went inside.

For the Easter season, the cathedral was surprisingly empty. One person who looked like a tourist was wandering around the interior, but there was no one in the pews. Near the organ gallery a man and a woman were washing the stone floor with identical movements. Szacki breathed in the unique, unmistakeable smell of an old church, waited a moment until his eyes got used to the semi-darkness, and looked around. It was the first time he had been in here. He had been expecting monumental Gothic austerity, something like Saint John's cathedral in Warsaw, but in fact the Sandomierz basilica was not overwhelmingly stately. Szacki liked the fact that the architectural skeleton – the columns and ribs of the vault – was not made of red brick, but of white stone, which gave the interior elegance. At the slow pace that he always switched on automatically in churches, he walked between the pews and stopped in the middle of the central nave, beneath an imposing crystal chandelier. On one side he had the organ gallery, topped by the crown of the organ, and on the other the high altar and the presbytery – all in lavish baroque style. The marble font on a barrel-shaped pedestal, the gold framework in the side altars, each curling ornament, the chubby cherubs and dark oil paintings shouted to the spectator: hello there, we were made in the eighteenth century.

He zigzagged his way between the columns, looking without much interest at the sculptures and paintings of saints, and stopped for a while at the presbytery, which some local Giotto had actually quite successfully adorned with scenes from the New Testament. There Szacki saw the Last Supper, the Raising of Lazarus, Pontius Pilate, Judas and Thomas, a whole set of immortal images that apparently give two billion people a sense of security, peace and the awareness that they can do what they want because ultimately it's the prodigal sons that God loves best anyway. Yet another misguided hobby for the deranged, sod the lot of you. Szacki rubbed his face with his hands; he felt dead tired.

Abruptly he turned away from the altar – after all, he hadn't come to the cathedral to admire second-rate European art. He started walking rapidly down the central nave, between the pews, towards the organ gallery. Beneath the chandelier he tried to get past the man, who was robotically washing the floor, steadily wielding his mop like a metronome.

"Not on the wet," the man warned.

Szacki stopped. The man broke off what he was doing and looked him in the eyes. He had a sallow complexion, a sad expression and a black shirt buttoned up to the neck. A bit of a zombie, a bit of a tramp – a genuine Catholic, full of gladness and joy since God had laid before him a shining path straight to heaven. In silence, Szacki took a step back and walked along the very edge of the dry floor to the side nave. His steps drowned out the steady swishing of the mop, which had resumed its activity.

There could be no doubt where the famous painting was. On the western wall, on either side of the entrance to the vestibule hung four large canvases. The first two portrayed, in a naturalistic manner, two massacres – judging by the appearance of the attackers, it was a Tatar or Mongol raid. In the first picture the infidels were pulverizing the citizens of Sandomierz, and in the second some Dominicans, easily recognized by their white habits. On the other side of the entrance there was another massacre and a burning castle; this time it didn't look like the Tatars, so it must have been the Swedish invasion – no one was quite so keen on burning down and blowing up as the Swedes, who had a real passion for explosives, and a long time before Nobel's day too. And the fourth canvas? Prosecutor Teodor Szacki stood in front of it and folded his arms across his chest. Could it possibly have something to do with Mrs Budnik's murder? Should they really be looking for a religious madman? He turned round towards the altar, and mentally asked God for it not to be a religious madman. The worst cases are the ones involving madmen. A madman means miles of documents, whole processions of expert witnesses and arguments about whether or not he is aware of his own acts; sheer torment, and when it comes to the sentence, it's a lottery, regardless of the hard evidence.

Szacki prayed and thought. From the left, the whoosh-swoosh of the church cleaning was coming steadily nearer to him. This time it was the woman. She put down her bucket, started to mop, and got as far as Szacki's feet. She broke off her work and looked at him expectantly. She was just as radiant and full of the joy of faith as her partner; a shop selling accessories for suicides would have employed her on the instant. The prosecutor stepped back a pace and started walking towards the exit along a narrow alley of dry floor; there wasn't much sense in staring at the red shroud shielding the controversial painting. As a consolation prize, so there wouldn't be nothing to look at, there was a portrait of John Paul II hanging on the fabric.

Szacki knew what the picture showed – he had looked at it on the Internet. Charles de Prévôt may not have been a good painter, but he had a predilection for the macabre and a comic-strip talent for pictorial narration which appealed to the archdeacon of the time, who had commissioned the painter to decorate the cathedral. As Archdeacon Żuchowski was a true Christian and a sworn Jew-baiter, de Prévôt had documented Jewish crimes against the children of Sandomierz. The painting showed Jews buying children from their mothers and checking their condition like cattle at the market, there were Jews in the act of murdering, there were experts at extracting blood with the use of a barrel studded with nails, and there was a dog eating up the leftover bits thrown to it. What had stuck most firmly in Szacki's mind was the sight of the babies' little corpses scattered on the ground.

He failed to reach the door; between him and the exit from the side nave there were three metres of wet, freshly mopped floor. He simply wanted to take three big steps, but something made him stop. The silence. There were no footsteps and no swishing noises. The man and the woman were both standing still, leaning on their mops in identical poses, staring at him from a distance. His first instinct was to just shrug his shoulders and leave the place, but there was such sorrow in their eyes that he sighed and started looking for a way out along the dry bits of floor. His route was a winding one; feeling like a rat in a labyrinth, he reached the opposite side of the church – a long way from the exit. But it looked as if he had an open path to the altar now, and from that side he could get to the door. Reassured by his behaviour, the man and woman went back to work.

Walking close to the wall, Szacki looked at the paintings he was passing, which were also the work of the baroque cartoonist de Prévôt.

As he looked, he started walking more and more slowly, until finally he stopped. His Catholic upbringing wouldn't allow him to use the word "pornography" to describe what he was seeing, but no other word could have got the point across as well as that one. The large paintings had one single theme – death. The very realistic, gory deaths suffered by martyrs, in hundreds of different varieties. In the first instance Szacki couldn't understand why each corpse had a number, but then he noticed that each picture was supplied with the Latin name of a month, and he realized that it was a sort of perverse calendar. One little horror for each day of the year. He was standing in front of March, and the tortures were so inventive that they seemed to be trying to reflect the entire hopelessness of the cold, muddy start of spring in Poland. The 10th of March featured the demise of Aphrodosius, nailed to a tree with spears, and two days later a spade was chopping through the neck of Micdonius; then his eyes were drawn to their fellow martyr, Benjamin, whose entrails were twisting in a gory ribbon around the serrated something that had transfixed him on the 31st of March. In April things were a tiny touch better – someone was being thrown off an embankment into a river, some heads were being cut off, somebody was being dragged by a horse and someone else was being torn apart by wild beasts. One chap seemed to be being boiled alive; the look on his face implied more than just a warm bath. On the 12th of May he came upon Theodore. In fact his namesake could boast of rather a mild punishment – being drowned with a weight around his neck. Szacki felt absurd relief that this was not his patron saint – he celebrated his name day on the feast of Saint Theodore of Tarsus, a seventh-century monk and intellectual.

As he walked on, the pictorial horrors repulsed and attracted him all at once, like the victim of an accident lying by the roadside. He admired de Prévôt's inventiveness, as for 365 days surprisingly few tortures were repeated, though crucifixion and throat-slashing were definitely top of the bill.

He finally managed to reach the vicinity of the door and increased his pace, because the sexton in black was clearly trying his best to cover the last patch of dry floor by the exit. He stopped at November, as his birthday was on the eleventh. Wow, this particular martyr really did deserve canonization. Not only was he strung up on a hook in a very nasty way, just to make sure his legs were burdened with a weight and his body was stuck through with a spear. Szacki thought grimly what a dreadful prophecy it was, as if someone were trying to tell him there's always room for a little extra martyrdom.

The sexton cleared his throat in a meaningful way. Szacki tore his gaze from the vision of baroque pornography.

"I've found my birthday," he said pointlessly.

"That's not a birthday," replied the cleaner in a surprisingly jolly tone, "that's a prediction of how you'll end."

Outside it was like November – damp, cold and dark. Szacki buttoned up his coat and went out of the gate into Kościelna Street, then started walking towards the market square. He glanced into a camera – the very one that had captured Ela Budnik for the last time as she straightened her boot top, and then caught up with her husband in three skips. The idea of calling on Budnik flashed through his mind, but he dropped it.

VI

Outside it keeps on raining, as if the winter is bidding farewell to this land in weak, weary weeping. In here it's warm and dry, and if it weren't for the burning eyes of the man sitting in the corner, it would even be cosy. Not very tall, skinny, with his hands and feet bound, he resembles a child; only the ginger beard protruding from under his gag betrays the fact that the victim is a grown man. He stirs pity, but that doesn't change anything. In the distance the clock on the town-hall tower chimes four times to mark the full hour, and then strikes two. One more day. Just one more day. Unfortunately it can't be waited out here; there are still the dogs to look in on before going back up. Luckily, the second act is coming to its end now.

4

Saturday, 18th April 2009

The seventh, penultimate day of Easter for Catholics, and Easter Saturday for Orthodox Christians; the Sabbath in the entire Jewish world. Tadeusz Mazowiecki, independent Poland's first prime minister, is celebrating his eighty-second birthday. More recent former prime minister Jarosław Kaczyński claims that only his party, the right-wing Law and Justice, can save democracy in Poland. In the outside world the Somali parliament introduces shariah law throughout the country, and Bulgaria is in a panic because a well-known astrologer predicts an earthquake. In the Czech city of Ústí nad Labem hundreds of neo-fascists from the Czech Republic, Slovakia, Hungary and Germany celebrate Hitler's approaching birthday by attacking a Roma settlement. Łukasz "Flappyhandski" Fabiański defends his net poorly on his twenty-fourth birthday, so Arsenal lose against Chelsea and go out of the FA Cup at the semi-final stage. In Sandomierz thieves cut down six apple trees and a plum tree. The sixty-year-old trees were worth a thousand zlotys. In the evening there is a noisy party at the club located in the town-hall cellar, Soundomierz Rock Zone. This is the first fairly springlike day — it is warm and sunny, and it isn't raining.

"Listen to this. A rabbi and a priest are travelling in the same train compartment, reading in silence, all very civilized. A while goes by, and then the priest puts down his book and says: 'Just out of curiosity – I know you people aren't allowed to eat pork. But… have you ever tried it?' The rabbi closes his newspaper, smiles and says: 'You really want to know? Well actually, I did once try it.' After a pause he adds: 'And just out of curiosity – I know you people are obliged to be celibate…' The priest interrupts him, saying: 'I know what you're driving at, and I'll tell you straight away, that yes, I did once give in to the temptation.' They smile indulgently at each other's little peccadilloes, then the priest goes back to his book, the rabbi to his newspaper, and they read in silence again. Suddenly the rabbi says: 'Better than pork, isn't it?'"

Szacki knew this joke, but he laughed sincerely – he liked Jewish jokes.

"OK, here's another one…"

"Andrzej…"

"Last one, I promise. It's Passover, a beautiful day, so Moshe takes his lunch to the park, sits down on a bench and tucks in. A blind guy comes and sits next to him, and as it's the festive season, Moshe is feeling warm and loving towards all mankind, so he offers him a piece of matzo bread. The blind man takes the matzo, turns it in his hand, his face falls and finally he says: 'Who wrote this shit?'"

This time Szacki burst out laughing without any buts – the joke was excellent, and brilliantly told too.

"Andrzej, please! Teodor will think we're some sort of anti-Semites."

"This is a good Kielce region family. Have you told him how we met at the National Radical Camp rally? What a night it was, in the light of the flaming torches you looked like an Aryan queen… Aargh!"

Andrzej Sobieraj ducked as his wife threw a piece of bread at him, but he did it so clumsily that he banged his elbow on the edge of the table. He glared at her reproachfully. Szacki always felt awkward when he witnessed intimacy between people, so he just smiled weakly and smeared a generous helping of mustard on his piece of barbecued sausage. He was feeling odd, jostled by emotions he couldn't identify.

The husband of Basia Sobieraj – the principled pussy, as Szacki couldn't stop thinking of her, despite his growing fondness for her – was a fairly typical teddy bear. The kind of man that had never, not even in his best years, been a heart-throb women sighed over and dreamt about, but one they all liked, because they could have a chat and a laugh with him, and feel safe. But then of course they went for the enigmatic hunks, alcoholics and skirt-chasers, convinced that love would change them, and the reliable teddy bear usually ended up with a bitch who needed someone to kick around and do all the work. In spite of all, Basia Sobieraj did not look like one of those, and this teddy bear had made a pretty good match. And he looked like a nice, happy guy. He had a nice checked shirt, tucked into old, cheap jeans. He had a nice, stocky, slightly pot-bellied, beer-and-barbecue figure. He had nice, gentle eyes, a moustache that curled towards his mouth and slightly balding temples, two thinner patches in a forest of wavy, salt-and-pepper hair.

"Stop stirring it up," said Nice Andrzej to his wife, as he turned the pieces of sausage on the barbecue. "Of all people the prosecutor isn't likely to be offended by anti-Semitism. From what they write in the papers…"

Basia snorted with laughter, and Szacki smiled politely. Unfortunately, yesterday's press conference had gone running through the media, and unfortunately almost all of them had written about a "mysterious murder", about "anti-Semitic undercurrents" and a "Nazi undertone"; one paper had recited the history of the city in detail, and suggested in an editorial that "it is not entirely certain whether the investigator is aware of the delicacy of the matter he is having to deal with". And that was just the start of it – if they didn't solve the case quickly, or if some new facts didn't turn up soon to give the vultures something to feed on, it would just get worse.

"Why on earth are we talking about anti-Semitism anyway?" asked Andrzej Sobieraj. "Ela wasn't a Jew, and as far as I know she had nothing to do with them, she didn't even organize klezmer concerts – the closest she got to Judaism was a concert a few years back featuring songs from *Fiddler on the Roof*. So how can her murder be a fascist act? And why should the word 'Jewish' appearing in any given context immediately have to mean it's an anti-Semitic context?"

"Sweetheart, don't try to be clever," said Basia Sobieraj, brushing aside his reasoning. "Ela was killed with a Jewish knife for the ritual slaughter of cattle."

"I know that, but if we reject the hysteria, in that case wouldn't it be more logical to interrogate some Jewish butchers rather than those who hate Jewish butchers? Or are we so politically correct that we can't even hypothetically consider that the culprit is a Jew or has close connections with that culture? And as a result, has access to that tool, for instance?"

Szacki briefly considered the words coming from the cloud of smoke above the barbecue.

"It's not exactly like that," he replied. "On the one hand you're right, people commit murder with whatever's to hand. A butcher uses a meat cleaver, a mechanic uses a tyre lever, a hairdresser uses scissors. But on the other hand the first thing they usually do is try to get rid of that clue. And here the murder weapon was lying next to the corpse, washed and sterilized to boot, carefully prepared for us, so as not to give any circumstantial evidence except for one thing: to imply that this is some sort of filthy Jewish-anti-Semitic case. That's why we think it's a smokescreen."

"Maybe it is, but I'm sure you don't buy that sort of ritual razor-blade at the local supermarket."

"No, you don't," agreed Szacki. "That's why we're trying to find out where it comes from."

"With moderate success," added Basia. "There's a slightly worn inscription on the handle, saying 'Grünewald', and I'm in touch with a knife museum in Solingen in Germany to find out more. They claim it might be a small pre-war manufacturer from the district of Grünewald, which is in Solingen. They still make various blades, knives and razors all over the place there, and before the war there were dozens of workshops and artisans of that kind. Some of them Jewish, for sure. We'll see. It's in a perfect state, it looks more like a museum piece, part of someone's collection, than a *chalef* that's actually in use."

Szacki winced; the word "collection" made him think of the loathsome word "hobby". But at the same time it shunted his thoughts onto a new track. Knife means collection, collection means hobby, hobby means antiquarian, and antiquarian means... He stood up; he did his thinking better on the move.

"So where do you buy this sort of knick-knack?" asked Andrzej, saying Szacki's thought aloud. "At an auction? At an antique shop? At a secret den of thieves?"

"The Internet," replied Szacki. "E-bay, Allegro. There's no antique shop in the world nowadays that doesn't sell on the Internet."

He and Basia swapped knowing glances; if the knife was bought at an Internet auction, there must be some evidence of the transaction left. Szacki started mentally sorting the tasks that would have to be performed on Monday in order to check up on it. Lost in thought, he wandered off into the depths of the garden, leaving the Sobierajs and their house behind him. By the time he went back, walking right round the apple tree, he had a list ready; but instead of being satisfied with this new idea, he felt anxious. There was something he had overlooked, something he had failed to notice, he had made an error. He was absolutely sure of it, as he went over and over the events of the last few days, trying to find the flaw. But he couldn't. It was like having a name on the tip of your tongue that for all the world you simply cannot remember. An unbearable itch in the middle of his skull.

Now he could see the Sobierajs' villa, or rather cottage, in its full glory. It was in the Kruków district; in other words, a long way from town by Sandomierz standards, near the bypass. Past the chimney, on the other side of the highway, he could see the church with the unusual roof shaped like an upside-down boat. Szacki was finding it hard to get used to the idea that here having your own home did not mean, as it did in Warsaw, luxury and membership of the elite that had broken free of the high-rise towers, and that in Sandomierz this was the same sort of standard middle-class home as a fifty-square-metre flat in a big city. But so much more human. There was something natural about coming out of the sitting room onto the patio, about having a garden with a few apple trees, spending a lazy Saturday on deckchairs by the barbecue, and breathing in the first scent of spring.

He didn't know this world, but he thought it was lovely, and he envied those who didn't appreciate it and never stopped complaining about their house and garden, about the endless work they required, and that there was always something that needed doing. Even so, urban Saturdays in flats, at public swimming pools, in shopping centres, in cars and on smelly streets were like a punishment compared with this. He felt like a prisoner set free after forty years in jail. He didn't know how to behave, and had a strong physical sense of the discomfort of not belonging. Nothing about him belonged here. His solitude compared with their friendship – because he wasn't sure it was love – his cold big-city manner compared with their warm, provincial nest, his caustic quips in response to stories that rambled on pointlessly, his pressed suit compared with their sports clothes, and finally his can of Cola compared with their beer. He told himself that if not for the interview with Szyller, he'd be sitting slouched in a sweater finishing a second beer, but he knew himself too well. That was the whole point – Prosecutor Teodor Szacki never sat slouched in a sweater.

Now he felt down, as he slowly walked back towards Basia Sobieraj; her husband had disappeared into the house. The grass dulled his footsteps – either she couldn't hear him as he stopped right behind her, or she was pretending she couldn't. She was offering her freckled face to the sun, with her shoulder-length ginger hair tucked behind her ears; in the parting he could see the roots – typical Polish mouse, with a subtle trace of grey already. She had a small nose and lovely full lips, which, even without make-up, clearly stood out peachy-pink against her pale complexion. She was wearing a mohair polo neck and a long pleated skirt, and had her bare feet on a stool – a typical Polish stool with white legs and a greenish seat. She was wiggling her toes comically, as if trying to warm them up, or mark the beat of a song she was humming in her head. She looked warm-hearted and serene. Infinitely far from the women he had been dealing with lately, the owners of clean-shaven pussies who produced vulgar moans and liked rough sex in stilettos. Szacki thought of the date ahead of him that evening with Klara at a club and sighed out loud. Basia idly leant her head back and looked at him.

"Your freckles are showing," he said.

"I haven't got any freckles."

He smiled.

"Do you know why I invited you?"

"Because you noticed how horribly lonely I am, and you were afraid that if I top myself, all this Jewish shit will land on your head?"

"Yes, that's reason number one. And reason number two… will you smile again?"

He smiled sadly.

"Well, exactly. I don't know how life has turned out for you, Teodor, but a man with a smile like that deserves more than you seem to have now. Do you know what I mean?"

She took hold of his hand. She had the dry, cool palm of a person with low blood pressure. He returned the squeeze, but what was he meant to say? He just shrugged.

"In Sandomierz the winters can be dreadful in the usual provincial way, but now the spring's coming," she said, without letting go of his hand. "I won't tell you what that means, you'll see for yourself. And…" she hesitated, "and I don't know why, but I thought you ought to leave the dark place you're in."

He didn't know what to say, so he didn't answer. The build-up of emotion rising in his chest was slipping out of his control. Self-consciousness, sentiment, embarrassment, envy, grief, the pain of transience, pleasure at the touch of Barbara Sobieraj's cool hand, envy once again – he couldn't control the snowball of emotions. But he was very sorry that such an ordinary thing as spending a lazy spring morning with someone in a garden at home had never been his lot. A life like his was meaningless.

Andrzej Sobieraj came out onto the patio holding two beers, and his wife's grip loosened; only now did Szacki remove his hand from hers.

"I must be off to do that interview," was all he said, and bowed stiffly.

Szacki walked away rapidly without looking round; on the move, he automatically did up the top button of his graphite-grey jacket. As he was closing the garden gate he was already mentally formulating scenarios for his conversation with Jerzy Szyller. Nothing else interested him.

II

Everything lies in the graveyard now, and what's left seems very far away, veiled by feelings that are inconceivable. What a strong sense of regret and determination, what a thirst for destruction, the pure and simple desire for revenge. Strong enough to occupy one's thoughts non-stop, ad nauseam, to keep repeating in one's head every element of the plan; it seems there can be no question of a mistake, but the fear is no less for that, the tension doesn't disappear. I want to run away, but the plan doesn't allow for running away, I must wait. This waiting is appalling, the noises are too loud, the lights are too bright, the colours too garish. The ticking of the clock on the wall is as infuriating as the chimes from the town hall; every passing second drives me to distraction. I'm longing to remove the batteries, but that's not in the plan – a broken clock could be a clue, a piece of evidence, a pointer. It's tough, it's very tough holding out.

III

Szacki was just about to press the doorbell, but he withdrew his hand and slowly walked along the fence surrounding the property. Was

Szyller watching him? He couldn't see a face in the window, or the twitch of a curtain, nor were there any cameras. Was he having his coffee? Watching TV? Reading the newspaper? If he were waiting for the prosecutor conducting an inquiry into a murder case, he probably wouldn't be able to concentrate on everyday tasks. He'd be loitering by the window or standing on the porch, exceeding his daily quota of cigarettes.

Jerzy Szyller's house was on the slopes of Piszczele gorge, for where else should the home of one of Sandomierz's most distinguished and richest citizens be? Judging by the size of the neighbouring properties, the owner must have joined up two or three plots of land, thanks to which his tasteful Polish mini manor house was surrounded by a well-kept garden. No follies, no little paths made of granite slabs, no ponds or temples of Diana, just a few walnut trees, a new growth of spring grass, and a climber winding around the veranda on one side. If not for the distinctive portico supported by stout columns, and if not for the red-and-white flag hanging rather wistfully from a mast by the entrance, Szacki would have thought: Germany. Although no, in Germany there would have been some obvious stylization, the plastic windows would have been divided by gold strips, but there was something genuine about Szyller's house. The columns looked wooden and tired, the roof sagged slightly under the weight of the shingle, and the whole building was like a dignified old man who is doing very well, but has clocked up the years. A sort of Max von Sydow of manor-house architecture.

He pressed the bell and the homeowner answered so speedily that he must have had his hand on the intercom. So Szacki was right.

Jerzy Szyller was boring and monotonous; Szacki let him ramble on. Despite a show of openness and joviality, the man was extremely tense, a bit like a patient at an oncologist's, who's going to talk about anything at all rather than hear the verdict. Feigning friendly interest, the prosecutor was taking a good look at his host and his surroundings.

"Forgive me, please, for keeping the name of the place to myself, I don't think there was anything illegal about it, but naturally I wouldn't want to get anybody into trouble."

"But did you transport the whole house from the east, or just part of it?" asked Szacki, thinking Szyller used too many words – trying to drown out the tension in a way he had observed hundreds of times before.

"The mansion was pretty much destroyed, it was built in the mid-nineteenth century, and as you can imagine, after the war naturally no one took care of it, and it fell into ruin, but luckily enough for it the Belarusians never turned it into a state farm or the like, I think it was simply too small, and besides that, the land in the vicinity was barren. My specialists took it apart beam by beam, once it was here we had to replace and supplement about twenty per cent of the structure; the roof was recreated on the basis of some pre-war photos that had survived in the Wyczerowski family. In any case, the count and countess's descendants turned up here a couple of years ago, I must say it was a very nice…"

Szacki switched off. In a while he would shunt Szyller off this bloody tedious tale, but only in a while. For now he was registering things. The tone of Szyller's voice – low and velvety in greeting, it had imperceptibly got higher and higher. Good, let him get a bit anxious. He couldn't see a wedding ring, he couldn't see any photographs of women, he couldn't see any photographs of children, and considering the fact that Szyller was a classically good-looking, well-off man in his prime, that was strange. He could possibly be gay. His meticulous clothing and the impeccable, but refined elegance of the interior also spoke in favour of that. Instead of pictures in gilt frames, there were a few graphics and engravings. Instead of an ancestor with a sabre, there was a portrait of the homeowner, painted in the symbolist style.

Szyller finished his boring oration on transporting the house from Belarus to Sandomierz and clapped his hands emphatically. Plus one for the gays, thought Szacki, and awarded them another point a little later, when his host leapt up to fetch some chocolates, laid out – yet another point – on a small cut-glass platter. Minus one for movements – Szyller moved energetically and softly, but there was nothing camp about it; the softness had more in common with the movements of a predator.

He sat down, crossing his legs. He reached for his shirt cuffs in the typically male gesture of a man who has come home and wants to announce the end of the day by rolling up his sleeves. Yet he withdrew his hand before touching the buttons. Szacki kept a stony face, but he felt a sudden twinge of alarm. Something wasn't right.

"Let's start," he said, taking a Dictaphone out of his jacket pocket.

Szacki pretended to be bored, and to be plain about it, he really was a bit bored, but he wanted to put Szyller off his guard and let him give the game away. He had taken his personal details, told him about liability for making a false statement and politely expressed surprise that the interviewee was fifty-three years old – he really didn't look older than forty-three – and now for a quarter of an hour he had been hearing about Szyller's relationship with the Budnik couple. Nothing but big fat platitudes. He was rarely in touch with them, as you know, relations between businessmen and politicians aren't well regarded, ha ha ha, though naturally they knew each other and ran into each other at official events.

How would he define the nature of these relations? Sporadic, appropriate, maybe even friendly.

"And what about the victim?"

"Elżbieta," Szyller corrected him insistently.

Szacki merely pointed at the Dictaphone.

"Ela and I have known each other almost from the day she came back here."

He hadn't got used to the past tense yet, and Szacki didn't correct him.

"Since her marriage?"

"More or less."

"What sort of relationship did you and she have?"

"Well, you know, if you're looking for a sponsor for anything in Sandomierz, the list is quite short. The glassworks, me, a few factories, a few hotels, for want of anything better the restaurants and bars. There's hardly a day when someone doesn't ask. A concert, some children in need, some old folks in bad health, skateboards for the skateboarding club, guitars for a new band, drinks for a private view. I've sorted it out by having one of the accountants dispense a certain sum each quarter for, let us say, aims to do with Sandomierz. He chooses the projects, and naturally I approve them."

"How large is the sum?"

"Fifty thousand a quarter."

"Was the victim in touch with him?"

"Elżbieta," he emphasized again, "spoke to the accountant, or directly to me."

Szacki started questioning him in more detail, and taunted him with the word "victim" several times more, but couldn't get any worthwhile information out of him. He and Mrs Budnik knew each other, and had even been friends, he funded (or didn't, but more often did) her various crazy ideas, such as putting on a production of *Shrek* at Sandomierz Castle. Perhaps, so it seemed to Szacki now and then, the businessman from the Belarusian manor house had been a little bit in love with Mrs Budnik.

"Will you continue to make such generous donations to local cultural life?"

"Naturally. As long as I regard the proposed projects as worth it. I'm not a state institution, I have the luxury of supporting what appeals to me."

Szacki made a mental note to check what did and what didn't gain the noble gentleman's approval.

"I've heard you didn't love" – he paused almost imperceptibly to gauge Szyller's reaction – "Mr Budnik? That his activities at the municipal council weren't convenient for your business interests."

"Gossip."

"In every bit of gossip there's a grain of truth. I realize that for a thriving businessman who wants to operate with full transparency it might not be convenient for the city to be handing property over to the Church as recompense for centuries of injustice, only for that property to be traded outside the system of public tenders, to the eternal glory of all interested parties. Well, except for you, obviously."

Szyller gave him a vigilant look.

"I thought you were new here."

"New, yes; from Sweden, no," retorted Szacki calmly. "I know how this country works."

"Or doesn't."

Szacki made a gesture to imply that he agreed.

"I'm glad you're so agreeable. As a civil servant. It restores one's faith in the Republic."

Well, wouldn't you know, Mr Crashing-Bore can be witty too, thought Szacki. Except that he didn't have time for idle banter.

"Are you a patriot?" he asked his host.

"Naturally. Aren't you?"

"In that case it shouldn't bother you if someone acts to the benefit of the Church, the one true Catholic faith." Szacki did not think it appropriate to answer the question; his own views were totally irrelevant here.

Szyller stood up abruptly. When he wasn't huddled on the sofa, he looked like a big strong man. He was quite tall, broad-shouldered, a powerful build, the type on whom even a suit from the supermarket would look good. Szacki was envious – his own suits had to be made to measure so they wouldn't look as if they were hanging on a broom handle. Szyller went up to the minibar, and for a split second Szacki thought he was reaching for the Metaxa, visible in the distance, but he fetched out a bottle of some snobby mineral water and poured them each a glass.

"I'm not sure if this is really relevant to our conversation, but the biggest, most harmful idiocy in the history of Poland is the identification of patriotism with that paedophile sect. Excuse me for the strong words, but it only takes a little nous to see that the Church is not behind our greatest achievements, just the disasters. Behind the bloodthirsty myth about the bulwark of Christendom, behind the pornographic desire for martyrdom, behind a suspicious attitude towards the wealthy…"

That's where it hurts you, thought Szacki.

"…behind idleness, superstition, passive waiting for divine aid, finally behind sexual neuroses and the pain of all those poor couples who can't afford test-tube babies and who will never be granted the joy of offspring, because the state is afraid of that mafia of onanists in black skirts." Szyller had noticed that he was getting carried away, and got a grip on himself. "And so yes, I am a patriot, I do my best to be a good patriot, I want my actions to speak for me and I want to be proud of my country. But please don't insult me with suspicions that I place some Jewish sect above other superstitions and that I call it patriotism."

Szacki felt a touch of sympathy for the guy; no one had ever expressed his own views so aptly. He kept this thoughts to himself.

"Patriotism without Catholicism and anti-Semitism, you really are creating a new standard," said Szacki, once again steering the conversation onto topics of interest to him. He could see they were close to Szyller's heart too; the man noticeably loosened up, relaxed, and he could tell this sort of conversation had often been held in this house.

"Please don't be offended, but you're thinking in terms of politically correct stereotypes – you've been programmed to think the best citizen is the left-wing cosmopolitan with a short memory. And patriotism is a sort of shameful hobby that goes hand-in-hand with popular Catholicism, xenophobia and, naturally, anti-Semitism."

"So you're a non-believing, Jew-loving patriot?"

"Let's say I'm a non-believing Polish patriot and anti-Semite."

Szacki raised an eyebrow. Either the fellow didn't read the papers, or he had a screw loose, or he was playing some sort of devious game with him. Intuition told him it was more likely to be the latter. Not good.

"Surprised?" Szyller settled more comfortably on the sofa; it looked as if he were snuggling down in his own opinions. "Surely you're not going to pull out the Penal Code, you're not going to charge me for inciting racial hatred, are you?"

Szacki did not pass comment. He had more important things to think about. Besides which he knew Szyller would say his bit anyway. He was the type.

"You see, we're living in strange times. Since the Holocaust, anyone who dares to admit to anti-Semitism must be standing shoulder to shoulder with Eichmann and saluting Hitler – he's regarded as a deviant who dreams of splitting up families on the loading ramp. However, there's quite a difference between having a degree of reserve towards the Jews, their role in Polish history and their present politics, and inciting pogroms and the final solution, wouldn't you agree?"

"Please go on, this is very interesting," Szacki encouraged him, not wanting to get involved in an open quarrel. He would have had to reply sincerely that he was disgusted by any attempt to judge people in terms of the national, ethnic, religious or any other kind of group they belong to. And that he was sure every pogrom had its roots in the civilized debate about "a degree of reserve".

"Just look at France and Germany. By showing reserve towards immigrants from Algeria and Turkey do they at once become fascists and murderers? Or are they perhaps merely citizens who are concerned about their country's future, concerned about the expanding ghettoes, the lack of assimilation, the aggression, the alien element that is destroying their culture?"

"I don't remember anything about the Jews in pre-war Poland setting fire to carriages, organizing themselves into mafias and living on drug-smuggling," said Szacki, and mentally kicked himself for not holding back the wisecracks. Let him talk, man, let him talk.

"So you say, because you didn't live in those times."

"Indeed, I am a little younger than you."

Szyller just snorted.

"You don't know what it was like. A Pole and a Jew from neighbouring districts couldn't communicate because they spoke different languages. The Jewish districts were not necessarily like nice open-air museums of cultural interest. Filth, poverty, prostitution. Usually a black hole on the map of the town. People who were all too keen to live in a developing Poland, but who didn't want to work for it or fight for its good. Have you ever heard of any Jewish battalions fighting in the national uprisings? Of any Orthodox Jewish units in the Polish Legions? I haven't. Sit tight and wait until the Poles bleed to death, and then we can occupy a few more streets in the depopulated town. Yes, I think that if I'd been alive in those days, I wouldn't have been a fan of theirs, regardless of my respect for writers like Tuwim and Leśmian. Just as today I don't agree with the idea that every aggression-filled, xenophobic move Israel makes in the Middle East is immediately pardoned because of the Holocaust. Can you imagine what would happen if the Germans started fencing themselves off from Turkish settlements with a wall several metres high?"

No, Szacki couldn't imagine it. More than that – he refused to imagine it. Nor did he want to tell the man about Berek Joselewicz, who did command a regiment of Jews in the Kościuszko Uprising of 1794, and went on to fight in the Legions. He wanted to find Elżbieta Budnik's murderer, best of all with incontestable proof, to press charges, write out an indictment and win the case in court. Meanwhile, here he was in this annoyingly perfect sitting room, where apart from the tacky antlers above the mirror there was nothing to find fault with, listening to this man's woolly effusions about the world, and getting annoyed. He could sense that Szyller's committed rant was a well-practised routine, and he could imagine the guests at table, the wine that cost at least fifty zlotys a bottle, the scent of perfume that cost at least two hundred for thirty mils, the sirloin steak that cost at least seventy zlotys a kilo, and Szyller in a shirt that cost at least three hundred, toying with a cufflink that cost God knows how much and asking what would happen if the Germans… The guests agree and smile understandingly: how good he is at putting it into words, what an orator our Jerzy is!

"Those days are over, there aren't any Jews left, you can thank whomever necessary."

"Now really, you can do better than that." Szyller seemed genuinely devastated by Szacki's impertinence. "I am an anti-Semite, but not a perverted fascist. If I had divine powers and could rescind the Holocaust, aware that Poland would be left with its pre-war problems, I would rescind it, I wouldn't hesitate for a fraction of a second. But now that it has happened and can't be undone, it is a sad fact of life, a scar on world history, and if you were now to ask if the disappearance of the Jews from Poland was a good thing for it, then my answer to you would be yes, it was a good thing. Just as today the disappearance of the Turks from Germany would be a good thing for our neighbours."

"Yes, Polish children are safe at last."

"Are you talking about ritual murder? Do you take me for a fool? Do you think anyone in their right mind could take that nonsense seriously, that local legend with terrible, real consequences?"

"They say that in every legend there's a grain of truth," said Szacki, to goad him even more.

"You see, that's exactly what I'm talking about. Just one critical word and at once I am plainly a fascist, ready to march through the town with flaming torches, shouting that they've kidnapped a Polish child to make matzos. This is a country full of superstitions, distortions, prejudices and hysteria. It's hard to be a patriot here."

The modern anti-Semite broke off and pondered his own words, probably perceiving depths in them that even he found surprising.

"Szyller," said Szacki solemnly. "A truly Polish name."

"Don't mock – that name belongs to the old Polish aristocracy from Ukraine. Read the novel *Fame and Glory*, if you please."

"I'm not a great fan of Andrzejewski."

"It's by Iwaszkiewicz."

"I always get those socialist-realist queers muddled up," said Szacki, smiling stupidly.

Jerzy Szyller gave him a look full of disdain, poured out the rest of the water and went into the kitchen, most likely to fetch another bottle. Szacki did some thinking. He had talked to the man for long enough now to become familiar with his reactions, and reckoned his inner lie detector was tuned in. As well as that, he had let himself appear to be an idiot, which always helped. Time to move on to the really important matters. He felt calm, because he was sure he wouldn't leave Szyller's house empty-handed. He'd discover something. He didn't yet know what, but something for sure. And it would be something important.

As Jerzy Szyller and Prosecutor Teodor Szacki were having their long conversation, there were several things they didn't realize: Szacki that despite his intuition and expectations he was not coming close to a swift solution to the case, but quite the opposite – every minute spent on this debate was distancing him from its conclusion; and Szyller that the prosecutor's bored look was a mask, and that his growing conviction that the investigator was a typical incompetent official was acutely mistaken. And both of them were unaware that they belonged to a very small group of Sandomierz townsfolk who could have been, and yet weren't watching episode seven in the adventures of Father Mateusz, the TV priest-cum-detective.

Irena and Janusz Rojski were not in this minority; they were sitting side by side on the couch, regretting that it wasn't on the Polsat channel, where you could have a pee in the advert break, make a cup of tea and discuss what had happened so far. Artur Żmijewski, who played Father Mateusz, was just visiting the scene of a crime at a run-down care home, where one of the OAPs had given up the ghost with somebody else's assistance.

"Where did they film that? It's definitely not in our town. They make such a to-do, and then all he does is ride his bike about the market square, there and back again. I don't envy him riding it on those cobblestones."

Mrs Rojska didn't get drawn into the debate; she had stopped taking any notice of her husband's grumblings twenty years ago, halfway through their joint adventure. Nowadays her brain was so good at turning it into background noise that it didn't even drown out what the characters were saying on TV.

"Or the start? Did you see Father Mateusz opening a new cinema? A priest! A cinema! In Sandomierz! It's the Black Mafia's taken away our cinema near the cathedral. Soon as it turned out all that's church ground, they got hold of it and made it into a community centre, where bugger all happens, just so the bishop won't be shocked when he looks out of the window and sees the young people off to watch American films. And so then what? So then there's no cinema in Sandomierz. Except in *Father Mateusz*."

"Don't blaspheme."

"I'm not blaspheming. I never said a bad word against God, but I can say whatever I like about the clerics and the scriptwriters. Polish crime shows, honest to God, it's the same with crime as with everything else. What sort of a crime show is it, when bugger all happens, and on top of that you know from the start what's going on?"

"So why are you watching?"

"I'm watching because I want to see my town on the telly. And naturally I can't, because apparently they film it somewhere just outside Warsaw, and neither the church nor the vestry's actually here, just that bike and the market square. And the police station at the tax office, that's good. Besides, remember how we went for coffee and they were filming? We've got to watch, because we don't know which episode we'll be in, I'm recording them all just in case."

"Oh look, that's Marek Siudym."

"He's not in bad shape neither, I can't think why those scribblers have put him in an old folks' home."

"He's the manager."

"Oh, I see. Do you think our children will put us in an old folks' home too? I know it's not a nice subject, but maybe we ought to suggest it ourselves? I know we feel young, but I'm already seventy and you're sixty-seven, and you can't just avoid talking about it. Getting up to our second floor every day is a challenge for me. And I'm sure it'd be easier for them, there'd be someone taking care of us, so they'd have peace of mind. And actually the old folks' home doesn't scare me, as long as we're together."

Mrs Rojska grabbed her husband's hand; they were feeling the same emotion. On the screen, Artur Żmijewski was in his Sandomierz church outside Warsaw, asking the congregation to pray for the lonely and the afflicted, and to know love, saying that it is never too late to love and be loved. Mr Rojski stroked his wife's forearm; sometimes she wondered why her husband never stopped talking to her when they could communicate perfectly well without words. It was a mystery.

"You know what, I was thinking about Zygmunt."

"The one in the series?" The victim in the programme was called Zygmunt.

"No, our Zygmunt…"

"Strange, isn't it, how everyone with that name is at least seventy. Even on the telly. Can you imagine a baby called Zygmunt? No, they're always silly old codgers."

"I was thinking maybe we should go and pray for the lonely, for them to fall in love again. Zygmunt is so odd – he's aged about fifteen years since his Ania died, and I worry about him. And I was thinking there are lots of people like that."

For a while they watched the series in silence. Mrs Rojska thought about all her lonely friends, Mr Rojski thought about how his wife's kind heart would never cease to surprise him and that he was the luckiest man in the world, because this baker's daughter with the plaits down to her waist had once wanted him.

"So shall we go today? Say our prayers and get mass over and done with, then tomorrow we won't have to go."

"No, not today. I'd still like to make a meat loaf for tomorrow, and Krysia might drop in, and besides, you know what I think – you have to go to church on Sunday. We're not Jews or the like, keeping the Sabbath on Saturday."

He nodded; true, true enough. But what he found most convincing was the meat loaf – his wife could conjure real works of art out of beef; if the cow had seen them she'd have been proud to have given up her life for something so wonderful. At every opportunity Mr Rojski repeated the hackneyed phrase that if cholesterol were going to kill him, he'd go with a smile on his face. Because it was worth it.

"It seems dormant conscience is suddenly awake," said the on-screen Bishop of Sandomierz in the voice of actor Sławomir Orzechowski. "That is not pleasant, for it leads to a sense of helplessness, resentment and pain. And then He helps us to rise from our knees."

Irena and Janusz Rojski did not go to church that day; what decided it for her were her views about life, and for him it was the meat loaf.

Cuddled up to each other, they watched a lovely bird's-eye-view shot of Sandomierz in the final scene of the episode, and thought how peaceful and innocent their city was.

V

Beneath the façade of his bold and controversial opinions, Szyller was incredibly shallow, and his erudition turned out to be nothing more than a bit of dexterous juggling with stereotypes. Those were the conclusions Szacki reached as he listened to the man's arguments about Germany. As an honorary member of the Union of Poles in Germany he had a lot to say on the subject, but none of it was of any interest – nor was it all that positive; he suggested that the Poles were a persecuted minority there. On top of that, he had a particular way of talking that probably appealed to women, but which Szacki found im-mensely annoying. Regardless of the scale of the matter, he expressed everything with commitment and careful emphasis, in quite a raised tone, which might have made him come across as a virile fellow, sure of himself and his views, who knew what he wanted and usually got it. But actually Jerzy Szyller was just a self-focused egotist who loved the sound of his own voice, which was why he put so much effort into the lines he was uttering.

Verbal masturbation, Szacki thought to himself, as he listened to Szyller's family history. He was descended from one of the first members of the Union, hence his high standing and honorary mem-bership. He was born in Germany and had a small house in North Rhine-Westphalia, near Bochum, where the leadership of the Bund, as he put it, was located. But he spent more time in Sandomierz or at his flat in Warsaw, which he kept calling "the servant's room", as if it was meant to be funny.

"Do you recognize this symbol?" Szacki took a print-out of the "*rodło*" emblem from his briefcase, reluctantly, afraid he would wince at the next emphatic "naturally".

"Naturally! That's the '*rodło*', the symbol of the Bund – for us it's nigh on a sacred symbol. I don't know if you're aware of how it came into being – I actually had the honour of hearing it from the lady who designed it herself, Janina Kłopocka…"

"I am aware of it," Szacki interrupted. "I'm sorry if you find my question stupid, but in what form do you use the '*rodło*'? Flags, crests, letterheads, shirts, lapel badges?"

"We're not a sect, you know – naturally the '*rodło*' is on show wherever the Union makes an official appearance, but we don't hang it next to the White Eagle. Ostentation is never advisable."

Szacki took out a photograph of the badge that the victim had been holding. He had specially prepared a fairly ordinary one, which didn't suggest it was an important piece of evidence in the case. He showed it to Szyller.

"Do members of the Union often wear this sort of thing?"

Szyller looked at the picture.

"Only those who are actively involved, and perhaps distinguished members. You won't buy this from a Turk – you can only get it from the chairman of the Bund."

"You have one, naturally?"

"Naturally."

"May I see it?"

"Naturally."

Szyller stood up and disappeared into the house. Szacki waited, thinking with trepidation about all the paperwork ahead of him after this conversation. He'd have to listen to the recording, pick out the relevant bits, write them down and get it signed. And do a separate exhibit form. Jesus, why didn't he have an assistant?

"It's a strange thing…" Szyller was standing in the doorway; in the warm afternoon light his snow-white shirt looked peach-coloured.

"But you can't find it," added the prosecutor.

"No, I can't."

"Where do you keep it?"

"In a box with my cufflinks. I only wear it on special occasions."

"Does anyone know about it? Girlfriend? Close friends?"

Szyller shook his head. He looked genuinely surprised. That wasn't a good sign. Szacki would have preferred him to start scheming, saying it was in his jacket in Warsaw, anything.

"And may I ask where you got it?" he finally asked the prosecutor.

"We took it out of the victim's hand."

"Elżbieta," Szyller corrected him automatically, but the careful emphasis was gone from his voice.

"Elżbieta, the victim."

Szyller plodded over to the sofa, and sat down opposite Szacki without saying a word. He gave him an enquiring look, as if waiting for Szacki to advise him what to say.

"Where did you spend the Easter holiday?"

"On Sunday I was at my sister's house in Berlin, I flew back on Monday morning, and by one in the afternoon I was here."

"Where were you on Monday and Tuesday?"

"At home."

"Did anyone visit you? Friends, acquaintances?"

A denial. Szacki just gazed at length, and kept silent, planning how to continue the conversation, and suddenly a striking thought occurred to him. It was a stupid thought, without any foundation, born purely of his instinct, yet disturbing enough to make the prosecutor stand up and start slowly walking about the room, carefully looking around it. What he was looking for in this tasteful museum of the landed gentry were signs that a man of flesh and blood lived here – wine stains, photos on the wall, crumbs left over from breakfast, a dirty coffee cup. Some kicked-off muddy shoes, a rug to wrap round you in the evenings, a cap thrown on the window sill. He couldn't find anything. Either the house was never used, or it had been extremely carefully tidied. To remove dirt? Or someone's presence? Or evidence of inconvenient events? To avoid saying any more than what the host had to say about himself? At a hysterical rate the thoughts went flashing through Szacki's mind. If he was going to press Szyller, he must assume some hypothesis, suppose he was lying about a specific matter, and attack on that very point. Unfortunately, for the time being, the hypothesis that was pushing forwards the most firmly in his head was the most absurd one.

"Do you often have visitors?"

"I'm not particularly sociable. As you heard, I spent half of Easter alone. And this place is special to me, a sort of refuge. I like being here on my own, I don't want parties, noisy conversations, other people's smells."

The mantelpiece above the fireplace, the spot where dust and dirt usually collect seconds after cleaning, was sterile too. Szacki ran a finger over the varnished oak board – nothing. The bookshelf was the same. There was no television. Neither man had said anything for quite a while, and Szacki was feeling uneasy. He was alone in an empty house with a guy twice his size, who could perhaps be a murderer. He glanced at Szyller. The businessman was watching him alertly. If Szacki had been paranoid, he might have thought he was following his movements, getting ready to attack. Szyller noticed the prosecutor's gaze, and adopted a slightly startled expression.

"Do I take it this doesn't look good?" he asked.

"When did you last see the victim?"

"I had a meeting with Elżbieta about two weeks before the holidays. We talked about the summer vacation – she wanted to set up a seasonal cinema in the Small Marketplace, and we chatted about how to persuade the residents. You know what it's like, people are always against. They'd like to have a lot going on, but not under their windows."

Szacki took a decision. You only live once – at worst he'd miss the goal and Szyller would write a complaint against him. Not the first, and probably not the last time in the white-haired prosecutor's career.

"Could I see the photograph that was standing on the mantelpiece?"

"I'm sorry?"

"I'd like to see the photograph that was standing on the mantelpiece."

"There wasn't one…"

"Are you going to show it to me or not?"

Szyller didn't reply, but his face took on a serious look. Oh well, that's the end of the little anecdotes for the prosecutor, we'll never be friends now, thought Szacki.

"I've been talking to people about you. Nothing but superlatives. A model citizen. A philanthropist. A businessman with a human face."

Szyller shrugged. If he had been trying to play the role of the preoccupied, mildly alarmed citizen, this was the moment when he dropped that pose. He finally rolled up his shirt sleeves, and the muscles of his tanned forearms twitched ominously. The local philanthropist took good care of his patriotic body, and no mistake.

"Highly cultured. Highly intelligent. It would seem you ought to understand your position. A brutally murdered woman was clutching in her tightly clenched fist a rare badge of a type that you own but cannot find. And you are unable to explain what could have become of it. Nor do you have any way of proving where you were at the time when the murder was committed. But despite all this you're lying. I find that very surprising."

"You are easily surprised, Prosecutor. Does such a childlike trait come in useful in your profession?"

Szacki shook his head in disbelief. What a cheap quip – maybe he'd overestimated Szyller.

"I ought to lock you up, press charges and then wonder what next," he said, almost laughing, for the second time in as many days – what a rotten town full of crooks! Bloody hell, did anyone tell the truth here?

"What's stopping you?"

"I can't see the reason why you would have killed your lover. Especially in that way."

"Don't be ridiculous."

"One thing at a time. I want to hear the whole story, one thing at a time. You can start with the photograph."

Jerzy Szyller sat without moving; the air was thick with his emotions, his hesitation, his panic as he wondered what to do.

"You don't understand a thing. This is a small town. They'll say for ever after that she was a whore, a loose woman."

"The photograph. Now."

Jerzy Szyller soon came to the conclusion that branding the love of his life as a whore was a painful thing, but not as painful as the custody cells in Tarnobrzeg. He fetched all the things that earlier on he had painstakingly tidied away. The rug she used to wrap herself in on the sofa, her funny azure-coloured dressing gown, the album with their shared photos, and finally the photograph from the mantelpiece, in a tasteful – what else – wooden frame. Szacki understood him; if he had a photograph of himself with anyone like that one, he would have treated it like a relic. It had been taken on the Błonie meadows in Krakow, where they were sitting together on a bench, with part of the Wawel castle visible in the background. Szyller looked like Pierce Brosnan on holiday, and Ela Budnik was hanging round his neck in a crazy, playful pose, theatrically bending one leg in the style of Audrey Hepburn and pursing her lips for a kiss. He was over fifty, and she was over forty, but they looked like a couple of teenagers, with happiness radiating from every pore of their skin, brightening the picture; there was so much love in this little snap that Szacki felt sorry for Szyller. He might be the murderer, or he might not, but surely his loss was unimaginable.

The prosecutor learnt the history of the affair with all the details, and although it was clear how important these events were for Szyller, how life-changing and profound, in fact it was a banal story. A woman who thinks she is more than she actually is, and who mistakenly interprets a mid-life crisis as imprisonment in a cage in which she cannot spread her wings. A long-standing marriage, quiet stability, small-town tedium. And a guy, petty businessman and petty anti-Semite, so firmly convinced of his own unique qualities and erudition that he manages to convince her of them too, and together they get it into their heads that they and their pot-boiler romance are what great literature is made of. But it's the usual, standard, boring stuff. With a cynicism that even Szacki himself found surprising, it occurred to him that it was only the plaster-white corpse that really gave this story grandeur.

"In the year-and-a-half of your affair, did the victim's husband come to have any suspicions, did she tell you something?"

"No, she never said a word. But in this relationship it was easy to hide things too. He kept very unusual office hours and did a lot of travelling. She had meetings with people from the arts at all sorts of times and in all sorts of places. Thanks to which we had some wonderful days in Bochum together on several occasions."

"Was she planning to leave her husband?"

Silence.

"Did you talk about it? It can't have been pleasant for you. Knowing that every night she got into bed with him, kissed him goodnight and did what married couples generally do."

Silence.

"Mr Szyller, I realize that Sandomierz is a small town, but it's not quite so small. People must occasionally get divorced here, while others come together and start a new life. I understand that in your situation it wouldn't have been difficult. No children, freelance occupations. In fact she could have just sent him the papers by post."

Szyller gestured vaguely, as if to say there were so many complicated nuances to this matter that it couldn't be put into words. Szacki was reminded of how Budnik had made him think of Gollum, for whom nothing had any meaning but his "precious". What would he have done if he had found out someone was taking his precious away from him? And not just anyone, but a familiar adversary, a man whose views he and Ela had probably laughed at in bed together, whose emphatic way of talking they may have mocked and imitated. Maybe to cover her tracks she had complained about having to go and see him, saying what an odd sort he was, you know, trying to be such an alpha male, but a boor under the surface, but what can you do? Thanks to him we'll get something done for the children. And suddenly he finds out she didn't sit it out at his place with a martyred look on her face, talking about the poor little children, but rode him in a sweat, squirmed underneath him, begged him to fuck her harder and licked his sperm off her lips.

I'm off. Goodbye. You were right, you correctly sensed throughout our relationship that you would never have me entirely. I'm too good for you – I always have been.

Is that enough for murder? Absolutely.

"On Monday I was expecting her."

"Sorry?"

"On Easter Monday she was supposed to be coming to me and staying for good, and on Tuesday we were going to leave and never return."

"Does that mean she was going to tell her husband about you?"

"I don't know."

Holy fuck! Szacki got out his phone and called Wilczur; the old policeman answered at once.

"Go and arrest Budnik on the double, and I need someone for security on Słoneczna Street, for Jerzy Szyller. We're going to do a search at Szyller's and then confront Budnik. Chop chop."

Wilczur was a pro. He just said "Got it" and hung up. The businessman stared in amazement.

"What do you mean, 'a search'? I've told you everything, I've shown you everything already."

"Don't be naive – people show and tell me things every day of the week. At least half of it is a smokescreen, half-truths and plain old lies. Considering your degree of intimacy with the victim..."

"Elżbieta."

"...as well as a search I should have the garden dug up and you locked up until all the issues are explained. Which I might do anyway."

"My lawyer..."

"Your lawyer will be able to write a complaint," snapped Szacki; there was anger rising in him that he couldn't restrain. "Do you have any idea what crucial information you have been concealing? Your lover has been murdered, and you, who know facts that could be vital, sit quiet, because someone's going to say nasty things about her? What sort of a citizen and patriot are you if you don't give a shit about justice – which I'll remind you, is defined as 'the mainstay of the power and stability of the Republic'! Nothing but a common small-town anti-Semite – it's enough to make you throw up!"

Jerzy Szyller leapt to his feet, and red blotches appeared on his handsome face. He moved rapidly towards Szacki, and just as the prosecutor was sure they were about to come to blows, his phone rang. Wilczur, no doubt to say it was all arranged, good.

"Yes?"

Szacki listened for a while.

"I'll be right there."

He ran out, colliding at the garden gate with a policeman in uniform, and told him to guard Szyller.

VI

Prosecutor Teodor Szacki sat down on the sofa in the Budniks' sitting room, because he had genuinely started to feel weak. The blood was throbbing in his temples, he couldn't fix his eyes on a single point, he had a strange tingling in his fingers and a nasty, metallic taste in his mouth. He took a deep breath, but it didn't bring him relief, quite the opposite, he felt a stabbing in his lungs, as if the air were full of tiny needles.

Or maybe it wasn't his lungs, but his heart? He closed his eyes, counted to ten and back again.

"Is everything all right?" asked Basia Sobieraj.

Everyone had been suddenly uprooted from home. Sobieraj was wearing jeans and a black fleece, Wilczur was in strange brown trousers that looked as if there were no legs inside them and a thick polo neck, and the two policemen were sporting anoraks from the bazaar, so ugly that anyone could have guessed they were policemen. Once again that day Szacki felt like a cretin in his suit. And that was just one of the reasons.

"No, Basia," he replied calmly. "Nothing is all right, because a vital witness, and since recently the main suspect in the case of a highly conspicuous, shocking murder, despite being guarded round the clock by two policemen, has vanished. And although of course it is of no practical significance now, please, I implore you, satisfy my curiosity and tell me: how the fuck is that possible?"

The policemen shrugged in unison.

"Mr Prosecutor, we never moved a step, we swear. When we were hungry earlier on, we called the lads to bring us something, they can vouch for us. We've been sitting outside this place non-stop."

"Did he go outside?"

"About noon he went into the garden a few times. Did some trimming, put on the sprinkler, tightened a screw in the letter box. It was all noted down."

"And then?"

"He hung about the house, and when it got darker we saw some lights come on and go off."

"Was someone watching the house from the escarpment side?"

"But there's a two-metre-high wall there, Mr Prosecutor."

Szacki looked at Wilczur. The inspector tapped ash into a pot holding a rubber plant and cleared his throat.

"We've got all the exit routes covered, we're checking cars and buses. But if he took off on foot through the bushes, it looks pretty black."

Oh well, there was absolutely no way of doing it on the quiet.

"Inform the regional police stations in the surrounding area, I'll issue an arrest warrant, you draft a wanted notice and arrange via Kielce to get it to all the media as fast as possible. It's a fresh trail, the guy's not a pro, just an ageing town councillor, we'll get a dressing-down from everyone of course, but it should work. At least we've got a suspect, that's something solid, and we'll try to present it as a success for the forces of law and order."

"It won't be easy," muttered Sobieraj. "The media will jump on it."

"All the better. They'll trumpet it far and wide, and every shop assistant will know who Budnik is before he gets hungry enough to go and buy himself a bun."

Szacki stood up suddenly and his head began to spin. He automatically grabbed Sobieraj's arm, and the woman looked at him suspiciously.

"Relax, there's nothing wrong with me. Let's get to work – we'll fill out the forms at the prosecutor's office, you get the press release ready, we'll touch base in half an hour, and in an hour I want to see it on the TV news ticker."

Before leaving he cast an eye over the Budniks' bourgeois sitting room. Once again a little alarm bell jangled in his mind. He felt like someone staring at two pictures with ten tiny differences to spot.

He was certain something wasn't right, but he didn't know what. He stepped back into the middle of the room, the policemen went past him and left, and Sobieraj stopped in the doorway.

"Is it a long time since you were here?" he asked.

"I don't know, about a month ago, just briefly, for coffee."

"Has anything changed?"

"Something's always changing here, or rather it used to. Ela used to move the furniture around every few months, change the lighting, add flowers and fabrics, and created an entirely new flat out of the same basic elements. She claimed she preferred making controlled changes than waiting until her soul rebelled and started looking for changes without involving her."

He gave her a protracted stare.

"Yes, I know how that sounds now."

"But apart from the fact that the room looks different, or has a different decor, is there anything missing? Something that was always here?"

Basia Sobieraj took a careful look around.

"There used to be a bar for doing pull-ups in the kitchen door frame – Grzegorz did exercises on it. But it was always falling off – they must have thrown it away at last."

"Anything else?"

"No, I don't think so. Why?"

He waved to say it didn't matter, and together they left the small house on Katedralna Street, right in the shadow of the church, which was huge from this angle; its severe Gothic lines stood out sharply against the starry sky. There was a photo of Ela Budnik hanging in the hall from ten or fifteen years ago. She was very beautiful, very girlish, brimming with life, as they say. And very photogenic, Szacki told himself, as he thought about the photo on Szyller's mantelpiece.

VII

It was coming up to nine in the evening. Basia Sobieraj had finally gone home, the boss had left them earlier, and Prosecutor Teodor Szacki was sitting despondently in the office, listening to the din of young people and the muffled sounds of disco music; the entertainment had started at a club across the street. He felt ill at ease, and for a couple of hours had been feeling physical anxiety, physiological fear, which did not originate from any actual threat but was just there, flooding his entire body – his arms were afraid, his neck was afraid, and so were his internal organs. It would have been quite funny, if it hadn't also been tiring and protracted, as if a short stab of terror of the kind that everyone knows had been going on for hours. The more he thought about it, the worse he felt.

He started walking about the office.

Written out in brief, presented to Misia – who had come from home with sandwiches and a thermos of tea laced with raspberry juice – and stuck in the file, the case hypothesis seemed almost one hundred per cent certain. Grzegorz Budnik has been left, or has found out about his wife's affair with Jerzy Szyller. The jilted man's fury, regret and pain, and on top of that his awareness that this could be the ruin of the political career he has spent years building, is bound to lead to a row. During the row he squeezes her neck a bit too hard and Elżbieta Budnik loses consciousness. Budnik panics – he's killed his wife. He watches *CSI*, he knows his prints are on her neck, so he decides to stage the throat slashing, and decides while he's about it to stir up hysteria based on Catholic-Jewish relations – he's from Sandomierz, he knows the subject. He may even be surprised when litres of blood pour out of his wife, and perhaps when it's too late he realizes she was still alive. He knows the town, he knows every passage through the courtyards and he knows where every camera is located. He takes advantage of this knowledge to plant the corpse outside the old synagogue without being noticed. But when Szyller gets back to Sandomierz, he cracks. He knows that if the investigator finds out about the affair, he will become the main suspect. Once again he puts his knowledge of the town to use, this time to escape from it under the very noses of the policemen guarding him.

The story had its weak points: the site of the murder was a mystery, so was the means of carrying the corpse, and the murder weapon, too, was not the sort of thing you keep in the kitchen dresser next to the dessert forks. The question of the badge found in the victim's hand wouldn't let Szacki rest either. Never for a moment did he think it incriminated Szyller – things like that don't happen in reality, and Szacki was convinced the culprit must have had some reasons for wanting to destroy Szyller. But Budnik? He must have foreseen that diverting the investigation towards Szyller would instantly rebound on him.

However, despite the gaps it sounded credible, despite the physical absence of the suspect it looked miles better than only twelve hours ago, when they hadn't known a thing and were considering the option of looking for a nutcase with a religious and nationalist obsession. There was some solid evidence, and they could tell the media they were looking for a suspect, a person with a first name and a surname. They could also expect that Budnik would get caught, any day, any hour now.

Yes, so much for theories. In practice Szacki felt torn apart. He was trying to convince himself that he was confusing two different things, that his anxiety was purely personal and that his body was making him pay the price for the move, for the break-up, for being alone, for all the changes – all for the worse moreover – of the past few months. He was trying, but inside he was virtually yelping like a bloodhound. Something wasn't right.

He desperately didn't want to be alone this evening. Earlier he had stood Klara up, who was going to drag him to some village disco at the town hall, but now he called her and said he would come. He'd have to tell her they weren't going to carry on with this relationship – he needed to get a bit of order into his life.

VIII

He stopped off at home to put on a pair of jeans and a sports shirt, but even so he felt like an old codger, going out with Klara to the cellar bar at Sandomierz Town Hall, as if escorting his older daughter to a party. He knew about date-rape drugs and crystal meth from his practical experience as a prosecutor, but he had never had anything to do with the world of clubbing from personal experience. Was there some sort of code in force here, some unwritten rules? What was he to do if some child plastered in make-up offered to suck him off? Say no thank you politely? Call the police? March it off to the parents? And what if someone wanted to press drugs on him? Instantly charge them? His head was full of questions when he found himself in the small, low-vaulted brick cellar.

The place was crowded, but picturesque, with a grate draped in chains hanging from the ceiling and part of a stone sculpture of some religious figure in the corner – hence the name of the club, Lapidarium – and there could be no doubt this was the basement of a fine old building. There were a lot of people, but not so many to stop him from pushing through to the bar; Szacki got a beer for himself and one for Klara, while also taking a look at the assembled company. Well, it was a surprising company. No plasticky little girls, no kids with shiny lip-gloss and tits on show, no gel-boys in opalescent shirts, no white G-strings glowing deathly pale in the ultraviolet stroboscopic light. There wasn't a stroboscope anyway, or any ultraviolet light. What's more, even Szacki's age group was quite strongly represented – there were several couples of the roots-and-recession type who could already have children the age of the youngest partygoers.

He watched Klara, who had joined a small group of her friends. They were all the same age as her, about twenty-six or twenty-seven. One of them told a joke and the rest burst out laughing. They looked attractive: a guy with the look of a network administrator with round glasses and thinning fair hair, two girls in jeans, one flat-chested and broad-hipped, the other busty and slender – they looked funny together. And Klara. In jeans, a wine-red, low-cut V-necked top, with her hair tied in a ponytail. She was young and lovely, maybe even the prettiest girl in the room. Why did he take her for a dumb bimbo? Was it just because she was more feminine than his wrinkly ex-wife, with whom he had spent the past fifteen years? Was every display of femininity, every high-heeled shoe and painted fingernail going to seem vulgar to him from now on? Was he quite so badly brainwashed since the era of his wife's ghastly Ikea slippers for 4.99 that had been lying next to his bed ever since Ikea had first appeared in Poland?

He went up to the group, who looked at him with friendly curiosity during the introductions. Klara, strangely enough, seemed proud of having such an old granddad in their midst.

"My God, a real prosecutor, we won't be able to smoke any grass now," joked the flat-chested, broad-hipped girl, Justyna.

Szacki's face changed into a mask of stone.

"You won't be able to smoke grass because you can't possess grass. The law on the prevention of drug addiction, paragraph sixty-two, point one, stipulates a penalty of loss of liberty for up to three years for the possession of narcotics or psychotropic substances."

The company fell silent and looked hesitant as Szacki took a large slug of beer. Piss, as it always is on tap.

"But don't worry, I know a few good lawyers, they might even manage to get you a cell of your own for the second half of the sentence."

They burst out laughing, and a relaxed conversation began. Klara started telling them something about starting the procedure for her doctorate – he was stunned, he didn't even know she had a degree – but she was interrupted in mid-sentence by the noisy entrance of the support band. Szacki almost dropped his beer in amazement, and the feeling stayed with him to the very end of the concert, the best he'd been to for ages. They turned out to listen to and play some shit-hot music out here in the sticks. The support band started off sounding very punk rock, then came down towards the melodic style of Iron Maiden. The next two bands – as far as he understood, both had their roots in a well-known group called Corruption, who turned out to be from Sandomierz – also played hard rock without any frills, rap-style interludes or moaning about me and you baby, yeah, yeah, yeah.

With every track there seemed to be more people, everyone was bawling louder and jumping higher; as more and more endorphins accumulated in the cellar and the sweat began to condense on the metal grate, there was something of the tribal experience about it, which reminded him of the old Warsaw clubs he used to go to for rock concerts centuries ago. The first band was definitely better musically – here and there it came close to Soundgarden, and here and there it was like Megadeth, but flatter, without the surprises. The second one appealed to Szacki's taste, pounding out fast, fresh energy in the style of Metallica's *Load* and *ReLoad* albums. They sang in Polish, they had great lyrics, everything about them was a million times more interesting and a trillion times more genuine than the plasticky stars that filled Radio ZET's airwaves.

Somewhere up above, the world keeps turning. The traffic cops on the bridge are checking the cars leaving the city, and there are patrols carefully trawling the side streets with their roof lights off, on the look-out for a small figure with red hair. Jerzy Szyller is standing in the dark kitchen, watching the men on guard in a navy-blue Opel Vectra outside his gate. He is wearing the same shirt with the rolled-up sleeves and doesn't feel like going to bed at all. Leon Wilczur is watching *Alien 3* on Polsat and not smoking; the inspector never smokes at home. Barbara Sobieraj and her husband are having the tired conversation of a veteran married couple, and although it is about the emotional topic of adoption, even so it is stale with routine and the conviction that as ever it will lead to nothing. Judge Maria Tatarska is reading *The Secret Garden* in the original, telling herself she is practising her English, but in fact she just wants to read it again, and be moved to tears again. Maria "Misia" Miszczyk is eating a smoked sausage – by now she's sick of all those cakes, which she has made her trademark – and looking at a picture of Budnik on Polsat News. The picture was taken by the police during his recent interview and Miszczyk thinks a politician's job must be bloody awful, as Budnik looks so gaunt, half the man she remembers from the past. And that sticking plaster too. Mr and Mrs Rojski are sleeping peacefully, unaware how few couples there are who still sleep together under the same quilt after forty years of marriage. Two hundred and twenty kilometres away, in the Warsaw district of Grochów, Marcin Ładoń – at the same time as millions of other fourteen-year-old boys – is frantically masturbating, thinking about everything except the trip to Sandomierz awaiting him in the week ahead. And Roman Myszyński is having yet another dream about a china-white corpse coming after him inside the synagogue, walking stiffly like a dummy, but he cannot escape, because he trips over some stacks of documents written in Cyrillic.

Somewhere down below, Prosecutor Teodor Szacki was whirling frantically to the tribal beat of metal rock 'n' roll. With their arms locked, he and Klara spun round together until they lost their balance, drunk on beer and endorphins; her chestnut hair was stuck to her perspiring brow, her face was shining and her top was damp with sweat under the arms. Puffing and panting, they found enough breath to bellow out the chorus.

"O Lord, my life can't ever get no worse!" yelled Szacki, truthfully. "O Lord, my life is under the Devil's curse!"

Without waiting for the encores, he threw Klara her jacket and dragged her home to the flat on Długosz like a caveman with his prey. She smelt of sweat, beer and cigarettes, every cranny of her body was hot, damp and salty, and for the first time Szacki didn't find her moans and screams at all vulgar.

It had been a wonderful evening; even if he didn't fall asleep happy, at least he fell asleep calm, and his final thought was that he'd break up with the kid in the morning – why spoil such a great evening for himself and for her?

5

Sunday, 19th April 2009

Joseph Ratzinger celebrates the fourth anniversary of
becoming Benedict XVI, he and other Catholics conclude
festivities for the Easter Week by celebrating Divine
Mercy Sunday, and at Łagiewniki Cardinal Dziwisz com-
ments on the political situation by saying that it
is a condition for public life to master the art of
loving forgiveness. At the same time, MP Janusz Palikot accuses President Lech Kaczyński of alcoholism
on the basis of the number of miniatures ordered by
the presidential household. Marek Edelman, the last
surviving leader of the Warsaw Ghetto Uprising, lays
a bunch of daffodils at the monument to the Heroes
of the Ghetto on the sixty-sixth anniversary of the
start of the uprising. He has always done it at noon
on the dot, but today he must wait until the official
delegations have finished. Meanwhile, in the Czech
Republic preparations for the Führer's birthday continue, and as the result of a Roma house being set
on fire a two-year-old girl ends up in hospital in
a critical state. The police inaugurate the motorbike season, warning against bravado with the slick
slogan: "Spring is here, out come the vegetables".
Just outside Sandomierz there is a road accident — a
car smashes into an electricity pylon and goes up in

flames, killing a seventeen-year-old boy. It is sunny, but cold as hell, the temperature does not rise above twelve degrees, and at night it falls to zero.

I

Prosecutor Teodor Szacki couldn't find a condom. Or an empty condom wrapper. Or an open packet of condoms. Or any evidence at all to confirm that they had used protection during last night's ecstasies. But they always had before now – in other words she didn't have a coil, or take pills. There are fertile days and infertile days, there is being careful, and above all there's the bloody small-town Middle Ages of contraception, the oppressive need to put on a rubber. If there was a rubber. And that wasn't at all certain.

Szacki swept the room, searching every corner, feeling rising panic, wanting at any cost to assure himself that no, there was no chance he could have impregnated this charming girl from Sandomierz, fifteen years his junior. Whom, to cap it all – before becoming aware of the contraceptive catastrophe – he had dumped, as a result of which she had locked herself in the bathroom and was still in there, sobbing.

The door slammed. Quick as a flash, Szacki rose from his knees and adopted an expression full of sympathy. Without a word, Klara began to gather up her clothes, and for a while he even hoped there wouldn't be a conversation.

"I studied in Warsaw, I studied in Göttingen, I've done a lot of travelling, I've lived in three capital cities. I won't hide the fact that I've had various men too. Some for longer, some for shorter. What they all had in common was that they're great guys. Even when we came to the conclusion that we weren't necessarily made for each other, they were still great. You're the first real prick that has stood in my way."

"Klara, please, why say such things?" said Szacki calmly, trying his best not to think about the double meaning of her last remark. "You know exactly who I am. A civil servant who's fifteen years older than you, a man with a past who's been through the mill. What could you hope to build with me?"

She came up and stood so close that their noses were almost touching. He felt a terribly strong desire for her.

"Nothing any more, but yesterday I wasn't sure. You've got something about you that won me over. You're smart, funny, a bit enigmatic, handsome in a not-so-obvious way, you've got a sort of masculinity that appealed to me. And those suits are really great, adorably stiff and starchy." She smiled, but at once grew serious. "That's what I saw in you. And as long as I thought you saw something in me, from day to day I felt keener to give you more. But you saw me as a bimbo, a bit of country crumpet, a little slag from the provinces. It's amazing you never took me to McDonald's. Didn't they tell you all the village cocksuckers like going for a Big Mac best of all?"

"You don't have to be so crude."

"You're the one that's crude, Teo. In every thought you have about me you're a vulgar, crude, boorish misogynist and sexist. A sad little pen-pusher too, I grant you, but that only comes afterwards."

With these words she outscored him, then turned round abruptly, went over to the bed and threw off her towel. Ostentatiously she began to get dressed in front of him. It was nearing ten, the sun was high in the sky, high enough to light up her statuesque figure perfectly. She was lovely, slender, with feminine curves, breasts young enough to stick up pertly despite their size. Tousled after a night in bed, her long, thick, wavy hair that didn't need any artifice tumbled down her neck, and in the sunlight he could see delicate down on the peachy skin of her thighs and arms. Without taking her eyes off him, she put on her underwear, and he was beside himself with desire. Had she really never made an impression on him?

"Turn round," she commanded coldly.

He obediently turned round, comical in his four-year-old boxer shorts, faded from frequent washing, the only thing adorning his neglected white body. It was cold, he could see the goose bumps coming up on his skinny thighs, and realized that without a suit or a lawyer's gown he was absolutely defenceless, like a tortoise removed from its shell. He felt ridiculous. There was soft sobbing coming from behind him. He glanced over his shoulder, and saw Klara, sitting on the bed with her head drooping.

"And what will I tell them all?" she whispered. "I've talked about you so much. They said I should get a grip on myself, and I told them off, stupid girl."

He took a couple of steps towards her, at which she got up, sniffed, threw her handbag over her shoulder and left, without giving him a second glance.

"Aha, one more thing," she said, turning round in the doorway. "Yesterday you were charmingly insistent and delightfully careless. And to put it mildly, it was a very, very bad day to be careless."

She smiled sadly and was gone. She looked so beautiful that Szacki was reminded of the scene from *Camera Buff* when the wife leaves her obsessive film-making husband, who watches her go as if it were a scene he was filming.

II

The Cathedral Basilica of the Nativity of the Blessed Virgin Mary in Sandomierz was full. All the assembled believers were of one heart and one soul, if you believe the words of the reading from the Acts of the Apostles that were echoing off the stone walls. But – as is usually the case in church – no one was listening, everyone was just staring, lost in their own thoughts.

Irena Rojska was gazing at Bishop Frankowski, sitting in his armchair, and wondering what the new bishop would be like, because this one was only here for a while, filling in since the old one had gone to Szczecin to be the archbishop there. It might even be Frankowski, but that wasn't certain. People said he was too active on Radio Maryja, the highly conservative radio station. Maybe so, but Mrs Rojska remembered how he had defended the workers at the Stalowa Wola steelworks, how he had led the strikers along a secret tunnel into the church, and how the Commies had harassed him. No wonder he was hard on the Reds, and it hurt him to see that nowadays they were treated like good Poles, just as good as the people they'd put in prison. And where should he talk about it, if not on Radio Maryja? He could hardly do it on TVN – that was full of reality shows.

Janusz Rojski finally tore his wistful gaze from the pew where his wife was sitting. He had an awful pain in his leg from standing up, which seemed to run all the way from his spine, from his kidneys down to his heel. But what could he do? All the pregnant women and all the senile old ladies in the diocese had come to the cathedral today, and to ask his wife for her seat was idiotic. He looked up at the paintings, at some poor wretch being devoured by a dragon, and at another one who was so effectively impaled on a stake that the end of it had come out through his shoulder blade. Those fellows had to do their suffering for their faith, so I can stand up for an hour, he thought. He was feeling bored, and already wanted to go to the café for a Sunday coffee, sit down in a warm, soft place and have a chat. He breathed on his hands. Another hellishly cold day – the spring will never come.

Maria Miszczyk wasn't a believer, and even if she had been, her local parish was twenty kilometres away. Yet this morning something had tempted her to come here. The Budnik case wasn't giving her any peace and she had her mobile in her hand the whole time, switched to silent, so she wouldn't miss the vibration when they called to say they'd caught him and the nightmare was over. But Budnik lived next to the cathedral, this was his parish, this was where that blasted painting hung, thanks to which every now and then her beloved city became the capital of Polish anti-Semitism. Prosecutor Miszczyk was standing in the left nave in a crowd of people, and she could feel the gaze of John Paul II fixed on her, whose portrait adorned the fabric hiding the painting. And she wondered if he could feel the gaze of the Jews fixed on him, as they drew the blood from Christian children and stuffed babies into barrels spiked with nails. And what he would have had to say on the subject.

No one knew about it, but the non-believing prosecutor Miszczyk had once been an ardent believer, to such an extent that before taking her law degree, she had been a student at the Catholic University of

Lublin, and had wanted to find out as much as she could about her God and her religion. But the more she learnt, the less of a believer she became. Now she was listening to Psalm 118 with everybody else, listening to the words "give thanks unto the Lord, for He is good, for His mercy endureth for ever". And she remembered how once upon a time she had loved that psalm. Until she found out that in the Catholic liturgy several verses had been left out of it. That in its entirety it is a tale about having God's help to fight battles and get revenge, about wiping other nations from the face of the Earth in the Lord's name. "The right hand of the Lord is exalted; the right hand of the Lord hath done mightily." She smiled weakly. How strange it all is – here were the Catholic congregation in a church with an awful, Jew-bashing daub on the wall, praising their God to the skies in the words of a psalm that actually gives thanks for the victory of Israel over its neighbours. Yes, knowledge was the most virulent killer of faith, and at times she regretted ever having acquired it. At the end she sang the chorus with everybody else: "We thank the Lord, for He is merciful."

Depressed by her thoughts about religion, the memory of her lost faith and of everything that had once been in her life but had left nothing but a void behind it, Maria Miszczyk was one of the first to leave the church; she got in her car and quickly drove away. That was the reason why Prosecutor Teodor Szacki was at the crime scene before her.

III

Janusz Rojski must have had to make up for keeping quiet for over an hour, not counting the responses, because as soon as they were in the vestibule he had started talking, and hadn't shut up for a single moment since. It occurred to his wife that once they got to the café she would press a newspaper into his hands – maybe that would silence him.

"Do you think he really did poke about in his side?"

"Sorry? Who did what?"

154

"Saint Thomas, poke about in Jesus's side. Weren't you listening to the reading?"

"My God, Janusz, how should I know? If that's what it says in the Gospels, then I expect it's true."

"Because I couldn't help thinking it's quite disgusting, really. Touching his hands with a finger, that's one thing, but then he had to put his whole hand into his chest. Do you think it was empty in there, or could he feel something? His pancreas, for example, or his spleen? Do you have a pancreas after resurrection?"

"If you died at the age of thirty-three, then no, you don't – it's only after fifty that you find out you've got any organs at all. How's your leg?"

"Better," he lied.

"I'm sorry I didn't let you sit down, I could see it was hurting, but I've got such awful palpitations…"

In reply Mr Rojski hugged his wife and kissed her on her woolly beret.

"I'm still not entirely sure what to do about it," she continued – "maybe I should go for the operation."

"Why get chopped up for no purpose? Doctor Fibich said it's not life-threatening, just unpleasant. And even if they cut you up, they don't know if it'll pass, it might just be your nerves."

"I know, I know, please let's change the subject. Do you remember how we used to laugh at the fact that old folks talk about nothing but their ailments and pains? And now we're just the same – sometimes I bore myself."

"No, no, I don't think I do at all."

Mrs Rojska gave her husband a sideways look to see if he was joking, but no, the old boy had just blurted it out in all sincerity. To avoid causing him grief, she didn't pass comment. Instead, she took his arm; she was feeling cold, and wondered if it were old age or just that the spring was so feeble this year – here they were at the end of April, but the apple trees in the cathedral garden were grey, without a single flower. If it went on like that, her lilac probably wouldn't bloom until July. They stopped midway between the cathedral and the castle, beside the Second World War monument, which looked like an advertisement for a game of dominos. That morning they had debated going for a walk by the Vistula after mass, but now in silent agreement they had turned towards the town and started climbing up Zamkowa Street, which led to the market square; they didn't have to discuss where they were going, as they always went to the Mała Café. It may have been a little dearer there, but somehow it was different, nicer. And they sprinkled the froth on the coffee with icing sugar. One time, Mrs Rojska had actually spent quite a while wondering whether to say in her confession that throughout the entire mass all she'd been thinking about was that when this torment was over she'd be able to go and have her sweet frothy coffee.

"Do we really talk about our ailments all the time?" Mr Rojski switched on his running commentary again. "Maybe not, it's just that Thomas put me in the mood, somehow I had it there before my eyes, the image of him poking about in Jesus's side. Maybe it's because of those paintings, I don't know, I don't like standing next to April, that's where the very worst tortures are, that fellow impaled on the stake always grabs my attention, and he's got something trickling down that stake…"

"Janusz!" Irena Rojska virtually came to a stop. "Just you shut up about those monstrosities."

As if to emphasize her indignation, right beside her head, a blue-black raven landed on the wall surrounding an abandoned, tumble-down manor house; it was a really big bird, and it tilted its head as it looked at the old couple. They stared in amazement – it was only an arm's length away. The bird must have understood it had committed a faux pas, because it quickly hopped down on the other side of the wall. Mrs Rojska made the sign of the cross, at which her husband tapped his forehead knowingly. Without a word, they continued their walk up the hill, and then the raven came back. This time it jumped down on their side, marched past underfoot, and disappeared in the gateway of the abandoned property. It was behaving like a dog that wants to show its master something.

Mrs Rojska felt anxious and increased her pace, but her husband, whose eyes were ageing more slowly than hers, stayed on the spot, staring at the granite paving stones. The bird had left behind small, characteristic three-point tracks, as if it had deliberately dipped its claws in dark paint earlier on.

"Are you coming or not?"

"Wait a minute, I think something's happened."

There was a flutter of wings, and now there were several ravens sitting on the pitted wall. As if hypnotized, Mr Rojski stepped over a signboard warning that the building was in danger of collapse and went into the overgrown garden. Standing amid the bushes, the two-storey mansion was also partly covered in weeds and had been rotting away here for decades, until it had acquired the lifeless look so typical of abandoned buildings. The walls had gone green, part of the roof had caved in and the windows were like empty eye-sockets, making it look like the face of a water demon looming out of the duckweed for a moment to hunt down its next victim.

"Have you gone completely mad now? Janusz!"

Mr Rojski didn't answer; pulling aside the grey branches of the bushes he was walking slowly towards the house. His leg hurt like hell, so he could only shuffle along torpidly. The courtyard was full of ravens, which weren't flying, or cawing, just walking about in silence, staring expectantly. The house's empty windows made him think of the tortured martyrs from the cathedral again, their burnt-out eyes, grimaces of pain and mouths open for a scream. Behind him, his wife was making a fuss, scaring him with her palpitations and threatening never to make another meat loaf if he didn't come back instantly. He heard and understood, but he couldn't stop. As he went inside the house, the rotten floorboards didn't so much creak, as make an unpleasant squelching noise.

His eyes took a while to adapt to the semi-darkness; the windows were quite small, and partly boarded up, so, despite the sunshine, not much light could force its way inside – or at least not into the ground floor, because there was a bright glow coming from upstairs, and that was where Rojski headed. The ravens stayed outside; one, the biggest, stood on the threshold, cutting off the retreat. The old gentleman stopped at the foot of the stairs and thought this wasn't a good idea;

not many of the steps were left, and the ones that were did not inspire confidence. Even if he had been an extremely light, extremely brave cat he should have decided against it. Nevertheless, he started going up, mentally reproaching himself the whole time for being a silly old codger, telling himself that the days were long since over when after each adventure, once he had recovered, he could say: "Oh, what the heck, it always turns out well".

The banister was slippery with damp and mould, and it was impossible to get a grip on it with his bare palm, so he wrapped his hand in his scarf. The first stair broke as soon as he set foot on it, but luckily he was ready for that. The second one was solid, so was the third and they all looked the same up to the eighth, but just in case he left out the seventh, which had a strange bulge in it. After that it was worse. The ninth stair was missing, and so were the eleventh and twelfth. As for the tenth – well, anyway he'd come too far to go back, so he stood on it and quickly pulled up his painful leg. The stair gave a warning groan and creaked, then started to tip slightly and Rojski felt himself slipping on the rotten wood. Afraid of falling, quickly for his age he jumped across the hole, and that was the moment when he should have given up, but he had the floor of the upper storey at eye level, and that was his undoing. Wanting to cross the finish line as fast as possible, he rapidly surmounted two more steps, but his bad leg let him down and he lost his balance. Afraid of tumbling down the stairs, he threw himself headlong into the stream of sunlight falling through holes in the roof and a large French window. Something cracked, but unfortunately it wasn't a floorboard; the pain from his broken wrist flooded Rojski's body in a hot, sickening wave. Groaning, he turned over onto his back, and the sunlight dazzled him; as a reflex he shielded his eyes with the broken hand and felt a stab of pain, a terrible sensation, as if the bones in his forearm were being ripped out with pincers. He let out a loud scream and pressed his hand to his chest, breathing fast and heavily through clenched teeth; then he felt faint, and under his tightly closed eyelids the afterglow of sunlight fought for space with scarlet spots. Nevertheless he managed to clamber to his knees and open his eyes; the first thing he saw was a family of tiny mushrooms growing from a chink in the red floor. This sight was so absurd that he had to laugh. What a silly old codger, why on earth had he climbed up here at all? And how was he going to get down now? The fire brigade would have to fetch him down, like a cat stuck up a tree.

A piece of tar-paper struck him gently on the back. Rojski started to breathe more easily and stood up, banging his head on a hanging bit of roof. He cursed and turned around to discover that unfortunately the tar-paper wasn't tar-paper, nor was the bit of roof a bit of roof. It was a corpse hung from the ceiling on a hook like a side of meat, with the torso locked in a reinforced barrel studded with spikes. Above the barrel the body was as white as plaster, and below it was covered in a layer of congealed blood; the sunlight glinted gaily on the purple sheen. There was a raven perched on the cadaver's shock of red hair. It had one eye fixed on Rojski, as it half-heartedly pecked at a sticking plaster dangling pitifully from the corpse's forehead.

Rojski closed his eyes. The sight vanished, but the image remained beneath his eyelids for ever.

IV

I wonder if they've found the body by now. It's of no significance, I'm just wondering. Whether they find it today, or – doubtful – in a week is of no consequence. I switch on the TV, tune into the news channel and turn down the sound. That MP Palikot is drinking a miniature whisky and complaining about the president, and the Jewish Uprising survivor Edelman is laying flowers at the Heroes of the Ghetto monument. The same two images alternately. If they find the body, all that will be minor news.

V

Prosecutor Teodor Szacki had run to the spot before Wilczur got there, and climbed a ladder to the upper floor of the abandoned manor house straight after the police officers. The news had spread quickly and there was already a crowd of people on Zamkowa Street, with more descending from all directions. The Marshal, the fat policeman with a bushy moustache, clambered up the ladder behind him. Before Szacki had time to issue any orders, the Marshal began to shake with nausea, battled with it for a while, and then threw up all over himself and his moustache. Incredible, thought Szacki, but actually he couldn't blame the man. The sight was horrible, probably the worst he had seen in his career. Decomposing corpses, fire victims, drowned bodies, the victims of gang killings and fights with smashed-in skulls – it all paled in comparison with the corpse of Grzegorz Budnik hanging from a hook, until recently a wanted man with a warrant out for his arrest, the only suspect in the case of his wife's murder.

Szacki gazed at the image, surreal in its monstrosity; under attack from an overload of stimuli, his brain tried to process the information, but with some resistance, as if running at half speed. What was the most striking feature of all?

Definitely the barrel, a ghastly stage-prop that gave the scene a theatrical, unreal quality, thanks to which a part of Szacki was waiting for the applause, and then for the corpse to open its eyes and smile at the audience.

The face was definitely a riveting sight. Szacki had learnt on a criminology training course that the human brain is programmed to recognize faces, to identify the nuances of their expression, the emotions they display, and all sorts of changes that tell us whether to smile at another person or gear up to run away from them. That's why we sometimes see the Virgin Mary on a window pane, or a ghostly grimace on a tree trunk – it's the brain, endlessly seeking human faces everywhere, always trying to pick them out, classify them into familiar and unfamiliar, and recognize the emotions. Szacki's brain was agonized by the sight of Budnik's face. The distinguishing marks of the chairman of the City Council – morbid emaciation, sunken eyes, a shock of red hair and a red beard, that unfortunate cut on his forehead – had been distorted by the hook, stuck in the chin and emerging from the cheek. The mutilated muscles gave the face a strange, unsettling expression, as if Budnik had glanced into hell for a moment and seen images there that had changed him for ever. It crossed Szacki's mind that, depending on the killer's degree of sadism, this metaphor might not be far from the truth.

But the worst thing was the colours, mercilessly brought out by the sunlight, which was sharp by this time of year. Budnik's corpse was snow-white on top, drained of blood like his wife's body a few days earlier, but the bottom half of it shone blood-red; it looked like a perverse modern art installation, an iconoclastic artist's statement about contemporary Poland: Take a look at your national colours. Here's a naked Polish corpse, murdered according to a legend his ancestors invented to be able to kill others with impunity.

The entire floor was covered in blood as well, mixed with dirt; there was a brownish, dried-up puddle of it, three metres in diameter, with its centre right under Budnik's gnarled feet. In a spot near the stairs it was smudged, probably by the person who found the body.

"Should we unhook him?" asked the Marshal, once he had recovered.

Szacki shook his head.

"First the photographs, then the technicians have to gather all the evidence. This time the corpse is in the place where the crime was committed – there has to be something left."

Cautiously, watching out for the most rotten floorboards, Szacki walked up to the middle of the room. His impression was right – around the edge of the puddle, like on the rim of a coin, there was a sort of inscription, probably written with a finger. He quickly said a mental prayer for it to be a gloveless finger, and for the lunatic who had done this to be registered. He leant over the puddle and read it. Not this, please, he thought. Please, please don't let it be a nutcase who's been watching lots of American films and is playing cat and mouse with us now. On the edge of the puddle there were some letters carved in the dried blood: KWP, and straight after them three six-figure numbers: 241921, 212225, and 191621. It didn't mean much to Szacki, but just in case he took a picture with his mobile phone.

He forced himself to look up at Budnik's face again. Changed beyond recognition, the man looked even more wretched than a couple of days ago at his office; death had deprived him of the last remnants of his predatory, athletic look. Worst of all was that plaster – pitiful enough then when it had been stuck to his forehead, but now it was dangling wistfully, revealing a barely healed cut, the cherry on the cake of posthumous humiliation.

By the time Basia Sobieraj and Maria Miszczyk reached the spot simultaneously, the corpse had been taken down and covered with black plastic. Wearing disposable gloves, Szacki was looking through the dead man's wallet, while Wilczur stood leaning against an empty window frame, smoking.

Sobieraj took one look around the room and burst into tears. When Szacki went up to comfort her and put a friendly hand on her shoulder, she threw herself round his neck and hugged him tightly. He could feel her whole body shaking with sobs; over her shoulder he kept an eye on Miszczyk, hoping she wouldn't faint, firstly because he didn't want to catch her one-hundred-kilo body, and secondly because he was afraid she would fall through the rotten ceiling. But not a single maternal muscle twitched on his over-endowed boss's face; she cast an eye over the crime scene and fixed her gaze on Szacki. She raised an eyebrow enquiringly.

"The autopsy will be done today, and so will the crime scene inspection and tests to see if this blood includes Mrs Budnik's blood too," he replied to her unspoken question. "We'll get a new case hypothesis ready as fast as possible, and present an action plan. Unfortunately it looks like a madman – we'll have to have a psychological profile done, and review the databases to examine crimes with a religious motive. We can have a press conference tomorrow at noon."

"And what are we going to tell them?"

"The truth. What alternative do we have? If it's a madman, the fuss might help us. Perhaps he'll boast to someone, perhaps he'll accidentally say something that betrays him."

"Do you want to bring in the family to identify the body?"

Szacki said no; there was no point burdening others with this night-mare. He had all the necessary facts in the documents.

"Do the letters KWP mean anything to you?"

"*Komenda* – headquarters, *Wojewódzka* – regional, *Policji* – of police. Why?"

VI

Prosecutor Teodor Szacki couldn't bear chaos. The feeling of being lost in events and in his own evaluation of them, the feeling of being unable to keep his thoughts on one theme, of losing the logical thread, of helplessly, ineffectually thrashing about from thought to thought. You got a result by evolving one thought from another, by meshing them together, by creating a complex, precise logical mechanism, which eventually produced a fine, aesthetic solution. This time that was out of the question – his thoughts were rampaging in his head like a flock of nursery-school children in the playground. Budnik's death had dismantled all his previous suppositions, which he had had enough time to get used to. In a way, from the very start of the investigation, somewhere deep down he had been convinced Budnik was guilty of his wife's death, and that had given him peace, allowed him to look for the proof. Never before had his intuition let him down so badly.

God, how furious he felt. Angrily he kicked a can lying in the street, and a beautiful pregnant woman coming in the other direction gave him a reproachful look. She would be beautiful, she would be pregnant, as if to spite him. He was tired, because every time he tried to place one thought on top of another, Klara appeared, demolished the entire structure and forced her way into his consciousness. So what if she was pregnant? Maybe that would be a good thing – after all, last night had been great, maybe that would mean he'd be settling down with a beautiful young wife at his side? But what if he had just been overcome by the mood of the moment? What if she really was a dumb, plastic dolly-bird who had never attracted him and who had

163

once managed by some miracle to make a positive impression? And was it a good thing he had dumped her? And if she was pregnant, would she give him a second chance, or quite the opposite – would she change into a bitch out of hell making claims on him, getting maintenance out of him by the bucketload? So if she wasn't pregnant, should he be pleased or sorry?

He reckoned the long walk from the hospital to the prosecutor's office would sober him up, and the cool air would help him to gather his thoughts. But it just got worse. He turned from Mickiewicz Street into Kosely Street; in a moment he'd be there, he'd sit down in Miszczyk's office and present her with the investigation plan. The investigation plan! He laughed out loud. What a joke, the investigation plan!

There was a small group of journalists standing in front of the steps into the building. Someone said something, and they all moved towards him. Since his exchange of views with that pesky monkey in green had appeared on television, he had become recognizable. He straightened up and assumed a stony expression.

"Prosecutor, a word of comment?"

"There's going to be a press conference tomorrow, we'll tell you everything then."

"Is it a serial killer?"

"Tomorrow. Today I'd have nothing but hearsay for you, tomorrow we'll have information."

"Hearsay will do."

"No, it won't."

"The man suspected of the previous murder has been killed. Does that mean the investigation is at a standstill?"

"Not in the least."

"Should the schools be closed?"

Szacki was dumbstruck. He had been methodically pushing his way through to the entrance, but the question was so stupid that he stopped.

"Why the schools?"

"To protect the children."

"I'm sorry, from what?"

"From the blood ritual."

"Have you gone crazy?"

Prosecutor Teodor Szacki felt as if he had opened the door into a parallel universe, an alternate reality, which he had thought to be in the remote past, forgotten and untrue, strewn with the corpses of old demons. Wouldn't you know, you only had to peep through a chink to find out none of the demons were dead, they had just gone to sleep, and what's more it was an extremely light doze. And now they were wagging all their demonic tails with joy at the chance to come out through the door set ajar in Sandomierz and play with Prosecutor Szacki. Unbelievable. How deeply the stereotypes that substitute for thinking must be etched into the national consciousness, if sixty-five years after the Holocaust, sixty-three since the last pogrom and forty since most of the Jewish survivors were driven out in 1968, here we have a lunatic, born at a guess in the 1970s, who believes in blood rituals.

"I have not gone crazy and I'm not joking," the man went on, who with his diminutive physique and curly black hair reminded Szacki of a caricature Jew. He was wearing a tank-top. "And I don't understand why we haven't got the courage to wonder out loud whether by chance after all these years ritual murders haven't come back to Poland. I'm not saying that is the case. I'm just asking."

Szacki was waiting for someone to help him out by shutting up this clown, but no one was in a hurry to; the cameras and microphones just waited to see what he would do.

"You're out of your mind. Ritual murder is an anti-Semitic legend, that's all."

"In every legend there's a grain of truth. I remember that lots of Jews were condemned in legitimate trials for kidnapping and killing children."

"Just like lots of witches. Do you think witches have come back to the Most Serene Commonwealth too? Are they busy screwing with the Devil, squeezing the juice out of black cats and plotting how to dethrone Christ the King?"

The small group of journalists burst into servile laughter. The lunatic didn't have a notebook or a Dictaphone, and Szacki realized that apart from journalists there were all sorts of conspiracy-mongers here too.

"Political correctness won't change the facts, Mr Prosecutor. And the facts are: two dead bodies, killed according to the old Jewish blood ritual, practised for centuries in many places worldwide. You can swear it's reality, but you've still got two corpses in the morgue. And a Jewish ritual whose existence is beyond debate. There are documents, there are statements by witnesses, and we're not talking about medieval stories here – independent courts were still confirming the existence of this practice in the twentieth century."

"Let's not forget Piasecki," put in an ageing man who was standing at the back; his coat and hat gave him the look of an American reporter from the 1950s.

"Sacred words," the man with black hair responded excitedly. "A terrible Jewish crime, unexplained to this day. All the more deplorable since the victim was Piasecki's innocent son. They knew that would be worse for him than his own death."

"How do you know it was a Jewish crime if hasn't been explained?" asked Szacki impulsively.

"Excuse me, if you gentlemen could explain..." One of the hacks was feeling lost.

"Bolesław Piasecki," the black-haired man was quick to clarify. "Please look him up, he was a great Pole, active in the nationalist movement before the war, and after it head of PAX, the Catholic organization..."

"An anti-Semite and a Jew-baiter," grunted one of the cameramen, without taking his eye off the viewfinder.

As the black-haired man started telling the rest about Piasecki, it occurred to Szacki that after forty years of not believing in the weird and the wonderful, now he would have to start believing in genetic memory. What the hell were all these people on about? If it wasn't the pictures in the cathedral it was ghetto benches to segregate Jewish students, if it wasn't ghetto benches it was pogroms, if it wasn't pogroms, it was Piasecki, if it wasn't Piasecki, it was 1968, if not 1968, then – Szacki made a mental pause – it was sure to be Michnik and Geremek, it couldn't be otherwise. Those two influential people – the editor of the liberal newspaper *Gazeta Wyborcza*, and the former foreign minister, both from Jewish families – were always to blame for everything in some people's minds. He bet himself a decent bottle of wine that before five minutes were up, these Jewish-mafia hunters would get on to Adam Michnik.

"…in 1957 the Jews from the secret police kidnapped and murdered Piasecki's son. The prosecutor is surprised the crime has never been explained, and of course officially it hasn't, officially no Communist crime has ever been explained. Does that mean Father Popiełuszko is alive and well, and that no one was injured at the Wujek coal mine?" Oh, so now he's going to say the Communist secret police who killed the dissident priest and shot at the striking miners were all Jews, thought Szacki.

"The killing of young Piasecki may not have been explained," the man went on, "but strangely enough, it just so happens that the names that surfaced in this case were secret police officers of Jewish descent. I would also point out that in Polish tradition there is no custom of murdering children to punish the parents."

"There's no such custom in any culture," growled Szacki, as the familiar red curtain gradually fell before his eyes. He hated stupidity, which he regarded as the only truly harmful trait, worse than hatred. "Please don't talk nonsense. You probably aren't aware there are laws against that."

"You can't silence me," said the black-haired man, proudly sticking out his puny chest under the tank-top. "I know the authorities like it when there's only one right way of thinking. And nowadays the way of thinking of Messrs Szechter and the late 'lamented' Lewertow is the only correct one." Ah, here it is, thought Szacki – Michnik (his father was called Szechter) and Geremek (his father was called Lewertow) are indeed the villains of the piece.

"But luckily nowadays we can tell the truth," the lunatic continued. "If the blood ritual is back, and if Polish blood is soaking into the soil of Sandomierz, we can tell the truth. If we don't like the fact that the Poles are being pushed into the role of a minority in their own country we can say so."

Szacki felt tired. Very, very tired. So much so that he couldn't even be bothered to wonder what sort of wine he had won himself. He just replied from force of habit, from years and years of fatherly reaction, which bids one explain the obvious and keep saying that no, the sun does not revolve around the earth, and no, my dear child, you cannot have your own opinion on the matter.

"Among other things, it's thanks to Messrs Michnik and Geremek that you can say what you want nowadays. Unfortunately."

The black-haired man went red.

"Weeell, I see Mr Prosecutor is aware of what's going on after all."

Mr Prosecutor felt tarnished by being in the lunatic's favour. He could feel he was drowning. Drowning in the river of bloody Polish xenophobia, which never stopped flowing under the surface, whatever the historical moment, and was always just waiting for the opportunity to pour out on top and flood the surrounding area. It was a mental Vistula, a dangerous, unregulated sewer of bias and prejudice, just like in that drinking song about the Vistula flowing across the Polish land – "For the Polish nation has this special charm, everyone's love for it stays forever warm." Charm, more like harm – bugger the lot of them, on their patriotic hobby horse, the collectors of contempt.

Szacki was getting more and more wound up inside, and the tanktop-wearer was looking at him with the sympathetic smile of a man who has found his long-lost brother. The more he smiled, the more wound up Szacki became, until finally, he furiously spat out words he regretted before they had even squeezed past his larynx, but it was too late to stop them.

"Yes, right, I'm aware that Michnik and Geremek sold Poland up the river along with the rest of their Jewish gang. Listen up, because I'm not going to say this again. I am an official of the Polish Republic, and there's only one single thing I'm interested in: finding the perpetrator of these crimes and bringing him to trial. I don't give a damn if it's Karol Wojtyla come back from the dead, Ahmed from the kebab stall or a skinny Jew of your type baking matzos in the cellar. Whoever it is, he'll be seized by his lousy side-locks, dragged out of the miserable hole where he's hiding and made to answer for what he's done. I can guarantee you that, ladies and gentlemen."

All the blood had drained from the black-haired man's face, but the furious Szacki didn't see that, because he had turned on his heel and, feeling his hands go stiff with rage, entered the prosecution building. The door slammed shut. He didn't know that in the monitors of the cameras trained on him it looked just like the famous scene from *Camera Buff* which he had thought of that morning.

VII

"How about a nice profiterole?" Maria Miszczyk offered him a silver tray with some small cream puffs arranged on it in a neat pyramid.

Szacki felt like saying bugger the profiteroles, but they looked so appetising that he reached out a hand and put one in his mouth. And then another one immediately – the pastries were obscenely, unimaginably delicious. Considering the fact that there wasn't a single place in Sandomierz with good sweets – not counting the boxes of chocolates at the Orlen petrol station – and that for a week Szacki had been feeling like a drug addict in detox, he felt like jumping for joy and shouting: "Hallelujah!"

"Tasty," he delivered his sparing verdict.

Miszczyk smiled warmly, as if she had no doubts the profiteroles were perfect, but understood that it wasn't appropriate for him to go into pretentious raptures. She looked at him enquiringly.

"The good news is that we have more, much more," Szacki began his account. "Above all, we know that Elżbieta Budnik was murdered in the same building – the place is full of her blood. We also have material to test for fingerprints and trace evidence. Things aren't so good with the biological evidence and DNA material, the building is filthy dirty, bordering on collapse and has been inhabited by all sorts of animals for years. So that sort of test will be useless. For the same reason we can forget about odour analysis tests. The police provisionally put the prints through the database, but unfortunately nothing came up."

"A man?"

"It won't be possible to confirm that on the basis of the fingerprints. The trainer footprint is size 39.5, which doesn't tell us anything either."

"But you'd need a good deal of strength to drag someone upstairs."

"Not necessarily." Szacki set out the photographs taken at the crime scene in front of his boss. "Only part of the ceiling between the storeys is still there – where it's missing they found a pulley system, and considering the tracks left in the dirt we can be fairly sure it was used to haul the victims up there. Mrs Budnik and her husband were both small in stature, so a woman could have done it. Not a puny one, true, but it's possible."

"What was the direct cause of Budnik's death?" Miszczyk asked, reaching for a profiterole and biting into it too quickly; whipped cream blossomed on her lower lip in the shape of a cotton flower. Very slowly and very thoroughly she licked her lips; the gesture was so sensual that Szacki felt aroused, though he had never thought about his motherly boss in a sexual context before. Suddenly he saw the image of her riding him furiously, the folds of her ample body happily smacking together, her breasts swinging every which way, jumping and bouncing off each other like puppies at play.

"The cause of death, Prosecutor."

"Blood loss. He'd earlier been injected with a strong sedative, Tranquiloxyl."

"How did…" Miszczyk hesitated, "how did it look, you know, under the barrel?"

"Better than I was expecting," Szacki replied truthfully. "Budnik bled to death through severed arteries in the groin – the barrel was just for fun and effect, a stage prop. Of course the nails had cut and scratched him in several places, but they weren't the cause of death."

"And the numbers scrawled in blood?"

"Basia and I are going to deal with that this evening."

Even if Miszczyk was surprised to hear him warmly calling her "Basia", she didn't let it show.

"All right, now the bad news. But first a profiterole to improve the mood."

Without needing encouragement, Szacki reached for one. The small pastry puff was perfect. The fresh, chilled, slightly tart whipped cream melted in the mouth and blended with the egg-scented pastry, flooding his taste buds with ecstasy – Miszczyk's profiteroles were an absolute work of art, the Platonic ideal of all profiteroles.

"First of all, our suspect was bled to death in a way that made him look red and white, to the glory of the anti-Semitic legend of blood. Which means the media hysteria will soon be uncontrollable, and that fascist nutters and Jewish-conspiracy hunters will be descending on this place from all over the world, as well as fanatical defenders of political correctness. I've just had a taste of it downstairs."

He ate another profiterole, and decided to break up the bad news this way.

"Secondly, he was our one and only suspect. We don't know of anyone who would have had a motive to kill Mr and Mrs Budnik. I did consider the hypothesis that Budnik could have killed his wife, and then been murdered by her lover, Jerzy Szyller, in revenge. But that's unlikely. Szyller wouldn't have had any reason to replicate Budnik's modus operandi. I'd sooner believe Szyller murdered both of them. There was something odd and nasty going on between the three of them."

"And right now Mr Szyller…"

"Remains at liberty, but is under permanent police observation." Szacki could feel his boss's hard stare, and added that this time police observation meant that to disappear he would have to evaporate or squeeze through a drainpipe.

A profiterole.

"Thirdly, so far we're not entirely sure how the victims ended up at the crime scene. We're certain no car has driven onto the property, nor did we find any signs of anything being dragged through the bushes, no handcart or wheelbarrow tracks – there aren't even any footprints, not counting the ones left by the old man who found Budnik's body."

"So where did you get the size 39.5?"

"Printed in the blood upstairs."

And another. The profiteroles were like heroin – with each one he ate, Szacki needed the next one even sooner.

"Fourthly, the numbers scrawled in blood might indicate that we're dealing with a madman who wants to play at riddles, American films, heavy breathing down the phone and making himself a coat out of human skin."

"What do you think about that?"

Szacki made a face.

"I've studied cases of serial killings, and the murderers are only criminal geniuses in Hollywood. In reality they're disturbed individuals addicted to killing. It excites them too much for them to play at theatrical performances or little games with the investigators, and above all they apply themselves to planning the murder and then covering up their tracks. Of course they try, but they make mistake after mistake, and the problem with catching them comes from the fact that they aren't from criminal circles, known to the police, and it's hard to get a fix on them."

"In that case, what can this be about?"

"Honestly? I haven't the faintest idea. Definitely something other than murder for the sake of murder. Mrs Budnik was a local community worker, Budnik was a well-known municipal politician, both of them had strong ties to this city. The site of the crimes is right in between three of the biggest local monuments: the castle, the cathedral and the town hall. Both bodies were found in the Old Town. If I had to bet on it, I'd put my money on us finding the solution to the riddle in these old walls rather than in the mind of some madman."

"Would you bet a lot on it?" asked Miszczyk, reaching for one of the three remaining profiteroles.

"Not a very big sum."

She laughed, and a puff of cream flew down onto her unappealing foot, trapped in an unappealing court shoe. Miszczyk took it out of the shoe and started wiping it with a paper tissue; the foot was large and shapeless, and the toe of her tights was damp with sweat. Unfortunately, since the vision of her large, sagging breasts bouncing off each other, something had burst inside Szacki, and now he regarded this sight as perversely attractive.

"We have to check out the Jewish lead."

Miszczyk gave a loud sigh, but nodded with understanding.

"Whether we like it or not, we've got to look in that group, check up on descendants of the old Jewish community."

"They're going to fuck us rigid," said Miszczyk quietly. Coming from someone with the bearing of a royal nanny, this sounded very odd. "They're going to fuck us rigid when it comes out we're examining the Jewish community in search of the killer. They'll hail us as fascists, Nazis, prejudiced Poles seething with hatred who believe in the legend of blood. All the media are already jawing away about anti-Semitic provocation, and it's still Sunday. Tomorrow they'll really get going."

Szacki knew that was true, but he remembered yesterday's conversation with Sobieraj at the barbecue.

"We've no alternative, we can't ignore the theory that this could in fact be the work of a Jewish nutcase – a theory that does suggest itself, in spite of all. The victims are Poles, Catholics, patriots. The murders have been staged in the style of a Jewish ritual, admittedly a mythical one, but it's a well-known myth. This city is famous for tense relations between Catholics and Jews. And the people of Israel have come a long way from being the passive victims of history – now they're aggressors who fight brutally for their own cause and take revenge for being ill-treated."

Perfectly motionless, Miszczyk stared at him, and with every sentence her eyes grew wider.

"But you can relax, I'm not going to repeat this summary at the press conference," he said.

Only now did she breathe out.

They talked for a while longer about plans for action to take in the next few days and drew up a list of matters to attend to, and factors which could verify or exclude certain assumptions relevant to the inquiry. It was an arduous process of elimination, but Szacki didn't feel overwhelmed; at this stage there could be a breakthrough at any moment, thanks to some important new piece of information or an important turn of events. They tossed a coin to decide who would eat the last profiterole. Szacki won; as he was smearing the last bits of it against his palate and starting to think about a cup of mint tea, Miszczyk fired her final question.

"Apparently you've dropped Klara Dybus?"

This assault on his private life was very unexpected, and Szacki was completely tongue-tied. He wasn't accustomed to the speed at which information circulates in a small town.

"There are rumours going around that she's been crying and cursing all day, and her brothers are loading their muskets."

Fucking hell, he didn't even know she had any brothers.

"It wasn't a promising relationship," he said, just to say something.

She snorted with laughter.

"You didn't find a relationship with the best match in Sandomierz promising? All the perfect knights around here have already broken their horses' legs trying to climb her glass mountain. When she chose you, even the deaf could hear the suicidal thoughts emanating from hundreds of houses. She's beautiful, clever, rich – as God's my witness half the women round here would become lesbians for her. But you didn't think it a promising relationship?"

Szacki shrugged and made an idiotic face. What else could he do?

VIII

"The town itself fills me with sadness, the poverty and crudity are pitiful, there's nothing to drink and nowhere to eat, because all the restaurants are closed. At the People's Tavern I had a bad start and clashed with the waiter, but luckily I buried my pride and apologized. So I'm getting something to eat there. Things are worse when it comes to having a crap. There are two cubicles that they keep locked – filthy and stinking. There's no question of sitting. This is the side of living in this place that I find frightful, and I think in future I'll stop coming here."

Prosecutor Teodor Szacki was pleased that this particular comment from Iwaszkiewicz's *Diaries* no longer applied. He scooped up a tea-spoonful of the milky froth gracing his coffee and slurped it down, as specks of icing sugar tickled his palate. Either some anonymous Sandomierz genius had had the bright idea of sprinkling coffee with icing sugar instead of cocoa powder, or the café owners had seen it done somewhere, it didn't really matter which – the upshot was that the first sip of coffee at the Mała Café was always so delicious that Szacki had no desire to go anywhere else. This café was one of his favourites anyway – it was the epitome of the middle-class dream of "an unpretentious little café downstairs". The short menu offered toast and crêpes, coffee, tea and homemade cakes. There was a sofa, a few chairs, and just four small tables. The locals complained that the prices were as bad as in Warsaw, which always amused Szacki as he handed over just seven zlotys for a first-class latte here, actually far less than in the capital. He'd paid even less recently, since for some reason he had gained the status of a regular customer, which was as nice as it was surprising – he had never exchanged a single word with anyone here apart from placing his order; he just sat quietly in the corner, drinking his coffee and reading Iwaszkiewicz – sheer Sandomierz-style snobbery.

Iwaszkiewicz, or something else dug out of the little bookshop opposite. Which in its turn was the dream-come-true of those yearning for an "unpretentious little bookshop downstairs" – an antidote for shops in the Empik chain, which always made Szacki think of an overcrowded high-security prison. As if the books in there were serving a sort of sentence, not just living there while they quietly waited for a reader. This local bookshop may have been a little shabby, but at least in here he didn't feel like the victim of a prison gang rape, about to be beset by special offers and bestsellers, even though not all the new books have finished with him yet.

Right now he didn't have a book with him, but was sitting there with his eyes closed, warming his hands on his coffee cup. It was already dark outside – it was almost nine, and they'd be closing soon. Time to blow the whistle for the end of break and go back to squinting at a computer screen. Basia Sobieraj was sitting next to him on the sofa, cross-legged, flipping through a popular children's comic she had extracted from a pile of newspapers.

They had spent two hours sitting in his flat, trying through un-official means to find any sort of connection between the numbers left at the crime scene: 241921, 212225 and 191621. All good things come in threes, and all three numbers appeared at once on exactly three Internet sites. One was in Arabic, serving – as far as they could work out from the Roman-alphabet names scattered among the squiggles – for the illicit sale of drugs to increase sexual potency. One was Icelandic, and consisted of dozens of pages of figures published for IT purposes. And the third was in German, a bibliographical list where the figures appeared within index numbers. And that was all. In view of this total failure, they started studying the numbers individually, swapping jokes and observations as they did so. They tried to find phone numbers, and converted the figures into dates – thanks to which Szacki discovered that on 2nd April 1921 the first Poznan Fair had opened and Albert Einstein gave a lecture in New York on the theory of relativity, and on 4th February 1921 the Indian politician Kocheril Raman Narayanan was born, who lived eighty-four years – however, they couldn't find any point of contact. Anyway, the whole idea was pretty desperate, because only the first number could be converted into a fairly modern date.

Sobieraj folded the comic and put it back on the pile.

"I must have got older – it hardly makes me laugh any more," she said, and took a folded piece of paper from her fleece pocket. "Well, back to work, eh?"

"I thought we were having a break," he groaned, but he picked up the piece of paper, on which Sobieraj had written out the in-terpretations of the numbers that seemed the most reasonable. Just the pick of the bunch, after rejecting numerology, identity numbers on dating services and Internet auction numbers. On the page there were:

241921 – the symbol for "economic promoter for technological de-velopment" in the Ministry of Labour and Social Policy's classification of professions; the number under which Goldenline, a company that runs a community business service, is registered with the National Cooperative Council.

212225 – the patent number for some trendy Gucci slip-on shoes.

191621 – the number of the Polish patent for a tube for fibre-optic cables; and of an asteroid in the asteroid belt stretching between the inner and outer planets of the Solar System.

What a disaster. Szacki glanced at it and immediately closed his eyes again.

"We're not thinking the right way," he said.

"Hmm?" mumbled Sobieraj; Szacki had learnt by now that a polite "hmm" was her way of actively listening.

"We're just pretending to be doing something – let's drop this Google nonsense, as if we really believed the whole world was on the Internet by now. We're not after someone who murders IT guys by hanging them with network cables. It all has something to do with old traditions, superstitions, historic things. Google won't help us. We must think. Three six-digit numbers, relatively close to each other, but not arranged in order. We've established that local phone numbers used to have six digits, so let's check them in the old regional phone books. What else?"

"Police ID cards!"

Szacki opened his eyes. That was it. That had to be it. K-W-P, the Polish abbreviation for the regional police headquarters (as Miszczyk had reminded him at the crime scene), and three six-digit numbers. He set aside his coffee and immediately called Wilczur, who luckily was still at the police station. He told him to put the three numbers into the system and call back. Sobieraj listened with flushed cheeks as he gave the official orders in a cold tone of voice – she looked to him like a little girl with red hair on the trail of a mystery in a children's adventure story.

"What else?" asked Szacki. "What else is denoted by six-digit numbers? Tell me everything that comes into your head, the remotest associations, things that are right off the point."

Sobieraj glanced at him. If she wanted to ask a question, she thought better of it, and chewed her lower lip pensively.

"Concentration camp numbers. Germans, Jews, anti-Semitism. 'KWP' could be the symbol denoting a particular category."

"Good. To be checked. What else?"

"I think the numbers for the Gadu-Gadu instant-messaging service have six digits, but I'm not sure."

"To be checked. What else?"

Sobieraj bit her lip harder, frowned and leant towards him.

"Got it! The number of grey cells."

"The what?"

"The number of grey cells that die every time you give an order instead of doing the thinking."

"Somebody's got to organize the work."

"Well, I'm listening." Sobieraj laced her hands together, leant against the back of the sofa and began to twiddle her thumbs. She looked sweet, and Szacki felt he was getting to like her more and more. She was a bit like the girl who's your friend in the scouts, the kind with whom you can stay up all night on watch, and chat away with right through camp, but when it finally gets through to you that it was more than just a friendship, it's too late and she's been someone else's wife for ages. He closed his eyes and started imagining the figures. He saw a record book at a registry or an archive, but pushed the image away from himself – all the catalogue numbers in the world always include the year, so that couldn't be it. For the same reason, prisoners and detainees were out of the picture, and besides, their numbers weren't six-digit ones. He cursed himself for thinking in too normal a way. He had to give it a twist, he had to think the other way around. Break them up, maybe? Not six-digit numbers, but three-digit groups? 241 921 – 212 225 – 191 621. A bit like parts of national insurance numbers. A bit like mobile phone numbers without the operator's prefix. And what about two-digit groups? 24 19 21 – 21 22 25 – 19 16 21. He projected them in his mind, turning them every which way.

"There's a strange regularity…" he said quietly.

"Hmm?"

"There's a strange regularity," he repeated. "If we break the numbers up into two-digit ones, none of them is higher than twenty-five. Look."

He took a pen from his inside jacket pocket and wrote out the numbers on a paper napkin in the following way:

$$24\ 19\ 21$$
$$21\ 22\ 25$$
$$19\ 16\ 21$$

Sobieraj turned the napkin to face her.

"A magic square? A mathematical rebus? A sort of code? The Roman alphabet has twenty-six letters."

Szacki quickly wrote out:

$$X\ S\ U$$
$$U\ V\ Y$$
$$S\ P\ U$$

He and Sobieraj glanced at each other. It didn't look as if it made sense. But Szacki felt uneasy. Some idea had escaped him. Something had flashed past at the back of his head. When he changed the figures into letters? No, before that. When he was looking at the figures written out in a square, and Sobieraj said something about a rebus? No, first she had mentioned a magic square. Goodness knows why, but the idea of a magic square made him think of paper, mystery, a book read under the duvet by torchlight. What was it? Something for children, about a Jewish alchemist resurrecting the Golem in Prague by putting a piece of paper with a magic square into his mouth. My God, was the Kabbalah really coming into his investigation? It was a sort of lead, but that still wasn't it – some other thought had flown by when he was looking at those numbers, some remote association. Pairs of numbers. A magic square. The Kabbalah. Superstitions. Old wives' tales. The esoteric. Faith. He seized Sobieraj by the arm and pointed a finger to say don't speak – the idea that had surfaced was getting nearer and he didn't want to lose it. Numbers. The Kabbalah. Faith. Just a bit more. He held his breath, closed his eyes, and saw the answer looming out of the fog in his brain.

And just then his phone rang. Wilczur. The idea vanished, Szacki answered and listened to what the old policeman had to say. Sobieraj looked at him expectantly, placing her hand on his; Szacki found the sight of two prosecutors gripping each other's hand somewhat surreal, but he didn't pull his away.

"Well?" she asked as soon as he had finished the conversation.

"Well nothing," replied Szacki. "A lady chief commissioner from CID in Brzeg, a traffic police officer from Barczewo and a beat cop from Gorzów. Different places of birth, different names, no points of contact either with each other or with our case. And Wilczur promised his pal in Tarnobrzeg is also going to check the archive of militia IDs. There might be something there."

He felt like crying. His lost thought could have contained the solution to the riddle.

"Hmm," mumbled Sobieraj. "Yes, I hear you, Brzeg, Barczewo, Gorzów, places on the map. Do you think they could be geographical coordinates? You know, degrees, minutes and seconds?"

Szacki quickly downed the rest of his coffee and they almost ran back to his bachelor pad, where he could still smell Klara's perfume. Klara – the best match in Sandomierz.

By trying various combinations, on this quarter of the globe (latitude north, longitude east), they managed to mark several spots in the desert in Libya and Chad. Other experiments took them to the Namibian wilderness and the waves of the Atlantic Ocean.

"Let's try fixing a spot in Poland," said Sobieraj, leaning over his arm. Her ginger hair tickled his ear.

"Libya in Poland?"

"I mean let's see where these longitude lines cross Poland. You know, like *In Search of the Castaways*."

In Jules Verne's book it was actually about a parallel, but Szacki soon saw the point. Indeed, if all three numbers did denote geographical latitude, they would cross this part of the world. 19°16′21″ ran from Bielsko-Biała in the south, through the western suburbs of Łódź in the middle of the country, to the Vistula Spit on the Baltic coast. Then 21°22′25″ started further to the east, quite near Krynica Zdrój, ran right through the middle of Ostrowiec – here they exchanged knowing glances as this city was nearby – crossed the eastern districts of

Warsaw and ran via Mrągowo to the Russian border. 24°19'21" was entirely outside Poland, but still within its pre-war borders, passing slightly east of Lviv, Grodno and Kaunas.

"Ostrowiec is something," Sobieraj muttered into his ear, trying at any cost to prove that for a true optimist even a broken glass can be half full.

"And I know what that something is," said Szacki, standing up suddenly.

"Hmm?"

"It's a load of shit. A smokescreen. Lies. A great big load of shit the size of Australia, a vast pile of crap!"

Sobieraj tucked her hair behind her ears and watched him patiently, waiting for him to calm down. Szacki paced the room from wall to wall.

"In the American films some genius always shows up who tries to think like the murderer, right? He frowns, walks about the crime scene and in abrupt, black-and-white flashbacks we see how his mind attunes itself, how he works out exactly what happened." Something flashed between the wardrobe and the wall, something that looked like a silver wrapper, and Szacki had to fight the temptation to check if it was a condom wrapper, or an empty condom wrapper.

"Hmm?" This time Sobieraj supplemented her mumbling with an encouraging gesture. With one hand she tapped something out on the keyboard.

"Except that films follow a different logic from real life. They have a logic which has to reach a solution, a denouement so the killer is caught in an hour and a half. But now let's feel our way into the logic of a real case and of our murderer. He certainly doesn't want us to catch him in an hour and a half, so if he isn't completely and utterly fucked up he's not going to leave riddles we only have to solve in order to find him."

"Meaning?"

"Meaning either he'll leave a riddle that sends us off on a completely false trail. Or – which from his, or her, point of view has to be a more amusing solution – he or she will leave a riddle that makes no sense. The kind that has no solution and leads nowhere, but just makes us waste time looking at satellite pictures of the Libyan desert. And with every minute he or she is sure to be further and further away, safer and safer."

"OK," said Sobieraj slowly, rocking on a chair, with her hands entwined under her chin. "And what do you suggest?"

"Let's go to bed."

Sobieraj slowly raised one eyebrow.

"I haven't brought my lacy underwear, so if you'd be willing to postpone until another day…"

Szacki snorted with laughter. He really was getting to like her more and more.

"You people are terribly randy in this province."

"Long winters, long nights, there's no cinema and just boring stuff on TV. What can you do?"

"Sleep. Let's go to sleep, get a rest. Tomorrow we've got the profiler, the data will come through from the lab, recordings from the urban security cameras, maybe we'll get something extra."

Sobieraj turned her laptop towards him.

"First look at this."

He went over to her; the comment about the underwear meant that first he looked at her, differently, but he saw the same thing as usual. Jeans, thick hiking socks, a black fleece, no make-up. A textbook example of the one-hundred-per-cent Catholic girl guide. The only lace he could imagine in her context would have to be on the Virgin Mary's veil. But she smelt nice, he thought, as he leant over her – more of shampoo than perfume, but it was nice.

In the browser window the words *Konspiracyjne Wojsko Polskie* were entered – meaning the Polish Underground Army. Yes, of course, the KWP. Some scraps of superficial historical knowledge sprang to mind – the "cursed soldiers", post-war partisans fighting against the Communists, underground tribunals passing sentences, and anti-Semitic goings-on. Szyller?

"I'll leave you with the problem of whether this might be a smokescreen or not, and I am indeed off to bed now. I'll let you know when I've changed into something sexier. Kiss kiss."

She kissed him on the cheek in a friendly way and left. He waved to her, without tearing his eyes from the computer.

A few hours later, when he lit his first cigarette of the day at the open kitchen window, and the smoke mixed painfully with the sleep in his eyes, he already knew far more about the KWP. Enough to stick one more theory in the file, an ominous one, which assumed more than any other that the whole case involved bloodthirsty Jewish revenge. And which unfortunately provided for the possibility that it didn't have to stop at two corpses – quite the opposite.

Dawn announced its arrival as the first vague shapes appeared in the pitch-black courtyard, dark patches against very dark patches. Szacki was reminded of a few nights ago, when he'd been smoking in this very same spot, and to his vexation Klara's red fingernails had appeared on his fleece. He thought about that night, he thought about her, and how she had told him to turn around that morning as she clothed her statuesque body. The moisture forced from his eyes by tiredness and smoke was joined by a few tears of sorrow. Once again Prosecutor Teodor Szacki had fucked something up; once again he was all alone, with no one and nothing.

But maybe that was for the best.

6

Monday, 20th April 2009

Orthodox Christians are celebrating Easter Monday, and
Catholics finally have a day off, not counting those
of extreme right-wing views who are celebrating Adolf
Hitler's 120th birthday. The remaining People of the
Book are not being idle either: the Muslims are celebrating Mohammed's 1,442nd birthday and the Jews are
listening as the President of Iran delivers an anti-
Semitic speech at a UN conference on the fight against
racism. In Poland forty-eight per cent of Poles claim
there is no party in the Sejm — the Polish parliament
— that represents their interests, and thirty-one per
cent claim that none of the parties expresses their political views. India launches an Israeli-made spy satellite into orbit, Russia warns NATO that military ma-
noeuvres in Georgia are unnecessary provocation, and in
Italy Juventus are penalized for the racist chants of
their fans, and their next match will be played behind
closed doors. In Sandomierz a thirty-seven-year-old
man parks his Fiesta in a plumbing supplies shop on
Mickiewicz Street, and nearby the diocesan stage of the
XIII Bible Knowledge Contest begins. All forty-four
finalists have already won a one-day formative holiday
stay at a hermitage in Rytwiany. It is a little warmer,
but nothing to get excited about — during the day the

temperature is only about thirteen degrees, and to add insult to injury it's fine and sunny.

I

Szacki was having some idiotic dreams. Idiotic nightmares. He was back at the Lapidarium club again, but instead of rock music there was a non-stop stream of hits from the 1980s. *Wake Me Up Before You Go-Go* was still ringing in his ears as he reached for the bottle of water that always stood by his bed. As he gradually gained consciousness, the memory of the dream rapidly faded, but not rapidly enough to wipe the surprise from his sleepy face. Wham! had been playing, and he had been dancing with various women – Judge Tatarska, Klara, Weronika and Basia Sobieraj were definitely all there. Basia was wearing nothing but lacy red underwear, and it would all have been very sexy, if Adolf Hitler hadn't appeared – right on the words "you put the boom boom into my heart" – the real life Adolf Hitler, with a toothbrush moustache, in a Nazi uniform, a small, funny little man. He may have been small and funny, but he was a shit-hot dancer, copying George Michael's moves like the god of disco-dancing; the girls made room for him on the dance floor, everyone was clapping in a circle and Hitler was dancing in the middle. Suddenly he grabbed Szacki by the arm and they started dancing together – he could remember how the feeling of the inappropriateness of dancing with Hitler fought with the feeling of pleasure in his dream – Hitler danced superbly, sensually, letting himself be led a bit, and inventively reacting to every move. The final fading image was of a laughing Hitler throwing his arms in turns above his head, giving Szacki a flirtatious look and squealing "come on baby, let's not fight, we'll go dancing and everything will be all right". Or something to that effect. What nonsense – Szacki shook his head in disbelief as he dragged his rumpled, forty-year-old body to the bathroom. As he peed, he finally gave in to the demand rising in his throat and wheezed the words of the chorus into the mirror.

* * *

He resolved the eternal dilemma of whether to take a shower or eat breakfast first in a manner worthy of Solomon, by throwing on some clothes and going out shopping, to get a bit of fresh air and gather his thoughts before the meeting with the profiler. Basia had worked with him once before, but Szacki only knew him by repute; the guy came from Krakow, and in southern Poland he was legendary, renowned as much for being a genius as an eccentric. Szacki didn't like that, he didn't like stars; he always preferred people who weren't conspicuous but did their job carefully. A good investigator had to be like a consistent goalkeeper, who might not save a shot that was impossible to save, but didn't let the rubbish through either. There was no room in the justice system for a Barthez or a Boruc.

As he stood in the checkout queue at the co-op, his hand kept instinctively tapping out against his thigh the start of the Wham! hit – pa, pa, pa, pam pam – and his eyes went wandering over the charcuterie displayed at the cold counter. How sad it looked. He really had never seen such miserable sausages as in this shop. Most of them didn't look real – more like plastic imitations made on a broken injection press. And the ones that did look real were by contrast too real, changing colour, dried out or gone moist. On top of that, they had strangely low prices. So although he felt the urge for a bit of pepperoni to have with his breakfast, he went on standing in the queue, clutching a tub of cottage cheese, some pre-packed Jarlsberg, some tomato juice and two rolls, and listening to the conversation two women were having behind him.

"He's a good kid, but his favourite reading matter is the Gospel of St John, all those last judgements and horrors – for him it's as good as fantasy fiction. But the contest doesn't include John."

"Is the contest today?"

"Yes, at the institute. It's just starting – I even feel a bit nervous myself. We revised it all again yesterday, and he asked if Mary Magdalene was Jesus's wife. Where do they get it from?"

"From Dan Brown. Mary Magdalene's supposed to have manifested herself in Biłgoraj, isn't she?"

"What, at Palikot's place?"

The women giggled at the idea of Mary Magdalene appearing before the colourful MP who was from Biłgoraj, and Szacki smiled too. At the same time this conversation set something going in him, and he felt the familiar itch in his head. Dan Brown, yesterday's riddles, the magic stone, the Kabbalah. Once again something was eluding him; he should either sleep more, or swallow some magnesium.

"Would you like to try some cold meats?" said the checkout lady, smiling as radiantly as if she'd found her long-lost son. "We've got some delicious Żywiecka sausage, but rather than me going on, why don't you try a bit?" She stood up from her till and cut a hefty slice. "A bloke's got to have strength, not just eat that light stuff, like a model."

Szacki thanked her politely and chewed the sausage, though he hated eating anything before his first sip of coffee. The sausage was vile and unpalatable, despite which he smiled sweetly and took a hundred grams. He looked around discreetly in case there was a television in here by any chance; in forty years no one had ever been so exceedingly polite to him in any shop before. But no, there weren't any cameras, just him, the beaming checkout lady and the two high-school mums. One of them smiled at him, and the other blinked and nodded approvingly. Totally surreal. When he was dancing with Hitler, at least he'd been sure it was a dream, but now he was afraid he was going barmy. He paid up as fast as he could.

It was freezing cold again. Lured by the sun, Szacki had only put on a light top, and now he was shivering, despite which he dropped in at the little bakery too. He had to have a doughnut, though he knew it wouldn't taste good.

"Good day," said an old man as he passed him, tipping his hat courteously and bowing to Szacki.

Szacki returned the bow automatically, thinking things really were strange, and went into the bakery. At the till stood an old lady, entirely dressed in funereal black, and on seeing Szacki she moved away from the counter.

"Please, go ahead, I haven't made up my mind yet."

He didn't say anything, chose a large, oddly bloated doughnut and took a handful of change from his pocket.

"No need," said the shop girl, smiling. "Special offer today."

"What special offer?" he asked, unable to restrain himself. "Buy one, get it free?"

"A special offer for our prosecutor," added the old lady from behind him. "And for me, Natasza, that sausage roll, the well cooked one."

Szacki left without saying anything; he could feel his throat tightening and the muscles on the back of his neck tensing. He was having a dream about *The Truman Show*, but he couldn't tell the difference between dreams and reality, he couldn't wake up. He was going mad.

He marched rapidly back to the flat on Długosz Street, passing the shop where he had bought the food earlier, and bumped into a man emerging from it, who looked like a car mechanic in a suit. The man was clearly lost in his own thoughts, but when he saw Szacki, to the prosecutor's despair, he beamed all over.

"Congratulations," he whispered conspiratorially. "In our times it takes courage to say these things straight out. Don't forget we're all with you."

"We? What we, for God's sake?"

"We ordinary, real Poles. Good luck!" The man squeezed his arm in a familiar way and walked off towards the town hall; only now did the right cells start working in Szacki's brain. Please, he thought, don't let it be true. He dashed into the shop, pushed past a boy who was saying to his friend: "Hey, get this, they haven't got any fucking ice tea – what sort of a dump is this?", and got to the newspaper stand. The mystery was explained in an instant – he wasn't dreaming, he wasn't going mad, nor was he the hero of *The Truman Show*.

On the cover of a tawdry tabloid called *Fakt* he saw himself in his favourite graphite-grey suit, standing on the steps of the Sandomierz prosecutor's office. He had both hands raised in a gesture that yesterday had meant "no more questions", but in the picture it looked as if he was putting up a wall against some invisible threat, with a resolute *non possumus* drawn on his gaunt – now he could see that clearly – face. The headline *Mystery Jewish Murder?* and a short text left no doubt what the prosecutor was putting a stop to.

Prosecutor Teodor Szacki (40) categorically announced yesterday that he will track down the degenerate who has already murdered two people in Sandomierz. Residents can sleep in peace – in the absence of Father Mateusz he will solve the mystery of the possibly Jewish murder. The sheriff-in-a-suit yesterday gave his personal guarantee to *Fakt*'s reporter that he will catch the villain, regardless whether it is a Jew or an Arab, even if he has to 'drag him by the side-locks from the lousiest hole on earth'. Bravo, Mr Prosecutor! On pages 4–5 we present the details of both horrific murders, statements by witnesses and a graphic reconstruction of events.

Prosecutor Teodor Szacki closed his eyes. The knowledge that he had just become the hero of small-town Poland was horrifying.

II

Actually, he wasn't bothered about the lack of ice tea at the shop – he didn't really want any, or anything else for that matter – he just wanted to give vent to his disappointment and use the word "fucking". Right from the start, this excursion hadn't gone according to plan. At dawn he had found out his mother had put his favourite Abercrombie shirt in the wash yesterday, the one Uncle Wojtek had brought him from Milan, so he'd have to go in the extremely uncool sweatshirt he only wore for skiing, and even then he did his jacket up all the way. Unfortunately, when he got to school it turned out it didn't matter much anyway, because Ola was off sick and wasn't coming on the trip. He called her, she cried, so he had to comfort her, and meanwhile everyone had got on the coach, so instead of sitting at the back and drinking the vodka Walter had mixed with Cola, he had ended up in the third row next to Maciek, who had borrowed his PSP and played on it for so long he had to put it away in his pack before Kratos reached the next level. Then he felt ashamed, because what did he care? He could let Maciek have the Playstation for a while; it wouldn't do him any harm. And when he thought things couldn't be worse, Mrs Gołąbkowa had hovered over him, loudly praising the story he'd written about loneliness and drooling on about what a sensitive boy he was. Then she went off. Unfortunately, she didn't take Marysia and Stefa with her, who were sitting behind him groaning, and who spent the rest of the journey giggling into the gap between seats that he was about as sensitive as a toilet seat. No but seriously, if girls really did mature faster than boys, these ones must have had something genetically wrong with them. He gave Maciek the PSP and pretended to be asleep for the rest of the journey.

Sandomierz itself didn't have much appeal for him – he'd already been there in the autumn, when it was still warm. His father had taken him – since splitting up with his mother, his paternal role had alternated between periods of absence and periods of over-the-top toadying. Marcin wished that just for once his old man would stop trying so hard, but he didn't know how to tell him. He wanted to come over to his place and not find a slap-up meal waiting for him, not see a rented film and a new book in his room. He wanted to come over and see him in his underwear, with a five o'clock shadow, drinking a can of beer and saying, "sorry, mate, it's been a crap day, go and order yourself a pizza, and watch TV or something." At last it would have been a normal situation – he'd have found out he had a father, and not some plastic dummy following the instructions from a textbook on parenting after divorce. Of course he knew others had it worse, some people's fathers dematerialized completely, or just sent a text message once a fortnight. But so what. Even so, the whole thing was bloody awful – not them breaking up, because that hadn't surprised him, but the way they tried so hard now. His mother was just the same – he only had to frown and she'd be reaching for her purse to comfort her poor child from a broken home, even if she didn't have the money to pay the bills. He was ashamed that they were so feeble, that it was so easy to manipulate them, so easy that it didn't bring any satisfaction, like getting through a game that was too simple. It was lucky he had his violin – the violin was honest, it never cheated, it never made promises or greased up to him. It could reward him, but it could also be merciless, it was entirely up to him – yes, his relationship with the violin was the most honest deal in Marcin Ładoń's fairly short life to date.

Lost in cheerless thoughts and deprived of the ice tea he hadn't really wanted, he stood aside from the group, waiting to go into the Sandomierz underground vaults. Mrs Gołąbkowa was looking at him with tears in her eyes; she must have thought he was alienating himself again, sinking into solitude, poor boy, too sensitive for the modern world. In fact he liked her, but sometimes she was such an unrealistic cretin she evoked pity. What happens to them all? They're soft and indolent, they fall apart before your eyes like tissue paper in the rain, and then it's a big surprise their children don't respect them. Children – all right, he could count the virgins among his female schoolmates on a single hand. Including Ryśka, too stupid to spread her legs, and Faustyna from the Catholic family, sure to have been sewn shut with consecrated thread – that girl had definitely met with misfortune. And Ola too, but Ola was different, of course.

"Want a drop, Marcin?" Walter's eyes were already rather glazed, and Marcin reckoned there might still be a fuss about that. He drank a little "Cola", strong and reeking of vodka, then quickly put a fresh piece of chewing gum in his mouth.

"That's the second bottle. We had the first one on the way to Radom."

"Fan-fucking-tastic," he said, just to say anything.

Walter slugged at the bottle like an out-and-out alcoholic, so obviously that only a blind man could have failed to notice what he was using to lubricate his fifteen-year-old body. Marcin found his showing off embarrassing, and felt ashamed of taking part in this shabby performance, so he quickly moved nearer the centre of the group, which was now going down into the Sandomierz cellars. Despite their best efforts, some of his schoolmates had failed to hide their excitement at the adventure. Only the girls were impervious to such attractions; Marysia was holding onto Stefa with one hand to avoid falling over, while writing something on her phone with the other. God knows who to – they were all here.

"…in those days Sandomierz was a rich city, one of the richest in Poland, and the so-called staple right was in force, which meant that every travelling merchant had to display his goods for sale here, and as a result Sandomierz was a gigantic, permanently open shopping centre where you could buy anything." At the sound of the words "shopping centre" Marysia tore her jaded gaze from her phone, but soon went back to it. "The burghers of Sandomierz grew wealthy, and out of concern for their possessions and merchandise, and also for the sake of security, over several centuries they dug cellars under the city, which as the years went by developed into an enormous labyrinth. The connected rooms reached eight storeys deep inside the loess rock, with corridors running under the Vistula all the way to the castle at Baranów, and to other neighbouring villages. To this day no one knows how many of them there actually are."

The guide had a pleasant, cheeky voice, which didn't alter the fact that she was deadly dull, especially if you had to listen to the same story a second time over in only a few months. But even if she hadn't been boring, it wouldn't have changed the fact that Marcin had already found so surprising the last time – the famous Sandomierz underground vaults looked like the cellar in a prefabricated block of flats. Brick walls, concrete ceilings, terrazzo flooring, fluorescent lights. No magic, no mystery, no nothing. Extraordinary how they'd managed to screw up an attraction like that.

"And suddenly the Mongols surrounded the city," said the guide in a low voice, which made her sound silly instead of adding drama to her tale. "Halina Krępianka, inconsolable in her grief after losing her entire family, went to the enemy camp. There she told the Tatar chief she would guide them into the city along secret corridors, because she wanted vengeance on the citizens for dishonouring her..." The guide suddenly became embarrassed; she must have been unsure if the children understood exactly what she meant.

"Dishonoured her? So why did she run away, was she like stupid?" muttered Marysia.

"LOL," her best friend chimed in.

"The Tatars trusted the girl, and she led them a long way into the labyrinth of corridors, but meanwhile, the citizens walled in the entrance to the underground. All the invaders perished, and so did the heroic girl."

"Once they twigged, like that was when they really dishonoured her." Marysia was priceless.

"Ha ha, big LOL."

"…and to prove that every legend contains a small grain of truth, I can tell you that to this day you can dig up human bones near here, maybe the actual remains of the Tatars who were buried alive."

They shuffled into the next chamber, interesting in as much as it resembled a passage in a mine, and Marcin listened to the lecture on how the city was saved from collapse after the war. That was interesting, more so than legends about dumb-ass heroines. How the miners drilled shafts in the market square, how the houses in the Old Town had to be taken apart and rebuilt again, how the empty tunnels and cellars were filled in with a special substance to reinforce the rock, which was as full of holes as a sieve. He leant back against the wall; listening didn't prevent him from staring at the thin ribbon of a lilac thong sticking out of Marysia's hipsters. Maybe he was old-fashioned, but it bothered him a bit that almost all the girls did their best to look like tired old tarts. Good thing Ola wasn't like that.

The guide paused for a moment, and there was total silence.

In the quiet he heard a faint, distant howling that seemed to be coming from the bowels of the earth.

"Can you hear it?"

Marysia turned round to face him and pulled up her trousers.

"What are we supposed to be hearing, perv?"

"Sort of howling from deep in the ground. Oh, shush, shush, there it is…"

The girls swapped glances.

"O-M-G. Are you crazy?"

"Just listen, you really can hear howling."

"Howling like someone's dishonouring someone, or howling like the Devil? Coz I'm only interested in the first kind."

"LOL."

"Jesus, you're such a dumb bimbo. Just shut up for a while and listen."

"And you go and get cured, you psycho freak – I'm gonna tell Ola."

The girls giggled together and joined the group, which was moving into the next room. Marcin stayed put, pressed his ear to the wall in various spots, and finally found one where the howling was very clearly audible. It was a weird noise, which sent shivers down his spine – the long, modulated, almost uninterrupted howling of a tortured human being or animal. Whatever was emitting that sound must have been in a pitiful state. Though maybe he was just imagining it – maybe it was the wind, something to do with the ventilation.

The light went out, and there was only a gentle glow, combined with whispers, coming from the direction in which his class had disappeared. He lay down with his ear to the floor; something about the noise was still bothering him, something he hadn't fully heard. As he sought the best quality, he shuffled his ear across the cold flooring and heard the howling better and better; now he was sure it was coming from more than one throat. And apart from the howling there was something else, another kind of noise, familiar, animal...

He was just about to put a name to it when he felt a painful blow in his side.

"What the fuck..." The darkness was lit by the pallid gleam of a mobile phone display. "Marcin? Are you a complete twat-head?"

Marcin got up and brushed off his clothes.

"There's this howling..."

"Sure, pal, howling on a violin. Better have a drink, Vivaldi."

III

Chief Commissioner Dr Jarosław Klejnocki was sitting with his legs crossed, puffing on a pipe and looking at them with a calm gaze, hidden behind thick glasses. The glasses really were thick, thick enough to show the bulging shape of the lenses, and to make the bit of the profiler's face visible behind them seem much thinner than the rest. As well as that he had short grey hair, an equally short beard, below it a polo-neck top, a tweed jacket, suit trousers and black sports shoes in the style of House MD.

His clothes hung on him loosely, and it crossed Szacki's mind that he must have been fat until quite recently – he looked rather haggard, with a touch of surplus skin on the cheeks, and his way of dressing and slow movements testified to the fact that for years he had been used to his own corpulence. Which he must have lost to illness, or a compassionate wife who had realized she didn't want cholesterol to make her a widow prematurely.

Present in the conference room at the prosecutor's office, as well as Klejnocki and Szacki, were Basia Sobieraj and Leon Wilczur, who had earlier shown the profiler around the crime scenes. The windows were shielded by blinds, and pictures of the corpses were being projected on a large folding screen. Sobieraj was sitting with her back to the screen, refusing to look at it.

Klejnocki puffed on his pipe again and set it down on a special little stand, which he had produced from his pocket earlier on. If someone had held a competition to find the archetypal Krakow boffin, the chief commissioner would offer a simple choice – either first prize, or chairman of the jury. Szacki suddenly felt irritated. He could only hope there was some substance behind this ideal academic appearance, and not just clairvoyance.

"Can you imagine, I recently took part in a competition to find the most typical attribute of the Polish character. Do you know what I suggested?"

Bloody-mindedness, thought Szacki, smiling politely.

"Spleen," said Klejnocki emphatically. "Spleen – it covers certain generalizing features, and in a symbolic way it determines the nature of the community that, admittedly not all that often, employs it."

Fucking hell, this can't be true, thought Szacki. He couldn't possibly be sitting here listening to this lecture, no way.

"Spleen reflects a certain mental and psychological state that is characteristic on the banks of the Vistula. Embitterment, frustration, sneering underlined with negative energy and a sense of one's own lack of fulfilment, being on the 'No' side, and constant dissatisfaction"

Klejnocki broke off, shook the ash from his pipe, and pensively began to fill it again, taking the tobacco from a small velvet pouch the colour of the cloth on a billiard table. A scent of vanilla wafted about the room.

"So why have I brought this up?"

"We're wondering that too," said Sobieraj, unable to hold back.

Klejnocki gave her a polite bow.

"Of course, dear lady. I bring it up because I have noticed that apart from crimes of passion, there is also such a thing as, let us call it, a crime of spleen. Fairly typical for this place on Earth which, like it or not, we call our homeland. Passion is a sudden burst of emotion, a moment of over-excitement and blindness that removes all the brakes imposed by civilization. A red curtain falls before the eyes, and only one thought matters: to kill. Spleen is something else. Spleen builds up slowly, in small droplets. At first it just makes itself felt occasionally, then it changes into an unpleasant ache, it starts getting in the way of life, becoming an ever more irritating noise in the background, like a nagging toothache, except that we cannot remove the causes of spleen in a single procedure. Few people know how to deal with it, and meanwhile each moment adds another droplet of vexing emotion. Drip, drip, drip." Each "drip" was accompanied by a puff on the pipe. "Finally we feel nothing but bile, there is nothing else inside us, we would do anything to be rid of it, not to feel that bitterness any more, that humiliation. This is the moment when the sufferer casts everything to the Devil. Some people cast themselves – off a bridge or the top of a tall building. Others cast themselves at someone – a wife, a father, a brother. And I think we are dealing with an instance of it here." He pointed the pipe at the pale corpse of Ela Budnik.

"In other words we're getting down to specifics," remarked Szacki.

"Absolutely – surely you didn't think I was going to piss the whole day away like that."

Sobieraj raised an eyebrow, but didn't say anything. Wilczur didn't even bat an eyelid. Entirely motionless and silent until now, he seemed to realize the foreplay was over and it was time to get down to action. That meant he leant forwards in his chair – Szacki would have sworn he heard creaking, and it wasn't the chair – tore the filter off a cigarette and lit up.

"I admit this is a strange case," Klejnocki began, and Szacki thought, Here we go. He had always regarded the average profiler as a sort of psychic who provides so much information and multiplies the doubts so much that something has to fit. Then no one ever remembers the incorrect bits. "If it weren't for the fact that the culprit is obviously and undoubtedly one and the same person, I would suggest that in the case of the second killing you are dealing with a copycat. There are too many differences here."

"Such as?" asked Szacki.

"Both victims were bled to death – apparently a similarity. But let's look at the details. The male victim has precisely severed femoral arteries. In a way it's an elegant solution, the blood flows out rapidly, pours down the legs, and it's over. Whereas the female victim has her throat slashed so that it looks like a gill, which means lots of enraged cuts. He wanted to punish her, to humiliate, to disfigure, he wasn't impeded by the fact that there was blood pouring all over the victim's face and torso, and also spattering the culprit. Using that method to slash her throat, everything must have been covered in blood."

Szacki was reminded of the large crimson pool upstairs in the abandoned mansion.

"So the first crime was one 'of spleen', and in theory it should have closed the whole matter. Once the murder has been committed, the bile flows out with the victim's blood, there's peace, then a sense of guilt, pangs of conscience. Such are the dynamics. Why did he kill a second time?" Klejnocki stood up and began to pace up and down the room. "As well as that, both victims were undressed – apparently a similarity. But let's look at the details. The female victim is abandoned naked in a public place, humiliated once again, all of which clearly shows how strong the need to kill was. So we can exclude the idea that the culprit is a stranger or a random passer-by. The male victim is hanging in a secluded spot – more than that, the barrel can even be regarded as a sort of covering, after all, it didn't do great harm, it was more for appearance's sake. It looks as if this time the culprit was subconsciously ashamed of his action, while earlier he had wanted the whole world to hear about it. Why? For the time being we don't know, but I advise you to accept that the key to the whole puzzle is the first murder, and the motives behind it. The second is supplementary, so to speak, not pivotal. Please excuse my cynical tone, but I understand that at this stage your overriding concern is to catch the killer."

"You have said 'he' the entire time," put in Sobieraj. "Does the profile fit a man?"

"Very good question, I was just going to talk about that. Unfortunately you can't rule out a woman for several reasons. Above all, the victim was not raped. It is very rare for a man in a frenzy of desire to kill not to exploit the unconscious woman, because for her that means additional humiliation. As well as that, the victim's face is untouched, even though the killer cut her throat to ribbons with a sharp instrument. That might indicate a woman, because for women the face is a calling card, a manifestation of beauty which testifies to high value, fertility, a better position. Destroying this calling card is a stronger taboo for a woman than for a man. And finally what I was talking about earlier. The first killing is a typical murder with a strong emotional foundation, but the second has been committed as if with shame, out of obligation, because it was called for by a plan, of revenge for example. But women are far more systematic. A man would do the killing, the tension would leave him, and he'd stop. But a woman would tick off point one and start to implement point two. Of course I'm not saying that the killer is a woman, I'm just saying that unfortunately you cannot rule it out."

"A lot of help you are," remarked Szacki tetchily. "You can't confirm anything, or deny anything, everything's possible. That doesn't move us forwards."

"The victims did not die in the same place. What do you say to that solid fact, Prosecutor?"

"You're mistaken," wheezed Wilczur from the back.

"Rank does not guarantee infallibility, Inspector," bristled Klejnocki, evidently not accustomed to small-town cops holding a higher rank than he did.

"The tests showed that some of the first victim's blood was found under the second body."

"Perhaps they did, perhaps it was there. I advise you to check again, take samples from several places. Psychologically it is unlikely for a murder under the influence of emotion to have been carried out with such an effort. The second murder has been coolly staged, but the first was not, that's absolutely out of the question. If, however, the culprit went to the trouble of planting the blood of the first victim there, it means he's very anxious that you shouldn't find the place where she was murdered."

Szacki glanced at Wilczur, who just nodded in agreement. They would have to check.

"Thank you," he said to Klejnocki. "Confirmation will be very important for us."

"Will he or she attack again? Could it be a serial killer?"

"No, he doesn't fit the profile of a serial killer. As I said earlier, it looks more like the fulfilment of a plan, and of course revenge is the motive that suggests itself. So if the plan includes further victims, then yes, he will kill again."

"What is there to imply that?"

"The inscription left at the murder scene. If the whole matter were over and done with, he wouldn't be keen to play any little games."

"So it's a little game?"

"Or a way of communicating what the revenge is about. Often for avengers the death of the person whom they blame for their injury is not enough. Infamy is also important – the world must find out what the victims were punished for. Of course there is also a third possibility – after all, murderers exist, just as we do, on a certain meta-criminal level."

"I know where you're heading," sighed Szacki. "They watch the same films and the murderer has simply scrawled a few random numbers to confuse us."

"Exactly."

Klejnocki reached out a hand and switched off the projector.

"I'm sorry, but I can't look at that corpse any more."

Silence reigned in the conference room. Szacki was thinking that despite everything the meeting had been fruitful, and to be fair to Klejnocki he reasoned very logically, without letting an excess of theory obscure his view of reality.

"Assuming there is still someone on the list to be ticked off. Who might it be?"

"Someone connected," replied the profiler, just as Szacki thought he would. "First the wife, then the husband, I don't think it's the turn of a shop girl from Białystok now. A family member, maybe a long-standing friend, or someone from the same set-up. If you manage to discover what the whole matter is about, if you find the next person before he attacks…"

Klejnocki didn't have to finish, Szacki had been hearing the clock ticking in his head incessantly from the very start of this case, and now it had simply started ticking louder and faster. If they found the potential victim, they'd find the murderer too. Maybe a man, maybe a woman, certainly someone connected with the Budniks, someone familiar. Maybe someone he had passed in the street, or maybe even someone he already knew. He glanced at Sobieraj, who was asking about a few more small points, he glanced at Wilczur, who was talking on his mobile in the corner of the room. He thought about the others, about Szyller, about Miszczyk, about Sobieraj's husband, about the bizarre pathologist Ripper, about Judge Tatarska, about the guy who had accosted him that morning outside the shop. They were all in some way connected, they had known each other since childhood, they went to parties together, spread gossip, knew hidden facts and revealed secrets together. He wasn't paranoid, he didn't admit the idea of a city-wide conspiracy of silence, but he had noticed that he was being more and more careful to censor what he said to his new fellow citizens.

Until this point he had only sensed that the solution to the riddle lay in the walls of this old town that had existed since the dawn of Polish history. Now he was certain of it.

For obvious reasons the press conference happened without him; every question about Teodor "the Jew-baiting sheriff" Szacki was dismissed by Miszczyk in the same way – with the chilly statement that the prosecutor supervising the investigation was busy with his official functions. They had only had a brief conversation in advance about the front page of *Fakt*; his boss had laconically informed him that she had had a long talk with the prosecutor general, and it hadn't been a pleasant one. The facts – how appropriate – which ensured the investigation was not taken away from them and transferred to the regional prosecutors in Kielce were firstly that the prosecutor general had hated the tabloids ever since they published photos of him in his swimming trunks (with the headline *Justice at the Sauna*), and secondly that some mysterious citizen, high up in the power structure, had claimed that if anyone was capable of cleaning up this small-town mess, it was the white-haired prosecutor. Szacki was a realist, he knew what that meant – someone was very keen for him not to return to Warsaw. All right, he had no such intention.

He watched the press conference on television. It was a nightmare – half the questions revolved around Jewish ritual murders and half around serial killers. The fourth estate was finding it hard to hide its excitement at the fact that perhaps a real serial murderer had finally shown up on the banks of the Vistula. Correction: wasn't hiding its excitement. Most of the Teflon-coated presenters passing comment looked as if they kept one hand in their trousers all the time, and at the word "serial" they gave it a harder tug. It was an embarrassing display. He also noticed that the right-wing nationalists were raising their heads higher and higher; those ostracized for their political views had returned to favour, to add a bit of colour to the show. Various types of right-wing conservative, from parties such as the League of Polish Families and the Real Politics Union, sat there on TV, trying to dress bits of anti-Semitic propaganda in the robes of intellectual comment of the "I'm not racist, but…" kind, and the fourth estate was pretending to take it all at face value.

"One should ask oneself the question whether the people of Israel have always been nothing but the victim. Of course there is the nightmare of the Holocaust, but there is also the gory Old Testament, there's the bombardment of Lebanon and the wall dividing Palestinian families. I'm not saying the Jews are behind the events in Sandomierz – though in that particular city, where various incidents occurred in the past, it would be horribly symbolic. What I do say is that it would be foolhardy to pretend that there is any nation in this world that is entirely incapable of aggression. For in this particular instance an assumption of that kind could lead to an escalation of the tragedy."

Oh well, there's nothing to be done about stupidity; he decided to cut himself off from the fuss and focus on the proof. Once again he reviewed all the statements, old and new. It didn't look too good. The abandoned mansion on Zamkowa Street stood in a spot where no one could have seen anything, and of course no one had seen anything. Nor did any of the security cameras cover that spot. The six-digit numbers were not the numbers of old militia IDs (the militia were the police in the Communist era), and checking concentration-camp numbers and Gadu-Gadu instant messaging identification numbers had proved a blind alley, too. A small step forwards had come with Klejnocki's hypothesis that Mrs Budnik had not actually been murdered in the same place as her husband. Her blood was found in several spots, suspiciously evenly distributed, and the situation would certainly have been different if she had been butchered there. Szacki knew this was crucial information. If the killer was so anxious for them to stop looking for the place where the first crime was committed, it must indicate his identity. Which would confirm that he definitely wasn't a stranger to the victim. So Szacki gave orders to have the entire property carefully searched for the presence of blood. Perhaps the killer had made a mistake, spilt a little somewhere, indicating the direction from which he had come, maybe he had unwittingly left them a trail of breadcrumbs. Bread and blood – yet more twisted symbolism.

After the press conference he had another meeting with Miszczyk and Sobieraj, and they made a careful summary of everything. Almost everything, because Szacki withheld the results of his all-night research on the Polish Underground Army – the KWP. He certainly hadn't forgotten about it, but he hadn't added it to the documents as an additional case hypothesis, or presented it as an important lead. Why not? Because he felt that it cast too long a shadow on this chocolate-box city for him to be able to trust anyone who'd been brought up here and was in love with the place. Apart from that, he was getting more and more caught up in the idea that they weren't being entirely frank with him – that he was the outsider who only gets told as much as necessary, and not a word more. Perhaps that wasn't right where Sobieraj was concerned; the friendly feeling between them was getting stronger from one conversation to the next, and Szacki was finding the principled pussy's company a real pleasure. But she was from here, which meant he couldn't entirely trust her.

After the meeting he went back to the case files. He had to be sure he hadn't overlooked a single sentence, a single word, a single bit of a photograph. He had to be sure the solution to the riddle definitely wasn't hiding in the documents.

V

The big hand on the clock above the door was nearing ten, and he was still slogging over the papers, turning every piece of the puzzle in his imagination as various hypotheses projected themselves in his mind like films. Lost in another world, he was concentrating so hard that when his mobile rang just under his nose it made him jump. County Police HQ. Is that Prosecutor Szacki? Absolutely. He had totally and utterly forgotten he was on duty today – it was easy to forget about it in Sandomierz, because usually nothing happened that required the presence of a prosecutor at the site of the incident, just the occasional accident on the bypass. He listened to the duty officer, and had the same feeling he had that morning in the shop. It couldn't be the truth, surely someone was taking the piss.

"I'll be there in ten minutes," he said.

In the car he took a quick look at the city map – he thought he knew where it was, but he didn't want to risk it. It wasn't far – how could it be? Nothing was far away here.

He passed the bus station, turned left and parked behind a police car. The darkness at the back of the student hostel for the catering college complex was illuminated by the glow of torches. As soon as he switched off the radio, the sound of singing began to invade the car.

"… rivers of our tears and blood were shed. How dire it is for all whose freedom Thou hast removed. At Thy altars we raise our plea…"

Szacki rested his head on the steering wheel in a gesture of resignation. Please, anything but that. Please let's not have yet another patriotic shambles. With an undercoat of that Catholic, xenophobic drivel to boot. We're better, you're worse; we should be rewarded, you should be punished – he really couldn't see much difference between the patriotic hymn *God Thou Hast Poland* and the Nazi anthem, the *Horst Wessel Song*. The Nazi hymn was at least less whining and wailing. He did up his jacket, assumed the steely mask of a prosecutor and went out into the cold evening air, which smelt of fog and damp. He hadn't gone ten steps before the Marshal loomed out of the dark, barring his way in alarm.

"What are you doing here, Mr Prosecutor?"

"I'm out for a walk," said Szacki, taken aback. "The duty officer called to say there was an incident."

"Oh…" said the Marshal, waving. "Officer Nocul is a bit overzealous – there's really nothing going on. Some youths just got a bit drunk and were making some noise, the neighbours were afraid it was trouble."

"They got so drunk they lit flaming torches?" Szacki couldn't understand where the alarm in the Marshal's eyes was coming from. What was this all about? He strode past him decisively and headed for the gathering, which was now thundering out another patriotic anthem, *March, March, Polonia*. Oh yes, of course, he groaned inwardly, how could this incident possibly do without some crazy nationalists?

There was a group of about fifteen young men standing in the street, aged from roughly seventeen to twenty-five, some probably tipsy, some with flashlights and burning torches. At first Szacki wondered what they were doing here; he had heard rumours about the local nationalists, and that for some reason their traditional meeting place was the old Soviet soldiers' cemetery on the edge of town. Somehow the catering college complex didn't seem a likely spot for patriotic rituals, unless it had something to do with bread, hell knows. The mystery was soon clarified – right behind the college complex there was a small Jewish cemetery, and in the light of the torches he could see a pyramid several metres high, made from pieces of broken Jewish gravestones.

"The Pole will die for his homeland, for the nation," wailed the boys in black shirts. "He's willing to bear wounds and battle's devastation. March, march, Polonia…"

I wonder if they know that's a Ukrainian tune, thought Szacki.

His first instinct was to disperse the company before the media descended and wrote that the sheriff of Sandomierz and his trusty Praetorian guard were busy hunting down the perpetrators of Jewish ritual murder. Bravo, Mr Prosecutor! Keep it up! *Sieg Heil!* Incidentally, it's interesting that the tabloids the world over are all equally xenophobic. They know their boozy reader who knocks his wife about needs nothing more than to be shown an enemy whom he can burden with blame for his own failures. After a brief moment of hesitation, Szacki fought off his first instinct, nodded to the Marshal and told him to go and fetch Szyller as quickly as possible, and three Black Marias from Tarnobrzeg.

"But what for, Mr Prosecutor?" The Marshal almost had tears in his eyes.

"Right away," barked Szacki, and there must have been something in his tone of voice that made the policeman jump to the police car in two bounds. But shortly after he came back.

"The young people get bored, you know, they get crap into their heads," he started up again. "They've formed themselves a patriotic circle, it's better than drugs, that is."

"A patriotic circle, you say? They're just a bunch of fascist queers." From one moment to the next Szacki was getting more and more angry.

"But my lad is there, Mr Prosecutor. Why make a fuss? Let's just break it up and leave it at that."

Szacki gave him an icy look, and was just about to make a sharp remark, but he thought of Helka, who didn't want to see him, who was growing increasingly remote and was even fading in his memories. Who was he to dish out parenting advice? He felt sorry for the policeman, and in any other situation he would have told them not to bother him and to disperse the gathering. But right now, first of all he needed an exemplary punishment, and secondly he had already begun his, let's call it a legal experiment. Besides, he couldn't stand nationalists, hobbyists with flaming torches – fuck the lot of them.

"There's freedom of assembly!" a swarthy dark-haired boy, of very non-Aryan appearance, screamed at them. "We can stay here till the quiet hours and there's bugger all you can do to us!"

Szacki smiled at him. He'd find the right clause in the Penal Code soon enough, but for the time being he wanted on the one hand to lull their vigilance, and on the other to provoke them with his own and the police's presence.

"And freedom of speech!" added another, who looked more like the "*Lebensborn*" type. "We can say what we want, you can't close the mouths of Poles!"

Once again, it wasn't entirely true, but Szacki smiled at that too.

"All right, the waltz?" shouted the non-Aryan to his mates, and they all started singing to the tune of crooner Jerzy Połomski's megahit, popular at weddings.

"There was a goy, a cunning goy, who kept falling foul of the Yids… Then the Yids said 'oy', we're gonna have to deal with this kid…"

Szacki stifled a burst of laughter. This entire situation was surreal, no question, and the wedding hit converted into an anti-Semitic ditty gave it all some cabaret chic. The high-spirited gang reached the chorus.

"…the who-ole room fires with us, and hundreds of kikes bite the dust! We're gonna crack down on the scuzz, Arafat's troops are with us…"

On the one hand he felt satisfied, because they had just broken a paragraph of the Penal Code, on the other he felt soiled. He believed that every action starts with words, and that words of hatred lead to hatred, words of violence to violence, and words of death to death. Every massacre known to mankind has started with talk.

"…the blacks and the queers we'll fence in with wires. Commie trash, we'll send them to the gas, Nazi waltz on the Sabbath!"

Just as the last exclamation resounded, a police car pulled up and Szyller got out of it. In jeans and a black polo neck he looked like an old sea dog. He didn't even glance at the patriotic youth choir, but immediately came up to Szacki.

"What sort of a farce is this?" he barked.

"Sorry to bother you, but I need your help. I thought it would be better if you silenced your little rent boys before the pilgrims come flocking to this town as if it's the world's biggest museum of anti-Semitism. We've got enough problems already."

"What sort of nonsense is that? The fact that I am a patriot does not mean I know every berk in bovver boots."

Szacki went closer, the old trick of invading personal space.

"Why don't you stop screwing around, if you'll pardon the expression?" he whispered. "Do you think an investigation relies on nothing but polite chit-chat? We've gone through your finances and your philanthropic activities with a fine-tooth comb, and we know exactly what sort of organizations get money from you. Of course you'll deny everything for the statement, it'll turn out some accountant did it behind your back, and the only patriotic organizations you know about are rosary groups. That's for later. But for now why don't you go and tell your lads to go home before the drunken fascists get us all into trouble?"

The men glared at each other. Szacki had no idea what Szyller was thinking, and only had one concern – not to let it show that the whole story about the finances was a bluff. After a long pause the businessman turned away and went up to the "non-Aryan". They talked in low voices.

And that would have been enough, as far as the legal experiment went.

"Oh God, thank you, Mr Prosecutor," said the Marshal with relief. "I was afraid you were going to… but they're just kids. You have to understand it's different in our town, people know each other, they're friends, here it's about the whole community, we've got to stick together, haven't we? Even when they get stupid ideas into their heads, like celebrating that madman's birthday. Luckily they grow out of it."

Szacki had no idea whose birthday the policeman was on about, but he felt sorry that he'd have to cause him grief. The Tarnobrzeg Black Marias drove up from the direction of town, with their roof lights flashing but no sirens. They pulled up just as Szyller returned from his mission.

"Sorted," he reported coldly.

"I'll tell them to go home," said the Marshal, but Szacki gestured to stop him.

"Nick the lot of them," he said calmly.

"What?" screamed the Marshal and Szyller simultaneously.

"Nick the lot of them and lock them up for forty-eight hours. I can see fourteen people here – in the morning I want to see fourteen arrest sheets on my desk, not a single one less. The charges will be brought this evening."

"But Mr Prosecutor…"

"You son of a bitch…"

"We're not on quite such intimate terms yet, Szyller," Szacki drawled coldly. "And as you've just got yourself tied up with some ultra-right-wing nationalist organizations, I'd advise you to be courteous to the forces of law and order. Please take Mr Szyller home again – the preventive measures are still in force."

"But Mr Prosecutor…"

"Screw the cops! Screw the cops!" the patriotic song group began to chant.

"Give 'em the pig!" someone screamed. "Give 'em the fucking pig!"

Szacki turned round. One of the lads, the "*Lebensborn*" type, had pulled a pig's head from a black bin liner and thrown it straight at the monument. The head got stuck grotesquely among the broken gravestones, a pink ear swaying steadily. Right after the pig, a jar flew over the graveyard wall and smashed against the pyramid. Red liquid poured onto the gravestones, slowly filling the carved Hebrew letters.

"Blood for blood! Blood for blood! Blood for blood!"

"Please, Mr Prosecutor, I beg you!" wailed the Marshal.

"I start work at eight, Captain. Those arrest sheets had better be waiting for me."

The Tarnobrzeg crime prevention officers unemotionally handcuffed the defiant demonstrators and loaded them into the Black Marias. Szyller was driven away, the Marshal was in tears and the local residents watched the entire incident without emotion.

Prosecutor Teodor Szacki turned away indifferently and walked to his car. It was high time to call it a day and consider who from the outside could help him to unknot this provincial tangle of crime. He already had an idea.

Behind him, true to the best traditions of patriotic choirs, the arrestees were performing an encore to the tune of *The Internationale*.

"Let's bring Poland its rebirth, stamp on baseness, lies and muck. We're the mighty of this earth, we're the future, the nation's rock…"

What a country, thought Szacki. No original songs – nothing but covers and adaptations. How can things possibly be normal here?

VI

You can't have the old things in your life, you can only have new ones. The idea of any kind of return is impossible – even if we dreamt up a way to return and wrote it down on paper, we'd end up disappointed, because a return on paper is just a choice of bits and pieces, separate words, separate shades and separate scraps of emotion. The whole tide of that time is over, never to return. And so, as I wait for my next victim, I feel calm. I'm not yearning, not brooding, not feeling regret. I have to get on with practical matters, consider what's next. After all, you can only have new things in your life.

VII

The clock on the town-hall tower chimed four times to mark the full hour, and then struck eleven, without leaving out a single sound – at this time of night its thoroughness seemed like unnecessary cruelty. It was quite another matter that apart from the children and the policemen outside Jerzy Szyller's house, not many people were asleep in Sandomierz. Everyone was chattering. Mostly in the kitchen – that's the best place to have a natter, but they were also chatting in bedrooms, on sofas, and in front of turned-down televisions. They were all talking about the same thing. About the dead bodies they knew, about the suspects they knew, about the people-they-knew-who-must-have-done-it, about the people-they-knew-who-can't-possibly-have-done-it, about the motives and lack of a motive, about secrets, rumours, improbable explanations, conspiracies, mafias, policemen, prosecutors, and once again about the dead bodies. But also about old superstitions, about legends that never die, myths passed down from generation to generation, their one-time neighbours, and finally – about a grain of truth.

Ariadna and Mariusz were chattering in front of the information channel, which broadcasted nothing but bad news; in fact, he was doing more of the chattering, while she listened and rather sparingly disagreed. She didn't want to make a fuss that would wake up their small son, asleep in the next room, and besides, she couldn't be bothered to argue with her husband, ever since she had officially recognized him as the biggest mistake in her life.

"I don't get it. The painting's been hanging in the church for three hundred years, in the cathedral even. There were trials, they were condemned, before the war the procedure was still widely known. And now they're pretending to be so surprised the truth has come to light."

"What truth? Are you nuts? No one's ever proved it."

"No one can prove it's not true."

"Mariusz, for God's sake, it doesn't work like that. You don't have to prove innocence, just guilt. You don't have to study law to know that, it's... I don't know, it's the ABC of being human."

"It was a normal custom among the Jews. Get it? And not just here – apparently it was the same in France and other countries. And besides, who do you think drove those black Volga limos?"

"Let me guess: the Jews?"

"So where do we get the legends about children being kidnapped by people in black Volgas for their blood? Eh? Maybe something does fit here after all?"

"Yes, one lie fits another, it's all the same sort of nonsense. Every time a child got lost because the parents were drunk or couldn't be bothered to keep an eye on it, out came the vampires, Jews, Gypsies, black Volgas, whatever was the latest fashion. Can't you see it's just old wives' tales?"

"There's sure to be some truth in every old wives' tale, a grain of it, even just a tiny one."

"Don't give me that crap – blood isn't even kosher, no Jew would have touched a matzo with blood in it! Flipping heck, you're supposed to be educated, aren't you? You ought to know such things."

"It's because I'm educated that I know there's nothing black and white in history. And that you can tell everyone you're kosher and you keep the Sabbath, but do something quite different. Do you think that when Israel was fighting the war against Lebanon they stopped on Saturdays? Well, quite."

"But weren't you taught that historically it was the Poles who killed the Jews, not the other way around? It was the Poles who organized pogroms and random arson attacks, and during the occupation they liked informing on children who were hiding in the woods, or sticking a pitchfork in anyone who had miraculously managed to escape?"

"That's just one version of history."

"And in the other one they go about at night wrapped in their gaberdines, preying on children? God, it's incredible."

"But you can't deny that nowadays they do their hunting in a different way. Money's what reigns now, instead of those barrels full of nails. Which of the banks are in non-Jewish hands these days? Is there one in Poland that's Polish? That's a far better way to draw blood than using nails."

"Right. You'd better go and put a second lock on the door to make sure they don't abduct your son. A fat Catholic baby like him would make matzos for the entire town."

"Watch it, woman. I'm giving you good advice: watch it. Watch what you say about my son."

"Or it could be worse than that, they might open a bank account for him, that'd be a real tragedy – with every transfer the scabs would be getting rich at Kubuś's expense. By Christ the Lord, the King of Poland and the Universe, we won't let it come to that! Our Kubuś is always going to keep his money in a sock!"

Father Marek and his parishioner Aniela Lewa were chattering at the table in her kitchen. To be fair to them, as the good Lord had gifted Aniela with the grace of great faith and an even greater talent for cooking, energetic slurping was more often to be heard coming from her kitchen than essentially theological discussions.

"It's a sin, I know it's a sin, besides, it's late and I must go. But if you insist, then maybe just a very small piece, that bit on the edge, with the well-done crust, that's how I like it best. If Saint Thomas himself had had a piece of your cheesecake, he'd instantly have had another proof of the Lord God's existence."

"Oh, Father, what a joke!"

"It's thanks to this sort of joke I'll have to take my cassock to the tailor's again. But I really ought to be slimming down, the tourists are coming, they want to see Father Mateusz, not a big fatty."

"Don't say that, Father, you look very well."

"Too well."

"And what do you think, Father, is there a new fuss about those daubs in the cathedral?"

"Yes, there is. And I've been thinking about that lately, Mrs Lewa, I was thinking we ought to learn from those de Prévôt paintings that every murder, every form of hatred, every false suspicion, all of it is evil and we should guard against it. No fanaticism is good, no exaggeration, even if someone exaggerates in good faith."

"You put it so nicely, Father."

"But of course there are lots of interpretations where that painting is concerned. I was also thinking it has something to say about the issue of abortion which is so important these days – after all, the same problem existed in the past too, and it was said that they knew how to perform abortions."

"The Jews?"

"It's not clear if it was the Jews or someone else, and the infants were just left with them after abortion."

Stanisław Prawy, a qualified guide for twenty-three years who conducted tours of Sandomierz, was finishing his supper at the restaurant in the Hotel Basztowy. He had been invited there by the accountants from a building firm, whom he had just spent the entire day showing round his beloved city.

"Ladies and gentlemen, I may be getting old, but I was not alive before the war, so I haven't a clue what it may really have been like. But let us consider the logic of it. There are various religious sects in Poland and worldwide, are there not?"

"There are."

"And within those sects, as we see, unfortunately, on television, suicides occur, and murders occur too, don't they?"

"Yes, they do."

"The Satanists, for example, and others. And so is it logical to say there might also have been various Jewish sects in history?"

"Yes, there might."

"And might those sects have done some terrible things?"

"Yes, of course."

"And perhaps herein lies the truth. That unfortunately such things did occur, and the memory of those terrible incidents has been preserved in the painting."

Like all the town's ancient residents, who had once known real Jews, not just the wooden figurines in the souvenir shop, for one day Helena Kołyszko ceased to be a burden and became an authority on what life had been like in the past. And like most of those who had lived in the pre-war Polish-Jewish city, she couldn't remember any barrels, just sunbathing together in the meadows on warm days. As she was thinking about those warm days, downstairs her granddaughter was having a discussion with her husband.

"Sylwia says she's not sending him, why take the risk? Let the kid stay at home – no harm will come to him. After all, you know the local legend."

"Legend, my foot. Perhaps we should ask Granny – she remembers what life with the Jew-boys was like before the war."

"All right, let's go up and see her. But don't say 'Jew-boys', Rafał, that's offensive."

"So what am I supposed to say? Hebrews?"

"Just say it without the 'boys'… Watch out for that top stair… Granny, are you asleep?"

"I've had a good sleep already."

"I see you're blooming, Granny."

"Withering, more like. Give me a kiss, Rafał, my favourite grandson-in-law."

"Stop spoiling him, Granny. You can remember what it was like here before the war, can't you?"

"It was better than now. The boys used to look at me."

"What about the Jews?"

"Ah, the Jews were the best – Mojsiek Epsztajn, oh, how suave he was."

"And do you know, Granny, what sort of stories did they tell then? Because now they're saying things too, stuff about blood, and apparently they kidnapped children?"

"That's just idle chatter, but they used to tell stupid stories in those days too. I remember I had a friend, she wasn't terribly bright, and one Sunday she went to a shop a Jewish woman had on our street; her mother must have sent her for something. Because in those days the Poles were open on Saturdays and the Jews on Sundays, so everyone was happy."

"And your friend…"

"And my friend went to the shop on a Sunday, and as the church procession was passing by the Jewish woman closed the door to avoid causing offence, you see. And when that friend, I can't even remember what her name was – Krysia, I think – when she saw that she started to tremble, thinking they wanted to have her for matzos. There was a hullabaloo, and my mother just happened to be in the shop, so she saved the situation, spanked Krysia on the backside and escorted her home. But there was such a dreadful uproar that actually half the town must have believed it. The idea that matzos were made like that, and that Jews went round catching people was absolute stuff and nonsense – it's a shame to say it."

"But it's hanging in the church. If it wasn't true, they'd take it down, wouldn't they?"

"Because everything in church has to be the truth and nothing but, I suppose. Do use your head, Rafał."

"Well, yes, but the Catholic Poles didn't get on very well with the Jews before the war, did they?"

"And did the Poles get on well with the Poles? Have you young people just arrived yesterday from another planet? Do the Poles get on well with anyone? But I can tell you, I lived on one side of the market square, and there was a Jewish family on the other side, and they had a daughter the same age as me, whose name was Mala. And I often used to suffer from tonsillitis, so I had to stay at home on my own. Most of my friends didn't want to waste the day stopping indoors with me, but Mala always came by. And I always used to say: 'Daddy, go and fetch Mala, I'm going to play with her.' Mala used to stay all day and play with me. So I have very fond memories of her."

"And what became of her?"

"I don't know, she went away somewhere. Off you go now. And do think a bit, I say, because it's pitiful how stupid all that nonsense is. Blood to make matzos, I ask you…"

"Don't upset yourself, Granny…"

"Off you go, I say. I'm tired, it's late."

As soon as the young people had left, with a well-rehearsed gesture Granny Kołyszko removed a folded piece of newspaper that served as a lock for a small drawer in the sideboard, fetched out "Granma's Liqueur", half-filled a glass in a plastic holder and took a healthy swig, with the proficiency of someone who had knocked back her first drink at her cousin Jagódka's wedding in 1936, at the age of sixteen. Jagódka's mother had a shop and got on well with the Jews; she joked at the wedding that there weren't many Catholic Poles in the cathedral, "just a whole church-full of Jews came along". And when the procession went through the town, a whole group of wedding guests, all the Jewish girls came out: "Jagódka! May your life shine brightly!" She and Mala had walked along, holding hands and laughing out loud, and there were so many flowers – every tree in Sandomierz must have been blossoming that day.

But Mala had gone, Granny Kołyszko thought, as she downed the rest of the liqueur. She remembered her leaving. Doctor Weiss had gone away then too, the man who had treated her tonsillitis since she was tiny. He was thrilled with the Germans, saying they were a civilized nation, that he had never seen the like before… they wouldn't harm the Jews. Granny Kołyszko's father had tried to persuade him: "Don't sign, Doctor, don't own up." But he had insisted: "What do you mean? The Germans are civilized." Apparently he poisoned himself on the loading ramp at Dwikozy. He didn't board the train, he preferred to die like that. From the window she had seen them leading him away, and she had cried terribly, because she was fond of the doctor; the doctor had stared in at their windows as if he wanted to say goodbye, but her mother wouldn't let her speak to him. Then Mrs Kielman had been walking along with her twins, two four-year-old girls, so lovely. A German had fired at one of them, that little girl had been left outside their house. What sort of people, what sort of a nation fires at a crying child? A small child being held by her mother, and that man comes up and shoots. Her father came home that evening and told them lots of their friends were there, and they'd wanted to save someone, give someone a hand, but it was completely impossible, they were entirely surrounded.

And Mala had gone. The people who were there in Dwikozy said she had tripped and failed to jump across the ditch the Germans had dug opposite the station to test who was strong and fit. But how could Mala have failed to jump it? She was more nimble than all the women put together.

She had never had a friend like that again.

VIII

When they dropped him at the garden gate and wished him good evening, he almost jumped down their throats. Swine, bloody swine promoted above their station; common country bumpkins with straw coming out of their mouths. The prosecutor was no better. Got his socialist-realist queers mixed up indeed – not surprising, probably the only classics he knew were by Sienkiewicz, whose novels every schoolboy had to read.

He went into the house, threw his jacket on a hook, and without switching on the light poured himself half a glass of Metaxa. He had a weakness for the sugary Greek brandy. He sat in an armchair and closed his eyes. Before five minutes were up he was sobbing uncontrollably. He knew the theory, he knew he was still in the phase of disbelief and that this phase suited him, but sometimes pain broke through the disbelief, through the conviction that it was all just a game, a sham, and that when the show was over everything would be the same as before, a pain that drove him close to losing consciousness. At those moments all the images of the past few months flooded him in a wave, their happiest times, and definitely the happiest times in his life. Ela drinking coffee, the sleeve of her sweater pulled down so she wouldn't burn her hand on the cup. Ela reading a book, with her feet up on the armrest of the sofa, her hair gathered on one shoulder so it wouldn't get in the way. Ela winding hair round her finger. Ela joking. Ela babbling. Ela shouting at him. Ela, Ela, Ela.

Suddenly he sensed he was not alone. His eyes had got sufficiently used to the darkness to make out a ghost – a dark figure sunk into a chair in the corner of the sitting room. The figure shuddered and stood up, then slowly came towards him. On this side it was brighter; although the lights were off, there was enough yellow lamplight coming in through the fog outside for him to see the figure's features more and more clearly, until finally he recognized it.

"I've been waiting for you," he said.

7

Tuesday, 21st April 2009

At ten a.m. on the dot, Israel comes to a standstill
for two minutes as Yom HaShoah, Holocaust Day, is
solemnly commemorated. At Auschwitz the March of the
Living is held, and the Israeli deputy prime minister taking part in it compares Iran's political line
to that of Nazi Germany. Iranian public prosecutors
announce that they will demand the death penalty for
those caught producing pornographic Internet sites.
In Belarus the ice-hockey trainer whose club dared
to win against Alexander Lukashenko's team loses his
job — undefeated until now in the national championships, the president's team has only ever been
thrashed by the Russians. Poland's MPs receive a
government report on preparations for the Euro 2012
UEFA football championships (it's not bad), the tax
department refuses to allow cohabiting parents to be
accounted for as a couple, and the Wrocław firewomen
are complaining that they can't go on operations because there are no ladies' changing rooms. It turns
out communal changing rooms don't bother them, even
less their male colleagues. The weather is the same
as yesterday — sunny but cold.

"Anyway, I'll quote it to you, it has just been published in *Your Weekend*: 'Broad-minded female, 30, seeks gentleman or gentlemen, 55 to 65, interested in erotic experiments, with no strings attached, but with plenty of tying up.' And a sort of semicolon face to say it's funny. 'French without, chocolate starfish, two-hole snooker, bondage and a touch of pretend violence.' And again a sort of face with a winking eye. And my phone number. You can imagine what happens when it says in this sort of paper there's a woman looking for an over-the-hill bloke for erotic games, right? Half Poland calls. And the other half sends a text – look, here's an advert from the Internet two weeks ago: 'I like to talk dirty in texts, I'm bored out here in the country, I want a few dreams to wet my hasslebag…'"

"Hasslebag?"

"That's what they say in the borderlands for, well, you know what for. But that's not all. 'Write, I'll be sure to write back, and maybe I'll even send a text, lags welcome.' Of course, you know what lags are?"

"I'm a prosecutor."

"Well, quite. Then for two days solid, every fifteen minutes I get a message that's a vulgar summary of a porn flick, and what's more it's all so boring – I can't think why every other con has to write about sticking it through the bars. Have they got some sort of standard version? Is that the fashion? And don't tell me to change the number – I've spent a fortune doing that, and not a week goes by before the same thing happens again. But I'm in trade, I can't do without a phone, I've got customers, wholesalers. As it is, it's getting worse and worse, people keep complaining that they can't get in touch, but how can they if I've got a new number every week? I thought it would pass, but it hasn't. So I'd like officially to report a crime, I mean a suspected crime, and I hope that slag who goes with other people's husbands ends up serving time."

Prosecutor Teodor Szacki had a soft spot for ladies of the Communist-era queen-of-the-bazaar type who spoke too fast and were too expressive, maybe because they reminded him of his mother, and he knew that behind all those words, curls, rings and fluffy suits – always adorned with an amber brooch – there usually lay a heart of gold and an innate inability to do anyone harm. He felt all the more sorry that he had no good news for Mrs Zgorzelska, sitting on the other side of his desk.

"Firstly, you have to take this matter to the police – it comes under the Code of Misdemeanours, and even if I take down your report the police will deal with it anyway, so there's no point increasing the paperwork."

"Misdemeanour! That's a good one. And what about the fact that my sons' schoolmates always find out about it by some strange chance? And that my customers smile strangely, too? I've already reached the point where I'd rather they hit me, attacked me or something, and it was off my plate. But it's impossible to live like this. What's the maximum she could get for it?"

"If it's possible to prove she did it, one and a half."

"Years?"

"Thousand zlotys fine."

"What?"

"I'm sorry. There's been some talk about changing the rules to include stalking under the Penal Code and introduce a sensible deterrent, probably two or three years. But for now there's just paragraph 107 of the Code of Misdemeanours, which mentions malicious harassment."

Mrs Zgorzelska was shattered.

"But she's loaded with money. One and a half thousand? She'll pay up and send me a fax confirming the transfer. And what if it doesn't stop? Another one and a half thousand?"

Szacki gave a confirming nod. It wasn't the first time, when talking to injured parties, that he'd had to feel ashamed of the Polish legal solutions. Out-of-date, convoluted regulations that couldn't keep up with the times and were either curiously mild, de facto removing criminal liability from the culprit, or – the result of two decades of populist governments – absurdly punitive, causing the prisons in Poland to be full of people who shouldn't be in there, after taking part in drunken brawls where nothing had happened to anyone, simply because a penknife with a beer-bottle opener qualified as a dangerous instrument.

"But if she's punished for the same thing a second time, the judge can slap a sentence on her. From five to thirty days. It doesn't seem much, but I don't think your…" – he bit his tongue, he'd very nearly said "competitor" – "persecutor would be quite so desperate. Besides, after the first sentence you can sue her for the losses, but that means going to a lawyer."

"Sue someone in Poland," snorted Mrs Zgorzelska. "I'm almost fifty, I might not live to see the first hearing."

What could he say? That the most sensible thing to do was to hire someone to put the frighteners on the woman? He smiled apologetically and gave her a meaningful look. In actual fact this conversation shouldn't have been happening at all. As chance would have it, when he got to the office before seven, hoping to be early enough to avoid the journalists and use the time to review the case documents again, Zofia Zgorzelska was waiting on the steps. She was so frazzled and frozen that he didn't have the heart to send her away – he was clearly getting soft in his old age.

He got up, wanting to say goodbye, and just at that moment, the door opened abruptly without a knock, and there stood Basia Sobieraj, out of breath, still in her hat and scarf, her face flushed. She looked charming. It occurred to Szacki that with her heart problems she shouldn't run. And that he very much didn't want to hear whatever she had to tell him. It couldn't be good news.

II

The worst thing was the antlers. During his previous visit they had just seemed tacky, a typical small-town ornament – he'd seen them all over the place here. Now every wild boar's head and every deer's skull seemed to be laughing at him. Cool as a cucumber on the outside, inwardly he was seething with the desire to destroy, to seize the poker and smash it all to smithereens. So badly that his fingers were itching.

224

"She's seventy years old, why on earth should we have any doubts, Mr Prosecutor? This isn't Warsaw, people are friendly here, they help each other," repeated the policeman.

Small and slight, with a big nose, he looked like a comic-book kike. Szacki half-closed his eyes, to avoid seeing him. He was afraid that if he took just one more look at that red snout and those apologetic eyes he wouldn't be able to stop himself from attacking the man. The whole thing was like a bad dream. Two police officers had driven Jerzy Szyller home last night, parked outside his gate and got ready for all-night guard duty. Just after that, at about eleven, Szyller's neighbour, a lady with the strange Greek name of Potelos, had brought the policemen a thermos of coffee. She did that every day, because she had a kind heart and knew it was a thankless job – her son was a policeman in Rzeszów. She had given them the coffee, chatted for a while, droned on about her ailments and left, wishing them goodnight. Those words were prophetic – just one mug of coffee and the policemen had fallen into a very deep sleep, from which they had only woken up at seven a.m., so frozen to the marrow that the doctor said they had frostbitten ears, noses and fingers – which incidentally said a lot about the nature of the spring in the Year of Our Lord 2009.

"Is it possible that Szyller met up with her? That he went to her house and drugged the coffee?"

"No way. We had him under observation the whole time, we took it in turns to walk around the property. We only dragged him out to go to over to Sucha Street, where we met up with you, Mr Prosecutor. And then she came by, a short time after the door had closed behind him."

Something creaked behind Szacki. It was Wilczur.

"She didn't see anything, she doesn't know anything, she's in a panic. There are no signs of a break-in, but she isn't sure if all the doors and windows were locked either. We've sent the thermos and the coffee tin for analysis. I'd bet on the thermos – the lady says she wondered why it was standing on the tabletop, not on the draining board. But at that age, as you know, a person only wonders for a moment."

Szacki nodded to say he'd taken that on board. What pissed him off the most was that there wasn't even anyone to yell at. They had never had enough on Szyller to press charges and lock him up, and actually it was a courtesy on his part that he had agreed to stay indoors – any court would have overturned the decision to place him under house arrest in five minutes flat. And the fact that the cops had accepted coffee from the old lady next door, whom they knew well? So what if they had – he'd have accepted it too. The worst thing was not knowing what happened next. Had he run off? Had someone abducted him? He realized that in actual fact he was furious with himself. Maybe if he had thought quicker, put two and two together better, if he'd been able to notice something that he must already have seen, but the significance of which he had failed to understand – maybe, maybe, maybe.

"There's no sign of a fight," he said.

"None," muttered Wilczur. "Either he walked out, or he was carried out."

"I thought of that. Send the bottles from the minibar and the glass that was on the piano to be checked. Maybe they put something in his drink too. And left prints as well. That would make a nice change."

"Arrest warrant?"

"Out of the question, I've had enough humiliations for one case already. I don't want to find out in a while that the next main suspect is hanging on a hook somewhere. Send an announcement to the media to say we're looking for an important witness in the case, and we'll stick to that version. A witness, an important witness."

Basia emerged from Szyller's kitchen and stood next to them.

"Well?" she asked. "Do you think this is the next in a series? In theory it's the same style. The victims disappear from home without a trace, and a couple of days later they turn up drained of their blood."

"Take that back, this one hasn't turned up yet. Keep your fingers crossed for Szyller to be found alive, confess all, and for us to have it off our plates."

Click. Once again something clicked into place in his mind. Was it something he had said, or Sobieraj?

"But you're right, I thought of that. Only how can it be that Budnik evaporated in the Old Town area right under the policemen's noses, but here someone had to go to the trouble of knocking them out? Even though theoretically it's easier to vanish from here, through the courtyard, and on across the park."

"Someone didn't want to risk it."

"But earlier on he did? Why should abducting Budnik be less risky than abducting Szyller? Something's wrong here."

Sobieraj shrugged and sat down on the sofa. She looked pale.

"I feel a bit faint, but I should go and see my father in hospital," she said quietly.

"Here in Sandomierz?" he said in surprise.

"Yes, I feel awful – lately I've been there to see dead bodies more often than to visit him. But it's all because of him I ended up here," she sighed, and reached for a bowl of crispy snacks standing on the table. Szacki's gaze automatically followed her hand; her nail polish was a funny colour, very dark pink.

"Stop!" he bellowed.

She withdrew her hand and looked at him in horror. Without a word, Szacki pointed at the bowl, from which seconds before she had been about to help herself. There weren't any crisps in it, or salt sticks, poppy-seed pretzels, crackers, or corn puffs. There were – what else could there be? – some broken pieces of matzo, perforated and browned on the bumps in the usual way.

"Bloody joker," he muttered. "Strange he didn't pour ketchup over it – he must have been in a hurry."

They all leant over the wooden snack bowl as if were a sort of ritual vessel.

"What's the origin of the matzo, anyway?" asked one of the policemen.

"When they fled from Egypt, they had no time to wait for the dough to rise," explained Wilczur in his sepulchral voice, "so they had to bake some provisions quickly, and the result was matzos."

Something clicked in Szacki's head, and this time it was loud enough for him to understand what he should do.

"Put off your visit to your father," he said quickly to Sobieraj, "and do a thorough search here – this time it's not a mouldy old ruin, have them collect trace evidence, and get the matzos to the lab as fast as possible of course. I've got to fly."

"What? Where? Where are you going?" Sobieraj stood up, alarmed by his haste.

"To the church!" shouted Szacki and ran out.

Basia Sobieraj and Inspector Leon Wilczur exchanged surprised looks. Moments later she sat down, and he shrugged and tore the filter from a cigarette. He looked round for a while, trying to find a waste bin or an ashtray, and finally put the filter in his pocket.

III

These days the Cathedral of the Nativity of the Blessed Virgin Mary in Sandomierz was like a besieged fortress. There were journalists hanging around the railings, and access to the building was guarded by members of the clergy, trusted laymen and some hastily prepared signs saying "No photography", "No recording", "Do not disturb the peace of God's House" and "No entrance outside the hours of mass". Szacki went inside, taking advantage of the fact that a pensioners' excursion group was just emerging. He was ready to explain, and had even taken his ID card from his jacket pocket, but he wasn't bothered by anyone. Maybe they've recognized me as one of them, the fearless sheriff who doesn't kowtow to Jews, he thought grumpily as he walked through the portal. He stopped in the side nave, waiting for his eyes to get used to the gloom.

He was alone. Well, almost alone. A monotonous shuffling noise told him his old friends from his last visit were still there. Indeed, from behind a column separating him from the central nave the sad man emerged, and started to wash the floor; soon a wet trail separated him from the west wall of the church, where the vestibule, the organ gallery and the fine organ were located, and underneath it the none-too-lovely paintings by that eighteenth-century dauber and horror fan, Charles de Prévôt. Including the one shamefully shielded by a dark red drape. Szacki strode decisively in that direction. The sad man stopped shuffling and stared at him with an empty gaze.

"Not on the wet," he warned, the only effect of which was that Szacki waved a hand and stepped onto the wet floor without slowing down at all. He kept going, as defiant as the sheriff in a Western, except that he slipped, staggered, and had a hard time keeping his balance by desperately waving his arms about. He was only saved by grabbing the feet of a cherub on a column.

"I said not on the wet," the man repeated wearily, as if he had witnessed this scene hundreds of times before.

Szacki didn't answer, walked up to the drape, detached the portrait of John Paul II and set it against the wall.

"Hello, what are you doing? That's not allowed!" the man yelled. "Go and fetch the canon, Żasmina, there are hooligans in here again."

"Teodor Szacki, Sandomierz district prosecution service, I'm acting in the name of the law," cried Szacki, showing his ID to the man running towards him. And at the same time thinking that if he'd had a thousand guesses what the mournful woman washing the cathedral floor was called, he still wouldn't have got it right.

The man stopped, unsure how to treat the intruder. But also noticeably curious to see what would happen. Meanwhile Szacki had got a grip on the plush curtain, and yanked at it with all his might. Most of the curtain hooks gave way, the curtain breathed its last gasp in the form of a cloud of dust, and fell. Sunlight breaking through a high window landed on the storm cloud and changed it into a dazzling swirl of shining particles, through which nothing could be seen. Szacki blinked and took two steps backwards to get a better view of the enormous painting.

After all the stories, he had been expecting an impact– naturalistic slaughter, strong colours and definite shapes; sub-consciously he was waiting for the old superstition to come alive before his eyes, as if instead of an old canvas he was going to see a cinema screen, and on the screen a film, not so much about ritual murder, as about modern events. As if something would twitch, something would happen, and the solution to the whole conundrum would appear. Meanwhile there was an old canvas – well, it just looked like an old canvas, gone black, with cracked varnish, which the sunlight was bouncing off, so it was hard to make out the individual shapes.

The mournful floor cleaner must have been standing at a better angle.

"God Almighty," he whispered, and crossed himself vigorously.

Szacki moved in his direction, and instead of crossing himself reached for his phone and called Sobieraj.

"I'm in the cathedral. Tell Wilczur I need two officers here right away for security, the technicians as soon as they're done at Szyller's, and you and that wrinkled old dog as soon as possible… Never mind, it's a waste of time talking – just get over here."

He rang off and took a photograph of the painting with his mobile. Now that his eyes had learnt to pick the less black shapes out of the sea of darkness, he could compare the original with the reproductions. In this particular instance the size was significant. He had looked at reproductions in books or on a small laptop screen, but here the representation of ritual murder was about ten square metres, as big as a small room in a flat. At first glance it looked as if this painting had come out best for de Prévôt in terms of artistry and composition, though in narrative terms it was still true to the cartoon style of the tales about martyrdom. Szacki recognized the individual stages of the legend about the blood ritual. On the right, two Jews were busy getting supplies. One, clearly the richer, in a hat and coat, was offering to buy an infant from its mother. The other was enticing a little boy with something that might have been a sweet, or maybe a toy, while at the same time grabbing hold of him by the jaw with the gesture of a buyer at a slave market. On the other side, the Jews were busy putting to death or torturing (or both at once) a child laid on a sheet. And the central area of the composition was occupied by a barrel of course – two Jews were holding a barrel bristling with nails like teeth, resembling the open maw of a fantastical sea creature, with an infant's chubby legs sticking out of it. The dripping blood was being collected in a bowl by the ecstatic owner of a huge beak of a nose. De Prévôt wouldn't have been himself if in presenting this macabre scene he had not gone a step too far. There were some babies' corpses lying about on the ground, and the horrendous image of a small body being torn apart by a dog. There was a ripped-off leg protruding from the animal's mouth, and a second leg, some arms and a head were lying there for afters – all in separate pieces.

But Szacki hadn't taken the photo in order to have this moving work of art about his person forever. He took it because scrawled in red paint across the painting there was a Hebrew inscription:

$$עין תחת עין$$

The rusty letters shone in the sunlight like crimson neon, making a ghoulish impression; Szacki wasn't surprised by the mournful cleaner's reaction, but it also occurred to him that it was the typical reflex of a Catholic at the sight of Hebrew letters – to treat them as if they were going to come down from the painting, stride across the nave and put Our Lord Jesus Christ to death all over again, amen.

Moments later Sobieraj and Wilczur appeared, at the same time as the canon and the curate, whom Żasmina had gone to fetch. They were an astonishing couple. On hearing about the canon and the curate, Szacki had been expecting comedy characters, a tubby fellow and a young chap with sticking-out red ears. But here before him stood the spitting images of Sean Connery and Christopher Lambert, as if they had just stepped off the set of *Highlander* – both devilishly handsome.

After a brief fuss, all those present made it clear to each other that it was in everybody's interests to keep their mouths shut, and that was the only way to keep the situation calm. The investigators got on with the investigation, and the priests charged themselves with the duty of protecting the house of God, which allowed them to assume the role of spectators with impunity. They were not entirely placated, but they were less worried about the presence of the police and the prosecutors than about the prospect of a visit from the bishop, who was rushing to his cathedral from Kielce at breakneck speed, and was apparently very, very unhappy. And as he had a well-earned reputation as a hothead, they might find today's tribulations were still ahead of them.

"If it's not paint, but blood, we must check if it's human, do some DNA tests, compare it with the victims' blood and with Szyller's. Apart from that, every centimetre of the area around the picture will have to be screened. The inscription is high up, so whoever did it must have had to put up a ladder, get under the curtain, lean against it and hang up a bucket. That would give dozens of opportunities to leave evidence, and I must have that evidence. Even if it seems worth bugger all to us now, later on in court it might be worth its weight in gold as a small link in the chain of circumstantial evidence. So if any technician starts whining that it's pointless, tell him to get on with it."

Sobieraj gave him an acid look.

"Excuse me, but do you take me for a junior?"

"I'm just warning you that if some Kasia or whatever comes along who was at primary school with you, and starts insisting she's got to take her child to the doctor and isn't needed any more, because it's just a detail, then you'll tell her she's got to stay here until late and photograph everything, even if she's never going to speak to you again. Got it?"

"Don't teach me…"

"Thirty-nine."

"My age has nothing to do…"

"I've conducted thirty-nine murder cases, and twenty-five of them ended with a conviction. And I'm not asking you now, Basia. I'm giving orders. The prosecution service is a hierarchical institution, not a shining example of democracy."

Her eyes darkened, but she didn't say anything, she just nodded. Behind her Wilczur stood motionless, leaning against a confessional. The curate watched the scene with delight; evidently he knew Dan Brown not just from theory as Satan in a writer's skin, but had also devoted several evenings to a thorough study of his enemy. He cleared his throat.

"The first and third words are exactly the same. It must be some sort of code," he said quietly.

"I even know what sort," barked Szacki. "It's called an alphabet. Do you know Hebrew, Father?" he asked the canon without much hope, convinced that in reply the priest would cross himself and start performing an exorcism.

"I can read it. The first and third word is '*ein*', and the middle one is '*tehet*' or '*tahat*'. Unfortunately I don't know what they mean. '*Ein*' might be one, like the German, but then it would be Yiddish, not Hebrew." He must have noticed Szacki's look of amazement, because he added cuttingly: "Yes, we had Bible studies with elements of Hebrew at the seminary. But I didn't always pay attention – it was the first class of the day and we were usually tired in the mornings after the pogroms."

"I'm sorry," said Szacki after a pause. He genuinely felt bad – he realized that by responding to a stereotype with a stereotype he was behaving no differently from the drunken neo-fascists whom he had had arrested the night before. "I'm very sorry. And thank you for your help."

The priest nodded, and something clicked in Szacki's mind. It was starting to be unbearable – if those empty clicks didn't stop he'd have to consult a neurologist. What could it be about this time? The pogroms? The seminary? Bible studies? Or maybe he'd seen something out of the corner of his eye? Maybe his brain had made a note of something important that had eluded his conscious mind? He took a good look around the interior of the church.

"Teo..." Sobieraj began, but he silenced her with a gesture.

He noticed something that drew his gaze in one of the side chapels. It was a picture of Christ the Merciful, the same as everywhere, a copy of the one based on the vision of Sister Faustyna. Around the picture there were some votive offerings, and underneath it a quotation from the Gospels: "This is My commandment, that you love one another as I have loved you. J 15,12."

Click.

What's it about? Christ? Faustyna? The quotation? Mercy? That was just what was lacking in this case. Perhaps it was to do with John the Evangelist? The ladies in the shop had been talking about a Bible contest and he'd felt a click then too. Except that he'd had his head full

233

of Hitler and George Michael. God, how did that sound – sometimes he was ashamed of his own thoughts. Concentrate! A Bible contest – click. John the Evangelist – click. The seminary – click.

He tried linking these facts together, while staring non-stop at the picture.

Click.

He was a hair's breadth away from swearing as loud as he could bellow. How the hell could he have been so dumb?

"I need a copy of the Bible. Immediately!" he barked at the curate, who without waiting for the priest's permission, set off at a run towards the sacristy; his cassock fluttered in a cinematic way.

"Which books of the Bible can you think of that start with the letter K?" he asked the priest.

"There's no single letter K denoting a book in the Polish Bible," replied the canon after a moment's thought. "But the ones that start with a K are *Kapłańska* – Leviticus, *Królewskie* – Kings, and *Koheleta* – Ecclesiastes. In the New Testament we have the two letters to the *Koryntian* – Corinthians, and one to the *Kolosan* – Colossians. I think that's it, though in Latin nothing starts with a K – but with a C we have the *Canticum Canticorum*, in other words the Song of Songs in the Old Testament as well."

The curate had made the journey to the sacristy and back again like a seasoned sprinter, and had trouble coming to a halt before the small group assembled beneath the representation of ritual murder, wielding a vast A3-sized book bound in leather and adorned with metal fittings and gilding.

"Have you gone mad?" asked the canon. "Couldn't you bring an ordinary one from the bookshelf?"

"I wanted everyone to be able to see properly," panted the curate, though it was clear to all that he didn't find a plain blue Millennium Bible suitable for such a grand moment worthy of Dan Brown.

"Let's start with *Kapłańska* – Leviticus," said Szacki. "That's part of the Pentateuch, the Torah, right?"

"That's right," confirmed the canon.

"Chapter twenty-four, verses nineteen to twenty-five."

"Oh, of course… K-W-P," groaned Sobieraj from the back.

The curate found the right place, helping himself with a knee, and respectfully offered it to the priest to read out.

"If a man causes disfigurement of his neighbour, as he has done, so shall it be done to him – fracture for fracture, eye for eye, tooth for tooth; as he has caused disfigurement of a man, so shall it be done to him. And whoever kills an animal shall restore it; but whoever kills a man shall be put to death."

The canon had a deep, resonant voice, and uttered the words slowly, with the respect due to the Holy Scripture. They sounded ominous in the silence of the church, reverberating against the ancient stones and bouncing off the walls and vaulted ceiling, filling Sandomierz cathedral with sound and meaning. No one twitched a muscle until the distant echoes had fallen completely silent.

"Now for a book that starts with W – *Wyjścia*, or Exodus, chapter twenty-one, verses twenty-two to twenty-five," said Szacki.

The curate rustled the pages.

"If men fight, and hurt a woman with child, so that she gives birth prematurely, yet no harm follows, he shall surely be punished accordingly as the woman's husband imposes on him; and he shall pay as the judges determine. But if any harm follows, then you shall give life for life, eye for eye, tooth for tooth, hand for hand, foot for foot, burn for burn, wound for wound, stripe for stripe."

"And a book starting with P – I think it'll be *Prawa* – Deuteronomy, yes?"

"*Powtórzonego Prawa*," Wilczur corrected him from behind. Szacki shuddered; the voice just behind his back gave him a shock. And he was surprised, but only a little.

"Yes, of course. Chapter nineteen, verses sixteen to twenty-one."

More rustling. And a flush on the curate's face – he looked as if he was burning, filled with determination to cast off his cassock and swap it for Indiana Jones's jacket and hat.

"If a false witness rises against any man to testify against him of wrongdoing, then both men in the controversy shall stand before the Lord, before the priests and the judges who serve in those days. And the judges shall make careful inquiry, and indeed, if the witness is a false witness, who has testified falsely against his brother, then you shall do to him as he thought to have done to his brother; so you shall put away the evil from among you. And those who remain shall hear and fear, and hereafter they shall not again commit such evil among you. Your eye shall not pity: life shall be for life, eye for eye, tooth for tooth, hand for hand, foot for foot."

The priest read out the final sentence without looking at the pages of the Bible, but instead he cast his eyes over the faces of his audience, and finally suspended his questioning gaze on Szacki.

"That is all. It looks as if the meaning of the Hebrew inscription has been explained."

"Surely," remarked Sobieraj. "Our mysterious KWP has also been explained."

"Yeees," drawled Szacki. "But why aren't they in order? Strange."

"But what's strange?"

"The quotations aren't in order," replied the curate quickly, so no one would beat him to it. "In the Pentateuch first there's the Book of Genesis, then Exodus, Leviticus, Numbers and Deuteronomy."

"So it should be WKP? *Wyjścia* – Exodus, *Kapłańska* – Leviticus, and then *Powtórzonego Prawa* – Deuteronomy. Why have the letters been swapped?"

"I have no idea," replied Szacki. "But I'll find out. I must find a rabbi."

Basia Sobieraj glanced at her watch.

"You've got to be at the prosecutor's office in five minutes. You're interviewing Magiera – they've brought him in from Kielce specially."

Prosecutor Teodor Szacki swore hideously. Wilczur snorted with laughter, the canon gave him a reproachful look that was full of understanding, and the curate was delighted.

IV

SUSPECT INTERVIEW TRANSCRIPT. Sebastian Magiera, born 20th April 1987, resident at 15a Topolowa Street, Zawichost, currently de-

tained at Kielce custody centre. Education secondary technical, unemployed before arrest, occasionally employed as a gardener. Relation to parties: victim's son. No criminal record, informed of a suspect's obligations and rights, his statement is as follows:

I would like to change the statement made several times previously in the course of proceedings and to admit that on 1st November 2008 I unintentionally killed my father, Stefan Magiera, at his home, 15a Topolowa Street, Zawichost. I did it in an emotional state and in the heat of an argument, and I did not intend to deprive my father of his life. The cause of the argument was the fact that, despite repeated promises, my father refused to provide me, my wife Anna and our three-year-old son Tadek with accommodation at his house, which he inhabited alone, or to let us use a family plot of land which was lying fallow. This fact was having an extremely negative effect on our living conditions.

I met my wife at horticultural college in Sandomierz five years ago. At the time I was living alone with my father in Zawichost. I would like to mention that my father, a former athlete, was always abusing alcohol and was aggressive. Anna and I fell in love, and when she became pregnant, which was before we got married, I asked my father if she could come and live with us, because there was no room for us at her parents' flat in Klimontów. My drunken father insulted me and Anna, refused to let us live at his house and threw me out. To begin with, in spite of all we lived with Anna's parents, but once Tadek was born, we rented a room in Klimontów. Our situation was very bad and we didn't have any money. I had occasional work as a gardener, but I wasn't earning much. Once Tadek had grown a bit, Anna looked for work too, but without success. Throughout this time I kept trying to talk to my father, asking him to let us have at least one room, but he was unyielding, even after we got married in 2007, and continuously maligned me and my wife. We had problems because the benefits weren't enough to live on, especially when it turned out Tadek was suffering from asthma and needed expensive medicine. So we moved from the room in Klimontów into the welfare huts in Kruków, Sandomierz. The conditions there were not good. My wife Anna is very pretty and in 2007 she found a job as a model. She started travelling around Poland to do fashion shows, and I took care of the child. And I kept talking to my father, the whole time to no effect. My father kept repeating that he'd managed to win a bronze medal at the Munich Olympics through his own hard and persistent effort, and that I should follow his example.

Anna's job turned out to be unsatisfactory because the work as a model required some stripping. At first she modelled underwear at discos, then performances were added, such as wrestling in jelly and boxing with other girls. For her and for me it was very humiliating. At first she used to tell me about the other girls, about her female boss, who was unpleasant and aggressive, and about the woman's husband, who treated the employees disrespectfully and tried to exploit them. Then she stopped telling me, and I didn't ask, because I thought it was painful for her and she didn't want to talk about it. Besides which I felt ashamed, because I should have been the one supporting the family. That was an awful time, so I went to my father with the child and started begging him, and insisting that it was our last hope, that the land was just lying fallow, and he wasn't even getting any grants for it, nothing. And it wasn't just about grants, it could be cultivated, I could grow things there, I've always had a flair for that. And my father took pity and said all right, we could live with him, and he'd transfer the land to me, he didn't need it, because his pension was enough for him. He said we'd sort out all the formalities by the end of the year, and we could move in from 1st January. It was the summer of 2008 when we had that conversation. I admit that apart from my wedding day and the day Tadek was born, that was the happiest day of my life.

It was mainly me who took care of the preparations, because Anna was travelling to shows, and I admit that our relationship was deteriorating at the time. Not because we argued, but we didn't talk much. Now I think she held it against me that she had to do that job, but we had no alternative – we were spending up to three hundred zlotys a month on medicine. Nevertheless, I managed to borrow a bit from people too, to buy some gardening tools for the land. Things were even good with my father then too, we planned what I'd do together, I spent time at his place and he showed Tadek his discus, but it was still too heavy, the kid couldn't even hold it up. I was afraid my father would get upset, but *he just laughed and said it was nothing, never mind, he'd grow into it eventually.*

On All Saints' Day 2008, the three of us went to Zawichost to visit the family graves, and to see my father of course; I was a bit worried about the meeting, because since the arguments in the past Anna had hardly seen him at all. But it was nice, we had something to eat, we chatted and had a drink, but not much. I did most of the talking, saying what would happen with the land, but my father didn't pick up on the topic at all. He just switched on some music on the radio and said now Anna could show him how she danced as a model and how she did a display. She didn't want to, and I got upset and said it was out of the question. To which he, and I quote, said: "Since that tart gets undressed in front of everyone, she can do it in front of me too." And he said if she didn't do a dance for him, there'd be no home and no land, and I could go and play with my rakes with Tadek in the sandpit. And he started to laugh, and I realized it had all been lies – he had never really wanted to give us a place to live, or a piece of land, or to help me, or anything at all. Somewhere he had found out about Anna, and had just thought it all up to humiliate and degrade us, there was no truth in it at all.

And then I saw that Anna was starting to undress, doing it with such indifferent, mechanical movements. And my father was laughing even louder, saying he'd seen through her when we were still at college, but I had refused to believe him, so why didn't I look now, this lesson was entirely for free, worth more than the house and the land, because maybe I'd finally wise up. And at that moment I felt nothing mattered any more – not the future, nor my wife, nor the medicine for Tadek – and this red mist came down before my eyes, and I took that discus from Munich off the shelf and struck my father on the head with it, and then I hit him a few more times as he lay there.

In my defence I would like to add that I acted under the influence of shock, mental pain and strong emotions.

Prosecutor Teodor Szacki gazed at the heap of misfortune sitting in front of him. The boy was small and fair-haired. With large eyes and long black eyelashes, he looked like the ideal altar boy. He glanced at the text of his statement on the computer screen. He didn't let it show, but he was feeling the weight of responsibility – the fate of this boy and his family depended on him. And the point here was not how to classify the crime. It was evidently homicide, and even if an expert were to take pity and acknowledge extreme agitation, he'd still get a sentence from the higher end of paragraph four, which covered manslaughter: probably about eight years. The point was whether Szacki believed his tale or not.

"Where is your wife living now?" he asked.

"Well, after probate I inherited the house and the land, and she and our son are living there. Apparently she's even done well, my cousin wrote to say."

"Out of what?"

"She finally made the application to the Union for a land subsidy – there are people at the local administration who fill in the documents. Plus benefits. If I were already in prison, and not custody, I'd be able to earn some more, and send it."

Magiera gave him a beseeching look. He was squirming on his chair; he didn't know what the prosecutor's silence meant. Meanwhile the prosecutor's silence meant that he was trying to remember all the similar cases from the past. He couldn't remember exactly when he had first placed himself above the Legal Code for some higher good, trusting more to his own judgement than a merciless piece of legislation. Maybe there were mistakes in it, maybe it was unfair, but it was the cornerstone of law and order in the Polish Republic. The moment he realized he was slipping in between its paragraphs should be the moment he ceased to be a prosecutor.

He had a choice of two options. The first option was to buy Magiera's version of events and charge him with manslaughter, which would mean an easy defence of arguments set out in the case file in court. The defendant admits it, his wife confirms his version, there are no witnesses, there is no other relative of the father's or private plaintiff, and of course there is no appeal. He'd serve a few years and go back to Zawichost, where his wife would be waiting for him. Szacki had no doubt about that.

The second option meant, as it is termed, "establishing the material truth". Which in this case meant accusing both Magiera and also his wife of homicide as defined by paragraph one, in other words murder, and sentences from fifteen years and higher for both of them, while Tadek would be sent to a children's home. Both of them had left fingerprints on the discus. Neither of them had alcohol in their blood. By some odd chance the child had ended up at a neighbour's house two streets away before the killing happened. From the autopsy it appeared that Magiera Senior had died an hour and a half before the ambulance was called – they wanted to be sure he couldn't be saved.

But everything the cherubic little gardener had said about his life with Anna and his relationship with his father was true too – witnesses had confirmed it. Even the notary had testified that it was utterly despicable how the old man had come to see him as if he wanted to discuss the issue of the land, but really to make a fool of his son and his tart of a wife. And managing to disgust a notary is quite an achievement.

Magiera went on squirming, sweating and making pleading faces. Szacki was turning a coin in his hand, but there was only one thought in his head: the truth, or half the truth?

V

"There's a Jewish saying: half the truth is a whole lie," said Rabbi Zygmunt Maciejewski, as he raised a toast with kosher wine. It was delicious, but unfortunately Szacki couldn't drink a drop more if he didn't want to stay overnight in Lublin.

A few hours earlier, as he had travelled the narrow, potholed road from Sandomierz to Lublin, he hadn't placed much hope in the meeting ahead of him. He wanted to have a chat with someone who knew Jewish culture, to get some background information that, even if it didn't lead to a breakthrough, might help him at a critical moment not to overlook a piece of evidence left by their madman. And to understand whether this bizarre game had a subtext, a hidden meaning that he couldn't perceive because he lacked the knowledge.

Although he hadn't really thought about it, as he knocked at the door of a flat in the centre of Lublin he was expecting to see an amiable old man with a pointed nose and a white beard gazing with wise benevolence from behind half-moon spectacles. A sort of cross between Albus Dumbledore and Ben Kingsley. Meanwhile, the door was opened by a stocky man in a polo shirt, not unlike a hood from the Warsaw suburbs, looking equally intelligent and dangerous. Rabbi Zygmunt Maciejewski was about thirty-five and looked like the former boxer Jerzy Kulej – not Kulej now that he was old and an MP, but the Kulej of the black-and-white photographs in the days when he won Olympic gold medals. A triangular face with a sharply drawn chin, the pugnacious grin of a thug, the flat nose of a boxer, and above it deep-set, alert, pale eyes. And a receding hairline cutting into shortly-cropped black curls.

Prosecutor Teodor Szacki carefully hid his surprise at the Jewish teacher's appearance, but inside the flat he couldn't hold back, and must have made an astonished face at the sight of its decor, because the young rabbi snorted with laughter. The fact that the sitting room was crammed with shelves full of books in several languages was not unexpected. But that in between the symmetrically positioned bookcases the walls were covered in posters of life-sized beauty queens in bathing costumes seemed to him strange. Szacki was curious to know what lay behind the choice – they didn't seem to be Jewish girls, because only one of them, with a torrent of jet-black curls tied in a pony tail, looked like an Israeli army officer. He glanced enquiringly at Maciejewski.

"Miss Israels for the past ten years," explained the rabbi. "I put them up because I realized you have to provide other evidence besides Jewish jokes, Sabbath candles, haggling in gaberdines and violin recitals on the roof."

"Those Ukrainian models too?" asked Szacki, pointing at the slender blondes showing their curves in several of the posters.

"Did you think they all looked like Dustin Hoffman in *Tootsie*? In that case, come to Israel. But say a tender farewell to your wife before you leave. I'm probably not very objective, but I've never known sexier women. And that's a lot coming from someone who lives in a Polish university city."

The rabbi had a natural tendency not to keep anyone at arm's length for long, and although in Szacki's case it wasn't the norm, they were soon on first-name terms. Along the way he explained that he had inherited his Jewish descent from his Israeli mother, his first name from the great Jew Sigmund Freud and his surname from a Polish engineer, who forty years ago had gone on a four-day business trip to Haifa and never returned from there to the wife and two children he had left behind in Poznań.

"Just imagine, now I'm making friends with my half-siblings." Szacki couldn't imagine how anyone could fail to make friends with Rabbi Maciejewski who was all heart. "Even though throughout their childhood they kept being told a Jewish witch had stolen their father. I always cite it as an optimistic example, whenever someone asks me about Polish-Jewish relations. And I understand that's what we're going to talk about?"

However, they started with Sandomierz. With the murders committed in the city, which the prosecutor described in detail. With the cathedral, the old painting and the legend about ritual murder, which could in some way be the key to the case. (Though intuitively Szacki would have preferred to exclude this particular hypothesis, rather than confirm it.) With the inscription on the painting. The rabbi examined the photograph, and first of all frowned, muttering that it was strange, and that there was one thing he'd have to think about; importuned by the prosecutor, he explained that the words should be read as *"ayin tahat ayin"*, that literally they meant "an eye for an eye", and they did indeed come from the Pentateuch.

"The Christians and the Muslims often quote those passages as proof of the aggression and brutality of Judaism," explained Maciejewski, pouring the kosher wine. It was called *l'chaim* and was a decent table Cabernet. "Meanwhile this rule was never taken literally by the Jews. I don't know if you are aware that according to tradition, as well as the written Torah, Moses also received an oral tradition from God, in other words the Talmud?"

"Something like a Jewish catechism?"

"Exactly. The Talmud is the official interpretation of the Torah's written rules, which are sometimes, well, debatable. If, God forbid, I were sceptical about my faith, I would say it was a very wise move by the people of Israel – to quickly write down practical interpretations of some impractical rules, and regard them as the voice of God, except passed on during a chat. But as I am very God-fearing, we'll stick to the version that the wise God knew what to tell Moses to write down, and what to just say to him for remembrance."

"And what did he have to say on the issue of gouging out an eye?"

"He explained to Moses that only a cretin could take it literally. Here's a famous example: a person who has blinded someone in one eye is himself one-eyed. If the rule from the Torah were applied literally, as a punishment you'd have to gouge out the perpetrator's remaining eye, which would make him completely blind. Would that be a fair punishment? Of course not. And so tradition very soon explained that the point of the rule 'an eye for an eye' is fair, monetary compensation, proportional to the injury. Because in the case of losing a leg, the harm to a writer is not the same as the harm to a professional footballer. In other words, in Jewish law there was never a principle that the punishment for blinding should be blinding. Is that clear?"

"In that case, where does the belief come from?" asked Szacki.

The rabbi poured himself more wine; the prosecutor's glass was full.

"A lot of the credit for that is due to Matthew the Evangelist, who quoted Jesus as saying that once upon a time people were taught 'an eye for an eye, a tooth for a tooth', but now they're not to stand up to evil but turn the other cheek. A superstition was born out of this, which contrasts the merciful Christians with the bloodthirsty Jews. Which is even quite amusing."

"In other words, the Jews don't turn the other cheek?" asked Szacki, wondering to what extent the rabbi was open-minded, and to what extent politically correct, and whether he would send him packing when he found out he was actually testing a theory about a Jewish madman who had decided to play at ritual murders.

"No," replied Maciejewski curtly. "Rebbe Schneerson, the last Lubavitcher rabbi, was fond of saying that the best way to fight evil is to do good. But there are situations where this strategy does a poor job. There have been moments in history when we were the victims, but our mythology is not a mythology of victims. Just look at the Jewish holidays. Passover commemorates the drowning of the Egyptian army in the Red Sea. Hanukkah marks the successful Maccabbean revolt and the defeat of the invaders. Purim commemorates the fact that the massacre being planned for the Jews changed into the aggressor being put to the sword."

"And what about revenge?"

"The Torah and the Talmud are unanimous on this topic: vengeance is against the Law. You are not allowed to disseminate hatred, you are not allowed to seek revenge, you are not allowed to harbour a grudge, you should love your neighbour as yourself. The same Book of Leviticus, which your quotation comes from. But a few chapters earlier."

Szacki thought for a while.

"What about after the war? It would seem to me natural."

Rabbi Zygmunt Maciejewski stood up and switched on a lamp that was standing on the table – it was starting to get dark. In the half-light the scantily dressed beauty queens seemed more alive than before, more like real people lurking in the corners than pictures on the wall. And among them stood the young Jerzy Kulej in the role of the Lublin rabbi.

"I don't like talking about the Holocaust," he said. "I don't like the fact that eventually every conversation between Catholic Poles and Jews goes back to events from almost seventy years ago. As if there hadn't been seven hundred years of shared history before that, and everything after it. Just a sea of dead bodies and nothing else. That's why I put these models on the wall, whose presence seems surreal to me now, probably even more so to you."

Maciejewski stared out of the window, and there was nothing to imply he would continue the conversation. Szacki stood up to stretch his bones and walked over to him. A strange atmosphere prevailed in the rabbi's flat. Szacki felt his professional guard dropping, the cynicism and irony draining away. He simply wanted to talk. Maybe this resulted from the fact that for ages he had had to watch every word – in Sandomierz everyone was suspicious, and no conversation there was just a conversation. He stood beside the rabbi and felt an urge to tell him about his big dream: he had always wanted to walk about Warsaw as it once used to be, to sense and taste its diversity, to walk along streets where Polish mixed with Russian and Yiddish. He felt the need to express his nostalgia for otherness, and opened his mouth to speak, but closed it again, fearing that he would just witter on meaninglessly, because like every educated Pole he was desperately afraid of sounding like an anti-Semite. Suddenly he felt irrationally angry with himself and quickly returned to his armchair. He drank a little wine, and diluted the rest with mineral water. The pensive rabbi went on standing by the window; in profile he looked like the boxer brooding on a lost fight.

"I understand you have some reason for asking about Jewish vengeance," he said at last, coming back to the table. "To put it briefly, there wasn't really anyone to take revenge here, or anyone to take it on. Not many Jews, or Germans either once the Red Army came through. Some of the Jews, and I'm not judging anyone, I'm just stating a fact, were skewered by Polish peasants who were terrified they'd demand their property back. Some of them hadn't the slightest desire for revenge – revenge meant a risk, and a life saved by a miracle was too fragile to take any sort of risk. There were exceptions. Do the names Wiesenthal and Morel mean anything to you?"

"Wiesenthal yes, Morel no."

"Apparently during the war, here, in what was already Soviet Lublin, Simon Wiesenthal, our number one Nazi-hunter, and his comrades founded a secret organization called Nekama, meaning Revenge. I abhor revanchism, but I am capable of imagining a situation where a few survivors of the Holocaust are burning with desire for revenge to such an extent that they convoke a special organization. Perhaps it soon turned out they could operate openly, and something which came into being in Poland as Nekama later became the Historical Documentation Centre that Wiesenthal founded in Austria. Right?"

"Right," replied Szacki laconically.

"So on the one hand we have Wiesenthal," said Maciejewski, making an appropriate gesture, "and his revenge, involving hunting down Nazis. A clean solution. Then on the other hand, we are burdened by Salomon Morel. He was lucky enough to be saved from the Holocaust by a good Pole, thanks to which he could join the People's Guard, the Communist resistance, and when Wiesenthal was founding Nekama, Morel was organizing a militia for the Reds in this same city, Lublin. Later he became the commandant of the Zgoda labour camp in Upper Silesia, where the Communists detained mainly Germans and Silesians, but also Poles who were inconvenient for the regime. At this camp, established moreover at the site of a former concentration camp, almost two thousand people died, apparently as a result of Morel's deliberate neglect."

"And?" Szacki thought all this was very interesting, but it was of no help to him at all.

"And you have two faces of Jewish revenge in that era. On the one hand, Israeli officials tracking down SS-men in their Argentinean villas, and on the other, the compulsive satisfying of a base instinct for revenge. Base, but somehow understandable. Imagine you come home to your village, and there's someone living in your house who blackmailed Jews hiding during the war, and because of whose denunciation your entire family died in a camp. Your wife and children. Would you be able to restrain yourself? Forgive him? Love him as yourself?"

Szacki said nothing. He couldn't reply to that question – no one who had never been faced with such a choice could answer it.

"Do you have a family?" asked the rabbi.

"Yes, I do, I did have. Until recently."

Maciejewski looked at him closely, but didn't pass comment.

"In that case I'm sure you can imagine those emotions better than I can. For me it's an abstract, academic consideration. We only know ourselves to the extent that we have been tested."

"The Talmud?"

"No, the poet, Wisława Szymborska. It's good to get wisdom from various sources. In fact it's a quote from a poem about a woman, an ordinary teacher, who died saving four children from a fire. I like that poem and that quote, and I like the conviction that's behind those words: we never know how much good we have in us. I saw a documentary about an American Jew who went to Poland to look for his roots, and among the smashed gravestones and synagogues converted into workshops he found the peasant family who had saved his father. Then in Israel he asked the father why they'd never sent those Poles as much as a greetings card. And he got the answer: how? How do you say thank you for something like that? And the final question: in the reverse situation, would you have done the same? And the old man replied quietly: no, never."

"You're talking like an anti-Semite."

"No, I'm talking like someone who knows that history on the grand scale is a collection of little histories, each of which is different. Because in the reverse situation that old Jew might, as he says, have done nothing, but he might just as well have carried kasha to the barn to feed a fugitive, knowing his entire family could be shot at any moment. We only know ourselves to the extent that we have been tested."

Maciejewski poured himself more wine.

"I know hundreds of little stories like that," he said, sitting down again in an armchair opposite Szacki. "You know how it looks from the Polish side, all those shit-bag skinheads. But do you know how it looks from our side?"

Szacki shook his head, faintly curious to know what was coming next, but only faintly. He felt he was running out of time. That he should find something out and get back to work as soon as possible.

"It's like this – when a tour group comes here from Israel to visit the camp at Majdanek, they take their own bodyguards with them to the disco. And before they get on the coach to Warsaw airport, they have to listen to a talk on how to behave in case of an anti-Semitic attack. I was brought up in Israel, and I went on one of those tours, which mainly consisted of shocking us with the Shoah." Maciejewski pronounced this word in a guttural, sing-song way, and now Szacki realized that the strange, plucked tones he had heard from the start in his fluent Polish must be traces of Hebrew. "But not just that. It consisted to the same extent of bullshitting about omnipresent anti-Semitism, stirring up suspicions, xenophobia and the desire to retaliate. In fact, when it comes to building an identity on dead bodies we've done better than the Poles."

Despite the solemnity of the subject, Szacki burst out laughing and raised his glass.

"I'll drink to that, because if it's true" – here he paused – "you've achieved the impossible."

They clinked glasses.

"Does the abbreviation KWP mean anything to you?" asked the prosecutor, shunting the conversation onto the topics that interested him. He wanted to bring it to an end.

"No, why?"

"What about *Konspiracyjne Wojsko Polskie* – the Polish Underground Army?"

"I don't know, it rings a bell, but only a faint one. Is it something like Freedom and Independence, or the National Armed Forces?"

"Yes, exactly, they were one of the partisan groups known as the 'cursed soldiers.'"

The rabbi sighed and gazed at the dark window, as if posing for a photo session in which sportsmen pretend to be thinkers.

"Why do you ask?"

"Various clues imply that present events might be connected with it. Does it mean anything to you?"

"Yet another painful topic. The cursed soldiers fought against the Communist regime, some of them right into the 1950s. I've read about them, the whole issue has lots of overtones, over the decades all sorts of legends have grown up around it, and as is usually the case in Poland, there's no truth in them." The rabbi smiled unexpectedly. "By the way, I love your Polish characteristic of sticking to emotional extremities, either euphoria or black depression, great love or blind rage. With the Poles, nothing's ever normal. Sometimes it drives me mad, but even so, I like it – I've learnt to treat my addiction to the Polish character as a harmless vice. Anyway, that's not the point, the point is that your anti-Communist partisans are spoken about in extreme terms, too. For some people they were flawless heroes; for others they were harmful troublemakers who sought an excuse to fight and brawl; and for yet others they were bloodthirsty Jew-baiters who organized pogroms."

"Were there incidents of that kind?"

"Frankly, I don't have that much knowledge. Don't forget, these were generally right-wing units – the left wing more or less believed in the new regime. And this was the pre-war, National-Democratic right wing, streaked with anti-Semitism, especially in the case of the National Armed Forces. But remember too that since the Holocaust every act aimed against a Jew has been presented as an expression of anti-Semitism, which doesn't have to be true. The cursed soldiers fought against the state apparatus, against its functionaries, and Jews were killed in the fighting because there were a lot of them in the Communist secret police."

"I thought that was an anti-Semitic lie."

"The way facts are interpreted can be anti-Semitic, but not the facts as such. With regret, because it is not a very clear page in my nation's history, I admit that until the mid-1950s more than one third of the operatives at the Ministry of Public Security were Jews. That is a fact, and there's nothing anti-Semitic about it. Of course, presenting it as a Jewish conspiracy aimed at Poland is quite another story. Especially since most of them were common or garden Communists – they just had Jewish origins."

Szacki organized the new information in his head. He was pleased – the theory he had come here with was starting to gain flesh.

"Why quite so many?"

Maciejewski made a gesture of helplessness.

"Because any regime other than the German one seemed good to them? Because before the war, Communist ideology was already attractive to the Jewish poor? Because the regime by its nature preferred cosmopolitan Jews to patriotic Poles who disliked the Russians? Because there's just as much truth in the rumours of anti-Semitism among the Poles as there is in the ones about Jewish antipathy towards the Poles?" Suddenly the rabbi paused, and crooned sadly: "I wanted to be someone, because I was a Jew, a Jew who wasn't someone, was a no one through and through." Szacki recognized Jacek Kaczmarski's famous song about the Communist-Polish-Jew.

"Because for some people it was a means of getting revenge on their neighbours?" added Szacki.

"Right. Looking for the guilty parties is the simplest way of coping with trauma. If you point at someone who caused you harm, at once it's easier. There weren't any Germans, but the Poles were to hand. And the Reds, whispering in their ears that those National-Democrat gangs were organizing pogroms. It's no accident that the department for combating what the official terminology called 'banditry' was run by Communists of Jewish descent – the technique of inflaming and antagonizing always works well."

Szacki listened in amazement.

"I wasn't expecting to hear anything like that."

"Of course you weren't, you're oversensitive, like every educated Pole. You're afraid you only have to squeak and at once they'll fetch out the pogroms at Kielce and Jedwabne for you. That's why, unfortunately, like the rest of the world, you're incapable of making a reliable judgement. I myself am a Jewish believer and a patriot, but I regard Israel's politics as harmful. Instead of being the leader in the region, we're like a fortress inhabited by paranoiacs with a siege mentality, antagonizing nations that already hate us anyway. Presented, of course, as terrorists and Hitler's henchmen. Besides, I don't know if you've been listening to the radio today, but it's Holocaust Remembrance Day, and our deputy prime minister is at Auschwitz, exploiting it to compare Iran to Nazi Germany. It is so disheartening – some of our politicians, if they didn't drag out Hitler at every opportunity, would lose their *raison d'être*."

Szacki smiled to himself, because there was something very Polish about Maciejewski's commentator's ardour and ritual beefing about the authorities. It smacked of vodka, vegetable salad and smoked sausage laid out on a silver platter. Time to wind it up.

"Of course, you know why I'm asking about all this?"

"Because you're considering the option that it might be the work of a Jew, and you want to know if it's possible. If we were talking about someone normal, I'd say no, but anyone who has two people's blood on his hands is a madman. And with madmen anything is possible. And there's something else, too…"

"Yes?" Szacki leant forwards in his chair.

"Everything you talked about – Sandomierz, the painting, the quotes, the knife for *shechita*, the corpse in the barrel…" Maciejewski made his thoughtful boxer's gesture. "It's impossible to acquire all that knowledge in a weekend. In theory you'd simply have to be a Jew, and then one who's perfectly au fait with his culture. Or someone who studies it."

"Why in theory?" Szacki had switched on all his radars – there was something in the rabbi's tone that told him to be on high alert.

Maciejewski turned the photograph of the Hebrew inscription on the painting in the cathedral towards him and pointed at the middle letter in the middle word.

"That's *het*, the eighth letter of the Hebrew alphabet. It's written wrongly, but not so wrongly that you could explain it by dyslexia, for instance. It's the mirror image of a correctly written letter – the curve should be on the right, not the left. No Jew would write it that way, just as you'd have to be drunk or on drugs to write a B with the loops to the left. I think someone's just cunning, trying to resurrect enough demons to be able to hide among them. The question, my dear prosecutor, is whether in the crowd of phantoms and apparitions you'll be able to make out the face of the killer."

VI

The words about phantoms resonated in Szacki's head as he drove back to Sandomierz that night. As he passed the villages and towns of the Lublin region, he wondered how many of them had been Jewish shtetls before the war. How many Jews had there been in Kraśnik? In Annopol? And where had they ended up? In Majdanek, in Bełżec? Maybe some of them had lived until the death marches? An ignominious end, with no burial, no funeral rites, no one to see their souls off to the other side. If the folk beliefs were true, all those souls should be roaming the world, trapped for seventy years between dimensions. On days like this one, Yom HaShoah, could they tell they were being remembered? Did they then return to Kraśnik or Annopol, looking for familiar places, and did the Polish inhabitants glance over their shoulders, feel a chill more often than usual, and close their windows earlier?

Prosecutor Teodor Szacki felt anxious. The road was strangely empty, the dark Lublin villages looked abandoned, and from Kraśnik onwards there was fog trailing along the highway, sometimes hardly noticeable, like dirt on the windscreen, sometimes as thick as cotton wool, visibly parting before the bonnet of the Citroën. The prosecutor recognized his own apprehension by the fact that he was more focused than usual on the old car's moans and groans – a faint knocking on the left side of the suspension, a hissing from the hydraulic fluid pump and a grumble from the air-conditioning compressor. It was completely irrational, but he was eager not to have to stop right now in the fog and darkness.

He cursed and turned the steering wheel abruptly when a black figure loomed out of the fog; he only just managed to miss the hitch-hiker, who was standing almost in the middle of the road. He glanced in the rear-view mirror, but all he could see was blood-stained darkness and fog aglow with red lights. He was reminded of Wilczur's recording from outside the archive, and remembered the Jew dissolving in the thick fog above the Vistula.

To occupy his thoughts, he started mentally rewinding the conversation with Maciejewski, recalling the moments when he had felt the familiar tickling in his brain. Once when revenge for the death of a family came up, definitely. And a second time towards the end, when the rabbi had said it was impossible to acquire that sort of knowledge in a weekend. An idea had flashed through his mind at that moment, one that was valuable and not obvious. No, the point wasn't to look among experts on Jewish culture, no. Maciejewski had noticed a lot of details in Szacki's account, small points that formed a complete picture.

"And what about me?" said Szacki aloud, his hoarse voice sounding strange inside the car.

Have I noticed all the details? In this nightmare, have I failed to focus on the most visible things? When there's a corpse stuck in a barrel hanging from the ceiling, no one wonders why it has strange, deformed feet – but now it came back to his mind. When there's a naked woman lying in the bushes, and a little further off there's a butcher's razor, no one thinks about how she came to have sand under her nails. But now he remembered it – the corpse had not soil, not dirt, but yellow, seaside sand under its fingernails. How many of these details had he overlooked, how many had he regarded as unimportant? The whole incident in the cathedral, the quotation on the painting, "an eye for an eye, a tooth for a tooth" – he was following the obvious, intrusive trail of Jewish revenge. Just as the murderer wanted. Instead of acting contrary to his expectations by looking for mistakes in this whole performance, he was letting himself be led by the nose. Like the ideal spectator of an illusionist's show, who isn't looking to see what the other hand is doing, for fear of spoiling his evening's entertainment.

He was just passing through Annopol, so he only had to cross the Vistula, turn south, and in half an hour he should be there. The town was empty and wreathed in fog, despite which he felt safer in the presence of street lamps. So much so that he drove onto the hard shoulder and took out his mobile to get on the Internet. He found an online Bible, and as he was waiting for the link to load, he opened the window to combat his rising drowsiness. Cold and damp poured into the car, filling it with a strong, earthy smell of melting snow, a harbinger of spring, which was just about to burst onto the scene, eager to make up for the weeks it had lost.

Remembering the references, he found the biblical quotations. Why were they so long? It would have been enough to give the one verse containing the phrase "an eye for an eye", and the whole thing would have been clear. He wrote them all out in his notebook. The one from Leviticus was the shortest and simplest; it spoke about punishment for disfigurement and for death. "Whoever kills a man shall be put to death." Szacki was struck by the legalistic style of the phrase – paragraph 148 of the Polish Republic Penal Code started the same way: "Whoever kills a man shall be subject to a penalty of loss of liberty…"

The second quote talked about the penalty imposed for hurting a pregnant woman during a fight between men, which must have been a way of defining war or conflict. For causing a miscarriage the only punishment was a fine, but if the woman died, it was death.

Finally the third, from Deuteronomy, was the most tortuous – almost as bad as the modern Penal Code. And at the same time it was the strictest rule, aimed against bearing false witness, or – to put it in modern terms – against perjury. The Jewish legislator – which is really a strange definition of God, thought Szacki – gave orders for a perjurer to get the same punishment that would have been meted out if his lies were taken as the truth. In other words, if as the result of one man's unfair accusations, another man could have been condemned to death, and the matter came to light, then the perjurer would get the noose or whatever was used in those days. It was also curious that the severity of the regulation was dictated by the principles of deterrence. It was plainly written that "those who remain shall hear and fear, and hereafter they shall not again commit such evil among you". In a way, lying was treated as the worst crime of all.

Perhaps rightly, thought Szacki, and closed his notebook; he closed the window too, and did up his jacket – the night was damnably cold. What were the quotations about? About killing, harming a pregnant woman and perjury. Coincidence, or essential detail?

He switched off the light above the rear-view mirror, blinked a few times to accustom his tired eyes to the foggy darkness outside, and froze as he saw some dark figures crowding by the car. Feeling the panic rising in his throat, he started up the engine, and the headlights filled the milky mist with light. There were no shadows. Just a deserted town on the Vistula, a walkway made of paving bricks and an advert for Perła beer above a grocery shop.

He moved off abruptly, driving away towards the river. The fog swirled behind the Citroën's broad rear end.

Prosecutor Teodor Szacki didn't know it, because he couldn't have done, but he was just leaving one of the typical pre-war shtetls, a town occupied mostly by an indigent Jewish population, which in Annopol, just before the war, had accounted for more than seventy per cent of the inhabitants. There was a Hebrew school here, run by the Tarbut movement, cheders, a Talmud Torah Association and secular schools for girls and boys, and there was even a modest yeshiva, after which the boys continued their rabbinical studies in Lublin. There was a small commemorative stone left on the site of the old Jewish graveyard on the edge of the town, surrounded by a decorative path made of pink paving bricks.

VII

Disbelief had appeared on the girl's face, but she was still letting him keep his hand on her thigh – a good sign. For this reason, Roman Myszyński allowed himself to move it a little higher, onto the bit of skin above her lacy stocking top, except that there wasn't any lace there, or any skin. Oh no, don't say girls go out clubbing in tights these days. What is this, some sort of vintage party, or what? Was he just about to find out she'd got a spandex bra and hairy armpits? Couldn't he just for once in his life get a normal girl? Not once a month, not once every six months or even once a year. Just once, once ever.

"So you're something like a detective?" she asked, leaning towards him.

"Not something like, I just am a detective," he exclaimed, making a mental note never, ever again to offer anyone squid in garlic sauce on a date. "I know how it sounds, but it's true. I sit in an office, someone comes along, first he spins me a yarn – he's checking to see if he can trust me. And then," – here he paused – "and then he reveals his deepest secrets to me and I get a commission from him. You have no idea how complicated people's fates can be."

"I'd like to see your office. Reveal my secrets to you."

"Your deepest ones?" he asked, feeling the tackiness of that riposte dampening his desire for a thrill-filled evening.

"You have no idea!" she shouted back over the music.

Soon after, they were sitting in a taxi, which was taking them from the centre of Warsaw to his "office", in other words his small bachelor pad in Grochów. The place may not have been luxurious, but it was atmospheric, in a pre-war villa covered in creepers, squatting beneath the flat blocks of the Ostrobramska estate, known locally as Mordor. They were kissing passionately when his phone rang. A private number. He answered, mentally imploring all the gods in heaven for it not to be his mother.

For a while he listened.

"Of course I know, Prosecutor," he said in a businesslike tone, lower than usual, casting the girl a meaningful look. "Things like that aren't quickly forgotten… Yes, right now I'm in Warsaw… Right… Aha, aha… I see… Of course… I've got to grab a few hours' sleep, it'll take me three to get there, so I can be with you at eight… Yes, sure, goodbye."

With the gesture of a gunslinger he snapped the phone shut and put it away in his jacket pocket. The girl was gazing at him in admiration.

"What a thing," said the taxi driver, looking at him in the rear-view mirror, "for a prosecutor to be calling people at midnight. Normal, my arse. They're turning us into a proper Soviet Union. And they say they're liberals. Fuck the lot of them, sir."

8

Wednesday, 22nd April 2009

The Earth is celebrating Earth Day, Jack Nicholson his seventy-second birthday, Polish Prime Minister Donald Tusk his fifty-second, and car enthusiasts are commemorating the seventh anniversary of the demise of the Polonez. In Poland almost half a million high-school students are doing their final school exam; apart from that, the government announces that there will be a total ban on smoking in public places, a twenty-five-year-old mountaineer climbs up a wall to the top of the Marriott Hotel in Warsaw without any safety gear, and top prize for stand-up comic of the year is won by the Minister of Infrastructure when he declares that the A1, A2 and A4 motorways will be finished before Euro 2012. Poland's western neighbour opens a major trial of Islamic terrorists, while to the east the ice-hockey trainer who was fired because his players dared to beat President Lukashenko's team is reinstated. In Sandomierz the police arrest a man who accused a group of fourteen-year-olds of steal-ing seventy-four bottles of beer and some bottles of vodka at the bazaar and forced money out of them as compensation. Meanwhile, some real thieves purloin a handbag with 180 zlotys in it from an open flat. The owners were sitting on the balcony. And no wonder,

because although the temperature does not rise above
eighteen degrees, and at night it falls to two, it is
a beautiful sunny day.

I

Ever since the first high-school outing, when Marcin had ended up
on the coach next to Sasha – the only spare seat had been next to the
overgrown beanpole with the look of a murderer – the boys had been
linked by a friendship – perhaps not very close, but quite specific.
They didn't know much about each other, they didn't go round to
each other's houses, they didn't invite each other to parties and they
weren't even in the same class. They were both fairly independent,
and they both valued their own independence. Marcin was more of a
weakling, small with straw-blond hair and glasses, famous as well as
ridiculed for being a violinist who sometimes played, to his despair,
at school events. He did a bit of composing, and was turned on by
the idea that he might one day write the music for films, but the only
people who had heard his compositions were Ola and Sasha.

The rumours about Sasha were that he dealt in drugs and was involved with the Russian Mafia. The gossip was so widespread that even
the teachers treated him with astonishing leniency, probably fearing
that if they gave him too low a term grade some Mafioso in a rustling
shell suit would kneecap them in the school changing room. Reticent
by nature, Sasha kept quiet about this matter in particular, which of
course only compounded the gossip, and when someone dared to go
up to him and ask for some gear, Sasha first of all said nothing for a
long time, then finally leant down and said with a deliberate Russian
accent: "Not for you".

In reality Sasha didn't deal in anything – his greatest passion, un-
known to anyone, was documentary cinema, whole terabytes of which
he kept in his computer. Now and then he passed on the better and
more controversial bits of his collection to Marcin. Lately, thanks to
Sasha, Marcin had seen an unusual film about an American Jew who

went to Poland with his kids to look for the people who had saved his father's life. What struck him most was the sick old Jewish man, attached to various tubes, who had been living in Israel for sixty years, could no longer communicate, and just kept repeating that he wanted to go home. They told him he was at home, but he kept on saying he wanted to go home. "So Dad, where is your home?" someone finally asked. "What do you mean, where? Seven, Zawichojska Street," he replied. Marcin couldn't explain why, but he had found this scene very moving.

Sasha was standing leaning against the window sill with his arms folded across his chest, staring into space; in loose clothes including a light top he looked even tougher than usual. Marcin came up, nodded to say hello and leant against the window sill next to him.

"Pawn to e4," he said.

Sasha frowned and nodded approvingly.

"Knight to c4," he muttered.

They had actually been playing games of chess non-stop ever since they had met on the bus, when Sasha had been playing chess on his mobile. Now they had it set up so each of them had his own chessboard at home, and each day at school they swapped a single move. Except that Marcin had all day to think over and prepare his move, while Sasha's responses to moves Marcin had often spent hours working out took no more than a quarter of an hour. Once he had asked for time to think until the next break, and Marcin went about feeling proud for a week. But he never won – thanks to some Russian gene, Sasha was unbeatable.

"Listen, if I remember rightly, your old man's a crooked bully and all-round bastard on the take?"

"That's right, he is indeed a police officer," replied Sasha.

"On Monday I was on a school trip to Sandomierz."

"Bad luck."

"We went on a tour of these vaults underneath the Old Town – apparently they used to be on several levels, but now there's just a pathetic corridor left, or maybe that's all they show people."

"And?"

"And I heard this howling."

"In other words Marysia's finally found her clit. That's the end, no one's safe now."

"It was like sort of… sort of horrendous howling, from deep underground. As if someone was being tormented in there or tortured."

Sasha looked down at his friend. He raised one eyebrow.

"Yes, I know how it sounds," Marcin went on. "I know perfectly well. But I can't get it out of my head. You know what's been going on there lately – they've got a serial murderer on the prowl, they've already found two dead bodies and today I read that apparently people have stopped sending their children to school, it's hysteria. And you see, it's probably nothing, I mean, it's sure to be nothing, but what if? It'd be stupid, wouldn't it?"

"Howling, you say? All right, I'll tell my old man, he can tell the pigs there, maybe they'll find it useful. What else?"

"Howling, mainly howling, a bit like the wind, a bit like groaning, a bit like screaming. And one other sound, I couldn't identify it at the time, it was too faint, but this morning I heard a similar noise and I made the connection."

"Well?"

"Barking. Like a dog barking furiously, as if somewhere down in those vaults they were breeding hell hounds or, I dunno, as if werewolves lived there. Yes, I know how it sounds."

II

The conversation was short and fruitful, and Szacki was pleased he had managed to bring Myszyński here from Warsaw. An intelligent, quick-thinking guy, a little unsuited to the image he had created for himself. He was a good man, the kind that'll never do harm to anyone and will always be amazed if it's done to him. But he was trying to play the old stager, the cold, calculating cynic whose only interest in his work is professional, and nothing else. A perfectly decent role in itself, especially in this line of work, but it only makes sense if you can play it without being off key. Szacki could, but this guy could hardly do it at all. Luckily his acting skills were the least relevant thing here.

He left his office to wash a coffee mug, and did it in such a hurry that he bumped into Basia Sobieraj in the corridor. A small package fell from her hands. He quickly leant down to pick it up – the little cardboard box with a postage label was the size of a fat book, but it was very light, as if there were nothing inside. With a courtly gesture he returned the package.

"I believe you dropped this, madam."

To his surprise he noticed that Sobieraj was blushing like an adolescent girl caught performing an embarrassing and intimate act. Abruptly she tore the package from his hands.

"Please be so good as to look where you're going, sir."

He felt like giving a snappy reply, but the door of Miszczyk's office opened, the boss looked out and beckoned to him decisively, like a headmistress summoning a schoolboy. Off he went, still holding the empty coffee mug bearing the emblem of the Legia Warsaw football team. There was a man sitting in Miszczyk's office with the puffy face of an alcoholic and the look of a tramp, probably believing his sloppiness could pass for casual chic. He was unappealing. At the sight of Szacki he stood up and greeted him effusively.

"I'm a Polonia fan," he said, pointing at the mug.

"Sorry, a what?"

"You know… the other Warsaw team…"

"What do you mean? There's only one team in Warsaw," Szacki joked, but the other man didn't get it.

"The editor has come from Warsaw – he's writing a major report on our case," said Miszczyk, coming to his aid. "I promised he could have fifteen minutes of your time, Prosecutor Szacki, no longer."

Szacki bubbled up inside, but he smiled perfunctorily and suggested they deal with the matter at once, which would let him get back to work as quickly as possible.

To start with, the conversation centred on the investigation, the procedure that applied when the work of a serial killer was suspected, and various nuances of the Penal Code. Szacki answered the questions quickly and precisely; despite the journalist's efforts, he wasn't letting the interview change into a nice, non-committal chat, and he also ruthlessly blocked all the man's attempts to make things less formal. He was waiting for the inevitable, in other words a step in the direction of Jewish themes and Polish anti-Semitism. And sure enough, the inevitable came.

"I'm wondering about the sinister symbolism of all this – there's something extremely nasty about this bloodthirsty game with familiar themes. Here, in a city that's famous for a painting which is in a way an icon of anti-Semitism. Near Kielce, the provincial capital where the biggest pogrom since the Holocaust took place. All that seemed to be just old scar tissue, but meanwhile you only have to scratch the surface and what do you find? Some festering wounds that have never healed."

"I'm not interested in symbolism," quipped Szacki coldly.

The journalist smiled.

"That's so very Polish, don't you think? I am interested in it. Whenever a touchy topic comes up, at once someone will say 'why drag that up', or 'leave it alone', or 'why stir things up unnecessarily.'"

"I'm sorry, but I don't know what is typically Polish – my degree is in law, not anthropology. Besides, you're not listening to me. You can drag it up and stir it up to your heart's desire, I'm not urging you to leave anything out. I'm just informing you that as an official in the service of the Polish Republic I am not interested in symbolism, not even if it's nasty and bloodthirsty."

"Then why did you have those drunken yobs arrested who were holding an anti-Semitic demonstration?"

"One hundred and ninety-six, two hundred and fifty-six, two hundred and fifty-seven, two hundred and sixty-one and two hundred and sixty-two."

"I'm sorry?"

"Those are the paragraphs of the Penal Code which are applicable in this case. Above all, desecration of a place of remembrance, desecration of a burial site and incitement to racial hatred. My job is to prosecute persons who have broken the law. I'm not guided by any ideology or any symbolism in my work."

"I understand that's the official attitude. But unofficially what's your opinion of it?"

"Unofficially I have no opinion."

"Have you come across manifestations of anti-Semitism?"

"No."

"Are stereotypes obstructing you in conducting this investigation?"

"No."

"Do you know that in Sandomierz people aren't sending their children to school?"

"Yes."

"Do you reckon this is caused by the return of a belief in the legend of blood?"

"No."

"Do you know what they're saying on the streets of Sandomierz?"

"No."

"Or what the right-wing media are saying?"

"No."

"I don't understand why you completely refuse to talk about this – why all the panic? After all, you must be wondering what the source of these events is, their genesis. I don't know, have you read Jan Gross's book?"

"No," lied Szacki, knowing perfectly well he meant the famous book about the 1941 pogrom in Jedwabne.

"A pity. He describes the wave of post-war anti-Semitism, the anger of the neighbours at the sight of people who had survived the Holocaust, the hatred. I think that generation of post-war anti-Semites brought up the next generation, and they brought up the next one – to believe that the Jews are to blame for Communism, they have a worldwide conspiracy, and they control international high finance. And at the same time they were deprived of a counterbalance, in the form of an ordinary Jewish neighbour, with whom they would have gone fishing, whom they'd have known, thanks to which, on hearing those dreadful stereotypes, they'd have been able to shrug and say: 'Ee, that's bullshit, Szewek isn't like that'. And somewhere out of that generation your culprit has emerged, a carrier of the most dreadful

Polish stereotypes, ignorant, bearing grudges, burning with hatred for everything that's foreign. And here, on anti-Semitic terrain, this hatred of his has found its terrible manifestation."

The clock by the national coat-of-arms showed that Szacki had two more minutes of this torture ahead of him. He planned to get up as soon as fifteen minutes had been spent on this conversation, which was tiring, boring and infuriating him. He was worried that the energy he so badly needed today was now being wasted on not exploding, not arguing with this cretin, who only had one concern: to prove the thesis about Jew-baiting Poles. He was surprised that so far he had come across the greatest empathy, willingness to understand and common sense in the young rabbi born in Israel. Maciejewski was right: nothing but extremities, nothing was ever normal here.

"But what if it's the other way around?" he asked the journalist.

"Meaning?"

"What if it turns out the culprit is a mad Orthodox Jew, who has come here from Jerusalem with his gang, brought up in a spirit of antipathy towards the Poles, to murder Catholics? What if we find dead children in the cellar of his house, barrels filled with blood and a matzo factory?"

"That's... that's impossible... That would be awful. Here, in this country, which needs to face up to the black pages in its history. Which constantly has to be reminded of its own guilt. You cannot possibly give a scenario like that one serious consideration."

"My work involves giving every scenario serious consideration. I'll go further than that: it wouldn't stir much emotion in me if the culprit turned out to be a Polish bishop or the chairman of the Yad Vashem shrine. As long as we'd found him."

"Is it really all the same to you?"

Luckily the time was running out.

"Yes."

"You don't seem to understand your duties as an educated, thinking person. You have to declare yourself on one side or the other. Our side has to bear witness, to instruct and explain. Otherwise the other, the dark side will win over hearts and minds."

"What dark side?" bristled Szacki. "Can't you people simply provide information about what's going on? Does everyone here have to peddle some sort of twisted propaganda?"

"It's not all the same to us!"

"But it is to me. Your fifteen minutes are up."

III

He liked women, he liked that sensation when he met a new one and felt a shiver running down his spine, a thrill triggered sometimes by beauty, sometimes by sex appeal, a gesture or the sound of her voice, her smile or a sparkling riposte. Sometimes, very rarely, he felt a similar feeling, arising not exactly in his spine and not exactly in the pit of his stomach, in encounters with men. Once upon a time he had been afraid of it, but then he had realized it was admiration. A mixture of admiration, slight envy and a little excitement. A sort of boyish "Bloody hell, I'd love to be like that guy one day".

Roman Myszyński left Prosecutor Teodor Szacki's office in exactly this sort of mood. In his career as an archivist for hire, a tracker of family secrets hidden in yellowing pages, whenever he took on a new client and tried to make an impression on him, he did his best to be someone like that. Businesslike, but not taciturn. Professional, but not cold. Reserved, but not rude. Calm, but alert. Maintaining distance, but inspiring confidence. Teodor Szacki was just like that – the proud sheriff, who had seen a lot and knows a lot, but doesn't need to talk about it. A pale, as if diluted, unsettling glance, narrow lips, classic features. And that thick, milk-white hair, which gave him a unique, slightly demonic look. There was something sheriff-like about the prosecutor, a dash of Gary Cooper and Clint Eastwood, but also a touch of the archetypal Polish army officer, defiant indomitability and a rock-solid belief that he was the right man in the right place.

He also envied Szacki his mission. The evident conviction that he was on the right side, and that all his actions served goodness and justice. But who was he by comparison? Nothing but a pen-pushing historian, who in exchange for a few zlotys concealed their Jewish ancestors from moustachioed Poles and found them aristocratic roots so they could hang a crest above their television sets. In fact, for the first time ever he was finally doing something that had some meaning.

So he didn't feel any discomfort in connection with having so quickly returned to the site of his life's greatest trauma – the State Archive in Sandomierz. Maybe just for a moment there was a short stab of anxiety while he was looking for the relevant documents in the old synagogue's prayer hall. Once again he had to walk past the spot from which the drawbridge led to the window looking out on the bushes below the synagogue. He walked past it cautiously, feeling as if the zodiac signs painted by a Jewish artist were following his movements. But he soon shook off that impression and carried the mortgage record books to the reading room. Next to them he put down the material Szacki had given him – a short list of the people he was to check on, and print-outs relating to them from the national ID system to start him off, plus authorizations covered in stamps that guaranteed him access to all the data that hadn't yet ended up in the state archive. And a single sheet of paper on which it said what he was to look for: homicide, the death of a pregnant woman, perjury.

He took out his American notebook, a thick pad with yellow pages, and began to make a list of institutions to visit. He'd start with the Civil Registry and the parish records, and by sketching a short genealogical tree for each person. He didn't have to go further back than two generations, so it shouldn't be hard. Then the court records and the post-war newspapers – that was a piece of cake too. It might be trickier with the secret police documents – the people at the Institute of National Remembrance suffered from advanced persecution mania and paranoia. But perhaps there wouldn't actually be a need.

For now, however, first into the firing line came the property records. If the prosecutor was right, the key to the whole case was the abandoned mansion on Zamkowa Street, its present and former owners.

The phone call from Oleg Kuzniecow was like a voice from the world beyond, and it showed Szacki how fragile and easily disturbed his emotional balance was.

As soon as he heard the slightly sing-song accent of the Warsaw policeman who had been his friend and colleague for so many years, he instantly came unstuck. He was overcome with homesickness for his former life. Kuzniecow would fix a visit to the crime scene on a chilly morning, followed by coffee at Three Crosses Square, duty meetings at which the policeman would pretend to take him for a pestilential prat, and Szacki would seem to regard the commissioner as a useless layabout. Joint successes and joint failures, joint battles in the courtrooms, where Oleg was often the most important witness. Joint parties at his flat in the Praga district. Helka would be asleep in her room while the four of them drank together. Kuzniecow would tell jokes or sing Vysotsky's Russian folk songs, Natalia would tell her husband off for boring them to death and Szacki would pep up the conversation with a few genial jibes. Weronika would cuddle up to him – alcohol always had that effect on her, making her want to sleep, but even so, after getting rid of their guests they would find the time for some cosy, gentle, satisfying sex. She always fell asleep first, with her back to him. Moving up to embrace her below the breasts so he could feel they were there, fit his stomach against her back and nestle his face into the hair on the nape of her neck had been his last conscious gesture before falling asleep almost every day for almost fifteen years.

"But do you really want me to tell you about this?" He could hear the hesitation in Kuzniecow's voice. That was painful – in the old days Oleg would never have thought of censoring himself while talking to his friend.

"Of course, what do you mean? I want everything to be best for her, if she's doing all right, then Helka's all right too. Besides, you know, I'm curious."

"OK," said Kuzniecow after a pause long enough to be noticeable. "We went round to their place, I didn't even have to invite myself,

Weronika called to say they'd moved, Helka wanted to see us, and we must meet Tomek."

"So?"

"So I don't know what your place is like, if you're living in a palace by now with a garden and a view of the Vistula, but your ex has gone up in the world a bit. It might not be a villa in Konstancin, but it's a pretty pleasant semi in the Wawer district, tucked in behind Patriots' Street. There's a patch of garden with a hammock for Helka, and it's nice inside, you know, not Ikea style, more like leather suites and sideboards, you can see the guy's not a nouveau but from an old family."

"So what's he like?"

"All right, I'd say. Older than you, bigger build, less grey hair. Good looking I suppose; Natalia says he looks like the bloke in *Gladiator*, but from his later films. A bit of a bore if I'm going to be honest – I find all those legal advice stories rather tedious, but maybe we just have to go along with it."

We just have to go along with it. Pity you haven't found the time in half a year to come and visit me, mate.

"But Weronika seems, well, contented."

Censored. He was going to say: happy.

"Helka too, so maybe altogether it has worked out well, eh? I was pissed off with you before, because frankly I didn't know a better couple, but something must have been wrong, if you've sorted out your lives so well now. Ha, I think it gave Natalia something to think about, because she's started wearing lace and baking cakes. Yeah, there really is some truth in it, you've got to keep a bird on a short leash. Apropos birds, how's it going?"

"Bachelor life, not too dull, I had a surprise from a local lady judge the other day."

"A judge? Wait a moment. Five years for a law degree, two years pupilage, three years as an associate… Are you trying to say you've changed your life just to bonk birds over thirty? Is this a joke? But do I understand you've got a bit of variety there?"

"More or less." Szacki was finding this conversation tiring.

"God, it's the most fantastic feeling in the world to remove the blouse from a new body. How I envy you."

There's nothing to envy, thought Szacki, who knew what purely physical sex meant and, like every man, kept the truth about it to himself. The truth about the fact that a body reduced to just a body consisted of nothing but irritating imperfections. A sour smell, shapeless breasts in an ugly bra, pimples on the upper chest, stretch marks around the navel, the sweaty edge of the knickers, pubic hairs that got in between one's teeth, a corn on the side of the little toe and a crooked toenail.

"Bah!" he said, just to say anything.

"Yeeeah," said Kuzniecow dreamily. "But hold on, I called about something else. Just tell me how things are with Helka – Weronika said it's up and down."

"Yes, it is. She's coming to me this weekend, but actually, somehow, I understand she's pissed off with me for everything. I dunno, maybe I'll start coming to Warsaw more often." Szacki couldn't bear to listen to himself. He was getting lost, losing the plot, talking complete bullshit.

"Oh, quite, coming here more often's a great idea. We'll be able to go for a drink like the old days. Or maybe I'll drop in on you, what do you say? But not in the near future – you know what it's like."

"Sure, I know. Listen, if—"

"No, you listen, it's probably rubbish, but you might find it useful."

"Go on."

"My dearly beloved son Sasha told me he was yakking with his only mate. On Monday the mate was on a school trip to Sandomierz, and, aha, apparently the mate's extremely musical, he's got perfect pitch, he writes music, plays instruments and all that. That's important. He doesn't take drugs or drink, and that's important too."

As Szacki listened, he felt a slight tension in his muscles. Was it really God's idea of a joke to have the breakthrough come from his old crime-fighting partner?

"Apparently the mate went round some vaults under the Old Town – have you got something like that there?"

"Yes, it's a major attraction."

"And he claims that in those vaults, in a room with archaeological bits and pieces, he heard strange noises coming from behind the wall. Barely audible, distant, but quite distinct."

"What sort of noises?"

"Howling. Howling and barking."

V

The howling and barking really is unbearable. Even with ear plugs the air is quivering with unpleasant noises, I can feel it through my skin, I can feel it as I watch the drops of saliva whirling in the lamplight, I can smell it in the bitter, animal odour. It's one of those moments when I've already had enough, I want it to be over and done with so I can start all over again. I feel irritation and I feel fear, and I know each of these feelings is a very bad counsellor. I must make a call. Pointlessly I reach for the mobile and silently curse – of course there's no question of getting a signal in this place. I know I must go out, and I know I desperately don't want to come back down here. Maybe I don't have to? I know the way, I only have to set the machinery in motion and leave. If it all works out as it should, there won't be any traces left. I'll guide them here later, so they'll find it all, once I'm in a safe place.

VI

Szacki ran down the corridor at the provincial prosecutor's office beside himself with rage. Normally in this bloody hole everyone was always bumping into each other on the same three streets, but as soon as someone was needed, they all vanished as if it was New York, damn and blast it. Wilczur's number was constantly engaged, Sobieraj, whom he needed to reach the most urgently, had her mobile switched off, and Miszczyk had gone somewhere; he had managed to get Sobieraj's husband's number, but that was picked up by an answering machine too. Bloody provinces, a little bit of technology and they're lost – they haven't emerged from the age of smoke signals yet.

He noticed he was still running around with the stupid football mug, so he went into the kitchen and washed it, just to have something to keep his hands busy, and put it down on the draining board so violently that he broke a prehistoric office glass. He cursed out loud. And did it again when he cut himself picking up the pieces. The cut was quite nasty – he had blood flowing down his thumb into the palm of his hand. Bloody hell, where had he seen a medicine cabinet? In the front office perhaps.

But Szacki didn't get as far as the front office, because on the way there something sparked in his brain. He had made a mental jump from the medicine cabinet to a dressing, from a dressing to first aid, from first aid to ambulances, from ambulances to hospitals, and now he knew where to find Basia Sobieraj – at the hospital, visiting her sick father.

He was running out of the building with his cut finger in his mouth, but instead of getting in the car, he went back upstairs. Not because the cut seemed serious and he knew he'd better devote a couple of minutes to bandaging it. He went back guided by an irrational, sudden presentiment of danger. He went back to do something that in his long career as a prosecutor he'd only done once before now.

He went back for a gun.

With no time to put on a holster, he took a small Glock pistol from the safe, checked the safety catch and tossed it in his jacket pocket.

At the hospital he soon located the right ward – of course, all he had to say was that he was looking for Basia Sobieraj's father and the nurse pointed him in the right direction. He stood in the doorway and hesitated; the intimacy of the scene he found there made him feel awkward.

In the four-person room only one bed was occupied; there was an old man lying in it. On one side of the bed he had a monitor with coloured lines streaming across it and a stand with two IV drips, and on the other, at a slight distance, a clothes rail. There was a lawyer's gown hanging on it. A prosecutor's gown, beautifully ironed, with a carefully folded collar. It must have been pretty old, perhaps from several decades ago. The red trim was a little faded and the black of the worsted fabric had lost its intensity.

Basia Sobieraj and her father had their backs turned towards him. The father was lying on his side, presenting his back, buttocks and thighs to the world with the visible blue-and-purple marks of pressure sores. She was wiping his skin with a sponge wetted in a bowl full of some sort of solution, which was standing on a hospital stool.

"Don't cry, Dad, it's just your body," she whispered; her whisper was tired and resigned.

Her father mumbled something in reply which Szacki didn't catch.

He coughed quietly. Basia Sobieraj turned round, and for the second time that day she blushed a little. He was expecting to be told off, but she smiled warmly. She beckoned him inside, quickly turned her father over and carefully covered him with the bedding. She apologized for switching off her mobile, but she had simply had to be on her own with her father for a while, and hadn't wanted anyone to disturb her. Szacki told her about the howling and barking; luckily he didn't have to explain what it meant and what they needed. She took her phone from her handbag, which was hanging over the back of a chair, and ran outside, leaving Szacki with her father.

The old man was dying. It didn't take a medical degree to see that. The sallow skin clung tight to his skull, but hung loose on his neck and arms, and his faded eyes, as if coated in jelly, laboured to follow Szacki. Only his thick grey moustache was defying the laws of nature, shining healthily and embellishing the sick man's face. Szacki thought Sobieraj must have been a late child – she herself was under forty, but her father must have been about eighty.

"Mr Szacki," the old man stated, rather than asked.

Szacki started in surprise, but he went up to the bed and gently shook the man's hand.

"Teodor Szacki, pleased to meet you," he said too loud, feeling embarrassed that his voice sounded so forceful and resonant. It seemed to him out of place.

"Ah, at last someone who doesn't whisper as if they're in a mortuary," said the old man, smiling. "Andrzej Szott. Basia has told me a lot about you."

"I hope it was all good," replied Szacki with the most hackneyed remark in the book. At the same time he felt an itching in his head. Andrzej Szott. That name ought to tell him something. But he couldn't remember what.

"On the contrary. Though lately she's less abusive about you."

The prosecutor smiled and pointed at the gown.

"Yours?"

"Yes, it's mine. I keep it here because sometimes my mind rebels, and, how can I put it, floats off. The gown helps me to remember various things. Who I am, for example. You'll agree that sort of information can sometimes be quite useful."

He agreed with a polite nod, at the same time wondering why the old prosecutor had chosen his gown rather than a picture of his wife or his daughter. But he didn't wonder for long. If he could have chosen the one object that best defined him, wouldn't it actually be his gown with the red trim?

"You're asking yourself if you'd hang up your gown too," said Szott, reading his mind.

"Yes."

"And?"

"I don't know. Maybe." He went up to the gown and ran a finger over the striped woollen cloth.

"This one," said Szott, pointing with a flick of his finger, "is unique. It saw the last double death sentence to be carried out in Poland."

"Krakow, 1982."

"That's right. Do you know who was hanged?"

Click. And now he knew what the old man's name should be telling him. He turned round and went up to the bed.

"My God, Prosecutor Andrzej Szott. This is an honour, a great honour, please forgive me for not realizing at once, I really am very sorry."

The old man smiled gently.

"I'm glad someone remembers."

Incidentally, thought Szacki, Sobieraj really is pretty good not to have spilled the beans that her old man put away Sojda and Adaś. Either she's not accustomed to anyone here not knowing, or – which is also possible – Mr Szott was the perfect prosecutor, but not the perfect father, not eagerly mentioned by his own children.

Now he took a different view of the small wrinkled face, the weak smile under the moustache and the pale eyes under dark brows. So that's what Prosecutor Andrzej Szott looked like, who had prosecuted one of the most famous and most shocking criminal cases in the history of Poland.

"What year was it?" he asked.

"1976. A harsh winter."

"Is Połaniec in Sandomierz county?"

"Staszów county, right next to it. But in those days it was all the same administrative area, Tarnobrzeg province. I worked here, and the trial was here too. The Tarnobrzeg provincial court based in Sandomierz, that's what it was called then. They had the provincial administration and the sulphur mining in Tarnobrzeg, but nothing else, it was all here in Sandomierz."

Yes, Połaniec, and that village just outside Połaniec was called Zrębin; with each successive name Szacki remembered the books he had read about that case. Facts came back to mind and images appeared. It was Christmas Eve, Sojda...

"What was Sojda's first name?"

"Jan."

...Jan Sojda, known as "the King of Zrębin" – there's one like that in every village – had taken the whole village by coach to Midnight Mass at the church in Połaniec, but instead of going into the church they'd all got drunk together on the bus, it was a sort of Zrębin Christmas tradition. There were thirty people on that bus, but none of them knew at the time they were part of a bigger plan. In keeping with this plan, a friend lured a couple called Krystyna Kalita and Stanisław Łukaszek out of the church on the pretext of a family incident. The young people had just got married, she was eighteen and she was pregnant. Krystyna's brother was with them, a boy of twelve. For ages the "King" had had a grudge against the Kalita family, all the more so since Krystyna and Stanisław's wedding, when someone had accused Sojda's sister of stealing some meat – a valuable commodity in those days. So when the couple learnt that they were needed at home quickly, they asked if they could get a lift back on the bus, but Sojda refused – those scum could walk five kilometres back to Zrębin in the snow.

And so the scum had started walking. Soon the bus full of revellers headed after the young people and caught up with them halfway. First they ran down the kid, and at that point it could still have looked like an accident. But not once Sojda and his son-in-law Adaś had dived out of the bus and beaten Stanisław Łukaszek to death with a wheel wrench. The pregnant girl ran off into the fields, begging her uncle – the Sojdas and the Kalitas were blood relatives – to spare her, as they'd already killed her husband. They didn't – they beat her to death with the same wrench. There was still the twelve-year-old left, Miecio, injured but alive. They laid him in the road and ran a car over him several times to fake an accident. They did the same thing with the couple's bodies. Then they put them all in a ditch and went back to the church to secure themselves an alibi. Before that, all the revellers had taken part in a strange ritual, and had pledged an oath to Sojda that they'd keep silent. Each of them had kissed a cross, sworn on it and shed a drop of blood onto a piece of paper.

The investigation into the apparent road accident went on for months; something smelt bad about the case, but no one suspected the stink had anything to do with premeditated murder. Instead, they thought it was that no one wanted to admit driving while drunk. It was night, it was slippery – an unfortunate accident. On this charge Adaś was arrested – for causing a fatal accident. During the investigation some new facts appeared, but other facts disappeared too – for example a witness vanished, who was the only one to claim that on Christmas Eve some murders had been committed in cold blood. He drowned in the stream that ran through Połaniec, which was only a few centimetres deep. There was one thing nobody suspected – that out of thirty normal people who had witnessed the monstrous murders of three people, including a pregnant woman and a twelve-year-old boy, not a single one would breathe a word, in the name of village solidarity.

Nobody except Prosecutor Andrzej Szott.

"In a way it was a case similar to yours," said Szott, as if commenting on Szacki's thoughts. "From what Basia has told me."

"In what way?"

"An old hatred. You have to live in the provinces to be familiar with that sort of hatred – in the big cities it doesn't exist. Now people see each other, now they don't – they have to make an arrangement to see each other at all. But in the country they're all peering in each other's windows every day of the week. So if your wife's unfaithful, even if you sort it out between you, every day in the street and every week at church you're going to keep seeing the guy she sucked off. The bile accumulates, the hatred grows, and even if you don't do anything, you'll say what schmucks the X-es are. Your son hears you. And when he has a fight with X's son at school it's not for himself, but for you, too. In other words it's stronger. And so it goes on, brick by brick, until finally someone is killed, disappears, drowns. Do you think Zrębin is the only place in the world like that? I doubt it."

"Yes, but I don't know if there's any comparison. That was a case of drunken slaughter, this is very intricate work."

"Drunken slaughter? Don't make me laugh. They got two vehicles ready, one just to cover their tracks. They got the cousin ready to lure them out of the church. They got a crucifix ready and a safety pin for the drops of blood, they got the money ready for bribes to keep silent. They made up an alibi. Sojda had spent weeks getting it all ready, maybe months even, ever since the accusation of stealing the meat at the wedding had pushed him over the edge. And I think there are villages where vendettas like that are prepared for years, where it gets passed down from generation to generation."

Szacki felt anxious. Why? Because Szott had mentioned hatred passed down from generation to generation? That was his theory too, that was why he had told Myszyński to dig around in the archives. Yes, maybe that was it. But he felt anxious – the itching usually appeared when he had overlooked something, not when his theories were confirmed. Did the Zrębin case really have something in common with the stylized murder of the Budniks? In the Zrębin case, what was more shocking than the actual murders was the conspiracy of silence. A terrible, incomprehensible conspiracy of silence. A conspiracy dismantled by Szott.

"Where did you get the idea of catching them out in the court room?" he asked the old prosecutor. "Why the delay?"

"Those people had already got used to endless interrogations by the militia and the prosecution, but they kept repeating their version of events like parrots – no requests or threats had brought any result. We could do that until the day of the trial, the investigation had been dragging on anyway, we had to write an indictment, all the deadlines had been shifted. It was a risky move, to go to court with a conjectural prosecution, counting on hard evidence emerging in the courtroom. The militia captain and I spent a long time wondering if it made sense to put all our money on one single card."

"But it worked?"

"Yes, the court was a new experience for them, so we and the judge started to put pressure on them in there; the hearings were behind closed doors, so the families couldn't listen in and work out matching stories. It started badly. The defendants dug their heels in, so did the witnesses, and some of them started revoking statements they'd made in the course of the investigation."

"And?"

"What works best on simple people? An example. We knew which of the witnesses was the stupidest, who got lost the most and made mistakes. And in doing so he made an appallingly bad impression and prompted natural antipathy. We put pressure on him in court, and he got so muddled in his testimony that the judge lost his rag and had him locked up as a punishment. When people saw their fellow villager being led out in handcuffs, they softened up. They were afraid of Sojda, but no one wanted to go to prison for him. Then another one in handcuffs. And another. And then one started to talk, followed by a second."

"They got quite high sentences, as far as I recall?"

"Eighteen people served several years each for bearing false witness."

Homicide. The death of a pregnant woman. Perjury.

Szacki felt his mouth go dry. By no coincidence it kept coming back like a refrain – homicide, the death of a pregnant woman, perjury. But for God's sake, what connection could a case from thirty years ago have with the present murders? The same premeditation. The same family of investigators. Church themes – in that case Midnight Mass, here the picture in the cathedral. Perhaps the same theme of hatred building up for years. Maybe a conspiracy of silence? He didn't know that, he hadn't a scrap of proof for it, but intuition had told him to get Myszyński without telling anyone else and ask him to investigate the people who in theory were on his side, with whom he was working.

But maybe it was a coincidence, maybe the crimes just had some similarities? Maybe it was a sign that he should follow in Szott's footsteps in his reasoning? What did Szott have that he didn't? What had enabled him to discover the truth about the Połaniec crime? He knew it, somewhere inside he knew it, it was on the tip of his tongue, the answer was hiding from him in a cluster of brain cells, playing at hide and seek – but it was there.

"Jesus, Dad, are you on about those Sojdas again? What's the limit?" Sobieraj had materialized in the room, automatically adjusted her father's pillow and pulled him upright. "If you understood what those numbers mean," she said, pointing at the monitor, "you wouldn't gas on so much."

She glanced at Szacki.

"Let's go. I've found a young man who knows all about our underground vaults. He did a doctorate on it at the University of Science and Technology in Krakow, but luckily he's at home in Sandomierz right now. We're to meet him near the seminary – apparently there's a way in there. Off with you now." She started shooing him out of the room like a naughty child, but Szacki avoided her and went up to old Szott.

"Thank you," he said, and pressed the prosecutor's hand. It didn't even tremble; his gaze had become mistier and more absent, and the keen smile had left his face. Szacki said goodbye to the man who was one of very few people in Poland to have seen the death sentence carried out. He must come back here one day to ask what that was like. Did he believe in the death penalty? Did he believe some crimes were unpardonable?

On his way out he brushed a hand against the old prosecutor's uniform.

"You're going to inherit a fine gown," he said to Sobieraj.

"She won't get it," whispered the old man so quietly that Szacki guessed the words rather than heard them.

"Why not?" he asked, returning to the bed.

Sobieraj was standing impatiently in the doorway, and rolled her eyes tellingly.

"Because she doesn't understand."

"What doesn't she understand?"

The old prosecutor beckoned, and Szacki leant low over him, with his ear almost touching the dying man's lips.

"She's too good. She doesn't understand that they all tell lies."

VII

They parked by the Opatowska Gate; the Sandomierz Senior Clerical Seminary was situated bang opposite, in a fine set of baroque monastery buildings once occupied by the Benedictines. Unfortunately that was the extent of Szacki's knowledge about this place, which he had never visited, though Saint Michael's church had often been recommended to him as a must-see for tourists. Maybe because he didn't like the baroque, or maybe because it was located on a busy road outside the Old Town walls, the church had seemed to him less inviting than others.

At the monastery gate he saw Wilczur, next to whom stood a handsome blond boy, like a young Paul Newman, with a backpack slung over his shoulder. Szacki shuddered – the blond boy reminded him of someone. Not just the actor – there was something else familiar about his face, a hint of someone he knew well.

"Prosecutor Teodor Szacki," Wilczur presented him, as soon as they had run across the road.

The blond boy smiled broadly and punched Szacki right in the diaphragm. The blow was like a battering ram – Szacki doubled up and fell to the ground like a sack of potatoes. Kneeling, with his nose to the pavement, he urgently tried to catch his breath, but the air seemed to stop at his teeth and refuse to come through a millimetre further. Red and black spots began to dance before his eyes, he was afraid he was going to faint, and at the same time he wished he would – then he'd stop feeling the sickening pain that was flooding his entire body.

The blond boy squatted next to him.

"Remember, pal," he said in a barely audible whisper straight into Szacki's ear, "I've got another hand too, and my old man and my big brother have two more each, and we really hate to see our kid sister cry. Got it?"

Szacki managed to inhale the minimum amount of air necessary, just enough not to lose consciousness. He glanced at the boy, managed to raise one hand from the pavement and stuck up his middle finger right under his nose. The boy laughed, grabbed his hand and pulled him to his feet.

"Marek Dybus, very nice to meet you," he said with effusive sincerity. "Sorry about that – I tripped unfortunately."

The prosecutor nodded. Wilczur and Sobieraj stood side by side with stony expressions on their faces, which surely meant they were having trouble suppressing their laughter. Without a word they followed Dybus as he led them into a building standing slightly to one side, right next to the stone wall surrounding the grounds of the seminary on Zawichojska Street, which ran downhill towards the marketplace and the Vistula. The three-storey tenement was topped with gables in the baroque style, but apart from that it looked like a contemporary building. He asked Dybus about it.

"Yes, it was put up between the wars as the Junior Clerical Seminary, in the late 1920s I think – it's called Nazareth House. Though so far, laypersons have been in charge of it for longer than clergymen. During the war it was where the Gestapo tortured their prisoners, and after the war it housed the secret police, then the militia and the prosecution service. Sojda was interrogated here – have you heard of that case?"

"Yes."

"The building was only handed over to the diocese in the 1990s, so now it's a hostel, or whatever they call it, for clerical students, with accommodation for the lecturers too."

"Why are we going in here?" asked Szacki, following Dybus inside the building and then down some stairs into a narrow basement.

"Because this holy building full of clerical students also contains the gates of hell. When they built it, they accidentally came upon the medieval tunnels, and luckily, instead of just filling them in with concrete, some clever inter-war Pole installed a door." He took some headlamps from his backpack and handed one to each person.

The torches were small, but they gave out surprisingly bright, white light. Dybus looked like a seasoned potholer in his, Wilczur like a ghost and Sobieraj like a nursery-school Christmas decoration. From the faces they made as they looked at him, Szacki could guess that unfortunately he did not look like a seasoned potholer either.

"Button up," said the young man, as he unlocked the door, which looked no different from all the others. "It's pretty cold down there, never above about twelve degrees."

In single file, they went inside an underground corridor made of red bricks; it didn't look old, and there were some sort of dusty jars on the ground. They walked a few metres, turned once, then again, then went a short way down some wooden steps, which also didn't look as if they remembered the days of the Tatars. There Dybus opened another door and they went through it, into a small vaulted room the height of a flat in a housing block and about ten, maybe twelve square metres in size.

"Good, now a few words of explanation," their guide began, twisting the band of his headlamp to one side to avoid dazzling them. "We're seven metres underground, almost exactly underneath Żeromski Street. In this direction there's the Opatowska Gate and the Old Town, and that way goes to the Vistula. Auntie Basia said someone heard strange noises in the tourist area, except that section is completely cut off from the rest of the underground. That means you can hear something there, but without a pickaxe it's impossible to go any further in from there – all of it is either filled in or walled up, or flooded."

"Flooded?"

"Not with water. I won't go into detail, I'll just summarize so you know what it's about. Sandomierz is built on loess, and loess is a great kind of soil, because it's hard as well as malleable, so on the one hand you can build on it virtually without foundations, and on the other you can dig tunnels in it with your fingernails without worrying about pit props and supports. That's why, for as long as this overgrown village has been here, our ancestors dug cellars underneath it. Shallower ones for potatoes, deeper for valuables, deepest of all for shelters. They dug out the entire hill like moles, making corridors on more than a dozen levels, running for tens of kilometres. And that's how it happened. Occasionally something has caved in, but for a city built on Swiss cheese, it's doing pretty well. But loess is also not such a great material, because when it's affected by damp it behaves like a lump of sand thrown into a bowl – it collapses instantly, snap bang and it's gone. And in the 1960s Sandomierz suddenly started to crumble, as if it were built on shifting sands. Why was that? Thanks to civilization. The city had had a sewage system installed, the sewers leaked, and the leakage was dissolving the Old Town hill. Catastrophe. Got it?"

"Yes. It's very interesting, but time—"

"Just a moment. They brought in experts from Krakow and miners from Bytom. The miners took the Old Town apart, bored shafts, made a map of the vaults and flooded the ones underneath buildings and roads with a mixture of loess and water glass, which solidifies to make something like pumice, a sort of stiff, lightweight construction material. And then they rebuilt the Old Town."

"Except that the rehoused intelligentsia were left in flat blocks, and Commies were moved in," wheezed Wilczur. "That's why it looks like a slum nowadays – tramps and dirty windows."

"Which is not entirely relevant to our considerations, but of course we thank you for that comment," said Dybus with charm. Szacki liked this boy – he had good, lively intelligence. And to think he could have married into such a likeable family. He thought about Klara's honey-coloured body and felt a stab of regret. Maybe there was still some way to rebuild the relationship?

"Some of the remaining cellars were converted into the tourist route, and the rest of the underground was cut off from the city, but it has survived, and in fact no one was interested in it – everybody was convinced it was just a few damp cellars. It was only we" – there was a note of pride in his voice – "who started doing more careful research. And it turned out that even after the work to flood some of the tunnels under the Old Town, there was still a labyrinth down here. Without any exaggeration, it really is a labyrinth – we spent a year coming down into in these vaults almost every day, and we only managed to inventory about twenty per cent of the corridors. Let's go – follow me in single file."

They set off, and walked along another bit of vaulted corridor; beyond it there was just an unpleasant, low-ceilinged tunnel, as if drilled out of dried, brownish mud. Szacki put a finger to the wall, and it felt like sandstone to the touch. He only had to scratch a bit with his fingernail for tiny grains of yellow sand to fall off it.

They reached a fork.

"And now listen up, I must tell you a few rules. First of all, I'm in charge, and I'm not at all interested in your titles and ranks." Szacki cast an eye at Wilczur, who seemed strangely tense; perhaps he suffered from claustrophobia. "Secondly, if by some miracle we were to be separated, then at every intersection or crossroads there's an arrow carved at the height of a metre pointing the way to the exit by the seminary. But as the arrows are only in territory that we researched, we won't get separated. Thirdly, run away from damp places with visibly leaking or dripping water. It means the loess there is unstable and could bury you. Got it? Right, let's go."

Szacki didn't have claustrophobia, but he felt uneasy. The corridor was low and narrow, its sandy structure gave no sense of security, and he felt as if there wasn't enough oxygen in the cold, slightly musty atmosphere to satisfy his lungs. He breathed deeply, but hardly took in any air. Though possibly his diaphragm had been knocked out of shape by Dybus, and was having trouble getting back into place. He could still feel a pain under his ribs at every step.

For several minutes they walked on in silence. They took a few turns, but all the corridors were identical to one another. Disturbingly identical – the mere thought of the possibility of being left alone down here and losing his way was enough to make his skin creep.

"OK, we're there," said the young guide, and suddenly stopped at a wall made of planks. There was one missing, and they could see grey concrete behind it. "Behind this wall is the tourist route, the room with various archaeological exhibits. If there really is something going on down here, and if someone in there heard noises, we should be able to hear them even better."

They fell silent. There must have been a group going along the tourist route, because they could hear footsteps, muffled talking and laughter, then the high-pitched voice of the tourist guide, who was talking about somebody's extraordinary heroism. After a while all the noises moved away and they were left in unpleasant, dense silence. Szacki shuddered as he felt something move across his fingers – it was Sobieraj's hand. He looked at her in surprise, but she just smiled apologetically. She didn't let go of his hand, and it was rather nice. But only for a short time – then all other feelings were abruptly displaced by a pang of fear, as from the maze of black corridors they heard a distant, but distinct, bestial howling.

"Holy fuck," said Dybus.

Sobieraj sighed out loud, and squeezed his hand tightly.

"Can you tell where it is?" Szacki asked, pleased there was no tremor audible in his voice.

"The echo could be misleading, but I'd bet on the west, towards the synagogue and Saint Joseph's church. I've got it all mapped out as far as the ramparts, we'll see afterwards."

Now they were walking much more slowly and cautiously. First Dybus, then Szacki and Sobieraj, still clinging to his hand. The taciturn Wilczur brought up the rear. It crossed Szacki's mind that they should get the old policeman out of there. If he really did have claustrophobia and had a heart attack in these vaults it would somewhat complicate their outing.

"Where are we now?" he asked. They had gone about a hundred metres and the tunnel was going downwards in a gentle arc; until now they had passed one intersection and one side branch, filled in with loess rubble.

"Under the walls – to the left we've got the Old Town and to the right Podwale, the ramparts. Do you hear that?"

The howling sound came again; if it really was louder, then it was only by a little. Sobieraj glanced at her watch.

"What's the time?"

"Almost three."

They slowly went on, and the faint, unearthly howling was audible every time they stopped. At one point they heard a distinct metallic noise, as if someone had dropped a spanner onto a concrete workshop floor. Dybus stopped.

"Did you hear that?"

"Let's go," Szacki urged, dragging Sobieraj after him, but her hand slipped out of his sweaty palm.

"Oh my God," she drawled in a hollow tone that made everyone look at her. Slowly she raised her hand, and in the white light of the torches they could see it was all red with blood. The woman crumpled, and was clearly about to be sick.

"Basia, hey, calm down," said Szacki, gently pulling his colleague upright. "Nothing's happened – I cut myself at the office, I'm sorry, I didn't have time to put a plaster on it. I couldn't feel it bleeding – I'm sorry."

She gave him a look of hostility, but also relief. Without a word she took a thin silk scarf from her pocket and provisionally bandaged his hand.

"I don't know if we shouldn't send someone better qualified down here," she muttered. "Strange vaults, strange howling, we don't know what we're looking for, and now that blood, it's a bad sign."

"We're looking for Szyller," said Szacki. "So far in this case every time someone has disappeared, they've been found later on trussed like a piglet."

287

"You mean a lamb," Wilczur corrected him. "Pork's *treif*."

"*Treif*?"

"Not kosher."

"In any case, this time we've got a chance of finding someone sooner than that."

"How on earth do you know this has anything to do with it?"

"Howling, barking, it all fits."

"Have you gone mad?" Sobieraj made her surprised-and-outraged gesture, which suited her very well. "Where does barking fit into it?"

"Well, what have you got in that painting in the cathedral? Children being kidnapped and murdered, rolled in a barrel of blood, and the remains thrown to dogs to devour. What haven't we seen yet?"

"Oh God," groaned Sobieraj, but not because this information had shocked her. This time the howling was more distinct, and they could also hear furious barking. Distorted by the winding corridors, the noise sounded hellish and made their flesh crawl, their hair stand on end and their muscles tense, as if waiting for the signal to run.

"We haven't gone all that far," cried Dybus. "Maybe we'd better get the hell out of here."

"Quiet," commanded Szacki coldly. "What are you expecting? The Hound of the Baskervilles? A beast from hell breathing fire? A dog is a dog. Have you got a gun, Inspector?"

Wilczur opened the flap of his jacket; next to his sunken ribcage there was something swinging in a holster that looked like a classic police Walther.

"Let's go. Quickly."

They set off. As the unearthly animal noises got rapidly closer, Szacki couldn't shake off the sensation that he was standing in the middle of a road, caught in the headlights of a speeding car, and that instead of jumping aside he was starting to charge towards it. It's a dog, it's just a terrified dog and the acoustics of a small space, that's all, just a dog, he kept repeating to himself. Walking ahead of him, Dybus suddenly stopped, Szacki's momentum meant he fell on top of him, and after that everything happened quickly – too quickly, unfortunately, and too chaotically.

Dybus had stopped because around a bend in the corridor some steps began, cut out of the loess, leading in a steep spiral downwards, into inky darkness, from which the furious barking was coming, not just loud, but deafening by now. Perhaps he wanted to warn the others, perhaps he wanted to establish what to do next; his intentions ceased to be relevant as soon as Szacki pushed him and he fell headlong with a short cry. Szacki wobbled and fell to his knees, but by some miracle he managed to keep his balance and froze in a bizarre position: his feet and knees remained at the level of the corridor, but he was leaning his hands against the wall of the staircase – for want of a better word. Someone behind him, maybe Sobieraj or maybe Wilczur, grabbed him by the tail of his jacket, and he was just about to sigh with relief when right in front of his face the muzzle of a furious dog appeared – black and shaggy, with mad eyes, it was covered in dust, drool and caked blood. I wanted the Hound of the Baskervilles? Well, I've got it, thought Szacki.

The dog, a mongrel the size of an Alsatian, didn't go straight for his throat, but froze a few centimetres from his face, barking deafeningly; it couldn't get its balance on the narrow steps and was just scratching at them with its claws, sending up a stifling cloud of dust. Shocked and stunned, Szacki took one hand off the wall to shield himself from the startled animal's teeth, and that was his second biggest blunder of the day – the biggest of all was still ahead of him. The moment he waved his injured hand, wrapped in the blood-soaked scarf, in front of the dog's nose, the animal went crazy. And just as only a split second earlier Szacki had been propped up and had the chance to keep his balance, as soon as the dog violently bit him, he lost it entirely. He howled in pain as he and the dog rolled down the stairs, finally landing on something soft, which must have been Marek Dybus. Of course, his headlamp had fallen off, and now it was lighting up his fight with the monstrous, frenzied mongrel from a strange angle. The whole time he had one hand trapped between the animal's jaws, while he tried in vain to push away its head with the other. He kept yanking at its wet coat, bellowing and screaming, but the dog was not going to let go, it just bit down harder and harder – he could clearly feel the layers of tissue tearing under the pressure of its jaws. Acting more on instinct than reason, he let go of its head and reached into his jacket pocket for the Glock. Writhing violently as he tried to yank his body from under the dog's paws, which were now clawing at his belly instead of the loess, miraculously he released the safety catch, stuck the pistol in the animal's mouth right next to his own hand and fired.

His roar of pain merged with the deafening, ear-splitting bang of the gun; a cloud of tissue, which the shot blew out of the dog's skull, fell on Szacki's face in wet, sticky drops. At the same moment, the white light of a headlamp appeared at the foot of the stairs, illuminating something that Szacki couldn't see, but which kept on barking like mad. Under the headlamp a flash of fire appeared. One, two, three.

The barking changed into the quiet whimpering of a dying animal.

Inspector Leon Wilczur approached Szacki and helped him to get up; a little further off Dybus was scrambling to his feet, and at the top of the stairs he could see the light of Sobieraj's headlamp. It looked as if everyone was all right. Well, almost.

"Bloody hell, I think I've shot off part of my finger."

"Show me, Teo," said Wilczur matter-of-factly, addressing him by name for the first time ever, and pulled Szacki's hand roughly, making him hiss with pain. "Got any water?" he asked Dybus.

Dybus took a bottle from his backpack. Wilczur bathed the prosecutor's hand; it looked nasty. The glass cut on his thumb was still bleeding, on the back of his hand there were deep marks left by the blasted mongrel's fangs (Szacki had never liked dogs), and the torn flesh between his thumb and index finger showed unmistakably which way the bullet had gone before penetrating the dog's brain. The old policeman examined the wounds with expertise, then told Dybus, who was still in shock, to take off his shirt; he tore it into strips and carefully bandaged Szacki's hand. The prosecutor was impressed by the policeman's sangfroid.

"OK, can we go back now?" asked their guide and expert on the underground, whose restless eyes implied that he was on the edge of panic. "I for one am not venturing a step further into this Mordor."

"There's no question," said Szacki; in fact he wanted to throw up – the bile was accumulating in his mouth in a sour wave, but once again the professionalism he had developed over the years prevailed. "I've got to see the place they ran out from."

"But how?" Dybus's voice was hysterically plaintive. "There's no more howling now."

"But there is a trail of crumbs," said the prosecutor, and pointed at the floor, where the claws of the racing dogs had carved out symmetrical grooves.

They left the two carcasses behind them and headed onwards; this time Szacki was at the head of the group. He was desperate, determined at any cost to find out what lay ahead at the end of the corridor.

VIII

"Do I have to?"

Weronika knew this cross, sulky question didn't mean that Helka wasn't missing her father, because she was missing him, in a way that was unimaginable, inconceivable, burning through the little girl's soul over and over again. She knew, because she was from a broken family herself. Her parents had divorced when she was already at college, but even so it was the worst memory of her life. Divorcing Teo had been painful; now and then she felt a wave of anger flood her, she wanted to lay hands on him and scratch his eyes out for betraying her and cheating her. But there was nothing to compare with the time when her father had taken her to Wedel's chocolate shop and café on Szpitalna Street, and informed her that he and Mum weren't going to be together any more. She had never been to Wedel's ever since.

It wasn't that she didn't miss him. If in the blink of an eye Helka could have teleported herself onto her father's knees, she certainly would have done it. This was a rebellion, a denial, a way of testing how much she could get away with. A way of stretching the emotions that tied her to her parents to the limits of endurance, testing them to see if they would break. And also a display of loyalty to her mother, a way of saying: Look, I accept your life, I like Tomek, it's Daddy who's bad, Daddy left us, let's punish him.

And of course Weronika felt like stepping into those comfortable shoes, taking her daughter in her arms to have her on her side, for the two of them to get even with that evil prick together, shoulder to shoulder. But that was a harmful, easy way out. Helka had nothing to do with it, and she shouldn't have – let her build her life with her mum and her dad right behind her, even if her mum and dad were no longer standing side by side in an embrace.

"Yes, you have to. But anyway, you want to, and I can't understand what you're so het up about."

"Coz of all those hours on the bus. I could go kayaking with Tomek. It's warm already. He promised we'd go once it warmed up."

She smiled, but she was getting annoyed. She found her daughter's deference to her new partner immensely irritating, even though she should have been glad of it. The stories told her by friends who had brought children into a new relationship made her blood run cold, but in her case it seemed to be a sort of idyll. However, she felt annoyed whenever she heard this sort of response from her daughter. She hadn't a clue why – she'd have to talk to the therapist about it. Or maybe she didn't have to, maybe she knew that actually she still loved Teodor; she was still tied to him, she didn't really give a shit about Tomek and knew this whole relationship was just for show, calculated to rub that white-haired bastard's nose in it. And here, all of a sudden, in the middle of this put-on relationship, in which she hadn't had a single decent orgasm yet, her daughter was gushing in rapture over some guy who left her cold. Bugger it all.

"I'll tell you what, Helka. You'll go and you'll have a good time, and you'll see some new places, and you'll do your best pout for Daddy, like you did for me on Monday, so he'll know his daughter's growing up too. You'll be able to distract him a bit – the poor man's stuck in the office the whole time getting bored, so he could do with a bit of a laugh. Well?"

IX

The pain in his injured hand was unbearable, travelling up his arm in waves, as if the stupid hound were still hanging there, and Szacki was sincerely hoping that was the end of the thrills for today.

The dogs' claw tracks led them to a small room, similar to the one near the seminary where they had started their expedition. There they found three amateurishly welded-together cages, some dog shit, a lot of blood and the corpse of Jerzy Szyller. The discovery prompted various reactions. Dybus was violently sick – he must have turned his digestive tract inside out. Auntie Basia switched off her headlamp to get rid of the sight. Wilczur lit a cigarette. Szacki, feeling overwhelming exhaustion brought on by the adrenalin flowing out with his blood, sat down on one of the cages and held out his hand for a cigarette. Wilczur obligingly tore off the filter and handed him a lighter. Szacki wanted to object and ask for one with a filter, but he gave it a rest and lit up. The smoke settled the nausea that had been rising in his throat, and by blowing it out through his nose he could block up his olfactory receptors for a while, giving him a breather from the charnel-house stink. He found to his surprise that an unfiltered Camel tasted better than the ordinary ones. Bah, it actually had a taste.

"Where are we?" he asked, also because he wanted to occupy Dybus's mind with something; he had no desire to allay a panic attack, a hint of which he could see in those restless eyes.

Dybus took out a map covered in incomprehensible coloured lines and spread it next to Szacki.

"I've never been in this exact spot before, but somewhere here," he said, showing a point on the map just outside the city walls, not far from the junction of Zamkowa Street and Staromiejska Street. Not far from the abandoned mansion. As far as Szacki knew, there was a meadow in that spot.

"There's nothing there," he said.

"Not now," agreed Dybus. "But at one time there was a whole district. Except that most of the houses were wooden, so there's nothing left.

This room must have been left behind by some wily merchant who realized robbers were more likely to look under the tenements than under the poor people's houses on the ramparts."

"We'll have to check if there's a way of getting from here towards the mansion on Zamkowa Street, the cathedral and Budnik's house on Katedralna Street. I think we've just discovered how the corpses teleported themselves from one place to another."

"Are you sure?" said Sobieraj, who had recovered a bit, but was still as white as chalk.

"Yes, I think so. One thing's been bothering me since yesterday, namely Mrs Budnik's body. There was sand under the fingernails, a sort of yellow, seaside sand. At the time of the autopsy I didn't take much notice of it, I told myself maybe she liked digging in the earth, or it was sand from the crime scene. But this morning I checked the bushes below the synagogue, and her garden too, and in both places there's just ordinary black earth."

"Unlike here," muttered Wilczur, and scraped at the wall; there was a bit of yellowish loess left under his long fingernail.

"Exactly." Szacki went into a corner of the room, as far as possible from the corpse, to stub out his cigarette.

Only then did he do what he hadn't had the courage to do until now, which was to look straight at Szyller's corpse, while at the same time lighting it up with his torch. The patriotic businessman was only recognizable because he had been chained to the wall high enough to prevent the dogs from devouring his face. The rest of him, from more or less the level of the ribcage downwards, was torn to bloody shreds. Szacki didn't even want to guess where exactly the pieces fitted, which were scattered all round the room. The experts, the experts would deal with that.

"Can we go now?" asked Sobieraj quietly.

"We're not achieving anything here anyway." Wilczur stood up, creaking, and glanced at his watch; there was still a sort of nervousness and impatience about him that were completely unlike the usually so phlegmatic policeman. "We'll have to send in the experts, floodlights, evidence bags. They'll have to examine this room and the whole area – I think this is also the place where Mr and Mrs Budnik ended up, there's bound to be some evidence in here."

"Possibly even more than we imagine." Szacki turned his head slowly, lighting up the room. "Until now we've been operating on the murderer's terms, we've found everything cleaned up and prepared for us, but we've discovered this place too early."

"How's that?"

"That crash we heard before the dogs got to us – look, there's a sort of timing mechanism on the cages which opened them before we arrived. Except that if it weren't for one schoolboy gifted with perfect pitch, we wouldn't be down here. Those dogs would have run about the underground, maybe they would have lived a bit longer, maybe they'd have eaten up the rest of Szyller, maybe they'd have got out of the labyrinth somehow and we'd have found them by the river, and had yet another riddle. But if we hadn't found them, we'd probably have been offered a pointer. Whatever, we're definitely here too soon, and definitely not in keeping with the killer's plan. We must take advantage of that, and get the technicians down here as quickly as possible."

"And tell them to be careful," added Sobieraj.

"Aha, I knew that pervert wasn't sitting here by candlelight!" they heard from a side corridor, down which Dybus had disappeared unnoticed. "Over here, I've found an accumulator battery!"

Szacki's brain cells heated to red-hot in the thousandth of a second needed to add two and two, but even so Wilczur was quicker than him.

"Leave it!" the policeman yelled horrendously – Szacki had never heard such a shout. But it came too late.

First Szacki saw a white flash, then he heard thunder, and then a shock wave hurled him against the wall like a rag doll. With his last vestiges of consciousness he was aware of a surprising sense of relief, a feeling of floating off into the darkness that meant it would stop hurting. Maybe for a while, maybe for ever – but it would stop.

It looked as if he had found out everything he could find out at the Sandomierz archive. Time to move on – luckily everything implied that he wouldn't have to leave the province to get all the information the prosecutor needed. Who knows, with a bit of luck the work might be finished tomorrow. How funny – a job for the legal authorities on a difficult case had proved simpler than the traditional hunt for crest-bearing aristocracy.

He could have left all the registers in the reading room and gone – that was the usual procedure – but this time he tucked them under his arm and went back to the prayer hall. Why? By now he must have been infected with the mood of a criminal investigation, which in laymen always prompts heightened suspicion, caution and paranoia. He didn't want to leave documents that were crucial to the prosecutor just lying there for anyone to look at them. Anyone – meaning presumably the killer himself, his associate or someone close to him. Apart from which, he was bothered that the main room at the archive still inspired some fear in him, which made him incapable of thinking about it calmly. Was he really quite so soft? One weird incident, one corpse seen through the fog from a distance and here he was, whining like an old woman.

So, at a brisk pace Roman Myszyński crossed the threshold of the heavy, steel door and went into the synagogue's main room. In the light of the afternoon sun, falling through the window, it didn't look scary – above all it looked dusty. The signs of the zodiac painted on the ceiling didn't seem grim or sinister, but just awkward, betraying the unskilled hand of their eighteenth-century artist. Nevertheless, he didn't feel entirely secure as he ascended the jolting staircase of the metal scaffolding – because the mortgage registers were kept right at the top, of course, next to the blasted drawbridges and the blasted windows from which you could see dead bodies.

He put the archive records down in the right place and stood next to "his" window, thinking of it as therapy. Oh, look – here I am, and there's nothing wrong with me. It's just a place, like any other, no sweat.

And just at that very moment a strange vibration ran through the scaffolding, every rivet, joint and weld of the entire structure seemed to creak, and the drawbridge broke free of its catch, fell and landed with a metallic crash against the window sill, as if inviting him to find a new corpse.

Roman Myszyński leapt and screamed with horror.

"Sir, have you gone mad, sir, or what?" Below him stood the archive manager, staring at him in disapproval.

"I never... I never... It's not my fault you've got tectonic movement here."

The disapproval vanished from the manager's face, and was replaced with a look of mild indulgence for a lunatic.

"Quite so, tectonic movement. Is there anything else I can help you with? Because if not," he said, smiling mischievously, "I'd like to lock up our local seismic research centre now."

XI

He knew it was bad. In his life he had seen enough documentaries about war to know it was very bad. Now his body was working in a different gear, there were more hormones in his veins than blood, biology was trying to give him the greatest chance of survival. But in actual fact his limbs had been torn off, his guts were gathering in puddles, he couldn't open his eyes, and when he saw this he'd be sure to have hysterics like at the front, he'd crawl along with the torn-off leg in his hand or try to shove his intestines back inside. Rather a pity that was how it would all end, but on the other hand, maybe there was an afterlife, or life began over again, who knows.

"Get up, Teo! We can't stay here!" White light dazzled him even through his eyelids, and he shielded his face with a hand, thinking that meant he had a hand – a good sign.

"What about my legs?" he asked senselessly.

"What about them? Get up onto them, we've got to get Marek out of here, there might still be a chance to save him. Quickly, Teo, please!" Tearful, hysterical notes rang out in Sobieraj's voice.

Szacki started to cough and decided to open his eyes. There was so much dust in the air that the light from the headlamps was carving cartoon-style, sheer white tunnels into it. Basia Sobieraj's face was covered in a thick layer of loess, and he saw her terrified eyes shining in the dust, her moist, nervously licked lips and a trail of thick snot trickling from her nose. He was dusty and carved up too, but he was intact, he could move all his limbs, his head and back just hurt dreadfully at the spot where he had slammed into the wall. With some difficulty he got up; his head was spinning.

"Wilczur?"

"He's bandaging Marek."

"Get out of here as fast as possible and call an ambulance. You've got a straight path to the dogs, then remember the arrows. Take care." He pressed his Glock into her hand.

"Have you gone mad?"

"Number one, other dogs; number two, the killer. Don't argue, run!" He pushed her towards the exit and, staggering, headed towards the torch-glow and agonized moans coming from the tunnel into which Dybus had disappeared.

Wilczur was leaning over the boy's body, with one torch on his forehead and another secured to the rubble that had piled up after the explosion, blocking the passage into the part of the caves beyond. Hearing footsteps, he turned to face Szacki; he was just as dusty as the rest of them, which gave his long, furrowed old face a ghostly look; decked with his moustache and his pale eyes it looked like a ritual mask. Szacki was struck by the fact that the policeman's eyes were full of genuine pain. As if he were sorry it wasn't he who had gone down the ill-fated corridor, but the young man who had his whole life ahead of him.

"He's still in shock, but if he's going to have any chance at all he's got to be on the operating table within the next quarter of an hour," said the policeman.

His estimate seemed optimistic. Dybus had open fractures of one arm, his fleece was visibly soaked in blood and his jaw was showing through a hole in his face. But worst of all was his leg, blown off below the knee. Szacki's eyes were drawn to the white, nastily shredded bone sticking out of the stump.

"I've put a tourniquet on his thigh and dressed the wound on his stomach, I think his spine is intact, because he's reacting to stimulus, I don't think any of his arteries are severed either, which is good. But it can't last long."

Szacki went back and looked around "Szyller's room", without even taking any notice of the corpse. He was looking for something to use as an improvised stretcher and his gaze fell on the doors of the dog cages. He removed them from their hinges, arranged them next to each other on the ground and jammed them together to form a structure roughly the size of a garden gate. Not a very big gate. Wilczur watched.

"Lucky he's shorter," he sniggered eerily, to which Szacki couldn't help reacting with the same snigger, which had nothing to do with black humour, but was a symptom of shock and rising hysteria.

They had to hurry.

They carefully shifted the groaning Dybus onto the stretcher and picked it up from either end; the weight was unbearable. The boy was strong and well-built, and the cages were made from reinforcing bars welded together. Nevertheless, they set off down the corridor, Szacki hobbling slightly. After a few steps he noticed the reason for the pain in his thigh – his suit trouser leg was gradually becoming saturated with blood.

Cursing, moaning and groaning, they reached the stairs and the dogs' corpses. This was more or less halfway, but Szacki was incapable of taking another step. The muscles in his arms were howling with pain and his hands were being rubbed raw against the bars. He didn't even dare imagine how Wilczur felt, who was thirty years older. But Wilczur wasn't interested in telling anyone how he felt – he just leant against the wall, wheezing. Szacki found a reserve of will-power. First he dragged Dybus, whose moans were getting quieter, up the stairs, then the stretcher, and finally helped Wilczur to come up.

"I can't do it," said the old policeman quietly, when he came back for him.

"Yes you can, just a little more."

"If I don't make it, there's something you must know..."

"Oh, bollocks, man – let's just get out of here."

Once they had got Dybus back on the stretcher, Szacki grabbed hold of it at the heavier end, where the boy's head was, and waited for Wilczur to lift his end. Reeling, battling the pain and dizziness, the nausea and the spots dancing before his eyes, forcing every cell in his body to strain itself to the utmost, hoarsely gulping in air, he moved forwards, dragging the stretcher, the injured man and Wilczur after him. His entire mind was focused on nothing but the thought of taking the next step.

"Left," groaned Wilczur from behind. "Left."

Indeed, he had moved automatically, without looking for the arrows. The need to retreat two paces depressed him. He was terrified that now he definitely wouldn't have enough strength, and he burst into tears. But, sobbing and sniffling, he forced himself to turn into another branch, and once again set his mind to focus on nothing but his steps. One, two, three. He was on the edge of losing consciousness, but he was miraculously being kept on this side of it by a sense of duty, responsibility for Dybus. When he saw lights skipping across the walls of the tunnel, coming closer from the direction in which they were going, it didn't even occur to him what it meant, he just took the next step. He couldn't trust the lights, he could only trust his legs. One, two, three.

Only when the paramedic dragged him onto the grass outside Nazareth House, only when he was laid on a stretcher and saw the blue sky above Sandomierz, with not a single cloud to spoil it, did Prosecutor Teodor Szacki lose consciousness.

9

Thursday, 23rd April 2009

In Turkey it is Children's Day, in Britain it is Saint George's Day, and in Canada it is Book Day. Seventy-six people are killed in two suicide bomb attacks in Iraq, and in Mexico a flu epidemic claims its twentieth victim. Nepal installs GSM transmitters below Mount Everest and Scottish scientists are looking for forty volunteers to eat chocolate. In Lublin, police officers trying to prevent defecation in public arrest a man and find a flare gun on him, and in his flat an arsenal of weapons dating from the Second World War. In Gliwice, a customer dies at the meat counter in a Biedronka supermarket and other shoppers have to walk around the corpse in a plastic body bag. In Poznań, a Rossmann's pharmacy insists that a teenager who wants to buy condoms must show his ID card. In Łódź, the ultra-conservative League of Polish Families party informs the prosecution service that naturist nights are being held at a swimming pool. And also in Łódź it turns out the policemen from an anti-terrorist unit have been earning a lot of extra money from gangsters. Only in Sandomierz is it deadly dull, not even the weather changes — it is sunny and chilly. The pressure falls and everyone is feeling sleepy.

I

Even if China is the homeland of the apricot, it is worth knowing that in Poland it is a fruit typical of the Sandomierz region, whose introduction to Poland we owe to the Cistercians. It was the monks in white habits who, after they had built their abbey at Jędrzejów in the seventeenth century and started to disseminate culture in the surrounding area, established the first apricot orchard just outside Sandomierz.

Out of boredom, Prosecutor Teodor Szacki read the entire article about apricots and their patriotic local history, realized *The Vistula Valley Weekly* had nothing better to offer him and put the magazine down on a stool next to his bed. That morning there had been hospital procedures, tests, drugs and conversations with the doctors to entertain him, but now he was bored to death and felt he was wasting precious time. He had taken anti-tetanus drugs and been vaccinated against rabies, he had let them smear ointment on him and bandage him, but he had refused painkillers. Yesterday he had had no such objections, had let them pump something into him, and had floated off into a ten-hour sleep, but today he was afraid of any kind of doping – he had to think fast and efficiently, he had to reanalyse the facts gathered to date and all the new ones that would result from the underground research. Forgoing the drugs had its price – the muscle pain was coming back, his grazed hands were stinging nastily, and above all he had a steady, shooting pain in his bitten hand, which now and then made him groan and clench his lips.

The phone rang.

"I'm sorry, but why do I have to find out from the Polsat news ticker that you're in hospital?"

Weronika.

"I'm sorry, but the prosecution service hasn't got control of the media yet. Soon perhaps, if Law and Justice wins the next election."

"Very funny."

"There's nothing wrong with me."

"I'm not asking if there's anything wrong with you, because I don't give a shit. I'm asking because my daughter called from school in complete hysterics saying her daddy's in hospital, and the only thing I could say to her was, 'Wait a moment, hold on, I'll just switch on the telly, maybe I'll find something out.' Are you really all right?"

"Bruises. But they pumped me full of something yesterday, I slept. I hadn't a clue there was anything in the media."

Basia Sobieraj entered the room. Seeing that he was on the phone, she stopped in the doorway, but he beckoned her to come closer.

"Well, just fancy that, there is. About you, about some underground explosions, about some shooting."

He cursed mentally. Who the fuck had told them about all that? Meanwhile Weronika was getting wound up in the familiar, all too familiar way.

"Underground explosions?" she went on. "Shooting? Have you gone completely off your head? Have you forgotten you've got a child? I know, midlife crisis, for fuck's sake buy yourself a motorbike or something, man, but don't swap your office for an underground shoot-out. It's enough for me that I'm a divorcee, I have no desire to be a widow. How does that sound? As if I were sixty."

"I don't think you can be a widow if you're a divorcee."

"You're not going to tell me who I can and can't be – luckily those dismal days are over. Just don't frighten me and upset me. You've got a child, right? Remember? Every-other-weekend Dad?"

"That's below the belt."

"Maybe. Try stopping me. And what now? Is Helka supposed to come to you tomorrow? Or have you nothing to offer for now except changing your potty and tending to your bedsores?" Her voice faltered.

He wanted to say something nice, to hug her over the phone, to admit that he missed her too and he felt regret, he was sorry as all hell. But he didn't want to do it with Sobieraj sitting there.

"Of course, let her come, I'll be out of here in a while, I'll be back in working order tomorrow," he quipped in an official tone, the coolness of which surprised even him. All the more Weronika at the other end. He could clearly sense that it caused her pain.

"Yes, of course. I'll send you a text tomorrow when I put her on the bus. Take care."

And she hung up. Sobieraj looked at him enquiringly.

"My daughter's mother," he explained, making a weird face as if to apologize for the fact that she'd had to be a witness to some long-forgotten bird screwing him around, but then, you know, the child.

"You look great," he said, to reinforce the false impression that the past had long since been in the past. "What about the others?"

"The old man's fine, he'll outlive us all. They did some tests and sent him packing with orders to drink half a litre of vodka and sleep it off. Worse news about Marek, as you saw for yourself."

"Worse news... meaning?" he asked cautiously, fearing the worst.

"He's alive, if that's what you're asking. If he'd got to the operating table a few minutes later they probably wouldn't have been able to save him." Sobieraj looked at him as if he was a hero, sat down by the bed and gently began to stroke his bandaged hand. "I went to see him, but they're keeping him in the ICU, in a drug-induced coma. His leg's been amputated, above the knee unfortunately, though apparently the worst injuries were internal, some problem with the vascular bed, I didn't fully understand what it was about. But they dealt with it, they put him back together. A strong, young constitution, he'll be all right, so they say."

Suddenly she began to cry.

"It's my fault, I dragged him in there. W-w-we sh-shouldn't have gone down there at all," she stammered, "we should have sent in the technicians, the specialists with floodlights and equipment. Teo, we're civil servants, not some sort of agents – what kind of a sick thing to do was that, anyway?"

"We thought there was a chance of saving Szyller."

"Then we thought wrong!"

"I'm sorry."

Just as he said that, Klara passed by in the corridor, embraced by an older man who must have been her father. She looked at him, but didn't even slow her pace. Nevertheless, for that brief moment Szacki locked gazes with her, seeking in her dark eyes forgiveness for what had happened to her brother. And the hope of a second chance? No, perhaps not any more. I wonder if she is pregnant after all, or not, he thought, when their gazes disengaged. That would be rather unfortunate in the present situation.

"Yes, sorry," whispered Sobieraj, probably more to herself. "Easy to say. Harder to think ahead of time."

"Especially since he wasn't meant to die, was he?"

Prosecutor Barbara Sobieraj nodded in silence, lost in her own thoughts. This went on a while, and Szacki didn't disturb her; he too had a few things to sort out in his mind.

"They say they're keeping you here until Monday. Just in case."

"I'm leaving after the evening round."

"Are you off your head?"

"I need my office, the case files and a pot of strong coffee. We can't let ourselves take a holiday right now. Besides, there's nothing wrong with me. But I do have a favour to ask you – there are three things I need."

"Yes?"

"One, I want to know all the new information as it comes up. Two, I want my computer with an Internet connection, and three, a TV with all the news channels."

"I don't know if it can be linked up in here…"

"Then have them move me to another room."

She got up, and only now let go of his hand. Perhaps it was to do with the emotions they had experienced together, perhaps he had a better appreciation of this world now that he'd come so close to leaving it, but he thought she looked very pretty. Her orange top combined with her carrot-coloured hair made a nice, lively contrast to the green-and-white hospital room, and her legs, revealed by her rucked-up jeans skirt, were much better than he might have expected from a woman of her age.

The spring had come. Basia Sobieraj smoothed down her skirt and left, without looking round.

II

Only a little further and the border between a precisely planned vendetta and homicidal insanity would have been crossed. Who knows, perhaps it will be, if the boy dies. I look out of the window, gripping the sill helplessly. How could this have occurred? How? Now I must think calmly whether it changes anything. Maybe not, quite the opposite – paradoxically, maybe I can feel safer now.

III

Prosecutor Teodor Szacki was feeling dreadful. Not because his entire body ached. And not even because every hospital worker who had helped him to move into the television room had felt the need to joke that he must be keen to see himself on TV. He was feeling dreadful because it was the first time since this case began – not counting the famous front page of *Fakt* – that he had bothered to check how events in Sandomierz were being reported in the media, and he had found out that he featured in far too many scenes. At the press conferences, sure, but there were also plenty of shots of him going in or out of the prosecution building; once he had been caught near the town hall, crossing the market square at a rapid pace, and once coming out of the Trzydziestka restaurant. The loss of anonymity, though surely only temporary, was painful, but Szacki's dreadful frame of mind was first and foremost to do with losing his own positive image of himself.

He didn't claim to be an amazing tough guy, but he liked to think of himself as a sheriff, who instead of a conscience has the Penal Code, and acts as its embodiment, guardian and executor. He believed in it, and on this belief he had built his entire public persona, which over the years had become his uniform, his official costume. It had taken over the way he dressed, his facial expressions, his way of thinking, talking and communicating with people. When Weronika used to say, "Hang the prosecutor in the wardrobe and sit down at table," she wasn't joking.

Well, the camera saw him rather differently. At the press conferences he looked like a prosecutor – stiff, businesslike, excessively serious, not flirting with the audience and not engaging in unnecessary exchanges. Next to him, Miszczyk and Sobieraj looked like assistants. Unfortunately he had a rather unpleasant, high-pitched voice – maybe not squeaky, but it didn't sound like Clint Eastwood.

The less official the situation, the worse it got. In the scene on the steps outside the prosecution building, when he had uttered the unfortunate words taken by some as a declaration of anti-Semitism, he was evidently losing his temper, and with it his control over his persona. An ugly scowl of aggression had appeared on his face, one eye had been blinking, the rapidly spoken words had run together, and there were moments when he was jabbering unclearly. He looked like the sort of person he always laughed at – a pen-pusher in a grey suit: aggressive, frustrated, lisping, incapable of constructing a coherent remark.

But most depressing of all was the clip recorded in the market square. Here he didn't feature as the refined champion of Justice, crossing the centre of the ancient city at a cavalryman's saunter. But as a thin, pale, prematurely middle-aged little man, tightly pressing his jacket flaps to his sunken ribcage to retain some precious warmth. Scowling, with his lips clenched, taking the small, rapid steps of a man who has drunk too-strong coffee and is now running to the toilet.

What a nightmare.

Wading through the information on the television sites, newspaper archives and information portals was a ghastly job, because the reports were incompetent, chaotic, given in a hysterical tone and reduced to the cheapest, shabbiest sensationalism. If Szacki hadn't been familiar with the case, based on the press articles alone he'd have made a decision to leave the county as fast as possible, or even better, the province, where a bloodthirsty madman was hunting down his victims, making the murders into gory rituals, and where no one – for God's sake, no one! – was safe.

Luckily he didn't have to plunge himself into this sea of glorified shit, because he was only interested in one thing, with the working name of alpha information. So what was the point? He understood the way the media worked well enough to know that basically it relies on consuming its own vomit. The circulation of information was so rapid that there was no time to look for sources or to check facts; the information itself became a source, and the fact that someone had posted it was enough of a justification for repeating it. After that, it only had to be repeated over and over, adding a word of comment from oneself or an invited guest. Staying with the vomit comparison, it looked as if someone had been given scrambled egg to eat and then brought it back up. Someone else had fried up a bit of bacon, eaten it and brought that back up. The next person had added salt and pepper to the vomit, eaten it and regurgitated. And so on and so on. The less scrambled egg there was at the start, the more garnish had to be added afterwards. Which did not change the fact that somewhere at the start someone must have broken the eggs – and that was who Szacki was so feverishly looking for.

He was looking because this case had involved a media furore from the start. He remembered his surprise when the first broadcasting van had driven up to the prosecution building – it had happened quickly, too quickly, especially considering how far Sandomierz was from Warsaw and Krakow. He'd been surprised, but he hadn't paid attention to this detail, because generally the biggest problem with this case, which was unduly rich in shocking, stage-directed events, was the fact that Prosecutor Teodor Szacki hadn't paid attention to the details.

Now he was correcting that mistake. He divided the case into several essential stages. Above all, the finding of Mrs Budnik's body, the identification of the razor as a knife for ritual slaughter, and the finding of Mr Budnik. And he was trying to find the point at which the dry facts had appeared the quickest, and then become fodder for the rest of the media. For a while he thought it was Polsat News; there, for example, they had talked about Mrs Budnik before eight o'clock. But in all the other instances Polsat was way behind. Radio Zet was quick, but not quite quick enough to be ahead of Polsat in the case of Mrs Budnik, or TOK FM in the case of Mr Budnik. TVN24 stayed on a fairly even keel, and was never significantly late, but it wasn't the first in any instance. But perhaps this was a blind alley? Perhaps the information wasn't coming from one single source?

No, he couldn't believe that, he bloody well couldn't. Too great a role in obscuring the case had been played by the media hysteria for no one to be controlling it.

Suddenly the monitor started ringing above his head. Szacki tensed – he had no idea what it meant, surely nothing good. In less than fifteen seconds a nurse came running into the room. She raced towards him, but soon slowed down, and the worry on her face was replaced by a reassuring smile. She thrust a hand under his hospital gown.

"Don't wriggle so much or the sensor falls off and it sounds the alert," she said in a very low, almost masculine voice. "Why scare yourself and the staff, eh?"

She sorted things out, winked and left. Szacki didn't wink back, because he was busy chasing after a thought that was racing across his brain cells. Alert. Why did that matter? Oh, of course – Alert. That was the name of the *Gazeta* newspaper's online service that gave readers the chance to send in information along with pictures and videos. A brilliant solution in the age of the dictatorship of information on the one hand, and budget cuts at newspaper offices on the other.

He took a quick look at the service, and naturally didn't find anything. He cursed aloud; his injured hand didn't like tapping at the keyboard and now the pain was radiating right up to his shoulder, which had its good side, keeping him in gear and not letting him float off into a doze or sink into non-essential thoughts.

Think, think, Teodor, he urged himself – not Alert, but there must be other services like it. He searched. On TVP's site it was called Your Info, on Radio Zet it was Infotelefon, but both the former and the latter were of bugger all use. He began to wonder whether there might be some news blogs, and shuddered at the thought of plunging into the abyss of Twitter, Blip and Facebook. He took another look at TVN24, which also had its own society of informers (he tried to imagine Facebook in the 1980s, and wondered how many people would have liked the Secret Police, and how many would have added it to their friends), which was called Kontakt24. It was the best organized of them all – here each user could run his own information mini-service in the form of a blog, the editors looked through the entries and the most interesting ones ended up on the front page of the service, or were even used on television, which was denoted in a special way. In turn, the news items on the service were tagged in a corresponding way, marking which users' information had been utilized.

From this angle he started to read all the news connected with his case, beginning with the oldest, the discovery of Ela Budnik's body. In Sandomierz, at the crack of dawn, bla bla bla, historical city, corpse below the Old Town, a mystery worthy of Father Mateusz, bla bla bla. Lots of people had applied themselves to producing the chaotic text. Sando69, KasiaF, OlaMil, CivitasRegni, Sandomaria…

Oh my fucking God.

One of those mentioned was a user with the tag "Nekama".

Szacki clicked to open his page. There were only ten entries, all to do with the Sandomierz murders. By each one there was a note to say they had been used by the online information service and also on air. Short and written in dry, simple language, they provided the most important information.

The first entry was dated 15th April and said: "In Sandomierz Old Town, next to the old synagogue building, the naked corpse of a woman has been found. The woman was undoubtedly brutally murdered, her throat had been slashed repeatedly."

Prosecutor Teodor Szacki stared at the screen and felt his heart pounding in his chest – another moment and the alert would sound to summon the nurse, who would surely be very surprised to find the sensor in its place under his gown. However, his excitement was not brought on by the content of the information, or even by the author's tag, but the time it had been published.

He remembered the moment when he got the call from Miszczyk to say he must show up on Żydowska Street as soon as possible. Klara had dragged him back to bed; a moment earlier he'd been standing by the window, watching as thanks to the approaching dawn the first shadows of the beings inhabiting the darkness had started to appear, heralding the new day. Myszyński had described the moment when he noticed the body in a similar tone. Even making allowance for the fog, it had all happened at daybreak.

He checked – on 15th April 2009 the sun had emerged over the horizon in Sandomierz at 4.39.

The entry on Kontakt had appeared on 15th April at 4.45. Which meant that its author was either the murderer, or one of the people who had taken part in the investigation from the start. Either one or the other; since yesterday he had had a growing conviction that he knew the killer, and that it had to be one of the people with whom he worked on a daily basis, with whom he drank coffee, looked through documents and planned what to do the next day. And even though he had been weighing this option since morning, this confirmation of his theory was making his heart thump like mad.

Now he needed the information from Myszyński, and he also had to call Kuzniecow. But above all he needed the documents. He needed the documents bloody urgently.

IV

OK, so he needed the documents, but this was a bit over the top. The delectable assistant at the Kielce branch of the Institute of National Remembrance, made of nothing but curves, but none of them superfluous, was pushing a cart full of documents towards him. She smiled in a friendly way and started unloading the files onto the table. There must have been about a hundred of them.

"Is all that definitely for me?"

"Trials of the cursed soldiers from Sandomierz county, 1944 to 1951, right?"

"Exactly so."

"Well, then all this is definitely for you."

"I'm sorry, I'm just making sure."

She gave him an icy look.

"Sir, if you please, I've been working here for seven years, I've done a master's, a PhD and a post-doc on the cursed soldiers, I've written over a dozen papers and two books. I can fetch these particular files from the shelves blindfolded."

His eyes smiled at the mention of being blindfolded – it reminded him of a joke, rather obscene but funny.

"And I warn you, if you try to drag up the joke about the blindfolded hunters and the shovel, I'll take away the documents, the security guard will see you out and next time you'll have to send a proxy. There's no academic degree that works on you chauvinist, sexist lot – you need a smack in the mouth and a kick in the balls to knock some manners into your stupid heads. Anyway, never mind – is there anything else I can help you with?"

He merely shook his head, afraid of betraying what effect that sort of temperament had on him – he'd give anything for her phone number now. The assistant glared at him, turned and walked off, showily swinging her hips.

"Just a moment! There is one thing…"

"As God's my witness, if it's my phone number or that sort of gambit—"

"On the contrary. It's to do with some information."

From his notebook he took a piece of paper with the list of names that interested him written on it, and handed it to the young woman.

"Budnik, Budnik née Szuszkiewicz, Szyller," she read aloud, broke off for a moment and looked at him suspiciously. "Wilczur, Miszczyk, Sobieraj, Sobieraj née Szott."

"Do those names mean anything to you?"

"Not all of them."

"But some?"

"Of course. Do I really have to have my academic degrees tattooed on my forehead or cut off my tits for one of you big male historians to take me seriously?"

"It would be an irreparable loss…"

She looked at him the way a butcher looks at a side of meat.

"…to disfigure a forehead with such an incisive, analytical mind behind it."

V

"Are you there, Commissioner?"

"Of course."

"Sorry it took so long, but I had to check it all precisely with the IT department."

"Right."

"So each of the entries from the user 'Nekama' was sent from the IP address that's the GSM gateway for the Orange network. The entries were sent from a Skyfire browser opened on a Symbian system."

"Which means…"

"Which means someone used their phone, a Nokia, to take pictures and write the words, called up Kontakt on the phone and sent it all to the Internet from that phone."

"OK, I get it, maybe you could give me the numbers so I can check them with Orange?"

"Yes, of course."

"Oleg, please, you know it doesn't work like that."

"It's the last time, I promise."

"Oleg, with you it's the last time twice a week! Can't you just once, just one single time do it the right way? Send an official letter with a stamp and wait for the answer? So I'd have something in writing, some sort of back-up, so I could say: 'Yes, Commissioner Oleg Kuzniecow from Wilcza Street is sending us an official letter too.'"

"Really, fancy saying such things to a relative."

"We're not related."

"What do you mean? You're my wife's cousin's sister-in-law!"

"You call that being related?"

"So has it come up on your screen yet?"

"I don't believe I'm doing this, but listen… it was all sent from number 798 689 459, a prepaid SIM card bought on the twenty-fourth of March somewhere in Kielce, not at a showroom, so I haven't got any precise data. The number has rarely logged on to the network, always to BTS number 2328 in Sandomierz, which is located… just a moment... on a water tower on Szkolna Street. The owner uses a Nokia E51 phone, the popular business model, on sale anywhere."

VI

He remained true to his decision to forgo painkillers, but on the way from the hospital to the prosecution building he told the taxi driver to stop at the Kabanos deli, where he bought himself a small bottle of Jack Daniels. Partly as a painkiller, partly for relaxation, and he could dose himself more precisely with that than with Ketonal. The first thing he did in his office was to pour a little into his Legia mug and knock back a few shots of the bourbon almost in one gulp – it stank of burning. Oh yes, he needed that a hundred times more than a holiday in Sandomierz hospital at the expense of the National Health Fund – despite the persuasions, insistence and threats of Dr Ross. He really was called that, and Szacki only stopped himself from asking about Dr Greene because he didn't want to annoy the doctor, who must have heard that joke from every single patient he had ever met in his entire career.

He fetched the case files out of the safe (the Glock was in police safekeeping for the time being) and spread the documents out on the desk in front of him. Hiding in them somewhere, he felt sure of it, was the answer to the question of who had murdered three people, who had been leading him by the nose for the past two weeks, and who had very nearly finished him off in those blasted vaults. Yes, it was hard for him to get yesterday's images out of his head, but that was good – very good, he thought. Good because it really was the only situation that hadn't been stage-directed, the only one that hadn't been nicely prepared for Prosecutor Teodor Szacki.

And so from a brand-new file he took out copies of the photos the technicians had taken today and spread them under the lamp. The entrance by the seminary, the blood-stained stretcher lying on the floor of the loess corridor, the narrow staircase, the carcasses of the mongrels, Szyller's body covered in dust, the dog cages deprived of their doors, and protruding from the rubble in the side corridor, Dybus's leg. Every glance at the photograph made his hand hurt more. But that was good, very good. He had to examine yesterday's expedition minute by minute, analyse every gesture and every remark made by his companions.

He sat down and started to write out everything that had happened yesterday.

After working for two hours he had filled several sheets of paper with writing, but only a few elements were circled in red. He wrote them out on a separate page:

LW scared and tense from the start. First time like that.

BS looks at her watch and worries what the time is, just before the sound of the cages opening is heard. Then insists on going back.

LW mentions that Szyller should be trussed like a lamb, not a pig, because pork isn't kosher. He also uses the word "*treif*". Knowledge of Jewish customs. Just as earlier at Szyller's house and at the cathedral.

Neither LW nor BS want to explore the vaults, they go on my orders.

LW and BS let everyone go ahead just before the encounter with the dogs.

BS insists on leaving "Szyller's room" ASAP.

LW ditto, he keeps staring at his watch.

LW didn't notice when Dybus left, but as soon as he did, he reacted violently, hysterically.

BS had no problem finding her way out of the labyrinth.

LW wanted to say something during the evacuation. To confess something important. He also noticed immediately that we had turned the wrong way.

BS admitted at the hospital that Dybus was not meant to be a victim, and was behaving oddly.

He tapped the red felt-tip pen against the page and thought. All these things were clues, very weak clues, maybe not so much clues as just flashes of intuition. But his intuition rarely let him down. He remembered that icy morning two weeks ago, slipping on the cobblestones in the market square and scrambling through the bushes to Mrs Budnik's corpse. Who was waiting there? Prosecutor Barbara Sobieraj and Inspector Leon Wilczur. Coincidence? Perhaps.

The old policeman could have retired long ago, or had himself transferred to another HQ, got a promotion. But he had decided to stay in this hole. Beautiful, yes, but a hole. Especially for a policeman. Szacki read the crime report in the *Echo* every day – the theft of a mobile at school was a big event round here. And yet Wilczur had stayed. Coincidence? Perhaps.

Each of them had vied to share with him their knowledge of the citizens, the town, and the relationships. In fact, everything he knew, he knew from them. Coincidence? Perhaps.

Each of them had hung about the sites of all these crimes, leaving evidence of themselves there and thus gaining an explanation for the presence of a hair or a fingerprint. Coincidence? Perhaps.

Both of them were from Sandomierz, they knew the town inside out, its major and minor secrets. Coincidence? Perhaps.

Or maybe he shouldn't be examining them separately? Maybe there was something else that connected them besides this investigation? What might they not have told him about? What might they have kept secret? After all, as Sobieraj's father, the old small-town prosecutor, had said, they all tell lies.

Nodding off now and then, Szacki suddenly awoke. Sobieraj's father had said something else too. When he was talking about the Zrębin investigation, he had mentioned how he and the militia captain had hesitated before putting all their money on a single card. Could it be? The age was right, old Szott and Wilczur could have been colleagues thirty years ago. And what if Wilczur took part in solving one of the most famous crimes in Communist Poland? That would also explain his unbelievably high rank – who had ever seen an inspector in a county CID?

Szacki stood up, set the office window ajar and shivered as he let in a cloud of air, which must have strayed into the neighbourhood in February and not found its way back yet.

Even if... Even supposing Wilczur and Sobieraj's father worked together on the Połaniec case. Even supposing in connection with this, both of them carry some sort of baggage. Supposing they're linked by a homicide, the death of a pregnant woman and perjury. Supposing it's a splinter off that case. Supposing Sobieraj is helping her father with some twisted criminal plan, vengeance, or fuck knows what, then...

Then what?

Nothing.

What was the point of murdering people who couldn't possibly have had anything to do with those events, because they were quite simply too young?

What was the point of committing murder because of an emotional triangle? The husband, the wife and that third man. Was there a fourth man, or woman? Wasn't that rather over the top, even for this highly sexed province?

And above all, what was the point of stylizing it according to an anti-Semitic legend? Sure, stirring up media hysteria always helps, but to put yourself to that much trouble? Those barrels, those vaults, those dogs – absolutely pointless.

Klejnocki, the profiler, had explained that it didn't have to be a smokescreen or the work of a madman – it could be a deliberate action which justified the killings in some convoluted way, explained, or provided the motivation.

The motivation. The motive. There wasn't even a hint of a motive, no suspicion of one, not a single thread for him to latch on to and follow along to the answer to the question: why? If he made any step at all in that direction, the answer to the question "who?" would be merely a formality.

He sighed, opened the window wider, poured the rest of the bourbon from his mug into a flowerpot and went to make himself some strong coffee. It was coming up to midnight, his body was clamouring that it was payback time, but he meant to keep reading the documents until he found the motive.

VII

The motive was already well known to Roman Myszyński, except that for the time being getting in touch with the prosecutor was rather low down on his list of priorities. Despite her pugnacious manner, the Senior Inspector at the Kielce branch of the Institute of National Remembrance was not entirely inaccessible, and instead of acquainting himself with her rounded handwriting, Myszyński was at her Kielce flat, getting to know some very different rounded qualities of hers, neatly packaged in an awesome red Chantelle bra.

What a pity, because if he had spent a few minutes on the phone to Teodor Szacki and summarized for him how a little hatred, a few lies and a few coincidences had led to the destruction of a Jewish family in Sandomierz in 1947, he'd have spared the prosecutor, already far too put-upon by life, a sleepless night.

But on the other hand he'd have deprived someone else of a peaceful night, so maybe there was a degree of justice in it.

10

Friday, 24th April 2009

Israel is celebrating its independence and breaks up a Palestinian demonstration against the "security fence", Armenia remembers the Armenian genocide in Turkey and the Catholic Church commemorates Saint Dode's Day. Research shows that fifty-three per cent of Poles do not trust the prime minister and sixty-seven per cent do not trust the president. MP Janusz Palikot compares the chairman of Law and Justice, the leading opposition party, to Hitler and Stalin. The Institute of National Remembrance admits it made an error and withdraws its demands to change the name of Bruno Jasieński Street in Klimontów. Earlier it had called the poet Jasieński a promoter of Stalinism, and his torture and death internal strife within the Communist Party. Football team Wisła smash Górnik 3-1 in a match that starts the twenty-fifth round, racing driver Robert Kubica does pretty well in practice for the Bahrain Grand Prix and the Silesian Stadium unveils a hedgehog mascot, still hoping that some-one will play there during Euro 2012. In Sandomierz a criminal act is reported involving the theft of a mobile phone from the trousers of a sixteen-year-old left outside the gym. The weather is without change, maybe a touch colder.

I

They were holding him on a lead like a dog and they were treating him like a dog too. They kicked, pulled, called him the vilest names and finally pushed him into a cage. Welded out of reinforcing bars, the cage was too small for him, he had to bend his head painfully at an improbable angle to fit inside it, but even so it wouldn't close; someone started banging the door to force it shut, the door struck his protruding hand, causing appalling pain; he managed to retract it, but the door was still thumping away, the monotonous sound was filling his skull. He didn't know what was happening, who they were or what they wanted from him. Only when someone opened a can of Pedigree Chum and he saw Szyller's face inside did he realize it was a dream, and woke up with a start.

Unfortunately, the pain in his hand hadn't disappeared, nor had the pain in his neck, caused by the fact that he had fallen asleep and spent the night with his head resting on the documents. Nor had the thumping gone, but it was quieter and had changed into insistent knocking at the door. Moaning and groaning, he dragged himself out of the swivel chair; at the door stood a pale and sleep-deprived, but clearly happy Roman Myszyński.

"I spent the whole night at the archive," he said with an odd smile, waving a wad of photocopied pages.

"Then you'll have a cup of coffee," mumbled Szacki in reply, once he had managed to unglue one lip from the other, and fled to the kitchen to tidy himself up.

Fifteen minutes later he was listening to an unusual story, which his special affairs archivist was telling him, not without flair.

"The winter of 1946 came early, because before the end of November it had already ice-bound and snow-coated land where, not long ago, smoke had been rising from the burning ruins. In alarm, people looked into their neighbours' terrified eyes, their empty larders and a future where nothing but pain, hunger, illness and humiliation lay ahead of them."

"Mr Myszyński, for pity's sake."

"I just wanted to set the mood somehow."

"You've succeeded. Less of the baroque, please."

"OK, anyway, a hard winter set in, the country was devastated after the war, there was no medicine, food, or men, but there were Communists, a new regime and poverty. Even in Sandomierz, which had miraculously escaped being reduced to a heap of bricks by either side. And there's a story about a Lieutenant-Colonel Skopenko, who stopped with the Red Army on the other side of the Vistula—"

"And he liked the town so much that he spared it, thanks to his strategic wisdom and his love of fine architecture," Szacki interrupted him, thinking that if Myszyński couldn't stop bogging his narrative down with digressions, it was going to be the longest Friday of his life. "I know, everyone tells that one here. I've also heard the alternative version, according to which the Lieutenant-Colonel had such a bad hangover he wouldn't let them use the artillery. Mr Myszyński, please get on with it."

The archivist gave him a sad look; the reproach of a wounded lover of a good anecdote that showed in his eyes would have melted the hardest heart. The prosecutor just pointed meaningfully at the shining red light on the Dictaphone.

"A harsh winter, people devastated, hunger and poverty. Of course, there was an empty space where the Jewish district used to be, and of course the best flats and tenements were occupied by Poles. But not all – from what I have managed to establish, a few Orthodox Jews came back after the war, though unfortunately they weren't welcomed with flowers, no one here was looking forward to seeing them again. All the real estate had been claimed, as had the wealth and possessions left behind for safekeeping, and every Jew meant a pang of conscience that perhaps not everyone had behaved as they should have during the war. I don't know if you've read Kornel Filipowicz's stories, but he does a very good job of describing the dilemma of feeling that even if you'd done a lot, it was always too little, there were always pangs of conscience. And if you hadn't done anything at all, had watched the Holocaust passively, or even worse, of course nowadays it's hard to imagine—"

"Mr Myszyński!"

"Yes, of course. So a few Jews came back to the smouldering ruins and had to hear stories of how the Torah scrolls had been used as boot liners, and how the remains of their relatives shot by the Germans had been dug up in search of dollars and gold teeth. Stories went round about the cursed soldiers, especially the ones in the National Armed Forces, who were hunting down surviving Jews. Some of them are true, I've seen the trial documents. A strange, dark time…" Myszyński paused for a moment. "Some Poles managed to kill entire Jewish families, and others, both cases from Klimontów, were prepared to risk their lives to keep on hiding Jews, this time from the anti-Communist partisans. Yes, I know, stick to the point. Anyway, the Jews had nothing to look for in a place like Klimontów or Połaniec. But Sandomierz was a city, and those who didn't fancy emigrating to Łódź came here and tried to make a life for themselves at any cost."

"But that was straight after the war. You were going to talk about the winter of 1946 to 47."

"That's right. That autumn a Jewish family arrived. Strangers, no one had seen them in Sandomierz before. He was a doctor, his name was Wajsbrot, Chaim Wajsbrot. With him were a pregnant woman and a child of two or three years. From what I've gathered, the fact that they were strangers helped them. They weren't returning to old haunts, so no one had to look them in the eye as former neighbours, or explain away the new sideboard in the kitchen – they were just plain victims of the war. They were quiet, they didn't cause any trouble or make any claims, and what's more he could help people. There had been a Jewish doctor in Sandomierz before the war too, a man called Weiss, who was greatly respected, and so naturally somehow people respected this one too."

"Let me guess – the house on Zamokowa Street is his, right?"

"The house on Zamkowa Street is nobody's, it belongs to the local council, but at one time it did indeed belong to Dr Weiss, and apparently, by that token Wajsbrot and his family moved in there. But that's just local hearsay, I haven't any written proof of that."

"But why is it empty now?"

"Officially, ownership issues; unofficially, the place is haunted."

"Haunted?"

"It's a scary place."

"Why?"

"We're just coming to that."

Szacki nodded. Unfortunately, he knew this was going to be yet another story without a happy ending, and he felt reluctant to hear it out, but he hadn't lost hope of learning something thanks to it.

"The winter went on, and people did their best to survive, Wajsbrot treated patients, and the woman's belly grew. The doctor was particularly willing to help children, people said he had a good touch, and preferred to go to him rather than to a Polish doctor. All the more because it turned out the Jewish doctor had something the others didn't have."

"What?"

"Penicillin."

"Where was the Jewish doctor supposed to have got penicillin from?"

"I have no idea, and I don't think anyone knew then either, because the penicillin was American. Had he brought it with him, or was someone smuggling it in to him, or did he have some unusual contacts on the black market? I don't know, it's all equally probable. But when he cured one and then a second child of consumption, the news ran round the neighbourhood like wildfire. Can I get a Cola?"

"Sorry?"

"I'm going to get myself a Cola. I'm going to the kiosk. I'll be right back."

"Oh, yes, of course."

Myszyński ran off, and the prosecutor got up to do a few stretching exercises – every muscle ached, literally every one. It was cold, so he began waving his arms energetically to warm up. Hard to say if it was this dodgy spring, or if the climate of the story had infected him. A harsh winter, snowdrifts among the wreckage of the houses in the Jewish district, post-war inertia and desolation. The weak light of a candle or an oil lamp shines from the window of the walled mansion on Zamkowa Street. The generously called "mansion" – it must already have been in ruins then, just as it was now, if they had let outsiders come and live in it. The doctor and his wife must have fixed up a room on the ground floor as their accommodation, maybe two rooms, but there can't have been any luxury. And there stands that ruin with yellow light in one window, a mother holding a child in her arms knocks at the door, the moon is full, the woman casts a long shadow on the silvery snow, in the background the dark bulk of the castle and the cathedral obscure the stars. A long time goes by before a pregnant woman with black curls opens the door and lets the worried mother in. Please, please come in, my husband is expecting you. Was that what it was like? Or was he getting carried away by his imagination?

The archivist came back out of breath and red in the face with five cans of Cola. Szacki didn't pass comment.

"And so news of the penicillin ran round the district," he said, switching on the Dictaphone. "And I guess it wasn't only concerned mothers who heard about it."

"Not only. Wajsbrot was visited by the cursed—"

"Let me guess: the KWP?"

"Exactly. They came to see him and they demanded a contribution for their fight against the Red invaders, a contribution in the form of antibiotics. Wajsbrot told them to get lost, and they gave him a terrible beating, but apparently somehow the local people managed to save their doctor. That lot threatened they'd come back and kill him."

"How do we know all this?"

"From the explanations Wajsbrot gave in his trial for espionage."

Szacki made a surprised face, but didn't say anything.

"In fact we owe most of our information to this trial. And which came about because the partisan commander couldn't swallow the insult of being refused."

"So he came back and killed him?"

"Denounced him. Which in turn we know from the trial of his comrades. Would you believe it? The major went so mental at the

Jew's refusal that he betrayed him to the loathsome Reds, which says a lot about the scale of hatred in Poland – I wonder where the queers would have fitted into it."

"Mr Myszyński…"

"OK, OK. It didn't take much, it was enough to mention the American penicillin and the secret police locked up Wasjbrot in seconds flat – this time the Sandomierz populace could only stand and watch. And it was just before spring, Easter was approaching, so was Passover, and so was Mrs Wajsbrot's date of delivery."

Szacki closed his eyes. Please, I beg you, anything but that, he thought.

"The doctor was in prison, apparently somewhere on the grounds of what is now the seminary, I don't know if that's true. And his wife wasn't a doctor, she had no penicillin, on top of which she usually kept behind the scenes, so she hadn't made friends with anyone in the town. Nevertheless, people helped her and didn't let her die of hunger."

"And what happened?"

"As I said, her due date was approaching. Wajsbrot's wife was of a frail constitution, as they used to say. The doctor was going crazy, he knew they wouldn't let him go, but he begged them to let her come to the lock-up for a few days so he could deliver the baby. I read the transcripts, they're shocking – he kept alternately admitting everything and then denying everything, anything just to suck up to the interrogator. He spilled some made-up names and promised to expose an international band of imperialist contacts if they'd only let him do that. Well, they didn't. Actually, judging by the sound of the interrogators' surnames, it was his own brethren who wouldn't let him."

"And Mrs Wajsbrot died?"

Myszyński opened a can of Cola and drank it in one go, then another one. Szacki was tempted to ask why he didn't just buy a two-litre bottle, but he let it go. He waited calmly for the archivist to gather his thoughts.

"Yes, but she needn't have. The townspeople liked the good doctor and sent the best midwife to deliver the baby. As bad luck would have it, the midwife came with her daughter, and she was superstitious. Both she and her daughter. Well, the rest is easy to guess. She entered the house, and the first thing she saw standing in the doorway to the cellar was a barrel of cucumbers, and of course she thought it wasn't a birth at all but a trap, that the Jews were lying in wait to kidnap her lovely little daughter, drain out her blood to make matzos and wash the newborn's eyes with it so it wouldn't be blind. So she took her child and left."

"But there was no one there apart from the pregnant wife."

"There aren't any ghosts either, but people are still afraid. She ran away. Another midwife came, but not as skilled, and the labour was complicated. Mrs Wajsbrot screamed all night, and at dawn she and her baby died. Apparently to this day you can hear her screams and the baby's crying on Zamkowa Street. Wajsbrot hanged himself in his cell the next day."

Roman Myszyński fell silent and straightened the papers lying in front of him, arranging them in a neat pile. And opened another can of Cola. Szacki stood up and leant against the window sill, gazing at the Sandomierz houses and the roofs of the Old Town looming in the distance. He had been in the house on Zamkowa Street, he had been in Nazareth House, the site of the former secret police torture cells. Corpses everywhere, ghosts everywhere – how many places like that had he been to in his life, how many places branded by death?

Myszyński cleared his throat. In theory Szacki should have been very keen to hear more – after all, this was just the background, now the archivist would match the heroes of today's drama with the heroes of the post-war drama and everything would become clear. Why was he hesitant to find that out? This information meant an arrest, the end of the case, success. He was hesitant because he was being consumed by inner anxiety, some sort of resistance. He couldn't define it, he couldn't name it. In a moment everything would jump into place, the scattered pieces of the puzzle would finally be fitted together, all the bigger and smaller clues would be explained. Despite which, though he didn't yet know the details, he was burning with a strange sense of fakery that is often felt by the audience at the cinema or the theatre. It may be well written, it may be well directed and acted too, but you can feel it's just theatre – instead of the characters you can see the actors, the spectators and the chandelier above the auditorium.

"Jerzy Szyller?" he finally asked.

"His father was the commander of the KWP unit, the one who informed on Wajsbrot and accused him of espionage. A curious character – before the war he lived in Germany and co-founded a Union of Poles there with some others. When the war broke out, he came here to fight and his name went down in the annals of the underground as a hero with lots of sabotage operations to his name, some of them highly spectacular. But then he realized he hated the Reds more than the Germans, so he went into the forest. They didn't catch him in the Stalinist era and after that he was no longer a public enemy, despite which he left for Germany and died in the 1980s. His son Jerzy was born in Germany."

"Grzegorz Budnik?"

"Son of the head of the secret police lock-up."

"The one who wouldn't let the doctor deliver his wife's baby?"

"He had more on his conscience than just that, but yes, that's the one. Budnik Senior lived to a ripe old age and died peacefully in the 1990s."

"What about Mrs Budnik? How was she connected with these events?"

"I admit that for ages I didn't think she was – I imagined she was only connected via her husband, and that's why she was killed. I reckoned that if someone's mad enough to track down the children of those to blame for a tragedy that happened seventy years ago, maybe he's mad enough to hunt down their families too."

Szacki nodded; the reasoning made sense.

"But for the sake of form I wanted to check all the leads – luckily I met a very capable archivist." Myszyński blushed slightly. "She worked her magic spells on various databases and guess what turned up? Mrs Budnik moved here from Krakow when she was still Miss Szuszkiewicz, but she was born in Sandomierz in 1963. Her mother in turn is from Zawichost and was born in 1936."

"In other words, when the Wajsbrots died she was eleven," said Szacki, and the remaining pieces of the jigsaw fell into place. "A little girl like that, brought up in a Jewish shtetl where she belonged to the minority and where she used to hear all sorts of stories, a little girl like that could have been extremely frightened when she saw a terrifying barrel in a ruined Jewish house."

Myszyński didn't comment; the truth was self-evident. There was just one thing left for Szacki to find out. One single thing. And once again, there was something catching him by the throat, as if it didn't want to let him pose that final question. It was senseless, the first time he had ever had such a feeling. Tiredness? Neurosis? Age? Were there some vitamins he was missing? It all fitted together so nicely. Three victims from years ago, three corpses today. An eye for an eye, a life for a life. The son of the partisan who informed on the doctor. The son of the secret policeman who wouldn't let him deliver his wife's baby but did let him commit suicide. The daughter of the little girl who through her belief in the legend of blood had condemned the doctor's wife to die in childbirth. But why now? Why so late? Earlier on it would have been possible to get the people who were really responsible – you can't punish the children for the sins of their parents. Was it a deliberate act? Maybe the killer had only discovered the truth this late on? That was really the last thing he had to find out. The question was taking shape on his tongue, but it was refusing to push its way out of his mouth. Fuck it all, Teodor, he shouted at himself mentally. You must find out who it is, even if you find the solution very unpleasant. You're an official in the service of the Republic, and you're just about to know the truth. Nothing else matters.

"So what was the fate of the Wajsbrots' other child?" he asked coldly.

"Officially, no such person exists. However, there is someone whose age would tally. I came upon the trail rather by accident, because this person had been rummaging in the Institute archives and their name was left in the signing-in book. This individual was brought up in an orphanage in Kielce; before that there's no trace of the person in the registers, or of any forebears – I did a thorough search. This person has an extremely Polish surname, a family, a daughter. And works in your profession, i.e. with the forces of law and order."

II

Everything has been accomplished, there's nothing left to do now but to start a new life. What sort of a life will it be? How long will it last? What will it bring? Will it be possible to fill the void with love and friendship? Somewhere, some day. I'm laughing. Love and friendship, that's a good one. Suddenly I feel immense regret for lost youth and lost love. Although I console myself with the thought that there's no such thing as real youth or true love... After all these black deeds there's no chance left of filling my soul with light. But it doesn't matter. Emptiness and darkness are not an unreasonable price to pay for peace, for the fact that finally I don't feel that stifling hatred. I shudder when there's a knock at the door. Strange – I'm not expecting guests.

III

"You're wrong, Prosecutor."

Teodor Szacki said nothing; in this particular function he didn't have much to do – it was purely a job for the police. Indeed, the Marshal was stammering and looking apologetic, but he performed all the duties stipulated by the law. He introduced himself, he introduced the legal grounds and the case relating to the arrest, checked the detainee's identity, searched him, took away his gun, handcuffed him and told him about his right to have a lawyer present and about his right to refuse to make a statement.

Inspector Leon Wilczur submitted quietly to the procedures without saying a word; after all, he knew them from the other end. He didn't look surprised, he didn't struggle or argue, or try to escape.

"You're wrong, Prosecutor," he repeated with emphasis.

What was Szacki to say? All his muscles ached, so did his ripped-up hand and now his neck too; he really was bloody tired. Reluctantly, he glanced at the old policeman. Without a jacket, just in his scruffy shirt, trousers and thin socks he looked even more pitiful than usual. An old codger, spending his day of sick leave in front of the television in a neglected flat full of dusty antiques. He forced himself to look up and meet Wilczur's gaze head-on, his dry, slightly yellow eyes. He had always thought there was antipathy towards the world hidden behind them, plain old embitterment and typical Vistula-valley frustration. But hatred? My God, how much emotional effort you would have to put into nursing your hatred for years on end to commit three murders in the name of revenge for things that happened seventy years ago. How much toil not to let that hatred die out or fade, not to lose sight of it for an instant.

The experts wouldn't confirm it, and quite right too, but for him Wilczur was a madman. He had seen various murders and various killers. Plaintive, obstreperous, aggressive, remorseful. But this? This was off his scale. What could be the point of killing the children and grandchildren of people to blame from years ago, even if their crime was awful and painful? No code in the world stipulated that children were responsible for the sins of their parents – that was the basis for civilization, the border between the intelligent human race and animals driven by instinct.

"'Fathers shall not be put to death for their children's sins, nor shall children be put to death for their fathers' sins; a person shall be put to death for his own sin,'" Szacki quoted the Book of Deuteronomy.

Without tearing his eyes from Szacki's for an instant, Wilczur twittered some incomprehensible words that sounded now sing-song, now husky, pervaded with a bluesy nostalgia – it must have been Yiddish or Hebrew. Szacki raised an eyebrow enquiringly.

"'For I, the Lord your God, am a jealous God, visiting the iniquity of the fathers upon the children to the third and fourth generations.' The same book, a few chapters earlier. As you very well know, Prosecutor, you can find a Bible quote for anything. But that doesn't matter.

What matters is that you're wrong, and this mistake could have terrible consequences."

"I could tell you how many times I've heard that remark from arrestees, Inspector, but why should I? You've heard it even more often, and you know even better than I do how much truth there is in it."

"Sometimes a little."

"Where the truth is concerned, a little is nothing."

He nodded to the Marshal to take Wilczur away.

"We'll meet tomorrow for your interview – have a good think in the meantime about whether you really want to complicate proceedings. Those killings, that stylization, that sick staging, that insane vengeance. At least be sure to answer for all that with style."

Wilczur was just walking by, his face passed centimetres from Szacki's and the prosecutor could clearly see the thickened surface of his eyeballs, the pores of his skin carved with deep furrows, the yellow stain of cigarette smoke on his moustache, and the sharp hairs in the nostrils at the base of his prominent nose.

"You've never liked me, have you, Prosecutor?" wheezed the policeman with unexpected regret, breathing his sour breath into Szacki's face. "And I know why."

Those were the last words uttered by Leon Wilczur in connection with the case in which he had been arrested on a charge of three murders.

IV

Szacki didn't go back to the prosecution building. He just had two short phone conversations with Miszczyk and Sobieraj; he didn't want to see them, he didn't want to explain and elaborate, he didn't want to react to their fulsome oohs and aahs and OhmyGodhowcanthatbes. The most important thing, in other words the results of Roman Myszyński's research, was lying on their desks, and that was enough to issue an arrest warrant, which Sobieraj would deal with later. A laconic statement was also to go to the media to say a suspect had been arrested.

The rest of it was really up to Wilczur. If he confessed, in three months an indictment would be ready, but if he dug his heels in, someone had a long and tedious circumstantial trial ahead of him. Most probably not him – there was a healthy custom that cases involving police officers and civil servants were sent to a different prosecution service. Teodor Szacki was hoping that this time, however, it would be possible to keep the case here, or ultimately to persuade the people at the regional prosecution office to give it to him somewhere else. He was eager to be the one who wrote the indictment and defended it before the court. He couldn't imagine it would be any other way.

Whatever, he didn't have to deal with that today – today he could rest. He couldn't remember when he had last been so incredibly, dreadfully tired. To such a degree that just plain walking was an effort; as he stood beneath the Opatowska Gate, opposite the seminary building where many years ago Chaim Wajsbrot had hanged himself, and outside which the little Leon Wilczur may have stood, hoping to see his daddy, he couldn't keep going, and sat down next to a tramp on a small bench. Just for a moment. The tramp looked familiar; he searched his memory for a while – yes, sure, it was the one who had accosted Wilczur that evening as they were leaving the "Town Hall" bar together; he'd wanted the police to look for his missing pal. Szacki thought of striking up a conversation, but didn't bother. He closed his eyes and turned his face to the sun; even if it wasn't providing any warmth, maybe he could sunbathe a bit; he couldn't stop worrying about looking so pale on TV, like an emaciated maggot.

He was feeling odd. The end of an inquiry and catching the culprit always brought with it a certain emptiness, post-investigation depression, withdrawal syndrome. But this time it was something else; at a rapid pace the void was being filled by anxiety, the familiar anxiety in his brain cells, signalling a mistake, an oversight, an omission.

He had no idea what it was about, and he didn't want to brood on it. Not now. Now he pulled himself off the bench and walked up Sokolnicki Street to the market square. He passed a bar selling pierogi, he passed the Chinese which he had never dared to peep inside, and stopped briefly at the Mała Café, wondering whether a frothy coffee with a sprinkling of icing sugar might not be what he needed. But no, he didn't want coffee, he didn't want waking up – he wanted a shower and bed.

He reached the market square just as the clock on the town-hall tower began its antics to mark two o'clock in the afternoon. He stopped for a moment and observed how the city was changing, gearing up for the tourist season, which would start, like everywhere else, on the long May weekend. He hadn't seen Sandomierz in this guise yet; he had come to live here towards the end of the year, when everything was shut, there wasn't a trace of the Polish golden autumn left, and the cobblestones in the Old Town were either wet, snowed over, or coated in ice. Now the town looked like a sick person waking from a coma, who isn't able to get up and run at once, but is gently testing to see what he can and can't do. The terrace of the Kordegarda restaurant was already up and running, outside the Mała the owner had set two small tables in the open air and outside the Kasztelanka two waiters were setting up a garden fence. In the distance, maybe outside the Cocktail Bar, someone was cleaning a large parasol with a Żywiec beer logo on it, and outside the Ciżemka Hotel a green ice-cream booth, which had been tightly boarded up until now, was opening its doors. It was still cold, but high in the sky the sun clearly had no intention of giving up and Szacki sensed that this weekend would be the first of the real spring.

But he wasn't tempted by any of the bars or cafés; he turned towards the Vistula, and a few moments later he was at his flat, for the first time since Wednesday morning. He wasn't bothered by the clothes lying about the place or the empty fridge; he took off his suit and buried himself in the bedding, which still smelt of Klara's sweet, youthful scent.

I can't understand why I'm not feeling relief, dammit, he thought. And fell asleep.

V

A few hours later he was woken by a phone call from Basia Sobieraj. She had to see him right away. "OK," he said, and went to take a shower, forgetting that where Sandomierz distances were concerned, "right away" meant "instantaneously". When he emerged from the bathroom, with water dripping from his hair onto the collar of his dark-blue dressing gown, Basia was standing at the door with a shapeless package in her hand and a strange expression on her face.

She gave him the package.

"This is for you."

He undid the brown parcel paper, and inside there was a prosecutor's gown, the blackness of which had long since ceased to be black; the redness of the trim had faded too.

"My father asked me to give it to you. He said he doesn't want to look at it any more, he wants to die looking at me, not that piece of rag, which was his costume his whole life. And he says I'm to give it to you, because only you will know how to make use of it. Because apparently you understand something that I don't – I don't know what it means."

That everyone tells lies, thought Szacki.

He didn't say anything, just put aside the gown and used his dressing-gown collar to wipe away a trickle of water running from his hair down his cheek. He gestured to invite Sobieraj inside, wondering why she had really come to see him. Did she want to talk about the case? About the murders? Dead bodies, sins and hatred? He thought bitterly that he was a good partner for that sort of conversation – it'd be hard to find a better one in Sandomierz.

He didn't feel like talking. He sat down on the sofa and poured generous helpings of Jack Daniels into some thin antique shot glasses. Sobieraj sat down next to him and downed her bourbon in one draught. He looked at her in amazement and refilled her glass. Once again she drank it in one go and blinked funnily; she was behaving like a child who's afraid to say he's broken a vase, even though he's about to give himself away. She tucked a wisp of hair behind her ear and looked at him with a nervous, slightly apologetic smile.

Please, not today, he thought. He really was bloody tired.

Nevertheless, he leant forwards and kissed his colleague, wondering if that was what he wanted or not. He liked her, he liked her very much, more and more by the day, but he wouldn't have said a romance was developing between them, or a passion, not to mention love. If he had had to put a name to the feeling, he'd have used the word "friendship".

But he decided to skip the theorizing for the time being. Still kissing her, he drew her towards the bed and started gently but methodically undressing her.

"If you don't want this, you know, tell me, otherwise I'll feel bad. I've never been in this situation," she said, raising her arms above her head to let him remove her thin dark red polo-neck, "and I don't really know how to behave. I just very much wanted to, but if you don't want to…"

"Tough, I'll force myself somehow," he said, running a finger down her freckled chest, which looked like a join-the-dots picture, jumped across the wire of a tight bra the same colour as her top, and came to her navel.

"Is that a Warsaw joke? I swear, I don't know if I can manage," she said, but laughed when he made a rascally face as he peeped into her knickers. Which, incidentally, were also a touch too small, cutting into her stomach and making a nice little fold of flesh above the elastic.

Click.

"Hey, that package you got on Wednesday…"

"Yes, all right, laugh at me, because I wanted to have something pretty for you. Just imagine, there aren't ten shops full of designer lingerie in Sandomierz. But of course it didn't occur to me that over the winter I've grown a size and, well, it doesn't look super-aesthetic, I'm sorry…"

He laughed out loud.

"Let's get them off as fast as possible before they make marks on you!"

"Oof, thanks."

They went back to kissing, they were both naked now, when suddenly Sobieraj sat up on the bed and shamefully covered herself with the quilt. He gave her a questioning look.

"God, I feel strange, as if I should be asking him for permission. To make it all right."

"OK," he said slowly, waiting for the next bit.

"I've never been unfaithful to Andrzej. Not that I don't want this, you understand, I want it very much, I just thought you should know. That I'm not just a pushover. And I'm terribly nervous. There are stories going around about you, there's Klara, and Tatarska was going into raptures too, and she's usually so stern…"

Now he understood, at this precise moment, what it meant to live in a small town.

"…and I've been with the same guy for fifteen years, and not that often either, and I'm simply afraid my repertoire is, you see, more for a chamber than a symphony orchestra. And I know how that sounds, I just wouldn't want you to judge me too quickly, do you see?"

"Woody Allen," he said, pulling the quilt over his naked body because he felt cold.

"What about Woody Allen?"

"This is like a scene out of Woody Allen – instead of screwing we're talking about screwing."

"Yes, I know, I know."

"So maybe let's take it ever so slowly, and see what happens next, eh?"

They took it ever so slowly, and that suited him very well after all the perverse acrobatics he'd been forced into by his lovers of late. Instead of striving and straining, he could slowly revel in intimacy, enjoy finding his own and Basia's pleasure; she turned out to be a sensual and intelligent lover, as well as funny and delightful in her self-consciousness. She tried various things with the caution of a little animal, but then quickly picked up speed, and not much time had gone by before they had advanced from the stage of mild moaning to the point where she was burying her head in the pillow to avoid alarming the whole of Sandomierz with her shouts. He suddenly remembered about her weak heart and was worried.

"Is everything OK?"

"Are you nuts?"

"I was thinking of your heart."

"Relax, I took some drugs. If the orgasm isn't too intense I might just survive."

"Very funny."

The orgasm was moderately intense, and luckily both parties survived it. Szacki cuddled Basia to him and thought that if they became lovers, it would be a completely new experience for him – usually he was the one who wasn't free.

"I'm still in shock," she whispered, "still at the stage of disbelief, it hasn't really sunk in yet."

"Just let me get warmed up and I'll show you."

"Silly, I meant Wilczur."

"Aha."

"I read what the archivist found, it all fits together, there are no gaps, as far as the motive goes. Then I remembered he was the first to get to Ela's body, he was there when the razor was found and he showed us the recordings from the cameras and coordinated the witness interviews – he could have been manipulating us however he liked. Especially you – you don't know this town, you don't know the people, you took things on faith that I probably wouldn't have swallowed."

"If you're so smart, he should have been locked up earlier."

"You know that's not what I meant. I think he must have had the entire plan worked out long ago, but the opportunity only came up when you appeared in Sandomierz. He could be sure the star from Warsaw would get the case. A star, but an outsider."

"On the first day he said he'd help me, he'd explain who was really who."

"I don't doubt it."

For a while they lay in silence.

"I find it horrifying – to nurse hatred for so many years. But when I read the documents from the Wajsbrot case…"

"Yes?"

"The post-war brutality – it never gets talked about here, and when occasionally a researcher or a journalist 'from Warsaw' drags it up, he doesn't even become public enemy number one, it simply isn't talked about."

"You're not the exception here. It's like that all over Poland."

"I can't stop imagining it. How those people came home from the camps, kept alive by the hope that maybe by some miracle their bathroom and kitchen had survived, that when they finally got there they'd make a cup of tea, have a cry and somehow manage to get on with life. Except there was someone else standing in their kitchen, their life wasn't convenient for anyone – a friend from school came back a week ago and they'd already tortured him to death, they'd hanged him on a birch tree. That is, I knew things like that happened, but Wajsbrot puts a face to those events, I can see him banging his fists against the wall of his cell in Nazareth House and howling, and his wife dying a few hundred metres away, because the midwife was terrified of a Jew. Do you think she can have died in Wilczur's arms? He must have been four or five then."

"That doesn't justify what he did."

"No. But it helps to understand it."

The phone rang. He picked it up and leapt to his feet.

"Yes, of course, I'm on my way, I'll be waiting at the stop."

"What's happened?"

"My daughter's coming to stay with me for the weekend."

"Oh, that's great – so you'll be bringing her over with you tomorrow?"

"How's that?"

"We made a date for a barbecue. Don't you remember?"

VI

The pressure of thoughts and emotions is making my head ache. I'm pacing from corner to corner, but the room is small and uncomfortable, I can't just go outside the usual way. I can't concentrate, I can't make up my mind, as ever I can't make up my mind. I know the most sensible thing would be to accept that this is the end, and to be done with it all. It's only an unnecessary risk that won't bring any advantage, and might ruin everything, everything! I know that, but I can't let it go, not this time. Besides – besides, maybe the risk isn't that great.

11

Saturday, 25th April 2009

International Noise Awareness Day. Egypt is celebrating the twenty-seven anniversary of Israel's withdrawal from the Sinai Peninsula, Iceland's Social Democrats and Greens are celebrating a win in pre-term parliamentary elections, and Al Pacino and Polish actor Andrzej Seweryn have birthdays. The world is starting to get hysterical about swine flu. In Germany an anonymous collector pays 32,000 euros for some watercolours by Adolf Hitler, depicting rustic landscapes. Polish pianist Krystian Zimerman causes a scandal in the USA by announcing during a concert that he's not going to play any more in a country whose army is trying to control the entire world. In his homeland the Law and Justice party demands an explanation from the Ministry of Defence as to why soldiers in the guard of honour do not take part in ceremonial masses; the Ministry replies: Because if they faint from standing to attention for hours on end, they could do someone an injury with their bayonets. At tax offices all over Poland it is open day, and next week the deadline passes for filing tax returns. At the District Museum in Sandomierz an exhibition of "tectography" and unique prints by Grzegorz Madej opens. It is dry, sunny, a little warmer than yesterday, but not above seventeen degrees.

339

I

He was nervous about the meeting with his daughter, and although he would never have admitted it to anyone, he went to fetch her from the bus station with his heart in his mouth; it was situated not far from the Jewish cemetery, where a few days earlier he had had the supporters of national socialism arrested. Incidentally, he was surprised that after getting out of the can none of them had taken the trouble to paint a Star of David on his door or just give him a smack in the gob.

Helka came flying out of the bus laughing and happy, full of the longing, admiration and empathy of an eleven-year-old. Empathy, because the bandage on his hand still looked suitably serious, and admiration because the television reports combined with the little girl's fertile imagination had created the image of a hero, oblivious to the dangers as he battles against evil and crime.

They had a very nice evening over pizza, and a wonderful morning, the major elements of which were a walk (including races and a game of badminton) by the Vistula and breakfast at the Mała Café, hot chocolate and sweet pancakes. Prosecutor Teodor Szacki gazed at his bright little spark with the chestnut hair, engrossed in reading one of the tatty old comics, who was just starting to pupate from a lovely child into an awkward teenager, and for the first time in ages he felt calm. Not tired, but calm. And, picking up with daughterly sixth sense that her father had a few rough days behind him, Helka spared him the sulks, hysteria and heart-rending crying that she wanted everything to be the way it used to be, or she'd never be happy again.

And then they went to see Basia and Andrzej Sobieraj.

The very idea of visiting Basia and her husband, not just with a child, but after yesterday's heady evening, seemed to him as bizarre as it was attractive, and the only thing preventing him from enjoying this perverse situation was the fact that he still had the conversation with Leon Wilczur ahead of him. He would gladly have put it off to Monday, but he couldn't. For if Wilczur decided to confess – and Szacki supposed that would happen sooner or later – it would add strength to the temporary arrest warrant. For the time being, however, he pushed the thought of Wilczur into a corner and cheerfully threw his squealing daughter over the Sobierajs' low garden fence, then jumped over it himself, which he thought very sporty, but could only do because the fence came no higher than his knees.

Helka and Andrzej Sobieraj very quickly found a common language, mainly thanks to the gadgets he showed her, things with which the little girl, brought up in a high-rise, was unfamiliar. She had already played with the secateurs and the lawnmower, and now it was the turn of the garden hose, which to her, judging by her lively reaction, was something like the holy grail – the ideal toy.

"At last you don't look like Joseph K."

Indeed, he hadn't made the same mistake as a week ago, and had come to the Sobierajs' garden in jeans and a thick grey polo-neck sweater; he left the suit he had to put on later for the interview in a cover in the car.

"At last you don't look like a girl guide," he retorted.

They were sitting together at a small table on the patio.

"Better save up for a house with a garden!" shouted Andrzej Sobieraj from behind the hedge. "This kid's got the makings of the owner of a garden centre!"

"Daddy, Daddy, I want a lawnmower!"

"For your hair perhaps!"

Helka ran up to the table.

"You've forgotten I want to have long hair. Down to here," she said, waving her hand at kidney height.

Andrzej Sobieraj came trudging after the child, clearly out of breath. Szacki watched him take a big slug of beer from a can, and wondered if the Sobierajs had had sex yesterday. On the one hand he would have been truly surprised, on the other he had learnt by now that contrary to popular opinion, it's the small towns that are a hotbed of all manner of debauchery.

"Come on, you can help me carry all this clutter into the kitchen," said Basia to her husband.

"For God's sake…"

"What about the dancing flower?" asked Helka innocently.

"Of course I'll show you the dancing flower," said Sobieraj, reviving. "And the prosecutor will help you with the crockery. The child's come from the city, let her have a bit of fun."

He and Helka went back into the garden to set up the dancing flower, whatever it was, while Szacki and Basia Sobieraj gathered up the plates and went inside the house to kiss. Only when joyful shouts announced the success of Operation Flower did they stop, and go back onto the patio with a baking tin full of cakes.

The dancing flower really did dance – it must have been constructed so that the water flowing through it tossed its head in all directions, producing a jolly, comical effect. Helka stayed by the flower to squeal, jump up and try in vain to escape the sprays of water, and Andrzej Sobieraj came back to the table.

"You've got a wonderful daughter," he said and picked up his beer can. "To your genes."

In reply Szacki raised his glass of Cola. At the same time he remembered what Basia had once told him about the fact that they couldn't have children. Did that mean she didn't use any contraceptives and was used to the fact that sex never meant procreation?

"When will you tell the media about Wilczur?" asked the breathless Andrzej in a whisper. Earlier they had agreed not to discuss the case in front of the child.

"We'll tell them the arrested man is a police officer on Monday. And the rest of it as late as possible," explained Szacki, never taking his eyes off the child, an old paternal habit. "We'll talk in general terms about personal motives, we'll deny the rumours about a serial killer and use investigation confidentiality as an excuse. The hysteria will die down, and then it'll be as usual. The inquiry will go on for months, and once it's possible to look at the files and find out Leon W.'s motivation, few people will be interested. There'll be some fuss at the time of the trial, but by then it won't be our problem any more."

"Why not?"

"These are our final days on this case," said Basia, who in contrast to her white-haired colleague was not suffering for this reason – on the contrary, she seemed delighted. "Teo still has to interrogate Wilczur before we can issue the arrest warrant, but soon the documents will be passed to another prosecution service – I'd bet on the regional one in Rzeszów."

"That's a pity." Sobieraj crumpled his can and threw it in a rubbish bag. "I'd have liked to hear from you what it was really like."

II

Changing into his suit took longer than the actual interview. Leon Wilczur was brought in, and confirmed his personal details, then announced that he was refusing to make a statement. Szacki thought hard for a while, then passed him the transcript to sign. Wilczur was an old hand who knew his options perfectly well, so no requests, threats and appeals to his conscience would have been any use. The strategy of saying nothing was ideal – if Szacki had been the policeman's lawyer he would have recommended the same, without even looking at the documents. The case was complicated and circumstantial, the historical motivation was exceptionally obscure and the investigators had hard work ahead of them looking for proof and witnesses – to start with they'd have to repeat all the functions performed by the police because Wilczur's presence invalidated them.

"Maybe, though?" he asked. "Three murders. Three victims. After so many years in the police, after solving so many cases, catching so many criminals, don't you think you should confess? So that justice can be done. Quite simply."

"You're wrong, Prosecutor," wheezed Wilczur, without even turning his head to face him.

12

Sunday, 26th April 2009

For Orthodox Christians it is Renewal Sunday, a holiday
similar to the Polish All Souls' Day, when feasting at
the cemeteries is meant to help the souls of the dead
to reach heaven. For prison guards in Poland it is
Prison Service Day. Cabaret star Jan Pietrzak and actress Anna Mucha are celebrating their seventy-second
and twenty-ninth birthdays, respectively. Swine flu is
raging. The media are talking non-stop about those infected in new countries, some Polish musicians report
from Mexico that "the streets look like intensive care
units", and the Minister of Health provides assurance
that Poland is well prepared. Belarusian President
Alexander Lukashenko arrives in Rome on his first
foreign trip since 1995. Polish Prime Minister Donald
Tusk signs a declaration agreeing to donate his organs
for transplant — to the disappointment of the opposition, only in the event of his death. The people of
Sandomierz are advertising their city at a tourist fair
in Warsaw. Meanwhile in the city an ethnic-rock band
called Jacyś Kolesie — "Some Guys" — is giving a concert, and the excursion boats are back on the Vistula,
but the big news of the day is the spring, finally the
spring is here! It's warm and sunny, and the temperature rises above the magic barrier of twenty degrees.

Saying goodbye to Helena Ewa Szacka was heartbreaking. The closer her bus departure time came, the worse the atmosphere, despite Szacki's efforts to provide first-rate fun. On the way to what was generously called the bus station, which was really a booth made of plywood and corrugated iron, Helka was quietly crying, and outside the bus she started to sob and clung on to her father so hysterically that he began to consider driving her to Warsaw by car. But then a portly lady came to the rescue, who was travelling with a granddaughter of a similar age to Helka; seeing the direness of the situation, she offered to look after the other little girl as well during the journey. And as soon as she caught the whiff of some entertainment, at once the "other little girl" cheerfully kissed her dad on the brow and disappeared inside the surprisingly decent-looking coach.

Even so, Szacki felt sad and downcast as he went back to – well, quite, to where? His home? That alien flat wasn't his home. His place? That was more like it – "his place" could be a home, but it could also be a hotel room, a bed in a hostel or a tent at a campsite. You could talk about any temporary lodging like that.

So he went back to his place, but it only took a glance into the box-like kitchen window for him to turn on his heel and set off down the steps that ran towards the river. He felt like going for a really long walk – he wanted to get tired, eat dinner, drink a couple of beers and sleep dreamless sleep.

God, what a beautiful day it was! Basia was right a week ago when she said you have to see the spring in Sandomierz. The spring had decided to make up for all its lost days, it had showered the branches, bare until now, with green mist, and on the ones that had already gone green, white flowers had appeared; in the air the sweet scent of blossom mixed with the smell of earth and a muddy odour of sodden meadows blowing in from the Vistula. Szacki inhaled them like a drug addict, trying to experience all of them at once, and each one separately; never in his life before had he seen any other spring apart from the faded urban variety, which seemed tired and used up from the very start.

He went down onto the common, and next to the statue of John Paul II – where there was a curious plaque announcing that here the pope had celebrated "mass in the presence of the restored Polish knights" – he went left and crossed the meadow towards the road to Krakow. Only there did he turn around and look back at Sandomierz. And then he thought: all right, there has to be more than a feeble grain of truth in the legend about Colonel Skopenko. He couldn't imagine anyone seeing the city from this perspective and then giving an order for artillery fire. It was beautiful, it was the most beautiful city in Poland, it was Italian, Tuscan, European, not Polish, it was a place you wanted to fall in love with at first sight, settle in and never leave. It was – it occurred to him for the first time ever – his city.

He tore his gaze from the tenement houses banked up above the Vistula escarpment, from the white block of the Collegium Gostomianum which sat next door to the Gothic red-brick Długosz House, from the town-hall tower and the cathedral bell tower, slightly hidden from this perspective. And set off along the road, casting the occasional glance at the soothing architectural splendour.

He took a slight turn along Piłsudski Boulevard, where a pleasure boat had appeared, so he sat on a bench for a while, watching the tourists getting on and off. Depending on the person, he either felt glad he wasn't them, or quite the opposite – he envied them their lives. He could amuse himself like that for hours. Then he climbed the mysterious, murky gorge that led up to Saint Paul's church, from where he took the road back to the castle, encountering on the way a crowd of people leaving Saint James's church after mass.

Unfortunately, he couldn't helping looking at the meadow spread out below, the exact spot underneath which a few days ago the explosion had thrown him against the wall and crippled Marek Dybus for life. That wasn't a good memory.

Nor unfortunately could he carry on pretending to be occupied by his daughter, views of Sandomierz, walks and the search for spring. He was mercilessly, exhaustingly anxious, shaken, frazzled – any word in any language suited him, as long as it expressed anxiety. Which he was feeling painfully with every fibre of his existence; regardless of whether he was playing with his daughter, eating or sleeping, he could only feel that one emotion. And he could only see one thing: Wilczur's face. And he could only hear one thing: "You're wrong, Prosecutor."

Nonsense, bloody nonsense, he couldn't be wrong, because all the facts – though fantastical – fitted together perfectly. So what if they were unusual? So what if the motive seemed fanciful? People have killed for stupider reasons, and Wilczur knew that better than he did. Besides, no one was forbidding him to speak. He could explain why Szacki was wrong. He could prove where he was at the time of the murders. He could gabble away endlessly, keep talking until they ran out of paper at the prosecutor's office. But he wouldn't do that, he wasn't stupid, the bloody old codger, damn and blast it all.

Last night, unable to sleep, Szacki had already put a name to what was bothering him. He was sitting in the kitchen, listening to his daughter tossing and turning, and scribbling out possible versions of events – now with a suspect behind bars at least. The versions had various nuances, but they all answered the question "why?" neatly, in typical crime-novel style. A great wrong, transferred hatred, revenge years later. Revenge planned in such a way that everyone would hear what had happened in the frosty winter of the Year of our Lord 1947. Just as Klejnocki had explained: infamy is an important part of a vendetta, a dead body alone is not sufficient compensation. And Wilczur had achieved his aim – all of Poland would be talking about him and how he had been wronged.

Yes, on the question of the motive it all made sense. It was less straightforward when it came to the question "how?" How did this skinny, seventy-year-old kill three people? Many of the relevant questions could be explained by the fact that he was an experienced Sandomierz cop. Always first at the scene of the crime, he dealt the cards and issued the orders. He controlled the interviews and police activities, he controlled the entire machinery of the investigation. He supervised the recovery of the recordings from the urban security system, at the same time proving that modern technology was not unfamiliar to him. Which explained the account with the information service and using the mobile phone to keep the media informed. It was just a pity they hadn't found the phone. He knew Sandomierz inside out, which could explain his familiarity with the vaults. It would be necessary to interview Dybus about that circumstance, once he recovered – who knew about their research, who took part in it, whether the municipal services or officials were involved in it. Supposing Wilczur knew the underground, and supposing the fantastical thesis that there were hidden entrances to it in various parts of the town were true, that could explain how the bodies were transported. Placing a policeman in the role of the culprit also explained something that had bothered Szacki earlier on, which was the badge in the victim's hand. Wilczur had pressed the "*rodło*" symbol into Ela Budnik's hand to direct suspicion towards Szyller, and for suspicion to bounce off him in turn towards Budnik, and for the love affair among the upper echelons of Sandomierz society to come to light. It fitted Klejnocki's theories about infamy.

But that was very little, still very little.

Szacki was now standing in the castle forecourt; he liked this place, and the view stretching away below the terrace on to the bend of the Vistula, worryingly broad at this time of year. He liked knowing that people had stood there for several hundred years, admiring the same landscape. Well, maybe a slightly finer one, not hideously disfigured by the glassworks chimney. There were lots of people around, who were spilling out of the neighbourhood churches after High Mass. Typically for a small town, they were wearing their Sunday best: the gentlemen in suits, the ladies in bizarrely coloured matching skirts and jackets, the boys in shining sports shoes, and the girls in black tights and evening make-up. There were a hundred potential reasons for mockery in each of them separately and in all of them together, but Szacki found the sight of them touching. All those years living in Warsaw he'd sensed that something wasn't right, that the ugliest capital city in Europe wasn't a friendly place, and that his attachment to its grey stone walls was in actual fact a sort of neurotic dependence, urban Stockholm Syndrome. Just as prisoners become dependent on their prison, and husbands on their bad wives, so he believed that the very fact of living among dirt and chaos was enough for him to bestow affection on that dirt and chaos. Prosecutor Teodor Szacki, the Varsovian. The Varsovian, in other words the homeless person. Now, in the forecourt of Sandomierz castle, full of sunlight and chatter, he could see that clearly. As someone from a big city he had no mini homeland, no happy childhood realm that was his place on earth. A place you can come back to years later to be greeted by smiles, outstretched hands and the same familiar, though time-worn faces. Where the features of the neighbours and friends who have already gone are there to be found in their children and grandchildren, where you can feel part of a greater whole, discover what it means to be a link in a long and sturdy chain. Here he could see this chain, under the suits and outfits from the local market, and he envied all these people for it. He envied them so badly that it hurt, because he could tell it would never be his fate, even in the happiest exile he would always and everywhere remain homeless, without a land of his own.

"Prosecutor?" Klara had materialized beside him in a floaty beige dress. He opened his mouth, wanting to apologize.

"Marek's doing better now, he has regained consciousness, and I even managed to exchange a few words with him. I saw you and I thought maybe you'd like to know."

"Thank you. That's wonderful news. I'd like to say—"

"It's all right, you don't have to apologize. Down there, with Marek, none of it was your fault. I just hope that old geezer breathes his last behind bars. And as for us, well, we're adults. We had some extremely nice times together, the way I see it. Thank you."

He hadn't a clue what to say.

"I'm the one to say thank you."

She nodded, and they stood without talking; the silence was awkward and in other circumstances they would probably have gone to bed to avoid hearing it.

"Aren't you going to ask me if I did a pregnancy test?"

"That's not keeping me awake. It would be an honour to be the father of your child."

"Well, well, so you do know how to behave after all. In that case…" – she stood on tiptoes and kissed him on the cheek – "…see you. This is a small town, we're sure to run into each other now and then."

She waved goodbye and rapidly walked away towards the cathedral. Szacki's thoughts went back to Dybus, to the underground, to Wilczur, to the case. And to the question nagging him like an itch: how? How the fuck did he do it? How? Even supposing he was familiar with the system of tunnels, even supposing there was an entrance into them at each gateway, how did that old man cope with the corpses? OK, so Mrs Budnik was light and her husband was scrawny too, but Szyller was a muscle-packed bull of a man. So what? Was he to believe Wilczur had anaesthetized him, then tossed him over his shoulder and crucified him underground? That he had put himself to the trouble of carting Budnik up to the first floor of the mansion on Zamkowa Street? And what about Mrs Budnik? He couldn't possibly have known she would decide to move out to live with her lover on that day at that time. Had he been watching the property? How? Through cameras?

And there was the inscription on the painting in the cathedral. Wilczur was a Jew, several times he had shown himself to be an expert on Jewish culture, and he could quote the Gospels in Hebrew by heart. Would he have made such an obvious error? Would he have childishly reversed a letter in a simple word? That couldn't have had any purpose in his plan. Did it mean he had an accomplice? That would also explain his silence. It would be the perfect strategy, but also a guarantee that he wouldn't give anyone away by accident.

Szacki's head was starting to ache, and he thought it must be from hunger; it was coming up to dinner time, and he hadn't had a bite to eat since early morning. He made his way through the scent of blossoming apple trees in the garden by the cathedral, climbed uphill to the market square, and without thinking about it, aimed straight for the Trzydziestka restaurant. The place he always went to when he had no desire to experiment, where no food critic would have lasted out until the dessert, and where they served the best buckwheat in the world. He refused to think how many times the nice waitress had set a piece of fresh chuck steak from the grill before him, served with prunes, a heap of buckwheat and a pint of cold beer. He refused to think about it, because he was afraid his liver might overhear.

"Our tables appear to be in different dimensions of time and space, Prosecutor," he heard a grouchy voice from behind.

He turned round and was struck dumb. At the next table sat his former boss, head of the Warsaw City Centre District Prosecutor's Office, whom he had always thought of as the least attractive woman on earth. Well, a single glance after several months apart confirmed his conviction that he'd always been right. Her grey face was just as grey, her brown strings of slightly wavy hair were just as brown, and rather than softening the dispiriting impression, swapping her grey office jacket for a red sweater only reinforced it. Janina Chorko looked like a woman who has sent a request to a charity that makes wishes come true for the terminally ill, and been dressed in something cheerful for her final hours. What a ghastly effect.

"It's good to see you, Madam Prosecutor. You're looking splendid."

Chorko was not alone – with her was Maria "Misia" Miszczyk, her husband – a surprisingly good-looking man, the George Clooney type – and their two children, aged about fifteen or sixteen; the boy looked like trouble already, and the girl, the A-student type, had slightly muted charms, but her eyes flashed with such intelligence that Szacki would have been afraid to pit himself against her in a battle of repartee.

Despite her mother's tendency to excess plumpness and her talent for baking cakes, all three were slender and looked fit. Szacki suddenly felt sorry that Chorko was sitting with them; it must have been painful for this worn-out, grey, lonely woman to see this lovely, happy family.

"I didn't know you knew each other," he said the first thing that entered his head, not wanting Chorko to notice the emotions written on his face.

"I don't know what that says about you as an investigator, Prosecutor," she remarked cuttingly. "You've failed to detect that your bosses were at college together."

Miszczyk burst out laughing, and Chorko joined in with her. He had never heard his former boss laughing before. And she had a lovely, joyful laugh, her wrinkles smoothed out and her eyes began to glow; even if she didn't become pretty, at least she stopped looking like a study aid for medical students.

"Hold on a mo," said Prosecutor Janina Chorko. "I usually keep my private life as far as possible from the world of crime, but now... This is Prosecutor Teodor Szacki, I told you, Mariusz, that if in spite of all you did want to study law, you must write your dissertation on his cases – some unusual stories, solved in an unusual way. This is my husband Jerzy, and some girl we've adopted whose name is Luiza."

"What do you mean, adopted?" said Luiza indignantly, drawing attention to herself.

"Because I can't possibly have produced a daughter who leans her elbows on the table like that."

"Aha, so it's a joke. Pity, I was just looking forward to finding my real family..."

"Please don't take any notice, it's her age."

"...after an adventure-packed search, which would finally give my life a meaning."

"Please, come and join us, let's have a drink, Janina's driving." Chorko's husband, as he had surprisingly turned out to be, smiled broadly and made room for Szacki on the wooden bench.

But Prosecutor Teodor Szacki was standing on the spot, not even trying to hide his amazement. It wasn't possible – he had worked with this woman for twelve years, always assuming she was an embittered spinster, who made discreet, embarrassing passes at him to boot. For twelve years he had felt bad about rejecting them, for twelve years he had regularly drunk her health, thinking the world was unfair, and that somewhere there must be someone, maybe not top class, but at least with both arms and legs, who would show her some mercy, bestow on her if not love, then at least a little sympathy, and would bring just a teeny bit of light into her grey-and-brown existence.

Evidently, he had worried in vain. Evidently, there are legends in which there isn't a grain of truth. In which everything is a lie from start to finish.

They all tell lies, Basia Sobieraj's dying father had said.

"Oh fuck!" he said out loud.

He didn't see the company's reaction to this unexpected opening remark, because suddenly, finally, one simple thought had brought the wall tumbling down, against which he had been banging his head from the very start of this investigation. Legends in which there isn't a grain of truth, in which everything is a lie. Everything! He started running through the scenes of the investigation in his mind, from the first misty morning below the synagogue, assuming that everything was a lie. The slashed throat, the razor, the blood ritual, the place where the body was found, all of that Jewish mythology and all the Polish anti-Semitic mythology, the mansion, the barrel, the painting in the cathedral, the inscription, and all those pictures that were so readily shoved under his nose.

"Oh fuck!" he repeated, louder this time, and set off at a run across the market square.

"I don't think I do want to study law," he heard Chorko's son remark behind him.

Never before had any thought process run through his head so quickly, never before had so many facts combined in such a brief flash into a single indissoluble logical sequence, which had only one possible outcome. It was an experience bordering on mania as his thoughts went leaping across his brain cells at epileptic speed, his grey matter shone like platinum from the information overload, and he was afraid something would happen to him, his brain wouldn't be able to process it all and would stall. But there was also something like drug-induced euphoria or religious ecstasy about it, an excitement impossible to restrain, emotions impossible to control. A lie, a lie, it was all a lie, an illusion, a smokescreen. In the crush of funfair attractions, amid the stage-settings of the crimes, in the excess of facts and their interpretation he had overlooked the most important details, and above all the most important conversation.

As he flew into the "Town Hall" bar he must have had a wild look in his eyes, because the grim waiter dropped his cool and timidly hid behind the bar. There was hardly anyone in there, just two families of lost tourists sitting by the wall; they must have been very hungry if they had decided to stay here for a meal.

"Where are those tramps who usually sit here?" he screamed at the waiter, but before the man could get the words out of his mouth, Szacki's hormone-filled nervous system had given him the answer, and he ran out, leaving some more astonished people behind him, who just like the company at the Trzydziestka swapped glances and tapped their foreheads.

He had had the most important conversation with a man from the outside, a clever man, who had evaluated the facts not against the background of the small-town hell of Sandomierz, but simply as facts. During that conversation, he had been irritated by Klejnocki, the profiler, had cringed at his style, the annoying pipe and the clever-clogs chat – once again, stage props had obscured the truth. And the truth was that Klejnocki had solved the Sandomierz riddle a week ago, but Szacki had been too stupid, too steeped in lies, too bogged down in the details to notice it.

He sprinted past the post office, ran down Opatowska Street, miraculously managing not to knock over an old lady coming out of a shop selling handicrafts, flew through the passage under the Opatowska Gate and, panting, stopped at a small square. He almost whooped for joy when he saw the same tramp as yesterday sitting on a bench. He ran up and grabbed the fellow, on whose small triangular face adorned with sticking-out ears a look of terror appeared.

"What do you—"

"Mr Gąsiorowski, isn't it?"

"Eee, and who's asking?"

"The Polish Republic Prosecution Service, that's who's bloody well asking! Yes or no?"

"Darek Gąsiorowski, pleased to meet you."

"Mr Gąsiorowski, you might not remember, but a few days ago we saw each other outside the 'Town Hall' bar. I was coming out with Inspector Leon Wilczur, and you accosted us."

"Oh yes, I remember."

"What was it about? What did you want him to do?"

"I wanted Leo to help us, because we've known each other for decades, and if we went to the police like normal, they'd laugh in our faces."

"To help you with what?"

Gąsiorowski sighed and wiped his nose nervously; he clearly wasn't eager for more mockery.

"It's very important," said Szacki.

"There's this one fellow, a fine fellow, who tramps about the district. He's my mate."

"A vagrant?"

"Not exactly, they say he's got a home somewhere, he just likes to roam."

"And?"

"And he's, I think it's a sort of illness, he's not all right in the head, you see, because when he roams you can set your watch by him. You always know what time he'll be in a particular place. That's to say, I know for example, when he'll be here, and then we'll meet up for a drop of wine and a chat."

"And?"

"And lately he hasn't come. Twice now he hasn't come. And that's never happened with him before. I went to the police, so maybe they'd find out, because he goes to Tarnobrzeg and Zawichost and Dwikozy and I think Opatów too. So they'd check, because, as I say, he's not all right in the head; he might have got that illness for example, where you don't remember nothing. Or he was walking along the roads, so maybe he'd had an accident or something – he'd want someone to come and visit him in hospital, wouldn't he?" He fixed his gaze on Szacki's bandage.

"Yes, he would. Do you know what he's called?"

"Tolo."

"Short for Anatol?"

"Yes, I think that's right. Or it could be Antoni, they sometimes say that too."

"And his surname?"

"Fijewski."

"Anatol's surname is Fijewski?"

"Yes."

"Anatol Fijewski. Thank you."

Szacki left Gąsiorowski and got out his mobile.

"Shouldn't I describe him or something?" called the fellow, getting up from the bench.

"No need!" Szacki called back.

As he looked at Nazareth House, standing on the other side of the road, his gaze slid across to Saint Michael's church, which adjoined the baroque seminary building.

Archangel Michael, vanquisher of evil, patron saint of all those who fight for justice, guardian angel of policemen and prosecutors, hear your faithful servant and let it be not too late. And just for once in this blasted country please let it be possible to get something done at a registry office after working hours.

13

It is World Graphic Design Day, Independence Day in Sierra Leone and Togo, and Cardinal Stanisław Dziwisz reaches the age of seventy. In the news, the economic crisis is supplanted by the swine flu, which in Israel is known as the more kosher "Mexican flu". The state of Iowa legalizes homosexual marriages, General Motors announces the end of the Pontiac and Bayern Munich the end of Jürgen Klinsmann in the job of coach. In Poland sociologist Jadwiga Staniszkis claims that President Lech Kaczyński will not stand in next year's presidential election, Communist-era minister Czesław Kiszczak claims that introducing martial law was legal, and twenty-six per cent of Catholics claim to know priests who cohabit with common-law wives. In Świętokrzyskie province there is a puma on the prowl. In Sandomierz a decision is made to build a modern sports pitch at High School II, and next to a different, existing pitch yet another mobile phone falls prey to audacious thieves — this time it was left on the ground in a plastic shopping bag. It's a lovely spring day, it's sunny and the temperature is higher than twenty degrees. It's dry, and in the woods there is a risk of fire.

I

Coming here was immensely, incredibly stupid – I feel fear, but above all anger. Anger that a stupid accident could end the whole thing now. It's true there's always a crowd of people at the registry office, a big crowd of applicants from all over the province, a random collection of people who have never seen each other before and will never see each other again. A crowd like this is on the one hand, safe; on the other, risky, very risky. I can feel waves of panic flowing through my body, and the numbered receipt I'm holding in my clenched hand is turning into a soggy scrap, so I'm sticking it in my wallet.

Ping, two more people ahead of me. Two more people! I can feel the panic battling with my sense of euphoria. Two more people, then just a short stop at the window, then I leave the place and… it's the end, the end at last!

The panic is winning. I'm trying to occupy my thoughts with something, anything to kill the time; I try reading the regulations on the wall again, and the official announcements; I try reading the instructions for working the fire extinguisher, but it just makes things worse, I can't understand the simplest words, my thoughts are racing, the hysteria's rising so I can't possibly do it. I feel sick, my hands are tingling, there are black spots starting to dance before my eyes. If I faint it'll be the end, the end! That thought starts drumming in my head, louder and louder, faster and faster; the more I refuse to give in to it, the harder it drums, the greater my fear, the bigger the black snowflakes falling thicker and thicker before my eyes. I'm struggling to squeeze air into my lungs, I'm afraid I won't be able to gasp out a word, I'm scared there'll be a commotion, and that will be the end! The end! The end! All for nothing, the rest of my life in prison, pain, incarceration, solitude. The end!!!

Ping, just one more person.

No, I can't do it, I'll just leave slowly and forget about this stupid idea. I turn around and take two steps towards the door, but my body isn't really obeying me, and a new wave of panic floods it, the nausea returns with increased strength, the fear pushes bile into my throat. Slowly, little by little, very slowly, I calm down, taking very small steps.

Ping, it's my turn right away – impossible, someone else has given up! It's a sign! I go up to the window on legs of jelly, I feel as if I'm glowing all sorts of colours, as if my panic is bright red, glaring out of the security screens. Tough, there's no turning back now. I hand in my ID card, answer a few casually posed questions, and wait for the lady behind the window to finish. I sign a receipt form, the clerk hands me a new passport, and its dark-red cover shines in the sunlight that's pushing in through the vertical blinds. I say a polite thank you and leave.

Soon he's standing outside the large, hospital-like Świętokrzyski County Registry Office in Kielce. And he thinks the perfect murder does exist after all – all it takes is a bit of work and some savvy. Who knows, maybe one day he'll tell someone about it, maybe he'll write a book, we'll see. Now he just wants to enjoy his freedom. He puts the passport in his pocket, wipes his sweaty hands on his fleece and smiles broadly as he saunters off towards Warszawska Street. It's a beautiful, sunny day, on a day like this even Kielce looks nice. Now he's calming down, relaxing, smiling at people heading at a rapid pace towards the registry office entrance, a pace that's right for the provincial capital. The policemen standing at the bottom of the steps make no impression on him at all – after all, they're in the right place, keeping order at the seat of power.

As his euphoria grows, he smiles more and more openly at the people he passes, and when Prosecutor Teodor Szacki answers with a smile, he doesn't immediately sense that something isn't right – it's just a nice, middle-aged guy, gone prematurely grey perhaps. That lasts a fraction of a second. In the next fraction of a second he thinks it's someone very similar, and that his hounded mind is playing tricks on him. And in the next fraction of a second he knows the perfect crime does not exist after all.

"Yes, can I help you, sir?" he says in an act of desperation, still trying to play dumb.

"I'm the one who can help you, Anatol," replies the prosecutor.

II

Later on, back in Sandomierz, during an interview that lasted for many hours, once the murderer had confessed everything, Szacki had to contend with a strange feeling. He had sometimes felt empathy towards the people he interrogated, sometimes compassion, and he had sometimes even respected people who had transgressed and had the courage to face up to it. But it was probably the first time in his career that he felt maybe not admiration for the criminal, but a feeling close to it, worryingly close. He was trying very hard not to show it, and yet, as he learnt more and more details of the crime, now and then it occurred to him that never before had he been so close to the perfect crime.

SUSPECT INTERVIEW TRANSCRIPT. Grzegorz Budnik, born 4th December 1950, resident at 27 Katedralna Street, Sandomierz, higher education in chemistry, chairman of the Sandomierz City Council. Relationship to parties: husband of Elżbieta Budnik (victim). No previous convictions, advised of the duties and rights of a suspect, his statement is as follows:

I hereby confess to the murders of my wife Elżbieta Budnik and of Jerzy Szyller, and to the abduction and murder of Anatol Fijewski. I committed the first murder, of Elżbieta Budnik, in Sandomierz on Easter Monday, 13th April 2009, and the motive for my conduct was hatred towards my wife; I had been aware for a long time that she was having an affair with Jerzy Szyller, whom I knew, and that day she had announced that as a result of this she wanted to end our marriage, which had lasted since 1995. That same day I put a plan into action which was designed to lead to the death of Jerzy Szyller and to my evading justice. I had this plan prepared for many weeks, but up to a certain point I did not take it seriously, it was a sort of intellectual entertainment...

Budnik talked, Szacki listened, and the figures jumped on the digital Dictaphone. The chairman of the City Council, and until recently cold corpse, described events rather unemotionally, but there were moments when he couldn't hide his pride, and Szacki realized that this intrigue, this one and only flash of genius that had happened in his office-bound life was this man's greatest ever success. Or rather, second greatest – the first was leading Elżbieta Szuszkiewicz to the altar. Budnik related his activities exhaustively with all the details, while Szacki thought about their former conversation when – as it turned out, rightly – he had been convinced of Budnik's guilt. And how he had reminded him of Gollum from *Lord of the Rings*, a character totally obsessed with possessing his "precious", for whom nothing else counts, not even the precious object as such, but just possessing it. Without possessing his precious, Budnik was nobody and nothing, he became an empty shell, deprived of all natural and social restraints, capable of planning and committing murder in cold blood. The scale of the crimes was terrible, but even more shocking was the scale of Budnik's obsession with his wife. Szacki heard about the underground, he heard about the preparations, about the starving dogs, and the weeks spent making himself look like the poor tramp in order to steal his identity, he heard explanations of the lesser and greater mysteries, the solution to which was obvious in any case, ever since he had hit upon the idea that Budnik had to be the murderer. But somewhere deep down in there he couldn't stop wondering: Is this real love? So obsessive, so destructive, capable of the greatest sacrifices and the greatest crimes? Can you really speak of love at all, until you come to experience emotions as strong as these? Until you realize that in comparison with it, nothing else matters at all?

Prosecutor Teodor Szacki was not able to expel these thoughts from his mind. And he was afraid, because there was something prophetic about them, something which meant he couldn't just regard them as theoretical. As if Providence were preparing the biggest test of all for him, and with his sixth sense he could tell that one day he would have to weigh up love on the one hand, and someone's life on the other.

As Budnik droned on, successive elements jumped into place, and the jigsaw started looking like a picture ready for framing. Usually at such moments Prosecutor Teodor Szacki felt calm, but now he was filled with a strange, irrational alarm. Grzegorz Budnik hadn't planned to become a murderer. He hadn't been born with that thought, and it had never been part of his existence. Quite simply, one day he had realized it was the only alternative.

Why was Szacki so strangely convinced that a day like that would come for him too?

III

Arresting Grzegorz Budnik was a bombshell, and on the news bulletins even the swine flu was put on the back burner; in Sandomierz no one was talking about anything else. The general commotion allowed Basia Sobieraj to keep her husband in the dark by saying she didn't know how late they'd have to work at the office, and so they ended up at Szacki's flat, so the married woman with a bad heart and a fifteen-year training period could discover her erogenous zones with the commitment of an A-grade student.

They had wonderful fun together, and at a certain point Szacki fell in love with Basia Sobieraj. Quite simply and frankly, and it was a very nice feeling.

"Misia said you were behaving like a lunatic."

"It could have looked like that, I admit."

"Was that when the penny dropped?"

"Uh-huh."

"You know it excites me?"

"What does?"

"The fact that you're a crime-solving genius."

"Ha ha."

"Don't laugh. Really, after all, the case was already solved, so how did it enter your head?"

"Because of a grain of truth."

"I don't get it."

"They say that in every legend there's a grain of truth."

"There is."

"But there are legends, such as that blasted anti-Semitic legend of blood, in which there isn't a single drop of truth, which are one hundred per cent lies and superstition. I'd been thinking about it just then in the market square, never mind why. And I remembered what your father had said. That everyone tells lies, and you mustn't forget they're all lying. And suddenly I thought about the case as one big lie. What it would mean, if you were to suppose there wasn't anything true in it, suppose it was all a creation. What would be left if you threw out all the stuff from seventy years ago, the ritual murders, ritual slaughter, Hebrew inscriptions, biblical quotations, rabid dogs, gloomy underground tunnels and barrels studded with nails. What would happen if I realized all the evidence and clues which had been driving our investigation from the start were lies. What would be left?"

"Three dead bodies."

"Actually no. The three dead bodies were a creation, a lie, the three dead bodies were to make us think about three dead bodies."

"Well then, three times one dead body."

"Exactly. I could tell that was the right way to think. But I wasn't quite there yet. I already knew there weren't three dead bodies but three times one dead body. I knew that to see something, I had to strip those bodies of all the theatrical scenery. I knew I should latch on to what came from outside, the objective things which weren't imposed on us, and hadn't been specially prepared, as had the badge in the victim's hand, for example."

"Ela's hand," muttered Basia quietly.

"Yes, I know, all right, Ela, I'm sorry," said Szacki, surprising himself with his tender manner, hugged his lover's slender body to him and kissed her hair that smelt of almond shampoo.

"And so what came from the outside?"

"You mean who."

"The profiler?"

"Bravo! Do you remember how the four of us sat together? You and I, Klejnocki and Wilczur. Under a huge picture of your friend's corpse projected on a screen. Once again the staging overwhelmed us. That picture, Klejnocki's irritating manner, his pipe, his boring twaddle.

There was a great deal happening at that point, we wanted a lot and quickly, and he said things that might have seemed obvious, his ideas seemed a bit thin, because he didn't know as much as you do, for example, about Sandomierz, about the Budniks, about the relationships between the people. But he said the most important thing for our investigation: that the key to the riddle is the first killing and the motives behind it. That the first murder was committed under the influence of the greatest emotions, and the ones that follow are just the fulfilment of a plan. The anger was vented on the first victim, the hatred and bile, whereas the second was simply, if you can say that, murdered. And I started thinking. If we don't treat the three killings as a whole, if we focus on the first, most important one, and forget the stage setting for the moment, the case is obvious. The murderer has to be Budnik. He had a motive in the form of his wife's betrayal, he had the means, and absolutely no alibi whatsoever, he fibbed in his statements and he deceived us."

"But who would have suspected a dead person?" Basia Sobieraj got up, put on Szacki's shirt and fetched some girly cigarettes from her handbag.

"Do you smoke?"

"One pack every two weeks. More of a hobby than a habit. May I smoke in here, or should I go into the kitchen?"

Szacki waved a hand, dragged himself out of bed too and reached for his own cigarettes. He lit up, the warm smoke filled his lungs, and goosebumps appeared on his skin; maybe the spring had arrived at last, but the nights were still cold. He wrapped himself in a blanket and started walking about the flat to warm up.

"Nobody suspects a dead person, of course," he continued. "Still, if it hadn't been for Budnik's corpse, the whole thing would have been obvious, because in Szyller's case, too, he was the most natural suspect. All that was left was to apply Sherlock Holmes's old principle that if we eliminate the impossible, what remains, however improbable, has to be true."

Sobieraj dragged on her cigarette; the cold was making her breasts, visible in the open shirt, look extremely enticing.

"Why didn't we notice that? You or I, or Wilczur."

"An illusion," said Szacki, shrugging. "Perhaps Budnik's most brilliant idea. Do you know what conjuring tricks usually rely on? On distracting your attention, don't they? While one hand is shuffling two packs of cards in the air, or changing a burning piece of tissue paper into a dove, you haven't the time or the desire to look at what the other one is doing. You see? We were the ideal spectators for his show for various reasons. You and Wilczur were local enough for everything to have too much significance for you. I was enough of a stranger to be unable to separate the important things from the unimportant ones. The whole time we were looking at the top hat and the rabbit – at pictures in churches, quotes from the Gospels, barrels, naked corpses on the site of an old Jewish cemetery. The less spectacular things escaped our attention."

"Such as?"

"Such as the loess sand under Mrs Budnik's fingernails. If you remove a mysterious symbol from someone's hand, the fingernails don't interest you. And if they had, we'd have started to think about the underground cellars sooner. Such as the second victim's feet, with a shiny coating of blood. You see something like that, plus that barrel too, and you don't stop to wonder why a town council official has carved-up, bruised, mangled feet."

"The feet of a tramp..."

"Exactly. But it was sitting inside me the whole time, all those little details, reminding me of their existence the whole time. Klejnocki's words, first of all. Your father's words, second."

"That everyone tells lies?"

"Those words too, but there were others that made me itch. At first I thought it was about passing on hatred from generation to generation, which in the context of Wilczur was obvious. But your father was talking about life in a very small town, where they're all looking in each other's windows, so if your wife is unfaithful, you've got to stand next to her lover in church. Bloody hell, somewhere in there I had Budnik at the back of my head the whole time, but I pushed away that solution, because it was too fantastical. Only when I started to consider that option did it all come together. Take the reversed letter on the painting – the rabbi in Lublin said no Jew would have made a mistake like that, just as we would never write a B with the loops to the left. That doesn't indicate Wilczur. It points at someone who had a good general idea, but had to keep looking at Wikipedia to add the details. And Budnik was pretty well clued up, he'd been interested in the painting, he had fought for the truth about it, he had a good enough grasp of the anti-Semitic obsessions to know perfectly well which strings to pluck.

"That wasn't his only mistake either. He had pressed the badge into his wife's hand because in that flood of bile – to quote Klejnocki again – he wanted to injure Szyller at any price, to incriminate him. It didn't occur to him that as soon as we got to Szyller, from the story of the love affair we'd come bouncing straight back to his doorstep like a rubber ball. Or maybe he did think of it, but reckoned Szyller wouldn't give the game away out of concern for his lover's good name? Hell knows. Either way, if Szyller hadn't gone to Warsaw, if I'd interviewed him a day earlier, he would be alive, and Budnik would have been in jail for a week by now."

Sobieraj finished her cigarette; he thought she'd come back under the duvet, but she did some more rummaging in her handbag and took out her phone.

"Are you calling your husband?"

"No, the Modena, to order pizza. Two Romanticas?" she said, fluttering her eyelashes in comedy fashion.

He agreed willingly and waited for Basia to place the order, then pulled her back under the duvet. Not for sex, he just wanted to cuddle and talk it all out.

"And that business with Wilczur?" she asked. "Was that a smokescreen? What was that about? They have let him go, haven't they?"

"Yes, of course they have. He told me he has an infinitely kind heart, so he isn't going to report his arrest to the Anti-Defamation League, and he won't make me into Poland's chief anti-Semite. Only because *Fakt* is going to do it for him."

She snorted with laughter.

"What a charming old boy. But is he really a Jew?"

"Yes, he really is. And that whole story is true, except that Wilczur didn't know as much about it as we thought – for instance, he had no idea Elżbieta was the granddaughter of the unfortunate midwife whose daughter was scared by the barrel. Budnik knew the most. The issue of Dr Wajsbrot and what happened in the winter of 1947 was a strictly guarded family secret. Which Budnik only learnt about when he fell in love with Miss Szuszkiewicz. His father, as you remember, was the head of the secret police prison who hadn't let Wajsbrot deliver his wife's baby. And, terrified by the coincidence, he had revealed all to his son on his death bed. The old man was afraid of a curse, he was afraid none of it was happening purely by chance, and that Dr Wajsbrot was demanding justice from beyond the grave."

"There's something in that," whispered Sobieraj. "However you look at it, there's something eerie about the fact that those people's fates were joined together again. Especially now that Budnik will live out his days in prison."

Szacki shuddered. He hadn't thought about it like that, but Sobieraj was right. It looked as if the curse doing the rounds of Sandomierz had taken control of him as well to do its work. He remembered the recording of the Jew disappearing in the fog – that was the one single aspect of the investigation that he hadn't been able to explain. And which he intended to keep to himself – there was no need for any trace of that recording to remain in the case files.

"Yes," he muttered. "As if some sort of providence—"

"Anti-providence more like…"

"You're right, as if some sort of anti-providence were helping Budnik. Strange."

For a while they were silent, hugging each other; outside the clock on the town-hall tower struck eleven p.m. He smiled at the thought of how very much he would miss those noises now if they weren't there. To think that not so long ago they had irritated him.

"Pity about that vagrant," she sighed sadly, and snuggled closer to Szacki. "There was no curse affecting him, as I see it."

"No, probably not, I have no idea – we certainly don't know anything about that so far."

"God, I shouldn't keep saying it or you'll be crushed under the weight of your own ego, but you're a real crime-solving genius, you know?"

He shrugged, although his ego was indeed lapping up this compliment with relish.

"Yeah, the next things I should have taken notice of were the laptop and the family photos."

"What laptop?"

"The polystyrene kind they pack takeaways in at restaurants."

"You call that a 'laptop'?"

"Yes, and?…"

"Never mind, go on."

"On Tuesday the camera caught Budnik coming out of the Trzy-dziestka restaurant with two dinners. That made no sense at all. Mrs Budnik wasn't there any more by then, and nor was there any explanation for why he needed two dinners. It only had to be linked up with the other facts. Such as the fact that if Budnik was meant to be the murderer, someone else must have been stuck on a hook in the mansion on Zamkowa Street. Such as the fact that one of the local tramps had been stubbornly looking for his lost vagrant pal. And then the family photographs."

"I don't get it – what family photographs?"

"Here the whole trick relied on making himself look as much as possible like the tramp, that unfortunate Fijewski. From his explanations it turns out Budnik had been preparing for the crimes for weeks, even months on end. Of course, it sounds like utter madness, but remember that until there was bloodshed, he could treat it like a perverse game, testing himself to see how far he was capable of going. He must have neglected himself pathologically, lost weight and lightened his hair a bit from reddish-brown to ginger, and grown a beard. The dodge with the sticking plaster was a stroke of genius: yet another way of distracting attention worthy of an illusionist, but it would have been useless if someone had started having doubts about whether the corpse on Zamkowa Street was Budnik's body. Why didn't we have doubts, and especially why didn't I? I'd seen the same skinny little man with a ginger beard and a plaster at the interview. The hook through the cheek made things additionally complicated. I saw that same face in the ID card I took out of the wallet lying by the remains. But unfortunately, the fact that there was no driving licence in there didn't set me thinking, and the ID card has been issued two weeks earlier. It didn't set any of us thinking, because in the past few hours we'd all seen Budnik's face on the television, from where? From a photo taken at the time of the interview. But could we have seen his face somewhere else? Of course we could, if we'd looked. But in the most obvious place, in other words his house, there weren't any pictures of him, only of Mrs Budnik. He knew we'd search the property carefully after his disappearance. He knew that if we feasted our eyes on his actual face in there, we might have some doubts. As it was, all we had to look at was a skinny face with a plaster on the forehead."

The doorbell interrupted Szacki's clarifications, and soon they were eating pizza and garlic bread, which – what a coincidence – was brought in a white polystyrene "laptop", just like the one Szacki had recently seen in the hands of the murderer on a fuzzy film recorded by a camera on the market square. The thought made him lose his appetite for this particular dish. Basia seemed to lose hers too, because not once did she reach into the container. Anyway, she didn't seem keen on the pizza either, although it was as delicious as ever. She ate one piece, took a couple of pecks at a second one, and put it aside.

"I'm sorry, I can't eat and think about all that at the same time – those vaults, Szyller… Now, of course, I understand more, the way he died… It confirms Klejnocki's words. Szyller was the most cruelly tortured, the hatred for him was the greatest. That also pointed at Budnik, didn't it?"

He nodded in agreement.

"Did he keep the tramp in the vaults too? And how? Did he go down into them from his cellar? I didn't even know there was anything except for that wretched tourist route, and soon it'll turn out you can get in there from every tenement."

"You can't. Budnik knew a little more than others by accident – he was interested in the history of the city, it was thanks to him that Dybus and his pals could do their research. The matter ceased to concern the other politicians when it turned out they weren't going to make a new tourist attraction out of it, but for Budnik it was pastime. A pastime which at a key moment turned out to be very handy. Of course it's not true that you can go down into the underground at any point. You know the entrance inside Nazareth House, and as Budnik explains it, and as we'll have to check, there's another entrance near the castle, by that meadow at the bottom, where there's a ruined building. That would make sense – with a bit of luck you could get from there to the synagogue through the bushes without being noticed, and you could also go through the bushes to the mansion on Zamkowa Street, and if you slip through the cathedral garden, you end up on the terrace at the Budniks' house. Hence his need to blow up the part of the underground tunnel that leads to that entrance. It would have pointed to Budnik, and then we could have started to look for him. In fact, he planned to be far away by now thanks to Fijewski's passport, but as we know: you can never be careful enough…"

"Admit it, the passport was a shot in the dark."

"Yes, but on target. Once I was just about certain whose identity he had stolen, it wasn't all that hard to make sure. But to convince several registry offices to check on a Sunday evening whether it was true, and when he'd call to collect it… I don't think I've ever run into a greater challenge in my career. Do you know what's interesting? That his biggest regret is Dybus."

"What a bloody nutcase. To think I knew him for all those years. How long will he get for it?"

"Life."

"And why? For what? I don't get it."

Szacki didn't get it either, not entirely. But he could still hear Budnik's words in his ears: "I wanted to kill Ela and Szyller, I really did, it gave me pleasure. After all those months imagining what they were doing together, after hearing those lies, the stories about business meetings with theatre people in Krakow, Kielce and Warsaw… You don't know what it's like, how that hatred grows day after day, floods you like bile; I was capable of anything by then, anything not to feel that acid consuming me, every minute, every second, all the time. I'd always known she wasn't really mine, but when she finally told me to my face, it was terrible. I decided that if I couldn't have her, nobody was going to have her."

Maybe it's better that you don't understand that, Basia, thought Szacki. And that I don't either, and few people do in general. And although Budnik's explanation had got through to him, although he did understand his motives, there was something in all this – dammit, he could only bring it up aloud in jokes; after all, he didn't believe in curses, nor did he believe that some sort of energy sometimes has to even out the scores for the order of the universe. And yet there was something unsettling about it. As if the old Polish city had seen too much, as if the crime committed seventy years ago was too much for these stone walls, and instead of soaking into the red bricks as usual it had started to ricochet off them, until finally it hit Grzegorz Budnik.

The clock on the town-hall tower struck midnight.

"It's the time for ghosts," said Basia Sobieraj, and slipped into bed.

It occurred to Prosecutor Teodor Szacki that ghosts certainly don't appear at midnight.

14

Friday, 8th May 2009

In the Jewish calendar it is Pesach Sheni, or Second
Passover, a holiday decreed by the Torah to take place
on the fourteenth day of the month *Iyar*, for those
who could not celebrate it at the right time, and a
symbol of a second chance granted by God. Benedict XVI
visits Jordan, where on Mount Nebo, from which Moses
saw the Promised Land, he talks about the unbreakable
tie that binds the Church and the Jewish nation. In
Spain some lucky devil wins 126 million euros on the
lottery, in California the world's smallest light bulb
is produced, and British Sikh policemen want bul-
letproof turbans to be invented. It is only a month
until the European elections, and according to the
polls in Poland the Civic Platform party is winning
against the Law and Justice party by forty-seven to
twenty-two per cent. Sandomierz is excited by a TVN
helicopter flying over the city, by the story of a
former secret policeman who persecuted the opposition,
and whose security firm now protects church buildings,
and — like the entire region — by the discovery in
Tarnobrzeg of Poland's first case of swine flu. The
police catch two sixteen-year-olds smoking "stupe-
fying dried plant material"; but meanwhile, Bishop
Edward Frankowski ordains seventeen new deacons, so

the balance is maintained. Spring is in full bloom;
in the morning it rained, but the evening is lovely,
warm and sunny, and it's impossible to find an empty
café table in the market square.

There was probably no better place in Poland to spend a lazy spring
evening over a pint of beer than in the shade of the chestnut trees
on the terrace of the Kordegarda restaurant, known to regulars as
the Korda. Slightly raised above the level of the market square, and
as a result slightly separate, it was the ideal spot to lose yourself in
watching the tourists milling around the town hall, the newly-weds
taking pictures of each other, the high-school children glued to their
mobiles, the kids glued to their candy floss, and the lovers glued to
each other.

Prosecutor Teodor Szacki was waiting for Basia to come back
from the toilet, and staring insolently at the people sitting around
him. As ever, he envied them all their lives, he was feeling mawkish
somehow, and wistful. Right next to him by the terrace railing sat
a couple of locals, in love with each other like teenagers, although
they must have been well over fifty. He was the portly manager type
in a scruffy shirt, and she was in a colourful top and had a bold sex
appeal that had come unscathed through decades of baking cakes
and bringing up offspring. They were talking non-stop about their
children, of whom they seemed to have three, judging by the vividly
described ups and downs of their lives – all around the age of thirty,
all in Warsaw. They didn't say a word about themselves, but just
kept reeling off colourful yarns about their daughters, sons-in-law
and grandchildren, what they were doing, what they weren't doing,
what was going well for them, what might go well or might not.
He was more positively disposed in a quiet way, she occasionally
got wound up in negative scenarios, and then he would clear his
throat and say: "What can you know about it, Hania?" Then she
would stop for a while, to let him enjoy the feeling that of course

Witek knows better, and after that she – well quite, what could she know about it? – went back to telling her story. Watching them and eavesdropping was a treat – Szacki was smiling, and at the same time he felt sad. It took several decades nurturing love and affection to get to be that sort of couple. He had destroyed his family, he was too old for a second one now, and he wasn't destined to grow into old age with someone with whom he had shared his entire previous life.

If only he were ten years younger. On the other side of the garden there was a couple just like that. They both looked quite young, but they must have been about thirty; in the first instance he thought "my generation", but he soon corrected himself. That's not your generation any more, Prosecutor – you know all Jacek Kaczmarski's opposition protest songs by heart, but for them music starts with Kurt Cobain. You were grown up when *Gazeta Wyborcza* published its first edition, as Poland's first independent newspaper, but to them it was just a rag their parents brought home. There aren't many generations in the world where ten crappy years make as much of a difference as in this instance.

The couple were all touchy-feely and totally absorbed in each other; their glucose level must have fallen really low for them to have decided to get out of bed. From snippets of conversation he understood that it was the man's birthday today. It's great to have your birthday in May, he thought, to have a barbecue party or meet up in a pub garden – in November he never had the chance. For a while he was tempted to offer his best wishes.

But he let it rest; dragging the birthday boy out of the tent created by his girlfriend's long chestnut hair would have been cruel. As soon as his neighbour sensed Szacki's gaze on him, he looked vigilantly around the café and Szacki quickly turned away. Something tickled Szacki's ear. The something was an absurdly large chestnut flower, being held by Basia. In the corner of his eye he just caught the man's smile, a smile that said yes, he too thought Sandomierz in May was the ideal place for lovers.

"Shall we go?"

He nodded, drank up his beer, and together they went down the steps onto the cobblestones of the market square. The setting sun was shining red at the top of Oleśnicki Street, coating everything in a crimson glow, including the walls of the old synagogue.

"We can't stay here if we want to be together," she said.

She smiled, kissed him on the cheek, waved a slender hand in farewell, and walked off at a rapid pace towards the Opatowska Gate, her skirt swirling around her bare, pale and – as he knew – very freckly calves. Prosecutor Teodor Szacki gazed after her for a while, and then walked towards the sun to catch its final rays. He stopped below the synagogue and watched as the orange light on the wall of the building was gradually displaced by a shadow from below. He was so absorbed in watching it that there was no room inside him for any other thought. Only as the sunset came to its end did he look around him.

Eighty years earlier in all the flats and all the houses in the district, for a quarter of an hour by now the candles would have been burning, lit by the women as a sign that the Sabbath had begun, and that everyone should stop working now, recite *kiddush* and start supper. He glanced down Żydowska Street towards the castle, and remembered the recording shown him by Wilczur, of the figure dissolving into the mist.

He shrugged and started walking in the same direction.

Author's note

I owe the origin of this book, like its predecessor, to my brother, who decided to tie the knot with Ola, a wonderful girl who happens to come from Sandomierz, and so I went there for the wedding, fell head over heels in love with the place and left knowing I had to write a novel set there. The fact that it is a crime novel and that the plot involves stereotypical attitudes that are still alive and painful, is due to Beata Stasińska, whom I take this opportunity to thank for all our conversations about all my books. Many thanks are due to everyone who helped during the several months I spent living in Sandomierz to research the book, above all Ola's parents, their friends and the invaluable Renata Targowska and Jerzy Krzemiński.

I used a lot of sources for this book, but the city of Sandomierz is the most important one of all, and I would recommend anyone who wants to know more about this magical city on the river Vistula to pay it a visit. Those interested in the sinister legend about ritual murder should read Joanna Tokarska-Bakir's essay *Legendy o krwi. Antropologia przesądu* ("Legends of Blood: the Anthropology of Prejudice"), published by WAB, Warsaw, in 2008. Another important source I should mention is *Sława i chwała* ("Fame and Glory") by Jarosław Iwaszkiewicz, the family saga I was reading while writing this book, and the careful reader will find echoes of it here. As a matter of form I should add that all the characters (well, almost all – my respects to Jarosław and Marcin) and all the events are fictional, and I am entirely responsible for any deliberate distortions or mistakes in the facts and the topography; also, making Sandomierz into a sinister capital of murder does not, God forbid, testify to my attitude towards this city, which I regard as the most enchanting place in Poland.

Sandomierz and Warsaw, 2009–11

ENTANGLEMENT

Zygmunt Miłoszewski

The morning after a gruelling psychotherapy session in a Warsaw monastery, Henryk Telak is found dead, a roasting spit stuck in one eye. The case lands on the desk of State Prosecutor Teodor Szacki. World-weary, suffering from bureaucratic exhaustion and marital ennui, Szacki feels that life has passed him by, but this case changes everything.

He must steer his way among a gallery of colourful characters: a flirtatious young journalist, an eccentric psychiatrist, a lecherous police colleague and a paranoid historian. Szacki's search for the killer unearths another murder that took place twenty years earlier, before the fall of Communism. The trail leads to facts that, for his own safety, he'd be better off not knowing.

PRAISE FOR *ENTANGLEMENT*

"Miłoszewski takes an engaging look at modern Polish society in this stellar first in a new series starring Warsaw prosecutor Teodor Szacki. Readers will want to see more of the complex, sympathetic Szacki." *Publishers Weekly*

"*Entanglement* has everything I want from a thriller. It opens with a murder and quickly develops into a fast-moving and tightly plotted whodunit with a host of colourful characters and vivid descriptions of contemporary Cracow. But it's the unsatisfactory personal life and emotional turmoil of its hero, State Prosecutor Teodor Szacki, that steal centre stage.' *Oxford Times*

"The character of Prosecutor Szacki has enough charisma and complexity to give competition to the likes of Mikael Blomkvist and Rob Ryan. Hopefully the first of many mystery novels from Miłoszewski." *Foreward Reviews*

£8.99/$14.95
Crime Paperback Original
ISBN 978-1904738-442
eBook
ISBN 978-1904738-633

www.bitterlemonpress.com